THE COLUMBUS CONSPIRACY

The mystery, deceit and crimes
of Christopher Columbus and the
500-years conspiracy to cover up
his true identity and mission

Karlos K.

COVER DESIGN

Portrait of Columbus: extract from the altarpiece "The Virgin of the Navigators", in Seville cathedral, by Alejo Fernández, c. 1536

The Nautical Chart, by Portuguese cartographer Pedro Reinel, c. 1504

CONTENTS

FOREWORD

"In te Domine speravi: non confundar in aeternum"
EPITAPH OF COLUMBUS TOMB

T he discoverer of the Americas is probably the second-best known person in the world and also the second about whom more has been written, after Jesus Christ. The deep fog of contradictions, deception and lies about the life of Christopher Columbus has proven a fertile ground for conspiracy theories and heated debates amongst historians, sparkling the imagination of many.

We may never find out his true name, but more importantly, why have so many, for so long, gone to such great lengths to cover up his identity and true mission? Who was Columbus and what was he doing? It must have been a massive and threatening secret, to justify the intricate web of deceit and manipulation weaved by monarchs, popes and chroniclers for over five centuries. This may be the longest lasting international conspiracy.

Columbus reflects, probably better than anyone else, the spirit of adventure, brilliance, courage and opportunism of the Age of Discoveries, the shift in global power it originated, as well as the political confrontation between Spain and Portugal at the end of the fifteenth century.

For centuries, the Arabs dominated the land routes of the silk road and the Italian republics of Venice and Genoa monopolized the Mediterranean trade up to the Pillars of Hercules, in the Gibraltar straight. Spices were more than a commercial commodity. They were claimed to have almost-magical properties, used as elixir to cure certain diseases and in concoctions for enhanced sexual prowess. They masked the flavor and odor of rotting food. They were exotic luxuries worth fortunes. Since the Romans, beyond those Pillars of Hercules lied the "Mar Tenebroso", the Sea of Darkness, full of monsters and dangers. The sun set down to the west by entering the water in boiling cascades at the end of the world.

In 1415, a tiny country of less than one million inhabitants in the western corner of Europe was setting off across the Mediterranean to conquer Ceuta, a display of courage and dare from the new founded Aviz dynasty. Less than a century later, at the end of the fifteenth century, The Portuguese had dominated the Atlantic winds and currents, rounded Africa, reached India and discovered Brazil. Over the following decades, Portugal would establish a global empire over which the sun never set, from Brazil to Japan. The spice and silk route shifted and with it the balance of power.

By the mid-1480's, Portugal was one of the most advanced scientific and maritime power of the time, attracting the most brilliant mathematicians and cosmographers to Lisbon. The Portuguese Caravelas relentlessly pushed south through the African coast, establishing trading outposts and looking for the passage into the route to the spices, gold and silks of the east. By 1470, Portuguese sailors had crossed south of the Equator, disproving the myth the fleets would fall into an abyss of boiling waters or that they would not be able to return north due to the globe's curvature. In 1485 the Portuguese Jew Abraão Zacuto created the Tables of Solar Declination at the Equator, which allowed to establish a boat's position based on the sun. And the great mathematician of the Junta dos Matemáticos, Pedro Correia da Cunha, brother in law of Christopher Columbus, was working on an estimation of the length of the globe's degree, which he achieved with such accuracy it would take 200 years to improve on his calculations. In 1488, Bartolomeu Dias turned the Cape of Good Hope, paving the way for the all maritime route to Asia.

But Granada would soon fall, thus removing the last bastion of Arab occupation of the Iberian Peninsula. With the Succession War and the Reconquista ended, the Spanish Catholic Monarchs turned their attentions to the Atlantic. This would set off the competitive race between the two countries to reach and claim...well, the world.

It was in retrospect a true Space Race, similar to the race to reach the moon between the USA and USSR in the 20th century (though with significantly more deaths). In 1482, Diogo Cão planted the first two "padrões", large stone pillars with an iron cross and an inscription, to mark the limit his caravels had reached. After these, the Portuguese sailors kept hauling stone pillars at marking points of their expeditions. These were men-sized stone pillars, transported thousands of miles from Lisbon and are a statement of intentions, like an American flag planted on the moon or the "greetings to the universe" in 55 languages of the gold record carried on the Voyager spacecraft.

Undoubtedly, the Age of Discoveries constituted a turning point in human history, jump-starting the shift from Middle Ages to Renaissance and henceforth the industrial revolution. It is, in the scientific and technical progress it required, the sheer courage and ambition it demanded and the overreaching social, artistic and cultural changes it unlocked, truly comparable to the Space Race – I dare say, the impact of the Age of Discoveries vastly surpasses the Space Race... it would require the next SpaceX mission to discover wild animals and plants and intelligent creatures in Mars to take the Space Age to the same level of social and cultural impact as the Maritime Age of Discoveries.

While cruising through the mysteries and lives of the Admiral who gave "new worlds to the world", we are spectators of a turning point in human history and the birth of the modern world.

Portuguese and Spanish fleets brought, in their return journeys, a display of colors, languages, cultures, spices and ideas that would melt the last bastions of the medieval ages. And, yes... also slaves, who would be the grounding force to colonize the American continent.

In the complex mix of medieval religiosity, knightly honor, mercantilism and scientific enquiry of the Age of Discoveries, lies a profound bridge from the middle ages into the Renaissance. In a short period of a few decades, the Age of Discoveries cracked wide open the medieval fortress, allowing the modern age to rush in and radically change the world.

At the turn of the century, the terrifying ocean had been conquered, giving humankind a new sense of technical power, free-will and self-belief. For centuries, the Pillars of Hercules in the Gibraltar strait marked the limit beyond which no sailor would venture. Legend has it that the Romans had engraved an inscription in the Pillars saying "Non plus ultra" (nothing further beyond). In the 16th century, the inscription was erased.

The mysteries around Columbus are deeply rooted against this complex background. They seem to originate from a mixture of political power games, opportunistic charlatans and religious quests.

Only recently has academic research started to clear the fog, recognizing the overwhelming evidence that Columbus was Portuguese, a secret agent of King João II in a Machiavellian plot the send the Spanish Kings into a wild goose chase to the west, protecting the Portuguese eastern route to India. The Tordesillas Treaty brokered by the Pope, dividing the world between Spain (West) and Portugal (East), was signed shortly after Columbus' first return.

The "Inheritance trials" of 1578-1608, after Columbus's grandson died without legitimate heirs, became a fertile ground for charlatans to attempt intricate cons, including forged documents from a supposed Genoese heir.

Some historians argue Columbus was of Jewish descent, from a family of "conversos". His mysterious signature may have a cabalistic meaning, hiding the key to his secret. Columbus benefitted from the key support of Jews like Luis de Santangel and Gabriel Sanchez in the financing of the first expedition. In his first expedition, Columbus used Abraão Zacuto's Solar Declination Tables, written in Hebrew. He enlisted dozens of Jews on the crew of his first voyage. The ships sailed out of Spain on 3 August 1492, the exact day of the expulsion of the Jews by Isabella's royal decree. Contrary to the usual practice, Columbus didn't spend the night before departure in vigil in a church. He required the crew to board, sealing off the ships before midnight. On the day of the expulsion, Columbus' ships set sail, a symbolic new Exodus in search of a new Promised Land.

All this could explain the secrecy and mystery around Columbus. But once the dust had settled, we would expect the veil of mystery to dissolve into the mist of time – but alas, that would not be the case. On the contrary. At the end of the 19th century, a stream of documents was made public by the City of Genoa, including forged collages with different handwritings and blank sections. In the twentieth century, the Spanish historian Ricardo Róspide supposedly found an important document about Columbus, but it was silenced (probably censored by the conservative religious dictatorships of Salazar and Franco). He confessed to a close friend that if he published what he had found he would face grave danger. Róspide died shortly after. The document or proof Róspide uncovered was never found.

It would be understandable that a conspiracy during the power struggles between the two superpowers of their time could be covered up for a few decades. But what is clearly inexplicable is that such censorship continued relentlessly for 500 years! What political, economic or religious interests could justify such secrecy?

So, there must be something else. There must be some enormous secret hidden behind Columbus's mysterious life, to justify five centuries of ongoing forgery, lies and censorship. What that secret is, we can only speculate. It is exactly at this point that this book crosses the fine boundary between facts and fiction.

This is not a history book, but a book of crossed stories inspired by the figure of Columbus. Facts and science can only take us so far on lifting the veil over Columbus' life, revealing only the tip of the iceberg. Beyond that, we can only guess, speculate and invent...

The facts, documents and artworks referred in this book are real, the speculations around them are fictional. You, the reader, will have to decide where the line between reality and fantasy lies. You, the reader, will have to establish your own "Tordesillas line" that separates the history from the story.

LISBON, JULY 2006

"God does not forgive the sins He makes us commit."
JOSÉ SARAMAGO, THE GOSPEL ACCORDING TO JESUS CHRIST

T he Delta Airlines nonstop flight from JFK to Lisbon touched down at 8.39am, 51 minutes ahead of schedule. This was remarkable, although not at all uncommon on the eastwards flights, thanks to the North Atlantic jet stream. According to the captain's information, they had moved within a 180 km/hour jet stream which helped the aircraft to reach a speed of more than 1.000 km/hour at cruising altitude, thus allowing them to make the 6h40m flight in less than 6 hours. Her body was aching from the sleepless night in the small seats, and she craved for a shower and a bed. Hopefully, her sister would be waiting in the airport to pick them up in Lisbon.

It had all started two years ago in a downtown Boston coffee shop, near the Common's, at the corner of Beacon and Charles Street. At least, that's what Savanah told her friends, although she herself was not totally sure. The little coffee shop had later been bought by a national coffee chain, but at the time it was a lovely local spot with the best espresso in town. It was owned by Paolo, a third generation Italian who proudly maintained the coffee shop opened by his grandfather, with aged photos in fogged and dusty frames of Tuscan countryside or Roman landmarks. Paolo himself decided it was good for business to maintain the flair and talkative attitude of the Italians – and with that, a penchant to talk up the young ladies that came to the shop. That said, he was a democratic *charmant*, seducing all women indiscriminately.

Savanah had arrived in Cambridge, Massachusetts a couple of weeks before, at the end of August 2004, to look up for a flat and settle down as a first year Harvard Business School MBA student. She had been to Paolo's a few times, enjoyed the slow and positive atmosphere of the place as well as the deep historical symbolism of the Boston Common's, the cradle of the United States. Paolo's flirts were a bonus, which she took at face value – good natured and inconsequential. That morning Savanah was in a good mood. She had finally settled for a small studio close to the Charles River, ten minutes cycling to HBS. It had the advantage of allowing her to be simultaneously close to Boston city center and the school. It was a bit pricey, but the money she had made as an investment banking analyst in Wall Street for the past three years allowed her to afford it. The MBA fees, though, were a different matter, but a great job at the end of the program would certainly pay off the student loans. Savanah had just turned 25, one of the youngest students of the MBA intake and a bright future ahead. Although not what men would call a "stunner", she had an elegant and athletic figure – not that she had had the time to go often to the overpriced gym in NY she insisted on maintaining during the past three years, but still remnants of the volleyball she played all the way from high school to the end of university.

She asked for a "doppio espresso macchiato, just a splash of skinny milk, take away". "Of course, bella signora, the dark roast blend as usual, sì?"

She could almost pinpoint the exact moment it happened. The day was hot and she was wearing a light summer dress, her bare arms showing her white, almost pink skin covered by a light translucent blond fluff. As she was leaving the coffee shop, a strong and tanned male hand held the door for her. As she exited, her bare arm fortuitously touched the tanned hand holding the door. It was just a light, unconscious touch. A scrape really, not a touch, because she kept on walking. But enough to make the tiny blond hairs on her arm stand. Perhaps what had caused the sensation was that the touch had been... unhurried. Not as hasty brush of two strangers in the bustle of the quotidian. As if time had imperceptibly come to a halt, a bubble of time encompassing only the white arm and the tanned hand touching in slow motion, leaving everything else – other people, smells, sounds – outside the selfishness of individuality.

On her wedding, she had retold that story, saying she had felt goose bumps on that moment – the funny thing was that she had not even seen the stranger's face. It was just a reaction of her skin to the chance touch of a hand, her nervous system suddenly awakened by the unexpected touch. But that was an exaggeration.

Maybe it had just been the reaction of her skin at passing from the cool shadow of the coffee shop into the hot day outside, a burst of sunlight suddenly hitting her body. As her eyes adjusted to the sudden explosion of light, she turned her head, a strand of blond hair falling in front of her eyes, to thank the stranger. An absent minded, casual, thank you, because her mind had not yet processed the tingle in the skin of her harm, the tint bristle hairs upended. That sensation was still an instant behind, trapped in that bubble of time. The vaguely familiar guy held the door for her, looking shamelessly into her eyes while saying "Without coffee I'm gonna feel like something's missing in the day". Savanah smiled and held his gaze, continuing the Al Pacino line, almost as an automatic response, in the spur of the moment: "Most of my scripts have coffee stains on them... that's how you know it's a Pacino script." The guy was obviously impressed. Like in all other things in life, Savanah believed that if you want to beat them, you must know more than them.

It turned out Hugh was a classmate and they had briefly met during induction day back in July. Hugh insisted walking her down the Commons as she headed towards the Park Street metro station. That warm September morning she found him a bit cocky, the type of overconfident sporty type that expected a girl to fall out for him and be grateful of the scrapes of attention he was dispensing on her. Tough luck. But then again, from her experience, at that age guys were mostly divided into two categories: dickheads who believed they would be masters of the universe, or sex-deprived losers who looked like puppies and couldn't hold a decent conversation with a woman without wetting themselves. Yeah, there were also the intellectual types and the sadistic, but those were the tail ends of the probability function... To be honest, she preferred the overconfident masters of the universe.

To her surprise, she found herself engaged at the end of the first year and married at the end of the second. They married on Sunday, 23 July 2006, in Savanah's hometown of Newport, Rhode Island. In September, a vastly well-paid job at Goldman awaited her in New York, while Hugh had landed his dream job as a hedge fund manager. Both knew what expected them over the next 10 years, but the reward at the end of the line was massive. It was said that when you enter Wall Street, a shot was fired on your back and you just had to keep out-running the bullet and never look back. Hugh was thrilled about the all thing. Savanah was a bit more cynical, although she liked finance and loved the buzz of being in the middle of the action, making things happen and the world go round. During her time at JPMorgan before the MBA, she had the habit of taking a solitary walk up and down the street eating her lunchtime sandwich, away from the rush and noise of the open-space office, while mentally planning the slides for the pitch books first-years were condemned to produce, chained to the production line 15 hours a day. In one of those lunchtime walks, it suddenly hit her – she smiled inward as she realized Wall Street was literally a street that started with a kindergarten and ended with the graveyard of Trinity Church... so fitting for the masters of the universe.

Anyway, Goldman was still a month away. Now Savanah and Hugh had three weeks to enjoy their honeymoon. They had finally agreed on a two-weeks tour of European cities and one week in Greece, island-hoping in a luxury sailing private tour.

As they waited for their luggage on the airport terminal and Savanah turned on her iPhone, a text message from her sister blipped on the screen. It had probably been sent while they were flying. Raven's text was short and a bit cryptic: "Sorry, can't pick you up. Urgent thing in Tomar, back tonight. Take a cab to the apartment and get a coffee at Antonio's next door. XX"

That was odd. But Raven was odd anyway, so nothing to be surprised. She was obsessed with Christopher Columbus, or Christopher Colon as she insisted. Savanah remembered fondly the lazy summer afternoons sailing with her twin sister in their godfather's boat around the Caribbean. He used to tell them stories about Colon's life and mysteries. Every summer since she could remember, they had sailed together, diving on Cuba's beaches, cruising the shores of Haiti and Dominican Republic, visiting the Cathedral of Santa Maria Menor in Santo Domingo where Christopher Columbus had been buried before being moved to Habana Cathedral and then to Seville Cathedral. Before that, the remains of the Admiral had initially been buried in Valladolid where he died and Las Cuevas Monastery in Seville. That was surely a record: 5 burial places. The famous explorer bones were as restless in death as in life.

Savanah and Raven both cherished those warm and breezy Caribbean holidays, hearing their godfather talk about the massive iron bell of Santa Maria, the ship from Columbus's fleet that supposedly crashed in the low tide reef off the island of Hispaniola, now Dominican Republic, and sunk – never to be found again!!

Still, Savanah found it a bit pointless to keep turning old and dusty pages in moldy libraries or spending hours looking at engravings in monasteries and churches no one really cared about nowadays. Yes, Columbus was a weird guy, with some crazy stories and mysteries, but the history books had settled that long ago. It was all in Wikipedia: "Christopher Columbus (1451-1506) was an Italian explorer, navigator, and colonist who completed four voyages across the Atlantic Ocean under the auspices of the Catholic Monarchs of Spain. He led the first European expeditions to the Caribbean, Central America, and South America, initiating the permanent European colonization of the Americas. Columbus discovered a viable sailing route to the Americas, a continent that was then unknown to the Old World. While what he thought he had discovered was a route to the Far East, he is credited with the opening of the Americas for conquest and settlement by Europeans." That's it, right? He convinced the Spanish Catholic Kings to finance his expedition to the Indies via a westwards route, based on Ptolomeu's view of a round Earth, thus contradicting the medieval myth of a flat Earth, and by doing so not only became the First Governor of the West Indies, but also contributed to taking humankind from the medieval Dark Ages into the Renaissance. His last days were sad, imprisoned by the Spanish in Santo Domingo and taken in shackles to Spain. In a very well received and widely circulated diary of voyage, the explorer and naturalist Amerigo Vespucci described in splendid and ravishing detail the geography, landscapes and costumes of the new lands and – as legend has it – used for the first time the expression New World, thus recognizing it as a new continent and not just scattered islands. A famous mapmaker, whose name she had now forgotten, had published a map where the new continent was named after the Latinized name Amerigo, which ultimately led to the new continent name of America. Perhaps if it had not been for that historical mistake, Colombia would now be a continent instead of a country.

Raven had finished her undergrad degree at UPenn in History and then moved to Lisbon to do her PhD research on Christopher Colon. Savanah felt a bit stiff about the fact Raven had been traveling between Rio de Janeiro, the Caribbean, Genoa, Lisbon, Seville and god knows where, sponsored by dad's money, while she was slaving away to make her way up the investment banking grinding machine.

Savanah pushed those thoughts away as unworthy, but they stubbornly reappeared once in a while, like a faint ghost making fun of her. But, heiii... Savanah and Hugh had only 3 days in Lisbon before flying out to Paris, and Raven couldn't spare the time to meet her husband and be with her twin sister? Gosh, not coming to the wedding had been bad, but this was a bit too much. Anyway, Raven had always been a head in the moon, fantasying about her mysteries and conspiracy theories, and Savanah had got used to take her eccentricities at face value. She had even made the effort to pretend to appreciate the loud, horrible satanic music Raven had played at a heavy metal band at high school.

Anyway, no matter. If Raven couldn't meet them, it meant more time for her and Hugh to be alone and enjoy the honeymoon. There was just a problem, as Hugh pointed out as they entered a taxi outside the airport terminal. "How are we going to get into the apartment to leave the luggage, without the keys?"

Savanah waived the issue aside a bit too hastily, transpiring some nervousness she attempted to hide, saying Raven had surely left them some clue to find the keys. The tiredness that had weighted on her bones just minutes ago was gone, and she was excited about exploring the city. Heading towards Raven's apartment in Alfama, she asked the taxi driver to take a tourist route through the river and the old town.

Savanah could feel the heavy late July heat rising from the ground, tempered by a light breeze from the Atlantic. The tourist route taken by the taxi driver bought them close to the Tagus, with a glimpse of the Vasco da Gama bridge. The sun reflected between the clear blue sky and the still waters of Mar da Palha, the wide estuary formed by the Tagus river, creating a reflective mirror that invaded the city in a hazy golden light, like sparkling liquid honey. As the taxi driver explained in a quite decent English, Vasco da Gama bridge, with 12km, is the longest in western Europe and is the unique setting for the Lisbon half marathon that every year closes off the bridge for close to 40.000 runners.

As they turned westwards towards the heart of the old town, they marveled at the stacking of houses in a multitude of colors, piggybacking on top of each other in the gentle uphill slope to St. Jorge Castle, as if competing to catch a glimpse of the river. The taxi driver continued his pleasant description of the old "bairros", the Moorish quarter, the Jewish quarter, until they reached their destination.

As they climbed out of the taxi, Savanah smiled... Raven's apartment was in a side-looped old building, freshly painted in pale blue, lying shoulder to shoulder against other old buildings as if supporting each other, in a steep street of Alfama. The sidewalk had an intricate geometrical design, the typical Portuguese cobblestone, worn by the erosion of centuries. It looked beautiful but deadly – specially for women in high heels on a rainy day.

In the ground floor of Raven's building, a rusted sign announced Café Antonio, a picturesque coffee shop and tavern, with two cast iron tables outside, and a front window where you could see small groceries, bread, fruit and vegetables.

Savanah and Hugh set down for a coffee, as instructed by Raven's text message. As they did so, a mustachioed man with a friendly round face, sweating abundantly (clearly the shop didn't have air conditioned...) came out of the store greeting her enthusiastically. "Menina Raven, já voltou!! An envelope was left under the door, found it as I opened the store this morning, it is addressed to you". The man, probably Antonio, gesticulated a lot as he talked, in a clear effort to make himself understood by the American girl. She hadn't said a word, but he was making an effort to address her in English. When he deposited an envelope on the table, addressed to Raven, Savanah laughed as she understood: the man had mistaken her for her twin sister. She was about to explain the confusion when she felt the touch of keys inside the envelope. Ah, Raven, naughty girl!

She probably left Lisbon in a rush very early that morning, so left the envelope with the keys addressed to herself under Antonio's shop door, anticipating he would confuse the twin sisters and give the envelope to Savanah as soon as she arrived.

So be it. She winked to Hugh and thanked Sr. Antonio, ordering some breakfast with a flush of gestures and a lot of pointing. Sr. Antonio was clearly used to talking to her sister in a mix of English and Portuguese. He still seemed to have no clue this was a different person.

In the apartment upstairs, as Savanah was taking a shower, Hugh called her up. "Hey, Savanah, who is Sarah?"

"What? Can't hear you, I'm in the shower."

Hugh came into the bathroom holding a piece of paper. Savanah came out of the shower and was drying herself with a towel as Hugh read the message. "Hi Sophia. I need to rush out to Convento de Cristo in Tomar... discovered something huge, will tell you everything tonight. Glad you found the keys with Sr. Antonio :-). See you soon, Sarah!"

"Long story, love. I am Sophia. For some reason, we grew up calling each other by those names. Raven calls me Sophia. I call her Sarah. It was also the names our godfather used for us, so it became a bit of an insider secret."

They left the Alfama apartment mid-morning, around 10 o'clock, for a leisurely sightseeing walk. Savanah had expected her sister to show them around town, so she had not really planned a route. They were heading towards Terreiro do Paço when Savanah's mobile rang. It was Raven. It sounded like she was driving, her mobile in loud-speak. Yes, they had found the keys all right. Yes, they were having a good time. No, there was no problem she had not picked them up. Raven sounded excited, maybe a bit nervous, and said something about an extraordinary discovery, a lost Book from Colon's library that might have been hidden in the Love Chapel in Tomar. Whatever that was. "I'm now arriving in Tomar and will be back to Lisbon tonight. It might be late, so don't wait up. Sophia, this changes everything, you will see! Love you, sis". And she hung up.

That evening, Savanah and Hugh lounged lazily in the balcony of second floor apartment, with some cold beer and a lot of kissing, enjoying that unique feeling of the city as it cools down from the daily heat. Down the steep street they could barely see a portion of the river. Uphill they couldn't see much, but could feel the imposing force of St. Jorge Castle dominating the city at its feet. The monotonous sound of the cicadas, the blue hue of the moonlight reflecting off the river and the respite from the daily heat lulled the city into a sleepy haze, in a long sensual groan, inviting mysteries and secrets behind closed doors. Savanah and Hugh moved to the bedroom, made somewhat noisy sex that could surely be heard on the street from the open window, and fell deeply asleep.

In the middle of the night, they were woken up by hysterical cries in the street. Someone was shouting. It seemed something distant, as the sounds of reality mixed with the stuff of their dreams, in a limbo between two worlds. As consciousness was fighting its way out of the sleepy mists, they were violently awakened by the sound of crashing glass. Hugh ran to the living room and cursed. Someone had thrown a cobblestone through the window. The stone caused a dent on the wooden dining table and laid on the floor, splinted in two. Fuck.

They heard steps running down the street. Morons. Assholes.

In the morning, as they were having breakfast after cleaning up the mess, Savanah looked fixedly to a spot in the ceiling, her mind still processing what the eyes were seeing. She was still a bit numb from the jet lag, in need of caffeine.

"Sons of a bitch, assholes, fuckers!" Hugh looked towards the spot where her eyes were fixed. A fist-sized hole in the ceiling, a nasty smudge on the otherwise white-painted ceiling. The cobblestone thrown from the street, following its inexorable elliptical gravitational path, hit the ceiling before crashing down into the wooden table and then the floor.

They only got the news when they walked out of the apartment, met in shock by Sr. Antonio, who run towards her, pale and hysterical, as if seeing a ghost. He started calling out, looking confused. It took Savanah some seconds to notice the buzz around them from a crowd further down the road.

Raven had never made it to the apartment. She had been found dead early in the morning, in the driving seat of her red Fiat Punto, in the steep street 300 meters away from her apartment, the door ajar and no signs of violence or fight.

A pool of blood soaked the seat and the floor. On her left wrist, a deep cut in the shape of a pentagram.

The police investigation was a dead-end. The time of dead was placed somewhere around 3.00-3.30 in the morning. The street had apparently been deserted and the neighbors asleep, as no-one recalled anything. The cobblestone thrown at their apartment window could have been around the time of Raven's death, but Savanah and Hugh weren't sure.

There were no fingerprints. The autopsy found traces of a strong sedative, Fentanyl, but no traces of injection or ingestion, suggesting the drug had been absorbed by nasal spray – willingly or administered. Fentanyl is the most commonly used synthetic opioid in medicine, but also widely used as a recreational drug and the most common cause of overdose deaths in the United States. It has a very rapid onset, although its effects last less than two hours. Fentanyl is 100 times stronger than morphine, and if Raven's assailant had pushed an impregnated cloth on Raven's mouth and nose, she would have been knock out almost instantly and unable to cry out for help. In any case, she had not overdosed. Raven died of the bleeding caused by the pentagram-shaped wound on her wrist.

The honeymoon was, of course, cancelled.

On the third day after the event, as Savanah and Hugh returned to the apartment after hours of bureaucracy in the American embassy to handle the repatriation of the body, she noticed a car parked on the street in front of the apartment. The man inside looked firmly at her, as if trying to ascertain if he had just seen a ghost, then drove away. He had shaven head, a goatee beard and a black Iron Maiden t-shirt.

Police investigation never found any relevant leads. No fingerprints, no visible marks of physical struggle or rape, no witnesses. The time of death, the presence of drugs and the satanic pentagram cut led the police investigators to consider the most likely scenario was a drugs-related crime or some satanic ritual suicide pact gone wrong. This was reinforced when a 112 emergency call [1] was linked to the death. As the police investigator explained to Savanah and Hugh, the call had been placed at 3.14am from Raven's mobile number. She didn't speak directly to the emergency phone line operator nor answered the questions, but the call recorded Raven saying something quite weird:

"High Goat, is Satan with you?"

After this recording and the results of the autopsy, the investigation winded down, although never officially concluded. Resources were pulled by other crimes with more likelihood of being solved... Savanah never mentioned this recording to her parents, to avoid increasing even further their distress. Just the suggestion Raven might have been using drugs or a victim of a satanic gang crime was enough for them to recriminate themselves for whatever parenting failures they invented. Parenthood is all about anxiety – parents never quite let go of the image of a tiny baby in their arms, totally dependent on them for even the basic survival needs, and carry that self-imposed burden of protection forever. Any failure of a daughter or son when adult is felt by parents as their own failure. Good thing that successes and happiness too.

SAGRES, JUNE 1460

(Columbus)

I was only nine when my father, a colossal man with reddish blond hair and blue eyes uncommon in those parts of the world, first took me to cross the 175 leagues from Madeira to Lisbon. At the time, I was not yet Christopher Colon.

It had been a last minute call to the mainland. Father had received ill-news that Infante Dom Henrique was sick and could die soon, so they had to make the voyage to meet the Old Man. Why he was taking me with him, no-one knew.

"I was born a king and a warrior" – father said in face of mother's protests – "At his age I already held a longsword and jested in tournaments to prove my skill. We now live in a land of sailors, so he must learn to live at sea. His sword will be the Compass, his armor the Caravela. He must learn to be one with the sea and the wind. The Old Man wants to speak to the boy."

As our ship entered the large mouth of the Tagus and approached the dock in Belém, what impressed me the most was the light of the city. The wide river reflected the clear blue skies filling everything with a warm, penetrating light. Lisbon was at the forefront of maritime exploration, a magnet that attracted cosmographers, mathematicians, adventurers and charlatans. The river was a forest of sails, the riverbanks lined with ships under construction exhibiting their ribs like skeletons of massive sea monsters. As we walked the shore towards the royal Paço, I marveled at the diversity of faces, variety of clothes and smells. The smells were the most memorable. Father had always told me that big cities stink. Indeed, a faint smell of rot and excrements hang over all things, but overpowered by the scents of freshly baked bread, exotic spices and fruit I had never seen, despite living in the fertile lands of Madeira island. My eyes turned everywhere, following the steps of strange men I had never seen – man black as charcoal with a deep blue hue and glistening white teeth, Arabs dressed in plain white cloths, Jews, Turks, Italians, Spanish. I could hear many languages with strange-sounding words, but somehow these people managed to communicate. Everywhere I looked, a wide assortment of priests and monks. Rough sailors, waiting for their next assignment, drinking the day away, playing cards or darts. Everyone seemed busy, talking loudly and gesticulating. Everywhere I looked, there were ships being built, the ships of the Infante being prepared to sail down the coast of Africa to Guinea and further south. Always further south. How could a small country of less than 1 million people command such large expeditions into lands though inaccessible just a few decades ago?

Father was at court, paying his respects to King Afonso, so I had been left outside to roam the city. João da Câmara, my older cousin, son of the governor of Madeira João Gonçalves Zarco, showed off his knowledge of ship-craft by explaining those ships under construction were a new form of vessel. The Old Man was always challenging his ship masters with new designs that could make the ships faster, with higher sterns than the old Mediterranean galleys, to be able to stand the rough waves of the open sea away from visible shore. This posed an immense problem – higher sterns and side decks meant they could not use oars to push the ship forward when coursing contrary to the winds. So they had adapted an Arabic type of sail, a triangular sail able to tack upwind: the lateen. The boats were also smaller, able to explore rivers inland, which required a broader hold able to take the provisions of water, salted meat and hard biscuit. The Infante had announced a large reward for the carpenters and tin-makers who could solve the problem of rotting water – the traditional container lined with black pitch to become water-tight turned the water insoluble a few weeks after storage, so they needed a new solution.

Our final destination was still several days on horseback, and father was in a hurry. The Old Man was dying and had summoned us in haste.

The Infante, grand master of the Order of Christ, lived in a self-imposed captivity of austerity in Sagres, where he had assembled the most prominent minds of that time in the School of Sagres. I had fantasized about a magnificent palace with extraordinary machines and great debates around opulent gardens... but when we arrived at that barren promontory at the southwestern tip of Europe, I was stuck by anti-climax. It was a barren wasteland atop a cliff battered by waves, with grey and somber men and barely any other sound besides the cries of the seagulls and the clash of the waves into the promontory. We entered the eastern gate of the ascetic fortress, passing the chapel of Nossa Senhora da Graça, dedicated to Virgin Mary, where mariners spent their nights in pray before challenging the Sea of Darkness. The only sign that this was the most active scientific and exploration center of Europe in that year of 1460 was the continuous movement of ships you could see heading towards Lagos, large galleys from the commerce in North Africa through Ceuta and ocean-going Caravels.

We were at the outer edges of civilization, away from the bursting trade ports of Venice and Genoa who monopolized the trade with Asia – spices, silk and precious stones –, away from the religious power of Rome – the only supranational institution in the world –, away from the cultural and artistic renovation of the Renaissance that was starting to take shape in central Europe. For centuries, the country had looked west, to the Sea of Darkness as the Arabs called it, to the vast sea where the sun sets on a curving line at night, to the pounding waves and the sheet of white foam... longing to conquer it.

As we were approaching the fortress, I noticed a wide circumference marked on the floor, with intricate signs similar to those I had seen on father's books. A steel rod (which I would later learn was known as "Vara de Medição" – the measuring stick or simply "the Stick") prompted from the dusty land in a straight vertical line to the skies, about 2 meters tall. From the center steel rod departed several radius-lines, dividing the circumference in sixteen zones, each marked with a geographic direction and a name, some of which I recognized as wind names. It was the Wind Rose, both a mystical and practical symbol of the Order. It would play a key role in my life's quest.

That night I barely slept in anticipation for the meeting with the Old Man in the morning. The cells inside the Fortaleza were simple, monastic, with a hard bed and bare furnishings. But the library..., heavens, the library occupied the entire center of the Fort, with sturdy wood tables filled with maps and strange nautical instruments I barely knew at the time.

It happened at dusk. It was still dark when father took me out into the promontory, the rocky cliff of Cape Saint Vincent. This is the prow of Europe. The first rays of sunlight appeared on the East, enveloping the world with a soft glow. The water was still as a lake, with a metallic quality that looked like liquid silver. A seagull floated on the water, slowly moving to the rhythm of the sea, indifferent to the destinies of men. It looked straight onwards, fixed on a distant point on the horizon I could not discern. What was the seagull waiting for? Uncomplaining, undemanding, just focused on its own selfish existence...

The Infante sat alone on the rocks, looking West, with the faint light at his back creating a halo of semi-divinity. He was clad in black, with a light black head-cloth fashioned like the moors, with a hanging strip you could use to cover your face against the burning sun or the whipping wind.

"Come closer. Only the boy."

I approached the Navigator and sat next to him, unable to look at his face. This was the Infante himself, what could he possibly want to talk about with a boy like me. We just stood there in silence. Then he spoke.

"What do you see?"

How was I supposed to answer such question? Was it a trick question, to test my knowledge, or an honest question to test my beliefs? As I tend to do when confronted with the unknown, I looked for an answer that would be unexpected, that could impress the Old Man and make him remember me.

"Beauty."

"It is, boy, it is. True enough. It is the beauty of the world God bestowed upon us, therefore invoking the marvel of His gift of intellect with which can perceive this sense of beauty. Keep your mind open to the beauty of the world. Do not trust what those ancient books tell you, unless you can understand with your brain or see with your eyes".

Then silence again, cut only by the languished sound of calm surf caressing the edges of the promontory below.

"And home."

"You mean, Madeira?"

"No. The far distant lands I will discover for you, my Lord, which by your grace and the King of Portugal I will have the pleasure of calling home."

"You are a strange boy. Too grown up for your age. Better that way. The weight of the quest me and your father will put on your shoulders is such that you need to grow fast. The sun rises to our backs and will describe an arch, burn from the South at noon and set on the West. Every day, the cosmic bodies are the only thing that is real, immutable, indifferent to the struggles of the lives of men. Do you know what the old books say? That the sun enters the sea and heats the water to the point of boiling and if a ship ventures close enough to the edges of the world, it will burn."

Silence.

"That cannot be."

"Why?"

"If the water boils, it evaporates and leaves an empty space. The water next to it enters the void and it also evaporates and so forth, until all water in the sea is gone and we should see the innards of the world exposed, with all water gone. That does not happen."

"Indeed, it cannot be. We shall sail further South and show them all. I know what they say on my back. A stubborn old man toying with dangerous dreams, chasing fantasies while sending men to their deaths by sea monsters or boiling waters. Boy, never doubt. Always further. Always further. There are no dangers grave enough that cannot be overcome by the promise of rewards. The little minds will always say you are wrong until you prove them wrong. Never listen to them. Never listen to the old theories that you cannot understand with your mind or test with your eyes. If you don't understand, look further. Never listen to the intrigues of the court mice, scheming behind your back while you push forward. God made the world and our enquiring mind to understand His creation. Exploring brings us closer to God. I have spent all my fortune and fallen in debt to set up this magnificent enterprise. So far, it has not yet paid off. But I do not worry too much. Others will come after me, keep pushing forward, and the rewards will come. They say to my nephew King Afonso that these maritime explorations are a waste of time and money - how wrong they are. We know today more about the world and the oceans than any European court. In this fortress, men of knowledge map the unknown world. Knowledge is power, and for a small country like ours, the only true power we can hope to achieve. What you know, you owe no one."

His feeble hands sat quietly on the Old Man's knees, as we sat on the rocks looking west. The only ornament he used was a ring on his left hand, a gold ring with a round sigil displaying an embossed hooked X, the north-eastern arm tilting up slightly.

I looked at the lone seagull on the silver still water, floating on the foam. Gulls never fly far from land or water. That one had the plumage of three or four years, an adult gull. It can manage about two leagues from land, at most. As if prompted by my attention, the lone seagull moved its head and opened the wings, gliding masterfully over the water and taking flight. It rose high up in the sky, wings stretched in solemn and majestic defiance of the earthbound limits of the two men seating on the rocks. The seagull hovered for a few seconds, static as it scanned the still waters down the reef, as if contemplating its chances of finding food. Then it dived straight into the sea, ready to continue with the gruesome business of daily life.

"So, boy", continued the Infante, "Have you seen the forbidden Book?"

"Yes, Dom Henrique.", I answered, knowing perfectly well he could only be referring to one book.

"Good, good…And has you father told you about the grotto in the Pyrenees?"

"Yes. A tremendous secret we must protect."

"Show me the figure engraved on the cover of the Book."

Solemnly, I picked up a stick and draw in the gravel and the sand. A rose and a cross joined in an embrace, the arms of the cross spreading wide as if trying to hug the rose. The Rosacrux engraved on the cover of the Book and on the Ark the Templars had for centuries been protecting.

"The Rosacrux, Dom Henrique. The arched cross is drawn on the sails of Portuguese Caravelas, the Crux still separated from the Rose. The Rose is kept hidden in the far lands beyond the boiling seas, until our Caravelas can re-unite the forbidden Book with the Rose."

"Very well", noted the Infante. "So you understand the importance of the mission"

The Infante motioned for my father to approach. There, in the cliffs above crashing waves and away from curi-ous hears, the two of them talked briefly. They seemed to know and trust each other, just confirming the final details of a plan that had been agreed in advance. Tough, austere men in manners as well as words. The plan had been set, there wasn't much to say besides trusting fortune and the strength of those they chose to face it.

"Ladislau, will the heirs of Henry Sinclair recognize the boy?"

"Yes, Henry. The boy has the mark, like me he has six toes on each foot"

The new day was dawning, the shadows of the night retreating hastily as the warm sunlight rushed in to fill everything. Nature was still yawning lazily, unaware of the plan set in motion by the Infante and my father. The full meaning of such mission would remain unclear to me for many years.

The Infante placed his hands on my shoulders as his eyes penetrated my soul. "Your father is from a noble Family. You are the son of a King. The quest me and your father are laying upon your shoulders is the most daring and challenging of all. Your fate is hard and most uncertain. Prepare well. And never listen to what the others say about you on your back. Never listen to them, for they have not been Initiated."

My father left early afternoon, heading back to Madeira. I stayed in Sagres for the following twelve years. Learning, studying and preparing.

The day after father left started at sunrise, as it would invariably do for the rest of my life. It became ingrained in such a way that even in my old years I would not be able to sleep beyond dusk. It never felt as a sacrifice, but rather as a blessing – I was being given the opportunity to participate in the most exciting, innovative and challenging enterprise of our times. I have always felt special, with a destiny to fulfill that required of me absolute dedication. Open myself to this destiny, embrace the sacrifice that God, my father and the Infante had bestowed upon me.

Indeed, I was special, son of a noble lineage with a grand mission. But I would soon learn that in Sagres, we were all special, each on his own way. Not all were noble, but each would prove to possess some unique quality. I learned to appreciate each of these friends. As I would find out many years later, the Old Man had a unique way of judging the men he carefully selected, of finding leaders who could strain further in the pursuit of great deeds. Bartolomeu Dias was stubborn, strong minded, well learned in the secrets of the sea. Pacheco Pereira was a brilliant cosmographer and mathematician, although I could not fathom how the skinny and sickly boy would ever survive on a boat. Diogo Cão was very much like me, proud and adventurous, rough and unrestful, maybe edging on the irresponsible sometimes and irascible when he failed to impose his will – but fearless and one of the most loyal men I ever knew. Gil Eanes was a charming philosopher chasing after girls in Lagos and looking for fortune. Gama was a cocky young boy, arrogant and auto-promoting, but a detailed and thorough planner, of soft noble manners he would learn to roughen up as he grew up. Pero da Covilhã came from a family of Jewish *conversos*, son of a merchant from the inner highlands of Portugal, who had learned to speak Arabic while accompanying his father in the trades with the Spanish Moorish cities. We all shared a sense of fate and pride... after all, we were being prepared to become members of the Order of Christ, command the Portuguese Caravelas, charter unknown lands and discover riches beyond our wildest dreams.

All these boys I met at the morning breakfast in the common room of Fortaleza de Sagres on my first day in June 1460, after the tedious morning prayers at the chapel. Dry bread and a bowl of warm red wine (spiced in festive days) in which to dip the dry bread. I was nine, a bit terrified by the novelty of it all, but also proud. Most of the boys in my table were a little older than me and had started at Sagres in January – I was 6 months behind. Probably the plan had been to start me when I was 10, but the Old Man illness rushed things. I was never the shy type. If anyone could bully others into submission, it was me.

Before we could break bread, the Old Man rose from the table he shared with the seasoned mariners and cosmographers who had the honor to seat with the Infante. Next to him, seated Jehuda Cresques, known as the Jew of the Needle, because he had invented the compass. On the Infante's other side, sat Master Abraão Zacuto, his trusted cosmographer and mathematician. He limped a bit and the back was noticeable curved. I would know later the Old Man often used a penitence belt with sharp thorns under his black habit. He addressed the boys, but I felt he was talking directly to me. The Infante had this unique capability of talking to a multitude but each of us felt he was addressing him in particular, with his long direct stares punctuating each sentence.

"The islands of Azores were on the Florentine and Arabic maps several years before we claimed them for Portugal. Indeed, any commercial fleet rounding the Atlantic coast from the Mediterranean to England or Flanders is likely to spot the islands in the horizon. But seeing land and plotting it on a map is not the same as discovering land. Discovery requires a more profound commitment, setting foot on it, understanding the locals and engaging in trade, understand their language and cultures, Christianize and educate them. Or if the land is uninhabited, colonize it."

"For decades the islands were seen from a distance at the west, fuming a grey smoke like if it was the end of the world. Frequently the passing fleets could witness massive volcanic explosions that cover the skies of ashes for miles. This is, most likely, how the western boundaries of the known ocean became to be known as the "Dark See" or "Tenebrous Sea". That was the realm of monsters. Indeed, when Diogo de Silves first set foot on São Miguel island, he discovered a strong sulfuric smell, the land dotted with holes from which smoke escaped continuously. The sailors started believing the islands were the domain of the Devil, the doors of Hell at the end of the world. The only way to face fears and prejudices is to break them. So I ordered a few dozen rams and sheep to be settled on the island. Beasts for the horny devil – it would befit the situation. A few years later, our men returned to the island to check if the rams survived. They had indeed, and reproduced happily. This convinced the people the islands were habitable and there was no devil. Settlement started and they now cook on those sulfuric hot holes..."

"Keep this story at your hearts. The domains of our Lord are infinite. But the domains of beasts, monsters and impassable obstacles are nothing but a reflection of our fears. There is no danger great enough that the expectation of gain and glory won't make men overcome it. You are the elite of Portugal, a new breed of men. Knights of the oceans who fight on caravels instead of on horses. God gave us a small nation as our cradle, but the entire world as our coffin."

NEWPORT, DECEMBER 2018

The corner office had taken to the red pen again. Another cull in the investment banking division of Bank of America. For thirteen years, Savanah had slaved away in the New York office, moving up to Managing Director. She had survived the sub-prime and Lehman's collapse at Goldman, so when the rebound came she was well positioned to make her move. In 2012, as investments banks struggled to rebuild the teams they had decimated just three years before, she landed a MD position at Bank of America, the new plain mortgages-to-synthetic CDOs colossus of American banking. It had been worth it: it was an adrenalin-filled fast paced job where she could do what she was best at – make things happen. And she got paid handsomely for it as well, to afford the Maldives annual holidays and the upper east side apartment. But she was growing tired of the treadmill, the grinding machine that never stopped.

Wall Street nowadays was different from when she started, back in 2001 as an analyst at JPMorgan. The great investment banks of old, the respectable houses whose names alone were sufficient to make corporate executives tremble, had closed after the Lehman Brothers collapse or forced to merge into the big commercial banks. Then they moved the Wall Street office into the midtown towers. Yes, it saved money and provided handsome real estate profits from selling the downtown offices, but... well, the glamour, the chutzpah was gone. Now, Wall Street was nothing more than a shadowy street with the fumes of the underground puffing out, more the scenery for Gotham City gangsters than for Kings of the World financiers. The former headquarters of the investment houses were being turned into luxury shopping malls, tendering for the Chinese tourists.

So, when another cull in the division was announced, she had volunteered to take the severance package and go. That's why this year she had arrived earlier for the Christmas holydays at her parent's house in Newport, Rhode Island. Instead of the usual endless succession of dinner parties and the glitz of the office silly season, she decided to take a few weeks off with her parents.

Hugh would join them later, for Christmas dinner. He had been quite supportive of her decision, although Savanah suspected he had second intentions. He had been gently pressing her, for some time now, to have a baby. Sure, she wanted kids... at some point... Hugh probably expected she would take the layoff as the right time to have a baby. Maybe. She was 39 now, the clock was ticking. The prospect of turning 40 in ten months' time, in October, was a bit... well, not daunting really, she was quite relaxed about the all age thing. But a bit, definitive, making her officially into the grown-ups' team. She kind of still though of herself as the young brilliant hotshot who had received several job offers from investment banks, strategy consultants and VC firms at the end of the MBA. She had gone through the grind, always first on the promotion line, up to MD. It felt like her real life had just began, now that she had the time for dinner parties, daily gym or running sessions, reading... She was now enjoying herself the way some of her teenage friends had, many years before. So it wasn't fair to start already talking about babies, right?

Anyway, in January she would think about that. Now was her time off, relaxing at the family home at Newport. She was in fact looking forward to the family's holiday routine: she went jogging in the cold mornings, alone with her thoughts, filling the lungs with the crisp December air. Then she would go sailing and fishing with her father, up to Boston bay. And in the late afternoons she would cosy up in the library, next to the fireplace, with the smell of uncle Santiago cigar in the air, a slice of cake mum liked to bake, and a good book.

To her own surprise, she found herself with Raven's old notebook, which had been stored away since her death. Between the pages of the notebook was still that strange piece of cut paper with a threatening message.

No one had dared touch Raven's belongings for a while, so the boxes had just sat in her old bedroom for a few months, until uncle Santiago cajoled mum and dad to organize her books and stuff, to get some closure. As mum was unpacking Raven´s papers, she found that notebook where Raven was taking notes of her thoughts and investigations – a notebook full of weird symbols and strange incoherent phrases. As she put it in the bookshelf unread, a loose piece of paper fell out. It was a nondescript white paper with a computer-printed message. It read:

"LEAVE GERMAN BITCH"

An uncomfortable though had probably been floating around the back of Savanah's mind all those years. More like a nuisance. She had been too busy to think about it, and everyone just wanted to forget what had happened in Lisbon. But as much as she wanted to wish it away, the memory clang and nagged her: that email that was on her inbox upon their return from Lisbon, sent by Raven mid-afternoon the day before her death. She had probably sent it from her mobile in a hurry, on a motorway service station on the way back from Tomar to Lisbon.

Raven's notebook started in a very organized way, as she took notes for her thesis. At some point, though, the notes became all messed up, with lines back and forth, esoteric symbols and maps and random words just hanging like threats on the page. Most disturbingly, from a certain point onwards, the pages were covered in pentagrams and stars. A page showed a huge pentagram with a bearded and horned goat's head in the middle, and a weird sentence next to it: "The Goat is in my way".

The written pages ended abruptly at about 2/3 of the notebook, followed by two pages ripped off, the irregular remains of the cut off pages still attached to the notebook's spine.

"What were you after, sis? Have you gone mad or did get yourself caught in some weird satanic cult?"

Raven's autopsy had determined no other cause of death besides the bleeding from the pentagram-shaped gash on her left wrist. No fingerprints, no signs of fight, just that horrible pentagram cut deep into her left wrist and traces of a powerful drug in her lungs. Had she done the cut to herself? Was it a suicide pact gone wrong? A drug-related assassination? Savanah could not believe any of that.

And then there was that note. "Leave German Bitch". Gosh. Raven was not even German! Sure, she and her twin sister were probably the stereotypical German, tall, broad shouldered, blond hair and pale skin. Could Raven's death have anything to do with a race agenda? That was just...

Savanah could not share these thoughts with her parents. Raven's death had been devastating enough. So she kept reading through the notes and waited for her uncle Santiago to arrive just before Christmas. Their uncle was not a common man, not just because of his position in the US Capitol but also due to his imposing figure, penetrating eyes and immense knowledge. During the summer school holidays, he used to take them sailing to the Caribbean and prod them about Columbus and the Templars and the role of women in the bible. The two girls loved his charades.

On the afternoon of Christmas eve, before Hugh's arrival and as her parents were busy preparing Christmas dinner, Savanah sat on the library with a book, cosy and warm next to the fireplace. The oak logs released a mildly inebriating smoke, filling the library with a bluish tone and a musty odour. Her thoughts were far away, lost on the kindling flames, as Rachmaninov played on the stereo. Uncle Santiago's choice, obviously. She had an easier music playlist, usually pop beats or beast mode power music when she went for the morning run. Or easy listening jazz during dinner parties. At most, she tolerated some Chopin or Liszt to help her concentrate. But uncle Santiago would always go for the "heavy metal" of the classics, Wagner, Beethoven, Rachmaninov. Rach 3, she could tell, was pounding from the Audio Analogue sound columns, an obsessive, compulsive music that always left her a bit agitated. Anxious. Like the soundtrack of a movie when something terrible is about to happen. Beethoven's 5th in Clockwork Orange.

Uncle Santiago used to say that Rach 3 is the K2 of pianists. The K2 is the second highest peak of the Himalayas, also called "Savage Mountain" and is the peak with the highest death rate of alpinists who try to reach its summit. Rach 3 is the summit of death for pianists who attempt to perform it.

Most people listen to classical music or go to the ballet or read intellectual books or attend art exhibitions because that is what their projected image of the self likes to do, the idea of who they are or how they like others to perceive them. Our true preferences are revealed by the choices we make when alone, the result of the intimate conflict between the true self and the imagined self. That was not the case with uncle Santiago, though. He really didn't care about how others perceived him. He was already at that point of his life when he didn't care about the imagined self or what others thought.

The family old cream-coloured Golden Retriever Leo,

short for Galileo, was lying lazily in the wooden floor next to the fireplace. He raised his aristocratic head from time to time, surveying his surroundings, before getting back to his rest. A hazy atmosphere filled the room, mixing the aromas of the musky oak logs crackling in the fireplace with uncle Santiago Cuban cigar. He was reading the paper, playing absentmindedly with the gold ring on the finger of his left hand, where you would expect a wedding band to be. A beautiful piece of distinguished aged gold with an embossed wind rose star that always reminded Savanah of Miró's drawings. Uncle Santiago had a friendly but imposing figure, a short man with muscled legs and arms like tree trunks, white-grey hair that had once been blond framing a round face and honeyed almond eyes, heavy beard trimmed to perfection. He sat on the couch with his cigar and a crystal cut glass of whiskey, probably Lagavulin or Talisker Dark Storm, strong peated whiskeys that taste like stormy seas and smoky seaweed.

Savanah finally managed to take herself up from her hazy numbness and decided to discuss Raven's notebook with uncle Santiago.

"My dear, those are intriguing notes indeed. Raven had a complex mind... there are complex crazy, and complex brilliant. The dividing line is tenuous. Complex minds are never easy, neither for themselves nor those around them. I have spent hours going through those pages..."

"So you have read it?"

"Of course. My job is to know, and to know you must invest time. You can make money running around like a busy bee in Wall Street, but that will just make you do better the things you already know, it won't teach you new things."

"Let's not have that conversation again, uncle. I hope we can have a decent conversation like we used to, when Raven and I were kids... Look, I guess part of the reason the police gave up on the investigation was because of those satanic pentagrams with the goat-headed demon Baphomet, weird symbols and nonsensical sentences found in her notebook. There were no marks of aggression or fighting, except for the pentagram-shaped cut on her wrist. Although they never openly stated it, I guess the police though she had lost her mind or was into drugs or some satanic cult."

"That's nonsense", answered Santiago quickly. "Many mistakes and wrong assumptions could be avoided if people had a minimum knowledge of history. The pentagram you are so worried about never had a satanic connotation until... well, until the church invented that, to cover up and justify the extermination of the Cathars and the Templars in the thirteenth and fourteenth centuries. You know the square and compass symbol engraved on the entrance stone of this house, right!"

"Sure", answered Savanah, picturing the image in her mind. "The freemasons symbol".

"Exactly. The tools of the Great Architect are the same tools we mortals have: the free will and the flame of consciousness. As above, so below – the human and the divine united. The square and compass represents this geometry: the universe is not chaos subject to the arbitrary whims of an exterior God, but a geometry we humans can understand through reason. Like Einstein said, "God doesn't play dice.""

"Yeah, I know the symbolism. You told me and Raven all about that when we were kids... But you know what I think about all the mysticism. The world is complex enough as it is, no need to add extra layers of complexity. Anyway, what does the freemasons' symbol have to do with the pentagr..."

"It *is* the pentagram! Look here."

Santiago took a pair of pens from the inner pocket of his jacket. On an empty space in his newspaper he drew a pentagram, highlighting the top and bottom open triangles to reveal the freemasons' square and compass.

"The 5 vertices of the pentagram also represent the Hebrew character "hei", which is the fifth letter of the Hebrew alphabet, and means God as an abbreviation for Hashem (meaning The Name). The pentagram shows in many churches, especially those associated with the Templars. The Vatican claims this is a simple reference to the five Holy Wounds of Christ, suffered during crucifixion. Two wounds in the wrists where nails fixed Christ to the cross. Two wounds on the feet where the nail passed through both feet to the vertical beam of the cross. And the final wound on the right side of Jesus, where his abdomen was pierced by the lance of Longinus to check if He was death. So the five pointed star is associated with the five Holy Wounds".

"But", continued Santiago, "do not be deceived. The pentagram symbolism is much older than this catholic justification. It is reminiscent of the ancient cult of the Venus goddess, a symbol of the feminine and fertility, and in this way it is intimately associated with the Templars' cult of Virgin Mary. The pentagram shows recurrently in Templar churches, namely Santa Maria do Olival church in Tomar, the headquarters of the Portuguese Templars, and Rosslyn church, the base of the Scottish Templars. Two very meaningful branches of the Templars... the northern path and the southern path. The freemason's square and compass appear in the emblem of Queen Leonor, wife of King João II, as well as in the decoration of the Convent of Christ in Tomar."

"Oh, come on, uncle. Portugal is such a nice, tranquil country...", commented Savanah, remembering her short honeymoon. "It's hard to imagine the country could be the stage for such intricate web conspiracy. Templars, Discoveries, Freemasons..."

"Surprising things come from where you least expect. I would not like you to think I'm just coming up with wild conspiracy theories. But the world is not black and white. History is written by the victors and the powerful, and for the past twenty centuries the roman church has kept a strong hold on how history is told. Secret orders were the only way to pass on messages that were otherwise censured by the church."

Savanah sat in silence for a while, contemplating the playful flames in the fireplace and the crackling sounds of the firewood. Then she asked, not wanting to let go so easily. "But then how did the pentagram come to be associated with Satan, the devil?".

"When the Templars were extinguished by Pope Clemente V in 1312 and persecuted by the French king Filipe IV, they were accused, amongst other things, of spitting on the cross in secret rituals and worshipping Baphomet, the devil... and that's how the Templar pentagram became associated with satanic practices. Indeed, a lie fed by the French King and the Pope of Rome. The true reasons behind the Pope's obsession to exterminate the Templars are... less obvious."

Savanah was not entirely convinced, but though it better to let go. Uncle had always been a bit secretive. She decided to prod him further regarding Raven's notebook. He clearly knew more than what he was saying.

"Ok, the Templars, sure. Uncle, just tell me what you think. What could Raven have discovered? What's all the mystery around Columbus?"

"A lot, actually, my dear. Starting by the man's name: he was never called Columbus on his time, but Colon, and continues to be called Colon in Spanish speaking countries. Colon means "member" in Latin. Columbus means "pigeon". So, a substantial adulteration..."

But that was just the tip of the iceberg. Historians were never quite convinced about the conventional view of Columbus as a poor, uneducated man from a family of Genoese wool weavers who inexplicably appears in Portugal – the old tale says he wrecked off the shore of Lisbon and swam 6 miles to reach land. Less than two years after washing ashore, penniless and illiterate, to Lisbon, this man becomes fluent in Portuguese, Spanish and Latin, masters cosmography, geography and mathematics, is admitted to the highly secretive senior counsel of king D. João II and his elite Board of Mathematicians and marries Dona Filipa Moniz Perestrelo, a "fidalga" of royal lineage, cousin of the elite Portuguese diplomats and discoverers, Vasco da Gama and Pedro Álvares Cabral. Dona Filipa was one of the twelve "donas comendadoras" of the All Saints Convent, where she lived, an elite place affiliated with the Order of Santiago. As a "dona" of All Saints, her marriage would have to be approved by the Grand Master of Santiago, who at the time was the King himself! A poor Italian wool-weaver or even ascending merchant would never have access to the Convent, reserved for the high nobility in a highly stratified society. How odd, or how convenient, that the log books of the Convent where the marriage of Dona Filipa must have been recorded, with the name of her husband, were never found.

This meteoric ascension in social and cultural status would be difficult today. It would be impossible in the 15th century. The traditional account, retold over and over again in schoolbooks, is ridden with contradictions, a well-orchestrated conspiracy that lasted for five hundred years and only recently is being revealed for what it is: a fairy tale.

All evidence suggests that Colon was a high ranked noble long before the expedition that made him famous. When Colon run away to Spain, fleeing from Dom João II rage after the 1484 conspiracy to kill the king, Colon was hosted as a 'hidalgo' (literally, son-of-someone, meaning, 'with high lineage') by the Duque of Medinaceli, a powerful Castilian noble. He is treated with the nobility title 'Don' in the 1492 Capitulações de Santa Fé, before he had even set foot on the Niña! So much reverence to a poor weaver, years before he supposedly gained fame and fortune by reaching the Indies!

Columbus cabalistic signature remains an unsolved mystery that eludes historians. When Bobadilla was sent to arrest Colon and remove him from commander of Hispaniola, he accused Colon of using a secret, cryptic alphabet to write coded letters, supposedly part of a conspiracy to rebel against Spain and establish a new kingdom in Hispaniola. Unfortunately, those cyphered letters were lost in the shipwreck of 1502. Nevertheless, Colon's books and letters are dotted with unknown characters, potentially from a secret cryptic alphabet. Was he communicating a secret message to the recipients of the letters, on the side of the main "official" texts?

"Huummm. Interesting.", interrupted Savanah. "But what have the Templars to do with Columbus, or Colon if you prefer? All these pentagrams in Raven's notebook and references to a Templars' treasure, the Grail".

"The Templars were right in the centre of the birth of

Portugal, as crusaders to expel the Arabs from Iberia. Later, in 1307, when Pope Clemente V extinguished the Order and the French King launched the ambush to kill or arrest them, the monk-knights fled from all over Europe and took refuge under King Dom Dinis in Portugal. This king not only protected them, but also promoted the rebirth of the Order, refashioned as the Order of Christ. Dom Dinis protected the Templars and transferred all the Templar properties in the country to the new Order, directly disobeying the Pope."

Columbus was most certainly a member of the Order of Christ. So Columbus was a Templar, maybe the Last Templar. The Templar's official mission was to protect the pilgrims to Jerusalem, but their ideology was charged with the dream of a "fifth empire", a new Promised Land ruled by the founding Christian principles, free from the self-serving and hypocrite bishops of Rome. In that, they share the spirit of the Portuguese Discoveries. When we talk about the religious motivations of the Age of Discoveries, we must distinguish the catholic "missionary" spirit to conquer, submit and appropriate, from the "spirit of discovery" that permeates the early Portuguese expeditions. The first intends to bring back, the second intends to go away.

"I dare say," continued Santiago, "that Portugal, in the outskirts of Europe, was the first attempt by the Templars to create a new, independent kingdom free from the shackles of Rome. The Portuguese Discoveries may well have been the second attempt to find that new Promised Land, the Avalon of Arthurian legends – the new Jerusalem that Colon is obsessed about in his Book of Prophecies."

"Ok. Then this note Raven wrote about Port-du-graal...", said Savanah

"Portugal as the port, the harbor of the Graal.", agreed Santiago.

Supposedly, the original nine Templars found, or were

offered, a great secret in Jerusalem. The Templar Order was established there, in 1119, and had their headquarters on the ruins of the Salomon Temple, in Mount Sion, next to the church of Haggia Sion. When the city was retaken by Saladino, the Templars had to flee the city and took this treasure, the Holy Grail, by boat. First to Malta and then to south of France, where a dynasty of Merovingian kings in the region is said to have protected the secret.

Santiago puffed away some smoke from his cigar. Galileo lazily got up and stretched out, jutting forward his well outlined snout and chest while pushing back his hind legs, tail pointed back in a straight line. His unashamed yawn, with closed eyes and wide open mouth baring his teeth and dark red gums, seemed to Savanah to be teasing her, as if showing off the absence of stifling social conventions of decorum in the world of dogs. He then walked out of the room, languidly, tail wagging contently, probably bored with uncle Santiago's long historic dissertation. Or he smelled the beef being taken out of the fridge in the kitchen and went to try his luck. You have to admire nature's attitude of 'don 't give a damn´ about good manners, taking the world as it is and living the present, sniffing, peeing and mating freely whenever they please, instead of always making a fuss about the past or the future. There are of course some hardwired genetic behaviors, but at least they are not consciously thinking about them, always anxious about the consequences. Human consciousness of the self and the world is the source of all sadness. And happiness. Tough choice...

Then again, dogs aren't totally free, are they? Leo can pee and sniff and mate and run, but only when allowed by his masters. Once he accepts a leash on his neck, his freedom becomes dependent on her father's whims. At least it guarantees shelter and a plate of food every day, and some occasional treats, fondling and hugs from all of us. But it wasn't Leo's choice, really... many many centuries ago, a great great ancestor wolf made the choice for him, opting to be tamed, trading part of its freedom for a higher probability of food and protection. Under that fluffy, cute forehead, his brain may well thank or resent that ancient Wolf-God who made the choice for him.

God is made up of the bits of free-will we give away, willingly or forcibly. Is that why Dog is spelled God the other way round? One's tameness and domestication opposed to the other's whimsical power? God is the Dog's harness. At least until the dog realizes he can walk away and piss and sniff and mate as he pleases, because God, as a nice loving parent, will always forgive the Dog's sins.

People have all types of different relations with God. It is a rather private affair. Some are true believers. Others have a sense of respect, going to the priest when there is a problem, like going to the doctor when something hurts. Some just keep the Sunday routine out of habit and not to look bad or cause gossip from neighbors. Others don't really believe, but kneel and cross themselves when they go to church on the occasional wedding or christening, just to be safe, because you never know. Some, like Savanah, are real, fierce atheists. Most, nowadays, simply don't care.

Savanah's brain was divagating, listening her uncle's voice continuing in the background, like ambient music. The sound is there but her brain is not registering. She was getting a bit bored like Leo, with all the historical references and controversies. Maybe she should go to the kitchen and seat patiently on her hind legs until mum throws her a succulent morsel of raw meat. What was the Wolf God that made the decisions for her, many centuries ago? There was a Norse wolf god whose name she once knew.

Uncle's long historical dissertation was sounding like a bunch of interesting titbits about a long gone past (as in 'dinner party interesting'), but hardly relevant for the present or the future. "Sorry uncle, what do you mean?", she asked, hoping he hadn't noticed her brain's temporary absence from the room.

"I mean no-one honestly believed the farce of the poor Genoese wool-weaver turned vice-Roy, but it kept being parroted away for the lack of a definitive alternative. However, there have been some academic breakthroughs around Colon since the turn of the century. Colon's life suggests a tangle of deeply conflicting loyalties, which may have driven him mad at the end of his life: to the Spanish monarchs, to the Portuguese king and to his Templar mission. So, speculation jumped out of Academia into the social media… conspiracy theories are running wild on the internet, especially after the DNA studies conducted in 2003 from the remains of Colon, his brother Diego and his son Fernando. These tests disproved any link between Colon and the many Columbus families previously identified as candidates for the Genoese thesis."

The traditional story became widespread because it is endearing: rags to riches just by sheer brilliance and perseverance. Colon has a mystical aura of social mobility, just like a Walt Disney story. All that is required to create a good lie is to create a plausible lie and repeat it exhaustively. As time goes by, facts are forgotten and the nicely fitting lie becomes an acceptable truth. Alternative plausible theories, for the lack of irrefutable proof, are simply ignored: better the devil you know than the devil you don't…

And once the white-beards in Academia sign off under a theory – out of boredom or tiredness or laziness, or just because the human mind has a horror of empty spaces and runs off to fill them in with whatever half-baked comfortable hypothesis is provided – then the bar of scrutiny is raised immensely for any alternative theories to replace the commonly accepted one and disprove the white-beards.

"Don't forget history is written by the victors.", said uncle Santiago, getting up and pacing to the window overlooking a frosty landscaped garden. Two red maple trees stood as sentinels on each side of the front gate, now naked of their colourful autumn red foliage.

After a few seconds hesitation, he voiced his thoughts. "The powers that control the pen can write, forge and manipulate documents to fit their chosen version of the events! In fact, many valuable documents about the Portuguese Templar past and the conspiracy of Columbus against Spain were likely destroyed or tampered with by the Inquisition or by the Filipes, the three Spanish kings who ruled Portugal for 80 years from 1580 to 1640. Without alternative documental evidence, historians resorted to whatever they could grab... The fable of the Italian Columbus is based in nothing more than circumstantial allegations, and in some cases tampered or forged documents."

Santiago doubts were a wide open field, full of question marks but no reliable answers. Savanah was about to point that out, but Santiago interjected ahead of her, maybe guessing her thoughts.

"I guess what I'm saying here is... well, look, just because we don't know what creates the mysterious crop circles in cereal fields, it doesn't prove they are made by UFOs. True, a poor Italian Columbus probably existed and was born in Genoa around 1450, he may even have made his way up to a peddler of copied maps and trader of sailor's gossip in Lisbon. But this Columbus and the Admiral Colon could never be the same person! The poor, commoner Cristoforo Colombo has nothing to do with the high-born *hidalgo*, vice-Roy and knight of the golden spurs Don Cristobal Colon, besides a similar name."

SAGRES, SEPTEMBER 1460

(Columbus)

T he Old Man died. The legacy of the Infante to the world is well registered in his personal signature: I.D.A., standing for Infante Dom Anriques, but also meaning "Ida", "Departure" in Portuguese. That's what the Infante did all his restless life: to go further, always further.

Even though he rarely sat foot on a Caravela himself, he probably suffered even more than his sailors, consumed by the anxiety of not knowing what was happening all those leagues away in the Sea of Darkness. He never married, living an austere life of seclusion, devoting his strength and personal wealth to conquering the seas. Brilliant, shy, harsh, moody, eccentric: men either idolatrize the Old Man or hate him. Many accused him of driving Portugal to ruin with his costly expeditions, that have, so far, brought little return.

The other boys in Sagres took up the nickname the Old Man has bestowed on me: "Alemão", the German, a name inherited from my father. Others though it was because of our tall stature, broad shoulders, reddish-blond hair and blue eyes, but I know the Old Man's reasons were different – a reference to my father's secret lineage that I am forbidden to reveal.

Mornings are often spent in Master Zacuto's chambers. A rigid looking Jew, actually quite affable after you gain his intellectual respect, who pretends to be despaired by the stupidity of the students in front of him. In fact, I think he enjoys the mornings of teaching as much as us. We are his sounding board, discussing his observations and helping him with the calculations.

He spreads his maps on the table, reverently and in silence.

"Which of you ignorant can tell me what is the shape of the world?"

"It should be round, Master" – replied confidently Dias "The masts of ships are the last things to disappear in the horizon, so the land must be curved"

"Oh, boy, you repeat well what you have been told. But can you think? Ehh, can you think? What if the ships lost in the distance are simply in a queue at the doors of Hell, trapped by demons at the edge of the world, a flat land surrounded by the lands of Satan, where ships are dragged slowly to the firing depths. Eeh? That would also explain why masts are last to be seen, boy. What else can those sleepy lazy brains conjure?"

I advance another explanation. "I once saw an eclipse. The shade of the world on the moon was a circle, so it cannot be flat".

"Well, indeed, but it does not mean it is not flat. It simply means it is not square. It could be a disk and still be flat. All the heavenly bodies we see in the sky, the moon and the sun, are round, but they could still be flat disks held afloat by divine forces. Never underestimate the power of tradition, it usually comes from sensible observations of reality. So... think about the shade. You will go to the Steel Rod, the Stick in our front yard and meditate how would shadows behave in a flat or curved surface."

These discussions advance us on the mysteries of cosmography and mathematics. I cannot say how all these calculations and abstract formulae will help us sail in the Mar Tenebroso, the Terrible Ocean. Still, the numbers have a certain beauty in them, a comforting certainty attained only by the initiated. I love that certainty of the cosmos, even though I often become restless with all the unanswered questions.

"The shade of a stick, with a specific height, has been taken by the ancient Greeks in two different places, known to be on a straight north-south line. The length of the shadows was taken at exactly the same time of day, at high noon, with the sun at the pinnacle. If the land was flat, the shades should be the same length. But the shades are of different length, and taking into account the difference of the shades and the distance between the two locations, you can reasonably estimate the curvature of the arch. This gives you the size of the longitude circumference of the globe. Also, our sailors have taken many readings of the angle of the sun at different places on our voyages, thus determining the latitude, with the corresponding distances to Lisbon. But as you know, by order of the Portuguese king, we never write true leagues, always double it up so that if a map or text falls in the hands of the spies from Genoa or Venice or Castella, they will be confused and unable to retrace our steps. Secrecy is the only reliable weapon."

"Ptolomeu's estimate for the equatorial circumference is smaller than the North South longitude circumference estimated by our cosmographers.", interrupted Dias. "How can the world be longer on its North-South axis but narrower on the Equator? It would look like an egg?!"

"You zest, but indeed. We have not yet been able to accurately estimate longitude degrees and thus the size of the equator circumference. We observe the skies and see round celestial bodies, never eggs, which makes me suspect of Ptolomeu's calculations for the perimeter at the Equator, but no one has yet been able to take an irrefutable measure".

Besides the theoretical learning in the central library, afternoons are spent amongst the seaman, learnings the eight winds: Tramontana is the north wind; Greco northeast; Levante east; Sirocco southeast; Auster south; Libeccio southwest; Ponente west; and Maestro northwest.

We also learn to keep time and course in the high seas. Distance at sea cannot be measured like on land. Water flows in one direction and the ship in another, there is no fixed point to measure distance. So, changing the hour glass to keep time is critical, because the pilot needs to know the time at which to take sun and polar star measurements to get the latitude. The speed of the ship is estimated by launching overboard a piece of wood tied to a rope. When the log passes the bow, the captain signals for us to start singing a spiel, until the log reaches the stern. That gives us time, distance and thus the speed of the ship.

Lagos is a marvel, teaming with buzz, carcasses of caravels and carracks under construction spread along the beach. Dozens of caravels are wrecked each year and new ones have to be built at breakneck speed, while looking for bolder designs. "The Old Man is mad, he wants the impossible!", the shipbuilders used to say. "Always more tonnage! He wants a ship fast with a low draft to enter shallow rivers and navigate near shore, but he demands hulls large enough to carry seventy tons of cargo! The largest caravel so far holds fifty tons!". Designing a ship entails hard choices and we have to push the limits of established patterns of shipbuilding. The three-cornered lateen sail is better for tacking back north from the coast of Africa against the prevailing 'nortada' winds. For coastal sailing, a shallow hull with a high length-to-beam ratio and lateen sails provides flexibility, speed and easier tacking upwind. But on the high seas with ravenous waves and whimsical storms, a deep hull and high bow with square sails offers the best odds of survival. In a large ship, the lateen becomes difficult to handle.

We experiment new designs, with wider beams to increase tonnage and mixing a square-rigged foremast with lateen sails on the other masts. Such a combination has never been attempted, and it will require the finest sailors to handle her. "The Jews of the Infante say the math works, but it won't be them on the ships in the middle of a storm!", the shipbuilders roared between closed teeth.

Large ships like that could only mean one thing: very long voyages in open water, far from land. The Old Man had in his mind more than short trade voyages close to shore...

We work often with the shipbuilders, discussing new boat designs and actively engaging in hard physical work building them. The best wood for shipbuilding grows in the colder northern countries. Oak wood is the best, producing long, straight and flexible planks with fewer knots. But it takes too long to grow, and is unsuited for our warmer climate. So, we are using pine from the Leiria forest planted by Dom Dinis. It is less flexible and has less lignin, thus rotting faster. The ships last half as long, but as most will wreck anyway, there is no point using oak. As the shipbuilders used to say, "Pine grows faster, so the Old Man will have his ships sooner"!

We seat with Cadamosto in Lagos, on a tavern drinking on a sunny afternoon. The man is tall and thin, long hair and singing voice. He talks as if always observed by women, with a flourish only an Italian could do without looking ridiculous. "If you don't know the innards of your ship, how can you control her? A ship is like a woman, you must touch the exact spot with the exact strength to make her turn the way you want. She is whimsical, fanciful, temperamental, and you must learn to control her – not by brute force, but by orchestrating the masts, the sails, the rudder, the ballast." The Venetian was on his early thirties, recently returned from expeditions at the service of the Infante. He explored the river Senegal, sailed up river Gambia and together with Diogo Gomes and Antonio da Noli discovered the islands of Cape Vert.

The other boys disliked Cadamosto. He was pretentious, condescending and a foreigner. But I sympathized with him, despite his flamboyant manners and incommensurate ego. I probably felt we shared a similar story, in some ways. Cadamosto was the son of a rich Venetian merchant, Giovanni da Mosto. He lived in the family's palace in Cá da Mosto, in the margins of the Grand Canal, until his father lost his fortune and was forced into exile. The son had to venture into international commerce and navigation quite young, trying his luck. In one of those voyages between the Mediterranean and northern Europe, his fleet docked in the Algarve – when Cadamosto heard the Portuguese crown offered licenses for exploration down the coast of Africa, he offered his services to the Infante. My father had also given up his fortune, delivering me a fate I could not escape.

Cadamosto now lives between Lisbon, where he established his trading with Flanders and England, and Sagres, where he lectures us and prepares his next exploration – although I suppose he will not make it, fully engaged in his flourishing commercial activities. In any case, he speaks excitedly and conveys a sense of adventure the old masters are unable to muster. He has sailed up river Gambia, almost 20 leagues inland – this is a central drive in Portuguese explorations, secretly exploring the rivers inland. Ancient maps show large rivers connecting the Atlantic African coast with the Indian ocean. But Cadamosto was forced to turn back due to the hostility of the region's inhabitants. He describes the African coast between river Gambia and river Geba[2] as the most beautiful scenery ever seen, as if it was the door of paradise, with fragrant flowers, blue-green calm waters and most beautiful women. He tells us of the luxuriant riches of the Bijagós archipelago, which he calls the "nursery of the Atlantic", so full it was with a variety of silver brimming fish.

But the most spell-binding tale of Cadamosto is his description of the night sky as the fleet approached the Equator.

"We were stranded in the middle of the Ocean Sea, without winds or currents. We feared we had entered what old sailors called the Cauldron of Fire, close to the Equator. Water turns red from the blood of all sailors who perished trying to go beyond Cape Bojador. The day had been a haze of heat, men sick with fever and diarrhea, the water and food supply we had taken earlier in Cape Vert were running low. After our unfortunate exploration up river Gambia, unable to trade with the hostile tribes, we were forced back down the river. I pushed further south, without stopping to replenish the stocks. Lads, I can tell you, a sailor has only one great voyage in him, and I felt this was the one – I had to push onwards, to find fame and fortune, for fear of not having another chance. At 5º North, the sailors could no longer depend on the familiar stars of the northern hemisphere. At night, every man on deck was conscious of the Pole Star almost disappearing in the horizon. The angle of the Northern Light to the horizon indicates the latitude, so we were approaching the equatorial line... will the ships turn upside down once we round the Equator, will they fall into an abyss of nothingness? But even if none of these old fantasies were true, very real problems face the fleet beyond that point. How can we navigate in the southern hemisphere, without the Pole Star, the most valuable and reliable reference point? Also, we still don't know if the compass needle works in the southern hemisphere, as the northern force that attracts the lodestone may be lost."

"I could tell the crew was approaching the point of mutiny and I would need to sail back soon. Desperately looking for signs of land, I searched the skies for high, puffy clouds turning vertical and dark, the sign of clash of earth and water. Only a miracle could still bring success to this expedition. And a miracle it was! In the evening, the boy at the crow's nest of the topsail cried like possessed "The Cross, the Cross of our Lord". I came out of my cabin as the sailors kneeled and prayed. There it was, in the clear night sky, a constellation of stars formed like the Cross of Christ, opening its arms in the southern sky and pushing us forward. I exhorted the men by claiming that "God wants us to push forward, for He has chosen the Portuguese to bring the true faith to these foreign lands". The sign is even more powerful, as the Cross maintains its position in the firmament, holding the South just like the Northern Light holds the North. We named it the Southern Cross. And so it was that we kept sailing, prompted by fresh winds."

CARIBBEAN SEA, JUNE 1502

(Fernando)

"You must have chaos within you to give birth to a dancing star."

FRIEDRICH NIETZSCHE

"I am the son of a king. My father accepted the ultimate sacrifice, in order to protect the Wind Rose and re-unite it with the Rose Line. I too sacrificed every-thing to bear this cross. So far I have failed, son. This is my last voyage and the last chance to complete the mission. I don't care what that dog Bobadilla says, or if I am forever for-gotten, if only I could take the Wind Rose and find the heirs... But I am old and sick. I'm not sure I can make it back to Spain. I am sorry, my son, to leave the work unfinished for you to carry on. It has been my burden, and it will soon be yours. I have failed, Fernando, I have failed."

Christopher Colon was prone to these ramblings. The ramblings of a genial, persistent and tenacious fool. My Father, the Admiral of the Ocean Sea. A proud and hard man, with an imposing presence. *"Tall, above the average height, with a long and authoritative face, aquiline nose, blue eyes, pale skin with flushed red cheeks. His beard and hair, blond during his youth, have quickly faded white from his hard labors (...) His bearing and appearance denote a venerable person of high statute and authority, worthy of all reverence. He is sober and moderate in eating, drinking and clothing* [3]*."* Although at the time, he wore his hair black, only later would I discover he was painting it to disguise the recognizable reddish-white hair.

This was his fourth voyage, which would prove to be the most extraordinary and dangerous of all. Mother had not wanted me to join the fleet, because I was too young. I remember the excitement as I boarded the *nau* [4] Capitana on May 9 of that distant year of 1502, in the harbor of Cadiz. Excitement and pride, for I was the son of the Admiral of the Ocean Sea. At the age of thirteen, I was embarking on an expedition to find the Straight referred by Marco Polo, the passage from the Atlantic to the lands of spices and gold: Cipango, China and India... At my age, Father had already sailed the high seas between Madeira and Lisbon. We left Cadiz on 12 May with 147 men and four ships: the flagship Capitana, the Gallega, the Viscaína and the Santiago de Palos.

I barely slept on the night before departure. I raised from my bed long before the call for Lauds and walked above deck. I love the silence before dawn. I still do. The night was dark, with no moon, just scattered stars in the cloudless night. I approached the bow of the ship, filling my lungs with the smell of pinewood and pitch mixed with sea salt. The high masts stood by, as generals ready for battle, topsail and jib yet unfurled. As I approached the bow of the Niña, a shooting star crossed the dark sky, leaving an incandescent trail behind it. It was a sign. But still today I am uncertain if the shooting star was a favorable or unfavorable omen...

At that moment, I felt Father's hands in my shoulders. We both knelt in silence, to make our confession and receive absolution, following the decades old tradition of the Portuguese sailors ever since Henry the Navigator obtained a Papal bull providing a general 'umbrella' absolution for those who died in discovery and conquest.

Many years have now passed, but I remember quite vividly the colors and smells encountered during the expedition, the excitement of meeting new civilizations as we sailed from Cadiz to Asilah, a fortified town on the northwest tip of the Moroccan coast, south of Tangier. It was dreamlike vision of whitewashed walls standing guard as the mouth of the Gibraltar Strait opened wide into the Atlantic Ocean. Seen from the water, as our fleet approached it, the city seemed a white painting against the backdrop of cream-colored sand beyond. The Portuguese garrison of the city was under attack and the arrival of our fleet scared the Moors away. I remember thinking Father was out of his mind, as we entered the city walls, for fear he would be arrested by the Portuguese. But to my amazement at the time, Father was received by the Lords of the city with much honor and respect. That was strange, but I attributed it to the relief of the Portuguese for our help.

We then called at Gran Canaria on May 20, to take water and provisions, and finally set sail for the Indies. Father navigational skills marvel even the most seasoned sailor. He managed to catch the favorable trade winds, the easterlies, as well as the undercurrent streams, so that we completed the crossing in only twenty days, even less than the thirty-three days of his initial journey. We arrived on June 15, with a rather rough sea and wind, to a tiny island so far unchartered [5].

I arrived exhausted and shaken by the perils and probations of the journey, but Friar Bartolomé de las Casas was surely worse than me. He was a friend of Father and a chronicler of the rising Spanish empire, but he surely was not cut out to endure the rough seas. He has written his memoirs of the expedition, describing the crew as "so worn down, shaken, ill and overcome by such bitterness that they want to die rather than live, seeing the four elements working against them and cruelly torturing them".

During that last voyage of the Admiral, in the lulls of

waiting when sea and winds did not allow us to sail forward, Father took to talking to me as if he needed to justify his deeds and impress me with his knowledge of the sea. He barely needed to do that, for I was truly convinced of his genius and divine mission. Probably because I had not yet lived long enough to be contaminated by the vicious intrigues of the palace, or because I was only mildly aware of the perfidious tongues that wanted to undo Father's accomplishments. Little minded men that saw only military conquest and commercial profit.

I always felt there was something special about my Father, a mission and a great sacrifice he had carried all his life. Indeed, as I would find out by the end of the expedition, Christopher Colon was, and myself after him, the heir to the southern arm of the Templar quest, continued by the Order of Christ. The Age of Discoveries launched by the Old Man – as father called the Infante, Henry the Navigator – was as much about commerce and empire as it was about the mission passed along generations of Templar masters.

The death of King João of Portugal – rumors spread he has been poisoned in Alvor – left Father unsupported, as the new King, Dom Manuel, abandoned the old Templar dreams and set his eyes firmly on the riches of the new empire. And in pleasing Isabella and the Pope, to marry the Castilian princess that could make him king of a united Iberia. In 1498 Vasco da Gama reached the true India sailing around Africa and returned to Lisbon with his ships full to the brim with spices and precious gems. That must have enraged King Fernando, who long suspected of Father's deceit. Soon after, the Spanish monarchs sent Francisco de Bobadilla to arrest Father in Hispaniola and return him to Spain in shackles, destitute of his position as governor. All this has taken a toll on my Father mental and physical health. He spent these past two years in isolated confinement at the Monastery of Santa Maria de Las Cuevas, near Seville, hallucinating and writing his Book of Prophecies.

I have now grown a wealthy and respected man. I struggle to maintain the secret of Father's mission. In doing so, I accumulated a collection of books, one of the largest collections of our times. They think the forbidden Book hides between these tomes... as Father taught me, the best way to hide something is to create a distraction. But I carry ahead of myself. I need to remember and reconstitute those extraordinary two years of the last expedition.

Not that these lines will ever be read by anyone. Mankind is not yet ready for the revelation. I need to remember for my own sake, to avoid going mad like my Father ultimately did in the last years of his life. I write only to myself, to make sense of the world, to fill the void of inaction as I wait... Wait for what? Mine is an ungrateful mission, just carry on the secret. I would much rather face the thrill of battles or the monsters of the sea to this wait. Action soothes the spirit, deceives the mind in believing you are in control of events. Waiting makes you feel powerless. But I must be patient. If indeed it is God's will that the Wind Rose be preserved and at some point revealed, it will be God to choose the appropriate time of the revelation. My duty is to preserve my Father's secret. My duty is to remember. So I have set myself to revisiting my old travel books, filled with wild annotations of foreign lands, exotic animals that impressed a thirteen-year old boy, along with Father's long monologues. I listened to him, partly to keep him company but mostly to learn. I knew Father pursued a great purpose, although I did not know at the time what it might be. I just knew I had to learn and be ready.

On 15 June, the night of our arrival to the western Indies, there was a great storm, and we were dogged by foul weather ever since. On Saturday we pushed forward to another island, then to Puerto Rico and finally reached Santo

Domingo in Hispaniola on Wednesday, 29 June 1502.

Christopher Colon, as he chose to present himself to the world, lied on his net, in pain from the gout [6], barely able to stand up in turbulent seas, almost blind from years of looking straight at the sun through the Astrolabe. Father had received strict orders from King Fernando and Queen Isabella not to stop at Hispaniola, where he had been arrested two years before by Francisco de Bobadilla – the dog, as Father referred to him. And yet, Hispaniola was exactly where we were. I could not fathom my Father intentions, nor did the crew. I don't know if out of spite for the new governor, Nicolas de Ovando, or because we indeed needed to, Father insisted on entering the harbor. He needed "to trade one of his ships for another because she was a crank and a dull sailor; not only was she slow but could not load sails without bringing the side of the ship almost under water. (If not for this), Father would be on his way to (...) cruise down the coast until he came to the strait [7]".

Father sent a delegation to Ovando, explaining we needed to trade one of the ships and also warning about a great storm approaching, asking to take shelter in the port. What signs had Father seen of such a great storm approaching? The seas were rough, but not more so than in the previous several days. And yet, the experienced sailors who had accompanied Father in the past look concerned. Diego Tristan, commander of La Capitana, told me that Father has an uncanny mastery of the elements. So, if he says a great storm is coming, we should take heed.

Unfortunately, Ovando refused entry of our fleet to the port and ignored Father's stark warnings of the storm. He probably feared Father would interfere with the convoy of ships getting ready to sail home-bound for Spain, including Bobadilla and the mutinous Francisco Roldan who had rebelled against the Admiral's rule in 1497/98. Did he fear Father would try something against Bobadilla and Roldan?

Or maybe Ovando wanted to keep Father away, as he oversaw the boarding of Father's personal possessions and gold into the small ship Aguja, the Needle, also part of the homebound convoy. The port was in a flush of activity, with final preparations for the departure of the fleet. Father was ravenous mad that Ovando refused us to enter port and insisted on sending off the fleet, ignoring Father's warning of the great danger that would soon assail us. A calamity was in the making, and Ovando stubbornly refused to listen to Father's warnings.

Prevented from entering the harbor, we sought shelter at the mouth of the Haina River and dropped anchor. No-one understood the commander's decision. Why had father insisted on dropping anchor here, despite the orders not to stop at Hispaniola. The storms that nagged us since the arrival on June 15 had passed. The skies were clear and blue, the azure sea flat and the breeze caressed the sails into a comforting lull. But Father had been ravening furious since the previous day, claiming a hurricane was forming. Very few had ever seen a hurricane. The natives called the phenomenon something like "aracan", which means "big wind".

Father commanded the four ships in our fleet to seek shelter in the west of the island, dropping anchor off the mouth of Haina River. Father always told me... the worst part of sailing is the wait. Days and days waiting for favorable winds, months waiting to sight land. Like life, in fact. An immense, endless, continuum of flatness and boredom and struggle, with the occasional moments of achievement. You only have the opportunity for do one or two great things in life, the rest is just enduring one day after the other, waiting. Practicing piano scales until you have the chance to perform a symphony.

So, we waited. The crew outside conspired the captain was mad or eccentric – there was no storm in sight and we should continue to Cuba where we could replenish our supplies.

As we waited, I was alone in the cabin with father and listened to the ramblings of a madman.

"I failed, Fernando. And so close! Finally, we know where the heirs of Prince Henry Sinclair are... The Corte-Real brothers [8] found the Scottish Templars in the New World in 1501 and are waiting for me to reunite the Wind Rose with the Rose Line! I need to go to La Isabella [9], my treasure is there, but the bastard Ovando does not allow us to approach Hispaniola. My health and vision leave me, I am discredited in the Spanish court and abandoned by Portugal... For 8 years I ruled the West Indies with an iron fist, establishing a base from where to complete the final mission. The round tower on fire signals the way, at 41º N. I must try, no matter how tired I am, I must reach La Isabella."

At the time, Father's words made no sense and were no more than delusional figments of his vivid imagination. La Isabella, his first settlement in the north of the island, was long abandoned, nothing more than a ghost town haunted by the souls of hundred sailors drowned with the lost fleet – Columbus thirteen ships wrecked by hurricanes in La Isabella in 1495/96, one fifth of its inhabitants dead, and Father's reputation tainted for having chosen such ill-fated location.

Father continuously mixed the practicalities of running an empire, the greed and power struggles, with a messianic destiny attributed by God to him alone. His self-imposed penitence in a solitude cell at the Monastery of las Cuevas, just added to the aura of mysticism and madness around him. True enough, Father has shown, time and again, an otherworldly command of the cosmic elements, a survivor blessed by fortune. I've witnessed during that last expedition how the sailors and captains looked at Father, in the aftermath of a furious storm and imminent disaster. It was more than his survival instinct and nautical knowledge, it was as if Father commanded the seas and the skies through witchcraft, a sorcerer protected by God or with a pact with Satan.

"I failed, but only to myself and to God! To the earthly princes and kings, I gave them everything! To Castella and that lunatic queen Isabella, with her mind full of Torquemada's intrigues and manipulations, I gave a new world! And how do they thank me? How do they thank the Admiral of the Ocean Sea? Ignorant, when I arrived in Seville those Spaniards knew of the ocean little more than casting a fishing rod and the court still believed the Earth to be flat. Eighteen years ago I offered those ignorant the opportunity to acquire the scientific and maritime knowledge of the Portuguese.

"They made me pass eight of them in discussion, and at the end rejected it as a thing of jest. Nevertheless, I persisted therein (...) I have placed under their sovereignty more land than there is in Africa and Europe, and more than 1,700 islands... In seven years I, by the divine will, made that conquest. At a time when I was entitled to expect rewards and retirement, I was incontinently arrested and sent home loaded with chains [10]."

"Oh, I tricked them all! I tricked them all but did not fail to give them lands and knowledge they would not have achieved without me."

"To Portugal, I gave my life. I left my wife and a young son in Lisbon to protect King João's route to India. Since 1484 my life has been a lie... Of that I shall never be ashamed! I did what had to be done. It was all to protect the Wind Rose and reunite the Book with the Rose Line. The Infante, King João... those were great men, true friends despite the sacrifice they asked of me. But now, all is lost! This new

King Manuel of Portugal, who grabbed his crown from the assassinated prince Afonso [11], seems to have forgotten me. He cares only for gold and riches. With illusions of greatness, he has put aside the true mission of the Discoveries and the purpose of the Order. He is mad, with grand visions of an empire that will quickly crumble if he stops supporting the sailors and starts playing court games with Spain. Vain... he aspires to become a high Lord, recognized by the courts of Europe, with big plans of buildings and palaces to honor his house. He is a greedy bastard, only seeing the profit and forgetting the Templar mission of the Order of Christ. The Order is dead... I am the last Templar, alone to complete the mission. You know what King Manuel did?! He expelled the Jews. Has he forgotten Zacuto, Vizinho and all the other Jews who contributed to the Infante's School of Sagres, or the Jewish merchants who financed the caravels? How dare this new king expel the Jews? I tell you, that will prove to be the biggest mistake of that country. The Jews are fleeing to the Netherlands, with their knowledge and money. We will someday see Dutch ships overthrowing the Portuguese from the lands that cost so many lives to discover. And all just because he wants to bed the daughter of the Spanish monarchs, with illusions of becoming the king of a unified Iberia. The fool! The Castilians and the Pope will never let him."

There was a fresh breeze coming through the cracks in the hull. Had the wind changed direction? There was a weightiness in the air, as if the waters had stopped moving in anticipation. The silence was heavy. There is never silence aboard a ship – it was a strange, heavy silence.

"Do you hear it, Fernando? The silence? Learn to listen to the winds and the seas, your life depends on it. The sea talks to us, the birds, the winds, they all talk if you are ready to listen. Those fools! Ovando ordered the treasure fleet to sail off to Spain, despite my advice. The hurricane is coming and those poor souls will die in vain. Fools, ignorant.

Does the dog Bobadilla think he can set his canons against the winds and order them to stop? Thirty ships, heavy with treasure, so much needed to set up an army to recover Jerusalem from the infidels. Thirty ships they sent into the sea, ignoring my advice. I just hope that dog Bobadilla drowns in the hurricane."

"I will show them all. This is the last voyage I have in me. I will explore Terra Firma in this new world and complete my mission, deliver the Book to the heirs of the Queen. And find a passage to the Indies through the center route. In my last voyage we reached the continent the Portuguese have been talking about. The land goes in Northeast-Southwest direction, suggesting the northern lands of Newfoundland and the southern lands of Vera Cruz [12] may not be joined. We may find a passage. We will have to sail South to circle the Sargaço Sea, and then West to find land and the passage. By finding it, I will recover my rightful place as governor of these lands, a title which as agreed with the Spanish will be of your brother Diogo when I die."

"Whatever those jealous bastards in Seville tell you, never forget who we are. Our family is the ultimate bearer of the Wind Rose. The proof. Your grandfather sacrificed his life and kingdom to protect the secret. I have also sacrificed everything to finalize the mission. In the mouth of the Red Sea, my father climbed the Mountains of Sinai and there he met the 12 Portuguese knights of Infante Dom Pedro, great-uncle of King João II. That's where the friendship began. Later, when my father was forced to abandon his kingdom to protect the secret, he took refuge in the Portuguese island of Madeira, where he became known as Henrique Alemão, Henry the German. My friends have since long called me 'Alemão' too. Fernando, I can tell you only half of my story and of that you can speak of only half. My origins must remain unknown and my mission shall be revealed only many years from now by future generations. Promise me you will preserve my signature. That is the key to the secret."

"We must accept with abnegation all the lies they will tell about me. And they will come, oh they will. Do not worry too much with the lies. Your sole concern shall be to carry on where I stopped. This ring I carry is the seal, the key that opens the ark that carries the forbidden Book. It will be yours, when I die."

Father's ring had always intrigued me, a gold piece he always wore on his left ring finger, with a round seal and an embossed hooked X, the top right harm tilting slightly upwards.

I remember sleeping uneasily that night, in the deceiving lull before the storm, waking repeatedly by uneasy, confusing dreams. The storm abated suddenly and mercilessly on the morning of 30 June.

We endured many great storms and probations afterwards, during the two years of the last expedition. But to me, that storm still resonates in my mind with biblical proportions. It was terrible.

There was little else we could do, except waiting for the storm to calm down.

"As the storm gained in intensity and night came with deep darkness, three ships were torn from their anchorages, each going its own way". We lost sight of the other ships. The caravel Bermuda, commanded by my uncle Bartholomew Colon, had broken anchor and was in grave danger, waves washing over deck. At the mercy of the sea currents, the commander wisely took it to the high sea to avoid crashing into hidden rocks nearshore.

For two nights and two days we weathered the storm. I could not sleep, soaked to the bones, unable to take food to my stomach, shaken side to side by violent winds and fearing our ship would break in half every time she crashed down from the massive waves. Every hour, father cried out from his cabin in the stern castle, to make sure the boys had not forgotten to turn the hour glass. "You must not forget to turn the hourglass promptly, we need to keep record of time, otherwise we will be doomed, unable to take proper measurements from the stars or the sun". Or he would urgently call the crew to move to starboard or portside to balance the sheep, in advance of a change of the winds. We had taken care to fill up the empty barrels with sea water, just to keep the vessel's balance, but still she veered dangerously in every wind change.

Father later described the storm quite vividly in his letters: "Everyone lost hope and was quite certain that all the others had drowned. What mortal man would not have died in despair? Even for the safety of myself, my son, brother and friends, I was forbidden in such weather to put into land or enter harbors that I had gained for Spain by my own blood and sweat".

When the storm around Hispaniola was over, we were all drained and miserable. After the winds calmed down, we realized the Capitana was the only vessel of our fleet still holding anchor. The three other ships of the fleet had broken anchor and were dragged out to sea. The position the Admiral had chosen to station our ship proved very wise, and I remember later listening to the crew whispering admiration at the Admiral for his great sense of the ocean and the elements (alas, how the human spirit changes like the volatile ether... these were the same men that in other instances resented Father's iron fist in command and volatile decisions. Fools, if only you knew how he had to juggle contradictory objectives). It is in these moments of hardship and tremendous peril that the true fiber of a man is proven. The ship had been battered endlessly by ravenous waves and furious winds, but she held.

Such was the violence of the hurricane that rumors spread amongst the sailors that "by his magic arts, (Colon) had raised the storm to take revenge on Bobadilla." I doubt Father had such powers to control nature and weather, but I do not doubt that if he did possess such witchcraft, he would not have hesitated to use it against Bobadilla, so raging furious he was not to be allowed to go ashore in Hispaniola.

We spent a few days resting bodies and souls, to overcome the strain of two weeks of almost continuous storms. The crew went fishing near shore, as much for the food as for the fun. For the first time since arriving in those islands, I could truly contemplate the sublime beauty of those regions, the rich colors, smells and sounds, all new to my senses. I was fascinated by God's creativity in all the diversity of nature. How crude and parochial we were in Europe, just a small fraction of the world's wonders, yet considering itself in any way superior.

Many surprising and unknown marvels of nature were in store for us during that fourth voyage, which father later called his "Alto Voyage", the highest and most ambitious expedition, simultaneously the culmination of his discoveries and confirmation of his downfall.

I marveled as a delicate sea animal glided graciously past us, a massive undulating form, like a carpet floating in the wind [13]. I touched its slick and slippery flat torso, the wide fins flapping like wings of a bird. It looked so frail and light, despite its size, floating effortlessly on the water's surface. The sudden appearance of this strange animal amused everyone on the crew. The sailors stabbed it with a harpoon and secured it to the launch with a rope, and "it drew the boat as swiftly as an arrow. (Those aboard), not knowing what went on, were astounded to see the boat running about without oars."

Later, we came across a sea-cow [14]. It is also unknown in Spain. It is a large, gray animal with a wrinkled docile face. Father says it resembles an African elephant, but me and most of the sailors have never seen one either, so we took to calling it a sea-cow. "It is as big as a calf and resembles one in color, but it is better tasting and fatter."

Father was at his best when challenged. In the face of imminent danger, his instincts and experience took over the ghosts inside his mind. But during the times of idleness, he fell back to his hallucinations. Illness and regret further weighted him down. Father was again burning with fever, with only intermittent periods of lucidity. I sat on his side, fearing his death, listening to his ramblings.

"For the Old Man and King João, I must hold the center. The Portuguese control the northern and the southern passages, holding Newfoundland and Vera Cruz [15]. So, I must hold the center. Keep Isabella interested on the western lands, promising gold and spices and a route to the Indies through an isthmus from the Atlantic to the South Sea. If such passage exists, I must be the first to find it and prevent those maniacs, Jew-haters, Pope-servants and churchmoths that cling to Isabella's dress from finding the passage. King João supported me in an uprising to take control of the Western Indies and protect the passage. Oh, but he died, he died."

I could not understand this insistence with the Portuguese. Had they not refused father's proposal? Why did he talk such nonsense? I spied the door in angst, for fear someone might hear his babblings. Surely Father didn´t mean those things... but then, why had he insisted on stopping at Asilah, on the Moroccan coast, just days after leaving Spain, to help the Portuguese garrison who was under siege from the Moors? It was a Christian's duty, he had claimed, but was there any hidden intention behind it?

"Father, we will find the passage into the South Sea, to reach Cipango. Calm down, you will make the passage. You will be vindicated and recover all your titles and wealth, to live as a great man and make mother very happy."

"Yes, Fernando. Take care of your mother, she is a splendid woman. You have her fiber, her stern calmness. Yes, find the passage... but do not wait much of it."

Two years later, upon my return to Spain, I found out what happened to the treasure fleet the Governor had sent out to sea, ignoring Father's advice. Shortly after those ships departed Hispaniola, the hurricane hit the ships with all its might. Twenty-five of Ovando's ships sank, four crawled back to Hispaniola, and only one ship actually made it to Spain – the Aguja, with Father's treasure. Truly a miracle. Approximately 500 men lost their lives during the hurricane, including Bobadilla. Father was delusional, but if it was not for his sixth sense of the seas, vast knowledge and stubbornness, our ships would also have been at the end of the ocean.

NEWPORT, CHRISTMAS 2018

*"Perhaps only in a world of the blind will things be what they
truly are."*

JOSÉ SARAMAGO, BLINDNESS

"**S**o, there you go", continued uncle Santiago, expelling a cloud of smoke from the cigar and seating
back down on his couch. The winter light was re-
ceding fast, already anticipating dusk. "Columbus life is a
mystery, and so is his signature".

Santiago took up his iPad and googled "Christopher
Columbus signature". Dozens of images popped up. He
pushed the screen towards Savanah:

She had seen it often enough. Raven's obsession had
started with that cryptic signature. Despite its overall
meaning remaining concealed to this day, Columbus himself
attributed a lot of relevance to it, to the point of insisting on
his testament that his heirs must continue using that precise
signature, as if it carried a hidden message for posterity.

"We can discuss forever the top part of the signature.
Its possible cabalistic meanings are endless. An interpret-
ation is 'Santo; Santo Alto Santo; Xristo Maria Yajé', meaning
'Saint; Saint High Saint; Christ Mary Joseph'. Or 'Servus Sum

Altissime Salvatoris', meaning 'I am a servant of the High Saviour'."

"I personally believe the top part of the signature is a clear Templar sigil. The Templars and their successor the Order of Christ invoked the Holy Spirit in their creed "Sanctus Spiritus Salvator", represented by three Ss. Not the material personas of the Father or the Son, with wills, demands and intentions, but a pure, ethereal Spirit. The disposition of the three S like a roof represent the "Roof of Solomon", the Salomon Temple where the Templar headquarters in Jerusalem stood and source of their name: 'Pauperes Commilitones Christi Templique Salomonici', the Poor Soldiers of Christ and of the Temple of Solomon. The 'XMY' may have a deeper hidden meaning, standing for Christ, Mohammed and Yahweh, invoking Saint Bernard of Clairvaux and Templar doctrine of the Temple protecting all faiths, Christians, Muslims and Jews."

Santiago raised the sheet of newspaper where he had scribbled the square and compass. Savanah now realized it looked eerily like a letter 'A'.

"And finally, the 'A' in the middle of the 3 'S'. It may represent an 'Ark' found by the Templars in the Temple of Solomon. Hence the A inside the 'S' arch. Which would suggest Colon had some type of treasure, an ark, he carried to protect and hide."

Savanah pictured the sigil in her mind. It would make sense for Columbus, the last Templar, to carry the Solomon Temple on his signature.

Oh, nonsense! Too much hocus pocus... She had always liked charades and treasure hunts. But she was a grown up now!

"Gosh, uncle. Don't Dan Brawn me here, we are talking about my sister's murder..."

Santiago's lips hanged open for a bit, as if deciding whether to proceed or not. In the end, he just said "Well, Dan Brawn got most of it right, actually, even though he didn't manage to uncover the whole truth".

Savanah needed something a bit stronger than her tea. She was angry at her uncle for mixing her sister's murder with all this crackpot efabulations, but even more angry at herself for not allowing the mental space to consider alternative views, as unlikely as they might seem.

After an uncomfortable pause, Santiago continued. "At least there is some consensus about the ': XpoFerens./' in the last line of Colon's signature. The ":" is used in most modern languages as a punctuation mark preceding a list of related ideas. It is named after the Latin word 'colon' or the Greek 'kolon'. In Latin and Greek 'colon' is not a punctuation mark, but a concept meaning 'member', or a 'part of a larger idea'. So it became used to name the ':' punctuation mark that precedes a list of arguments. 'Xpo' comes from the Greek Xpõ, meaning "Christ". Just like we write Xmas for Christmas, right? So, ': Xpo' means 'Member of Christ', or 'Member of the Order of Christ'. And 'Ferens' is a form of the Latin verb 'fero', meaning "to carry, to walk, to transport". So, ': XpoFerens' means "Member of the Order of Christ" but also "Carry Christ" or "Carry Christ's secret". Crispoferens is also a Latinization of Cristovão, the Saint who carried the Christ Child across a river.

Colon Christopher. Member of the Order of Christ. I carry Christ's secret.

The final dot and slash is a Hebrew 'semi colon' or 'imperfect colon', as if Columbus was saying that the ':' is a '. /', meaning 'This Colon is a false Colon', thus leaving a clear message of his fake identity.

"So, there you have it.", Santiago concluded. "Colum-
˙ through his signature, was affirming himself as a Tem-

plar, a member of the Order of Christ, and a carrier of a secret of Christ. What that secret might be…"

Santiago looked intently at Savanah, assessing her reaction. He got in return no more than a resigned roll of the eyes. Then, rather unexpectedly, Savanah burst into tears, sobbing profusely. This was not at all like Savanah, always quite self-conscious and composed.

"Sorry uncle.", Savanah said, trying to mop her tears and strengthen her heart.

"Don´t worry… what happened?"

"I just… Sorry. You talking about punctuation marks made be recall something Raven said when we were girls."

The image had stuck to Savanah's mind. They were 10 or 11 years old when in a rather ordinary day Raven came up with one of her crazy, genial comments. She used to drop these pearls like they were nothing more than worthless pebbles, but their parents treasured them. They had just finished homework, a comment on some reading assignment, and were leaving the room to play outside, when Raven said to mum, rather matter-of-factly. "My favourite punctuation mark is the comma, it provides dynamism to the sentence, as if you are pausing for breath before the next jump. The full stop is too definitive and the exclamation mark too dramatic, but the comma is just…like the background beat behind the music, unnoticed but crucial."

Mother and father made a big fuss of it. "Gosh, what a nonsense." Savanah had though at the time, riddled at all the attention the remark had caused. "Really? A favourite punctuation mark??" Savanah now recalled the episode, laughing between her sobs. She missed Raven. It had been nothing but an inconsequential, mindless child comment, but Savanah always got a bit jealous at her sister's easy, nonchalant geniality. She was ever the rational, all her achievements came from hard work.

It was quite ironic, though. Raven's favourite punctuation mark was the comma. Yet, her life had come to an abrupt full stop, due to the question marks she was raising about a Colon...

Savanah smiled sadly behind her tears, a dramatic dark humour image rolling in her mind. Raven's ghost from the afterlife, looking down at her own dead body, blood dripping from her fist, like the main character of a Greek tragicomedy, while an unseen chorus echoed in the night: "The comma was her favourite punctuation mark; the question mark has now become her least favourite."

Savanah shrugged the memory away, blocking the image.

"Bollocks! Sorry uncle... Ok. Look, I mean... That was all right for summer games and charades when we were kids. It's all good fun. But I just can't believe you actually take any of this seriously. I mean, you are a US General with a double degree in law and history. And Raven, what was she on about? This notebook is all over the place. I wouldn't be surprised to find here zodiac signs, voodoo fixes or aliens. I get lost in all this superstitious folklore. It's just... a mess."

"Well, Savanah", Santiago shifted on the sofa. She could not tell if he was looking uncomfortable or amused. "The world is not black and white, especially because millions of different people have conflicting views, ambitions, desires. Symbolism and mythology has always been a powerful way to manipulate the others and control multitudes."

"We agree there. That's my point. I am not a religious person. Religion just fills the void space of what science has not yet managed to explain, and over time the territory claimed by religion just shrinks and shrinks... Sure, it is difficult to face life without the purpose and meaning a mystical force can provide. But, well, it is what it is. The world is, life is, I am... and that's it."

"Discussing religious beliefs is just pointless, really, I have mine, you have yours...", interjected uncle Santiago.

"Oh, uncle, but it is not a matter of belief, is it? Hundreds, thousands, millions of people died on the fires of the Inquisition, countless wars, books censored or destroyed. All because of this God and His church! The killings, the lies, the atrocities..."

"...They were not committed by God or the Church, but by men..."

"In name of the church!"

"Which is not the same thing."

Savanah was not interested in the finer theological debate. Horrible thigs had been made. That was a big part for her having become an atheist.

"If He exists and allowed all these crimes to be perpetrated on His behalf, then He is a lousy, wrathful, power-thirsty God."

"Or so humble He willingly provided His creation with freewill, and stands away from interfering in that freewill."

"Fair enough. But I'm not talking about an idea, I'm talking about real things in the real world. I loathe the hypocrisy of the ecclesiastic hierarchy. All the rituals, the brainless rules, the mumbo jumbo that has been fed to people for centuries, all based on what... a book? The Bible is the biggest fictional best-seller ever written. A big farce, all those self-righteous church men praising the humble but living in riches. Throughout history bishops and popes advocated chastity but had mistresses and fathered children. And those indulgences, yeah you can sin around as long as you have money to buy a papal indulgency and all will be forgotten...

And don't get me started on the treatment of women by the church…"

"Are you done?", uncle Santiago eyed her from the top rim of his glasses.

"Yeah, I just… what was Raven doing?", sighted Savanah. "Did she get herself into some kind of sect and got herself killed?"

"Your sister was doing a serious investigation about a mystery that has eluded historians for five centuries. Columbus life is deep in a fog of contradictions. To see from another person's perspective, you need to use their glasses…"

Santiago took a long puff from his cigar, enveloping the library room in dense blue smoke that combined with the wood fire aroma. He took a sip from his whisky. 'Wisdom takes time to apprehend, it cannot be rushed', he seemed to convey.

"It seems to me", Santiago finally continued, "that your sister was looking for something. The notebook was not intended to transmit information or an argument to others. Raven was looking for something, and just jotting down ideas. If she suspected some kind of conspiracy, she might also have been concerned about writing her thoughts plainly."

"Uncle, why do I have the feeling you are not telling me everything you know?", Savanah said, getting slightly impatient. "I am lost. All this is new, different from what we have learned in high school, but Raven doesn't bother to explain or defend those alternative theories. I mean, you would expect a systematic side by side comparison of the competing theories, with arguments and counter-arguments."

"Well, you have a point there. So, why has your sister so quickly pushed aside such descriptive approach, to jump straight into much deeper quicksand? She was looking for something. As if the academic revelations since the turn of the century suddenly opened the door for a much wider hypothesis."

Savanah stared out of the window to the naked winter landscape, trying to decide if she really wanted to open a door she had resolutely kept closed for thirteen years. Uncle Santiago was not saying all he knew. He never did.

After several minutes of silence, interrupted only by the wood crackling in the fireplace and Rachmaninov 3 piano concerto, Savanah decided to bring up an issue she had pushed to the back of her mind, that email she found on her inbox after returning from Lisbon 13 years ago.

"Uncle, I have never shown this to anyone. Please don't comment with father and mother, that would bring back all the sad memories... When I returned from Lisbon to New York in 2006 after Raven's death, I found in my inbox an email sent by Raven in the afternoon before her assassination."

Savanah took her mobile phone, swiping through her google photos gallery to August 2006 for a screenshot of the email, which showed a single line:

"Go to Santiago to find ⧓ "

Santiago's eyes stared at the message. It seemed he was consciously making an effort not to convey any reaction, like a poker player. But then he smiled, saying "that devilish girl!"

Santiago took a few seconds to recompose himself, then added. "Well, if you read it at face value, I would say

Santiago refers to Santiago de Compostela, a northern Spain cathedral city that attracts millions of pilgrims every year walking the Santiago Paths to reach the cathedral where supposedly the remains of apostle Santiago are held. The symbol at the end is also quite straightforward at face value, it is a rune of the Elder Futhark alphabet used by the Vikings. Its Germanic name is Ingwaz and is a widely used symbol in medieval gothic magic to refer to "the God Ingwaz". So, if you take this literally, it means "Go to Santiago de Compostela to find God". Considering the religious links of Compostela to apostle Santiago, this seems a rather innocuous message."

"But...", prompted Savanah, knowing fully well that nothing in her uncle or actually her sister was innocuous.

"Well... reality usually has multiple meanings. We just have to be open minded to perceive them. The Viking rune can be decomposed into two other runes combined in mirrored images. Look here"

Santiago looked for another empty space on his newspaper to write down.

"So... The "God" rune in Old Futhart runes can be written as a combination of two other runes, the transliterations of the "K" and "S" sounds, and the respective mirror images. This would be K K S S. Quite interesting."

"Meaning...?", prompted Savanah, growing impatient.

"My dear, if you want to think like a symbologist, you will have to get loose of your excel spreadsheet. The mirrored KK would obviously stand for Kristopher Kolon, whom we know as Christopher Columbus. And the SS should stand for 'Segismundo Secret'".

"Meaning...?"

"Segismundo Alemão, in Portuguese 'the German'. There is evidence to suggest Columbus was in fact the son of Henrique Alemão, a Germanic noble who arrived in Madeira around 1450. He had a son, named Segismundo Henriques or Segismundo Alemão. Both disappeared in mysterious ways around the time that, out of thin smoke, a Christopher Colon appears in Seville."

"Uouu, uouu, uouu. Hold on. That's... Take a step back. I got lost, uncle", Savanah interrupted him, gesturing as if to swipe away the excess information. "What you are suggesting is that Columbus was in fact this Segismundo Alemão, son of a Germanic noble who for some reason took refuge in an isolated island at the westernmost extremes of the known world. Did I get that right?"

"Columbus himself tells us that, quite openly in his cryptic signature. The top part is a triangle formed with three "S" letters around an "A". This has received many interpretations, as we discussed. But the simplest explanations are usually the best. Why not take it at face value? He was really signing his true hidden identity: 'S. A. = Segismundo Alemão'."

"Huumm. Going back to Raven's email. This would be something like 'Go to uncle Santiago to find Christopher Columbus, the Secret Segismundo. Does this make sense?"

Savanah could sense this was not the end of the story, that there was something else. Rach 3 had ended on the CD player and a welcomed silence fell on the room. Savanah had several questions, but she would need to choose carefully as she did not want to get caught in an endless discussion about farfetched conspiracy theories. And daylight was long gone outside, so they would soon be called for dinner. She decided on two questions.

"The strange thing is... why was Raven writing to me in Futhark Viking runes?"

"That is fairly transparent, and you know it, right?", answered her uncle. Fair enough. If Segismundo Alemão was Columbus and the son of a Germanic noble, plus the representative of Dom João II in the Luso-Danish expedition that reached the Americas 15 years before Columbus officially claimed it for the Spanish monarchs, it would be fair to assume Columbus understood the Nordic runes. Besides that, it wasn't surprising for Raven to communicate hidden messages to her twin sister in Futhark runes, as they had learned them during the teenager summer holidays on the boat with uncle Santiago. Although Savanah had forgotten all about that.

The second question was a bit more difficult. Savanah looked again at the newspaper page with the double K. Would she dare to ask the question burning in her mind? She took the pen and wrote the mirrored KK, but joined together. And then superimposed the Greek orthodox square cross.

Savanah looked at uncle Santiago, straight into his eyes. He held her gaze for a while. Then he simply said "Some things are best left unsaid. The important things cannot be told, you must discover them for yourself."

With that, he clapped his hands, raising from the sofa and smiling to Savanah, as he headed out for Christmas dinner. Hugh had just rung the bell.

Savanah kept behind for a short while.

KK was Kristopher Kolumbus in her sister's urgent email, urging her to talk to uncle Santiago. Overlaying the mirrored KK with the Greek square cross, she faced a very familiar symbol. It was the wind rose of the sailors, pointing the 8 geographic cardinal points. More importantly, it was intriguingly similar to the "hooked wind rose" embossed on uncle Santiago ring, the gold ring he wore since she could remember on his left ring finger.

Raven had sent her a cryptic message in distress, the afternoon before her death, telling her to find the Secret Columbus, or Columbus' Secret.

Savanah could already hear Hugh making his best efforts to be the soul of the party, as usual, "dominating the scene" as he called it at dinner parties. As she walked out of the library for the Christmas dinner, Savanah's mind wondered momentarily away. "Why not? It's not like I have anything better to do right now. The baby can wait a bit longer..."

LISBON, JANUARY 2019

She was no longer an MD at Bank of America, so, although she could afford it, she decided to fly coach class instead of executive. On the other hand, she didn't need to take the red eye overnight flight. Having time more than compensated the small luxuries of executive class. She crammed on her seat on the 3rd of January TAP flight to Lisbon, flipping through Raven's notebook again, trying to make sense of it. She lingered slightly longer on the page with the goat inside a pentagram, with the handwritten statement on the side "The Goat is in my way!". What strange, hallucinated call for help was this?

She had gone through the notes already over the New Year break. One of the few things her quantitative mind could relate to were the references to distances and locations. There were several of these references in Raven's notebook, as if she was checking Colon's calculations. That was strange... why was this an issue at all? The quick biographies she had flipped through over the holidays suggested Colon could be a visionary but hardly an accurate mathematician or cosmographer, having grossly underestimated the size of the globe's circumference, writing he was in the Canary Islands but then anchoring in Madeira, or reaching Lisbon instead of Seville. He once wrote in the expedition log book that they were on 42ºN when they were sailing close to Cuba, which is a gross mistake (the correct latitude is 21º) ... it would be like being in Cuba but thinking to be in New York.

Is this credible? Can such a reckless and inaccurate

person find his way in four return trips in the endless and treacherous ocean, without GPS or satellite guiding system, just by pure... luck? That would be the same as Apollo 11 pilots landing on the moon four times by pure chance. It seemed Raven was also disconcerted by this, as she had several references in her notebook, noting divergences between Colon's private and public statements of locations or distances, with a side-note 'LOST??'. Out of curiosity and with time to kill, Savanah started compiling in her laptop all those references she could find, putting them into a neat table. In the end, what the laptop screen showed her was a rather different image from that tale of a madman driven only by vision, courage, intuition and sheer luck. The picture that emerged was of two totally different personas. Was Colon schizophrenic, measuring his location and distances at sea with astonishing accuracy on his personal logbooks and letters to close friends, but widely missing the mark on the official log book, letters to the court and other audiences?

Colon claimed he had reached India and maintained the deceit until his death. However, in a letter written in 1498 to the Spanish kings, Colon stated "Your Royal Highnesses know that, not long ago (before my travels), it was not known other lands besides those described by Ptolomeu". India is clearly shown in Ptolomeu maps and described in Marco Polo book. So, what "other lands" was Colombo referring to? If he truly claimed he had reached India, there would be no "other lands". Besides, he never referred to his discoveries as "India" but always as "the Indies".

Colon arrived from his first expedition in 1493, claiming to have reached India. The following year, he wrote a letter where he stated that the eastern point of Hispaniola (Dominican Republic) is about five time zones to the west of Cape St. Vicente. If he had written leagues or miles, he could still assume to be in India if grossly underestimating the size of the planet. But he wrote time zones! There is no misunderstanding possible. The globe is divided in 24 time zones and 360º, so each time zone corresponds to 15º of the equatorial circumference. In 1494, Colon had a very exact location of Hispaniola. Considering Colon statement of 'about five time zones', that means 67º – 82º. It would be plainly obvious he was very distant from the true India. Ptomoleu's map, which was clearly known to Colon and referred by him in audiences with the kings, marked the 180º of known lands from the Canary Islands to China, situating India 135º, or 9 time zones, east of the Canaries. That means, irrevocably, 225º or 15 time zones west (and thus even further west from Cape St. Vicente). Colon clearly places Hispaniola at 5 time zones west, not 15. He knew he had travelled only 1/3 of the distance to reach India!

In his first voyage he notes in the log book they had travelled 1142 leagues or 4568 miles, from the Canary Islands to Hispaniola. This indicates he was using Portuguese Maritime Leagues, PML, where one league equates to four miles (or 18º to the league). In the second voyage, he measured 1140 leagues, or 4560 miles. Considering Colon measured this as 5 time zones, then each of the globe's 24 time zones represents 912 miles at the latitude of Hispaniola (20º N), or 61 miles per degree. This would mean the full circle at this latitude is 21888 miles. The true measure is 23407 miles. He underestimated the distance by 6%, which is incredibly accurate considering the instruments of the time.

This also puts into question the key claim that Colon grossly underestimated the circumference of the globe by using an equatorial degree of 56 miles. His calculations in Hispaniola equate to 61 miles per degree (919*24/360). The equatorial degree must be larger than the 61 miles he himself calculated at the Haiti latitude!

And if this was not enough, how can we question his skills as a pilot and cosmographer if he always found his way back to the starting point, in the open ocean, and repeatedly reached Hispaniola and back? He ostensibly never provided the exact location of Hispaniola after the first expedition, so he was the only one capable of taking the fleet back in the second expedition – which he did without wavering.

Does this mean that when he supplied wrong measurements, he did so intentionally to hide his true route and intentions?

It is also remarkable the measurements of Colon were based on the PML, the Portuguese Maritime League. At the time, each nation used its own measurements for a league, so the globe's degree or time zone would be worth different leagues in different countries. In the PML, a league is equated to 6.173 km or approximately 4 miles. On 27 February 1493, on the return form the first voyage, he wrote Nina was 125 leagues from Cape St. Vicente (east) and 106 leagues to Santa Maria islands in the Azores (west). That means 231 leagues from Cape St. Vincent to the Azores island. The true distance is 1426 km, which means Colon not only had a very good idea of his location but also was using 6.173 km per league (1426/231), which is precisely the measure of the PML. Colon was using Portuguese measurements, because that is where he learned everything he knew about sailing and cosmography!

The PML is "18 leagues to the degree", meaning each globe degree at the equator contains 18 leagues. This means the 360° correspond to 40 001.04 km. The current true perimeter of the equatorial circumference is 40 075.017 km. How close the Portuguese estimate was, more than five centuries ago!

In his first voyage in 1492, Colon took a straight and direct route to Hispaniola, the shortest route possible, as if he knew beforehand the route he should travel. Then he returned in 1493 by a different route, taking the best route to the Azores which is still used today by cruising ships. And then returned to Hispaniola without error. How could he have done this if he had been lost or if he was not a master at cosmography and cartography?

Before departing for his second voyage, Colon left a letter addressed to his brother Bartolomé, who was in France at the time. Bartolomé Colon, who had never sailed to Hispaniola, later captained a ship that sailed from Spain to Hispaniola without error, based solely on the secret instructions left by Colon on a letter, arriving in Hispaniola on 14 April 1494. There is only one explanation: Colon left very precise and accurate measurements and indications. Colon and his trusted circle kept the information secret, while lying or confusing the information passed to the others.

Savanah's investment banker brain was used to order and structure, so it was quite stressful to make sense of all the disconnected data randomly compiled by Raven. The lack of historical knowledge didn't help either. She hoped the weeks planned in Lisbon looking through the books and documents Raven had used when reading for her PhD would help to make sense of the all mess. Professor Noronha, from Universidade Nova, Raven's PhD supervisor, had promised to help, although he was now retired. Luckily, Pedro, who had 13 years ago been a post-doc researcher and junior teacher at the university, was still there and would be able to give her a deeper view on what Raven had been researching.

Her fingers flipped through the pages of Raven's notebook, filled with drawings of stars, crosses, pentagrams and roses. The last two cut off pages felt like an amputated leg... it is not there, but the brain still feels it, can almost scratch the missing limb.

As she tried to focus and block out the noise of the

tourists in the plane returning from Christmas holidays, she dozed off to a restless slumber, her head dropping sideways against the window. She woke up a few hours later as the plane prepared for the final approximation to Lisbon airport. She had a nasty sore neck.

ROME, JANUARY 2019

Palace of the Holy Office

C ardinal Marcello Ferro sat at his immense mahogany desk, reading the Corriere della Sera. It was his brief time of respite before starting the daily affairs, which were many, as Prefect of the Congregation for the Doctrine of the Faith. The draft of the new constitution for the Roman Curia, the Praedicate Evangelium, was in its final stages and the theological and political discussions it involved required all his attention.

He had hoped for some time of peace and rest at the end of his life, but how could he have refused the invitation from his friend Jorge Bergoglio? The Pope had a herculean task to reform the Church and counted on him to supervise the work of the Council of Cardinals, gently prodding and nudging them forward. The group, created one month after Francis was elected, was supposed to advise the Pope on governance and reform, with the drafting of the new constitution a priority. But the work of the seven cardinals dragged out since 2013.

Lost on his thoughts, Cardinal Ferro failed to notice the silent arrival of Archbishop Jerome.

The Secretary of the Congregation cleared his throat, softly, to call the Prefect's attention.

"Marcello, disturbing news arrived from Lisbon", communicated the Secretary. "You remember the 2006 affair of the American girl?"

The Prefect raised his eyes from the newspaper. Of course he remembered and the Secretary knew that perfectly well. So, he remained silent, waiting for him to continue.

"Her twin sister landed today in Lisbon. We don't know yet what her intentions might be, but we must act diligently."

"Of course. Is father Paulo following the situation?"

"Yes. He will keep us informed."

"Very well."

The Secretary longed a little longer in the office, then added: "It may be better not to mention this to the Holy Father. We may need to keep... our options open. Some matters are better handled by the soldiers, unknown by the more... media-exposed offices of our Church."

He left, leaving an uncomfortable feeling in the air of the Prefect's office, as if a cold shadow had entered the room and pressed out the warmth of the sunny winter morning.

Cardinal Ferro moved from his desk towards the window, looking out of window. Anyone walking past the dark-saffron building of the Palace of the Holy Office and watching the Spanish cardinal, clad in his black Jesuit cassock, could not imagine the tough choices men in his position had to make.

The 2006 affair in Lisbon had been long before him becoming Prefect of the Holy Office. Still, the Book, the Q-source, remained elusive. The Church had furiously looked for it since the twelfth century, when rumours that the Templars had found the forbidden Book in the ruins of the Temple of Salomon started. The French Inquisition, then the Spanish and Portuguese, ravaged the Cathars, the Hussites, the Templars, the Jews... The protection of the doctrine against heresy was centralized by the Holy See in 1542, when Pope Paul III created the Supreme Sacred Congregation of the Roman and Universal Inquisition, commonly known as the Holy Office. It changed its name a few times until the current designation, remaining to this day as the oldest of the nine Congregations of the Roman Curia.

But the forbidden Book was never found, if it ever existed at all.

TOMAR, MARCH 1467

(Columbus)

I am now 16 and a fully appointed knight of the Order of Christ. Only anointed knights have access to the inner secrets of the Sagres School, as the Old Man established.

I am, therefore, a Templar.

My mind is restless. The Castle and the city of Tomar are asleep, but I remain awake, witness to the bright moon and the heavy responsibility ahead. Jerusalem has fallen to Saladin in 1187 and has, except for a short period of a decade, remained solidly under Muslim control. The pressure to the East increases and Constantinople is under threat from the Turks. The hopes of recovering the Holy Land are dim. We must protect the treasure the nine founding Templar knights found in the ruins of the Salomon Temple. It is my duty, bestowed on my shoulders by my Father and the Old Man, to carry this Templar treasure to safety. To take the Wind Rose to the Rose Line.

The Templars helped the creation of this nation, a tiny country distant from the political maneuvering that corrupts the heart of Europe. A country fiercely independent from Rome, turned to Africa and the Atlantic. The ties between the Templars and Portugal date back to the end of the eleventh century, before either the Templars or Portugal even existed.

Dom Henrique, cousin of the Dukes of Bourgogne and

uncle of Bernard of Clairvaux – today Saint Bernard – arrived in Iberia with his army at the end of the eleventh century, to help king Dom Afonso of Castella and Leon in the Reconquista war against the moors. As a reward, he received the hand of one of the king's daughters, Dona Teresa, and a county in the Atlantic coast, which would be the genesis of Portugal. Their son, Dom Afonso Henriques, was born in 1111.

At the same time as Count Dom Henrique arrived in Iberia, on the other extreme of the Mediterranean, the First Crusade captured Jerusalem from the Muslims in 1099. Ten years later, in 1119, a group of nine knights, including Hughes de Payens and André de Montbard (uncle of Bernard of Clairvaux and cousin of Dom Henrique), proposed to King Baldwin II of Jerusalem the creation of a monastic military order to protect the pilgrims to the Holy Land. The king accepted and granted the knights a wing of the royal palace on the Temple Mount, above the ruins of the Salomon Temple, to serve as the headquarters of the new Order. And thus were born the Poor Knights of Christ and the Temple of Solomon, the Templars.

Saint Bernard of Clairvaux, cousin of the Dukes of Bourgogne, a Benedictine abbot founder of the Cistercian Order and a very influential figure of the Church, advocated in favor of the new Order. Hughes de Payes returned to Europe in 1126 and, together with Bernard, worked to achieve the recognition of the new Order by the western Pope. Bernard was constantly sick, pained by anemia, stomach aches and headaches. Having lost his palate, he ate nothing but boiled vegetables. With a clear mind and honeyed tongue, he wrote innumerable letters and texts exhorting the reform of the church, exposing immorality and scandals. He also defended the rights of peasants, Jews and women through the veneration of Virgin Mary. These are the true founding principles of our Order.

Two years later, in January 1128, at the Council of Troyes called to discuss the possibility of a new grand crusade, the Pope announced the recognition of the Order of the Temple. Bernard of Clairvaux wrote most of the Rule of the new Templar Order.

The tale of parallel stories moved in tandem. On the same year of 1128, Dom Afonso Henriques went to battle against his mother and arrested her, claiming the title of count of Portucale. Immediately, he sent his cousin Bernard of Clairvaux the pledge of the loyalty of his nation, which, at the time, was only a dream – it would take 12 more years for Afonso Henriques to be proclaimed King in 1140 after the Battle of Ourique, and 15 years to be recognized by Castella in 1143 at Zamorra.

By mid-March 1128, Hughes de Payens, one of the original nine Templars, and a group of recently anointed monk-knights, arrived to Portugal. Barely six weeks after the new Order had been recognized by the Pope! This was extremely fast, considering they were travelling by horse, and implies the events were part of a grand plan. The knights carried with them a letter from Bernard of Clairvaux addressed to his cousin Count Afonso Henriques, addressing him as "Illustrious King of Portugal".

Soon after the knights arrived in Portugal, Afonso Henriques and Hughes de Payes attacked and conquered Santarem, continuing the push south of the Reconquista. The Moors that managed to escape took refuge in Lisbon.

In 1133, before the new country was recognized, Dom Afonso Henriques signed a document awarding several lands to the Templar knights in recognition for their support in the Reconquista war. He wrote "brother", next to his name in the signature.

Encouraged by this success and the later recognition of Portugal as a kingdom in 1143, the Templars knights with the help of Bernard of Clairvaux, launched a campaign to recruit new knights and launch a crusade to reconquer Lisbon from the Moors. From all over Europe, 3.000 knights were recruited, transported in a fleet of 164 ships, crossing the English Channel and descending the Atlantic coast.

The siege and conquer of Lisbon of 1147 was a tremendous multinational affair, linked together by the influence and power of the Templars. Lisbon was, at the time, a rich commercial city, at the southern frontier of Christendom. "You can find everything in the city in abundance. Gold, silver and iron. Good quality olives (...). River Tagus is so rich in fish that it is said the river is 2/3 water and 1/3 fish.[16]"

In recognition for his help in the creation of the new kingdom and the wars against the Moors, King Dom Afonso Henriques granted to Bernard of Clairvaux and the Cistercian Order a vast land in the center of the country, from Óbidos to Leiria, granting full power to make their own laws, administer justice and charge taxes. In 1159, the king awarded to the Templars the city of Tomar, which would become the headquarters of the order and of its successor, the Order of Christ.

The ties between the Templars and the Portuguese monarchs have been strong since the founding of the country.

The Portuguese kings were side by side with the Templar knights at the beginning, and remained loyal at the end. The sixth king, Dom Dinis, protected the Templars when they were extinguished in 1307, receiving the persecuted knights into a new order, the Order of Christ, against the Pope's orders.

And here, maybe, started the Portuguese maritime adventure! The Templars had a significant fleet, based in La Rochelle, to support the crusades. They also dominated the most advanced sailing techniques, including the astrolabe, an instrument to measure the position of the stars in high sea navigation, which they had learned from the Arabs. They are also said to have possessed ancient maritime charts brought from Egypt... However, after the order to extinguish the Templars and seize their possessions, not a single ship was found in la Rochelle! It is quite revealing that in 1307, when the Pope and France extinguished the Templars and their fleet vanished, the Portuguese king Dom Dinis created the first post of Admiral of the Seas. The same king ordered the plantation of a massive pine forest in Leiria to ensure wood for the Portuguese fleet. So, the Templar fleet disappears at the same time Portugal launches its maritime ambitions.

Since the dawn of this nation, there was a deep, silent conflict and antagonism between all the Portuguese kings and Rome, from Dom Afonso Henriques until today's King Afonso V. Almost 350 years during which Portugal remained profoundly independent from the papacy [17]. The first king, Dom Afonso Henriques, was excommunicated by the Pope because he insisted on choosing his own bishops and threatened to cut the arm of the Pope representative if he dared to extend the hand for the king to kiss. He thundered: "In Portugal we also have bibles and do not need Rome to teach us the Father, the Son and the Holy Spirit". In fact, a series of Portuguese first kings were excommunicated by the pope, even after the recognition of the nation: Dom Afonso Henriques died excommunicated in 1185, Dom Sancho was excommunicated in 1208, Dom Afonso II in 1220, Dom Sancho II in 1234, Dom Afonso III in 1277, culminating with Dom Dinis refusing to comply with the Pope's orders to arrest the Templar knights.

More than three centuries of Templar history lie on my shoulders, to complete the mission. I hope to be worth

But enough of the past. I look towards the future complete the mission my father and the Infante besto on me. I long to take to the sea. There is so much yet to discover! I now realize how tiny European kingdoms are, compared to the great world. The legacy of the Infante, although not yet bearing commercial riches to the crown, has opened a new world. Our ships have long abandoned dead reckoning and coastal sailing, using new or perfected instruments to sail in the high seas: the astrolabe inherited from the Arabs, the cross-staff and the Rule of Marteloio, a trigonometric table that allows to compute distance travelled along a course when tacking. Our ships sail to Guinea and Sierra Leone to the south and to the Antilles, Newfoundland and the Sargasso Sea to the west. Legends of sea monsters and boiling waters on the equator have been destroyed. The myths that the ships would slide south with no return if they went beyond Cape Nao [18] and that Bojador was the end of the world from which ships would fall off a cliff have been proven wrong. A systematic, scientific mind is emerging, refusing the blind acceptance of past knowledge.

How marvelous to live in this century of wonders and in the country that leads this great leap forward. Secrecy is of the utmost importance, because a small country like ours would never be able to defend these new lands against Spain, England or France should they know how to get there. The strict rule of secrecy imposed by the Infante is maintained by King Afonso and Prince João.

The first light of dawn is perceptible in the horizon. I must join my brothers for Vespers pray.

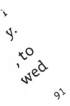

LISBON, JANUARY 2019

January in Lisbon was very different from New York or Boston. Although on approximately the same latitude, Lisbon enjoyed a temperate Mediterranean climate and a unique luminosity from the winter sun reflected by the wide Tagus estuary. Savanah had finally found a small beautiful attic room to rent in Lapa in a 1930's building with views over the rooftops to the Tagus at the foot of the hill. A short term let for three months. The owners, a young Portuguese couple that lived on the top floor of the building, could do with some extra income from renting out the attic. They had to share the same entry of the flat, but the views conquered her the moment the real estate agent showed her the attic.

Lisbon was fashionable and trendy, a recently discovered gem combining great climate, welcoming people and hipster cultural nightlife. The tax breaks for non-ordinary residents were a plus, making Lisbon an attractive cocktail for young Erasmus exchange students, foreign tech start-ups and retired couples from France or Finland. The real estate agent mentioned (three or four times actually) that Madonna had just bought a multi-million euro home in Restelo and moved to the city, which featured in her most recent video-clip.

Professor Noronha had retired more than ten years ago, but happily accepted to introduce her to the people in the history department of Universidade Nova. He had been Raven's PhD supervisor and when Savanah contacted him at the end of December, introducing herself and ing she would like to revisit her sister's work, he responded brightly:

"Oh, that would be lovely. You know, Raven was one of my most brilliant students. I quite enjoyed our discussions. It was rather sad... a terrible, nasty affair, what happened in the dreadful summer of 2006. But, yeah, I would love to show you around the department. I am retired now and quite bored of seating at home tendering the garden and feeding the seagulls. It would be something useful to do, for a change!"

Savanah had therefore booked the airplane ticked and headed to Lisbon, to Hugh's silent disapproval. She didn't really know what she was after, but, well, at least a change would do her good. She was enjoying the brisk sunny cold winter mornings full of light, setting herself to a daily routine of 10k run along the river before heading to the university. Her running track took her down the hill to the pedestrian riverside path and turning west towards Belém. Then, the way back. The last stretch uphill the steep Lapa street was a challenge that set her juices running for the day.

Professor Noronha met her at the lobby of the university and walked her around the history department, having already used his status as former head of the department to get Savanah an invitation as a short term guest researcher at the History department. He introduced her first to Pedro, now an Associate Professor with Aggregation, who had been a young post-doc and junior assistant Professor during ʼven's PhD 13 years before. Pedro accepted, politely but un-ʼusiastically, to guide Savanah around the bibliography ʼcuments Raven had used. He had a dovish guarded not looking straight at Savanah's eyes when talk-but focusing instead on some point on the wall ad a pale sickly white skin, which to Savanah ʼn this light-soaked city.

"Ah, and this is Ndunduba", said Professor Noronha embracing a joyous plump black woman, short, friendly face and bright eyes. Savanah could not place her age, she would not be surprised if someone told her the lady was either 40 or 60.

"Duma, how are you, my love?", continued Professor Noronha taking the woman's hand and patting her with affection. "Duma his, erhhhh... I'm her godfather. She is the real boss around here. Anything you need, forget about the professors or the secretary staff, Duma is the gatekeeper of the whole department, aren't you?". Duma giggled a bit, looking to Savanah with her wide lively eyes.

"Duma is the senior research assistant, she has been here, well, forever, right?"

"Yeah, part of the furniture already", stated Duma maintaining a broad smile on her round face. She smiled with her eyes. With her whole face, really. An honest, heart-felt smile. Not just the standard polite smiles you get from strangers.

"Please take good care of Savanah, she is Raven's sister... do you remember Raven?"

"Of course", Duma said shaking Savanah's hand. "How could I forget my lovely Raven?! You look just like her. You are most welcome, Savanah"

It took them the best part of an hour to go through the introductions and chit-chat, with most members of the small Discoveries History department taking the presence of Professor Noronha and his guest as an opportunity for an expresso around the coffee machine. "A proper coffee, velvety and creamy, not the American watery concoction" someone ventured. In her very pragmatic way, Savanah could not help but thinking this whole thing could have been done within less than 15 minutes, but... hey...

now in a Mediterranean country, time moved slower here, right?

Professor Noronha no longer had an office at the university, so he invited Savanah to join him during the afternoon at his home in Restelo for an introductory note on Columbus' "web of mystery and intrigue", as he put it. As they walked out of the campus, Savanah asked:

"If this whole story is a farce, how come did it start? I mean, if the man's name was Colon, how did he end up named Columbus?

Professor Noronha stopped walking and smiled broadly. "The fairy tale of Columbus was born out of secrecy and disinformation. Just add greed and trickery and you get the perfect ingredients for a Mexican telenovela!", he said.

Noronha started walking again as he explained. The swindler appeared 90 years after Columbus death. Baltazar Columbus, a rich Italian merchant, presented himself to the Spanish Council of the Indies as the heir of Columbus, during the successions and inheritance trial [19] of 1579-1609. After the death of the fourth Admiral in 1578 without any direct heirs, a legal battle ensued to claim the inheritance titles, riches and rights. A lot was at stake during those trials. Over the 30 years of the trials, several Italians tried to claim their links, often with the political support of the city of Genoa. `nton Colombo, from Placentia, was rejected for not being ꓳ to prove any relationship. Bernardo Colombo, from ꓳto, also failed the con, accused of producing a false ꓳy. The Genoese merchant Baltazar Columbus tried ꓳe genealogical link between Colon and his family ꓳg as his proof a 'testament' (Mayorazgo) sup- ꓳ by Columbus on 22 February 1498, which ꓳords 'I, Christopher Columbus, born in

ꓳry. Colon and his heirs go to great

lengths to hide his true origin, and yet, 90 years after it was written, a testament appears which so clearly and conveniently states the Admiral's place of birth. As it happens, the claims of this Italian merchant were dismissed by the court as a fraud and the Mayorazgo as a forgery: it is not "legitimate, nor authentic, nor solemn (...) after analysis of all the judges of the investigation Council, it was proven to be nothing more than a simple piece of paper". And yet, many continue to insist on using the Mayorazgo to support the Genoese theory!

The all story is hilarious. Baltazar Colombo also presented witnesses, including a monk that stated under oath to remember the birth of the Colombo brothers in the castle of Cuccaro. Colon was born around 1450, the monk statement was made in 1580. Even if the monk was a young man of 20 when he witnessed the birth of Colombo, by 1580 he would be...150 years old!

The true testament was written by Columbus in 1502, before embarking in his last expedition. However, this 1502 "true Mayorazgo" disappeared, replaced in the annals of history by the "fake Mayorazgo" of 1498...

The succession and inheritance trial was concluded in 1609, recognizing Nuno Álvares Pereira Colon e Portugal – descendent of the marriage of the third grandson of Portuguese hero Saint Dom Nuno Álvares Pereira with the granddaughter of Colon – as the true heir and fifth Admiral of the Indies.

That fantasy has later been arduously defended by th city of Genoa, to claim its own global hero.

Between 1892 and 1896, almost 400 years a Colon's death, the Italian Columbus Comission publish series of documents known as the Raccolta Colombi those documents, the Italians go to great lengths to d strate the existence of a Columbus family from Gen only thing the Raccolta documents prove is that there was a poor family of wool-weavers named Columbus (a rather common name), from Genoa... and so what??

Besides, many documents of the Raccolta are manipulated: manuscript copies without the originals, documents with insertions and collages of different sources. The lack of credibility of many documents led Ángel Duvale, a Spanish academic, to say that the Italians "should have eliminated those false documents".

Finally, in 1904, the city of Genoa published the Documento Assereto, a document supposedly dated 25 August 1479, presenting a Christofforus de Columbo, of unknown parents, born in Genoa in 1451, who was sent to Madeira to buy sugar... Moreover, the Documento Assereto is nothing more than loose sheets bundled together to look like a notarial booklet. The original document contains full empty pages, different handwritings and parts of text written over other text. It is a fraud!

LISBON, JANUARY 2019

Restelo

"Your questions are false if you already know the answer."
JOSÉ SARAMAGO

Professor Noronha lived in a nice house facing Rua dos Jerónimos. On the hill above, like a General surveying the wide expanse of the Tagus below, is Infante Dom Henrique's chapel, dedicated to Santa Maria de Belém, Our Lady of Blenheim. In that church, 500 years ago, Vasco da Gama spent the night before his departure, in prey and vigil.

Dias and Covilhã had done most of the hard work. Covilhã, the king's spy, had sent precious information about sailing in the Indic, from his overland travels. Dias oversaw the preparation of the fleet and joined the expedition to guide it through his route around Cape of Good Hope. But Dias was a sailor – and the last leg to India was not a discovery expedition, but a diplomatic and business affair. Gama was a noble, of the House of Viseu like the new King Dom Manuel, Count of Vidigueira and cousin of Columbus' wife Filipa, with the social standing and flair necessary to impress the Indian rajas and sultans, grabbing the trading lines so far monopoly of the Arabs.

On the morning of Saturday, 8 July 1497 Gama and the crew descended in procession down what is now the Empire Plaza into the Belém docks, where his Caravelas departed to India. In that spot of the old docks is today the Padrão dos Descobrimentos, a monument to the Maritime Discoveries.

It would be the longest ocean voyage so far, more than a complete circumference of the globe around the Equator, taking almost 11 months to reach Calicut.

We sat on Professor Noronha's living room, from which a well tendered garden could be seen to the back of the house. The room was cozy and had a faint smell of old furniture and leather, mixed with the aroma of the strong French Press coffee Professor Noronha poured into two large mugs.

"Columbus life has never been consensual amongst historians. It is strewn with contradictions", Professor commented as he added a hint of milk to each of the mugs.

Mostly, historians rely on documents produced decades or centuries later. The picture we have of the navigator is of an inspired, brilliant but mercurial and self-serving adventurer, lost at sea most of the times, an opportunistic man climbing up the social ladder who made his great discovery by pure chance and never recognizing his mistake of reaching the wrong Indies, a tyrannical governor obsessed with gold, prone to atrocities against his own crew, let alone the cruelty, genocide and enslavement of the entire native population.

Although part or most of these accusations may be true, the contradictions may simply be a cover up for something entirely different. This is a man who seems dissociated of reality, a lunatic living his own illusions of grandeur, unable to use nautical instruments and confused about measurements or distance... but at the same time capable of extraordinary feats, not least deceiving one of the most powerful countries of his time for almost a decade.

The voyages of Columbus are so memorable exactly because they are loaded with mysticism, delusion, obstinate courage and drama. If nothing else, Columbus was a most skillful writer and actor, turning his four voyages into epic adventures and his life into a true Shakespearean play.

"In 2006 we were just starting to unveil the tip of the iceberg.", said Professor Noronha, adding in a friendly manner. "Oh, but you are an American! Surely you have seen the writing desk of Christopher Columbus, taken to the United States in the early twentieth century and presently in Boalsburg, Pennsylvania at the Columbus Chapel of Boal Mansion Museum."

"Erhhh…my uncle took me and Raven there when we were kids. There is something about scallop shells, right?"

"Indeed, indeed, you remember right!"

Colon's personal writing desk shows three scallop shells on each side, plus another shell above the key lock, surrounded by eight-pointed stars. The scallop shells are obviously the symbol of Santiago, used by the pilgrims as they walk the Santiago Path. Filipa, Colon's wife, was from a lineage of knights of the Santiago Order. We can reasonably assume Colon himself was a member of the Santiago Order or its sister Order of Christ.

"Boal Mansion is a treasure of unresolved mysteries! Besides the Santiago shells on the Admiral's desk, there is also a genealogical tree of the House of the Dukes of Veragua, Colon's descendants, starting with the three original Colon brothers of the lineage… but without parents. The ivy line that follows the lineage just disappears out of the side of the paper, omitting the ancestors, as if the three brothers were born out of cloud of fog by magical summoning."

Professor Noronha then did some more searches on his phone and showed Savanah three flags. Her head was starting to swirl. Can you just pile up a bunch of coincidences and turn them into a conspiracy theory?

Queen Isabella in 1493 granted the Admiral an enlargement of the coat of arms 'that your family used to carry' (as is written in the royal decree). This means Colon's family already had a coat of arms. That original coat of arms of Colon's family, preserved in the 4th quadrant of the enlarged arms granted by Isabella, shows 5 gold anchors over a blue field. This original coat of arms can still be seen today in the palace of Diego Colon, in Santo Domingo, erstwhile Hispaniola. In the heraldic books of Portuguese noble families, there is a coat of arms very similar to this, with one gold anchor over a blue field: The Henriques family from Madeira island. There is a Segismundo Henriques born in 1451 in Madeira island, son of Henrique Alemão. Segismundo is reported to have died in a strange accident, with a sail mast on his head during a voyage to Lisbon. It is quite possible that Segismundo Henriques, after being allegorically killed by the chroniclers with a sail mast on his head and metamorphosing into Christopher Colon, changed his coat of arms from one to five gold anchors in a blue field. It's quite symbolic that Colon's original five anchors are disposed in the pattern of a saltire cross, or St. Andrew's cross, the diagonal cross used in the Scottish flag. The coat of arms of the Portuguese kings, maintained today in the Portuguese flag, includes five shields disposed in a Christian cross and within each shield are five silver dots (the five wounds of Christ) disposed in the same saltire pattern. Maybe just another coincidence: The flag of Scotland and Portugal, both countries with deep Templar traditions, and Colon's original coat of arms, all share the same saltire heraldic pattern (the St. Andrews diagonal cross) over a blue field.

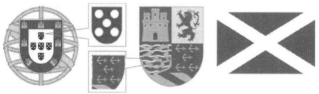

There was an awkward pause during which they both

sipped the coffee, as if checking who would make the next move.

"So, have you found Raven's Little Book of Lies?", finally said Professor Noronha.

Savanah's heart skipped a bit, her mind racing for a white lie. She didn't know Professor Noronha and suspected the key to Raven's assassination might be on her notebook, so she could not risk exposing it. She took a non-committal route "You mean, her little notebook? It was sent home with her books and documents, yeah... but it's all nonsense, isn't it? Those scribbles are just gibberish to me, I haven't paid it much attention. But why do you call it 'little book of lies' – you think Raven was making things up?"

Professor Noronha moved on his sofa, looking clearly uncomfortable. "Well, no, no, not really. She used to have the notebook to write down the contradictions and lies as she found them. We used to laugh a bit about that, how Colon and the Portuguese kings managed to conceal and confound so many for so long..."

"Well, there has always been a high level of speculation about Columbus.", conceded Savanah, "But do you really believe Colon deliberately lied and conspired to confound those who were sponsoring his voyages and giving him titles and riches? I mean... by now, we should have found some hard evidence, no?"

"The truth is, my dear, there is no hard and irrefutable evidence supporting any of the conflicting theories regarding Columbus life", admitted Professor Noronha. "The accepted tale of the Italian wool-weaver is based on documents many of which were almost certainly forged. As for the lack of solid evidence regarding his Portuguese origins, bear in mind three Spanish kings ruled over Portugal during a period of 60 years, from 1580 to 1640. They had ample time to hide, destroy and cover up all documents, re-writing history! Surely the Spanish monarchs pride would make them destroy any evidence that they had been so embarrassingly tricked. They would prefer to maintain the charade of a poor, adventurer and visionary Italian sponsored by Isabella and Fernando than to risk ridicule if the world discovered the truth. It is remarkable we have plenty of detailed accounts of Colon's life from 1484 onwards when he magically appears in Spain, but absolutely no documents before that. Colon was a detailed and exhaustive writer of his actions and thoughts... but nothing before 1484!"

"Professor, that's stretching it a bit too far, no? I mean... a conspiracy to cover up and destroy evidence regarding Colon's li..."

"History is written by the victors! Columbus discovered so many lands that if the Spanish kings had kept their promise of giving Columbus control of all he discovered, passing his titles to his heirs, then Columbus' dynasty would have ruled over a huge empire, probably richer and more powerful than Isabella and Fernando. So, the Spanish monarchs stripped Columbus of his power, sending Bobadilla to arrest and replace him as governor of Hispaniola – supposedly because they were concerned about mismanagement and disorganization of the colony..."

Savanah saw the logic of the argument, but was not entirely convinced.

"There are several highly suspicious events in Columbus life. Events which gain an entire new clarity if we consider he was not the poor uneducated wool weaver but instead a highly educated Portuguese noble setting up a plot to deceive the Spanish monarchs.", continued the Professor.

Professor Noronha raised his left hand and started listing some of those events, counting them on the fingers of his hand. Savanah listened to the succession of evidences suggesting Colon had a special relation of mutual trust with the

Portuguese king, whereas he repeatedly lied and deceived the Spanish monarchs.

When Professor Noronha finished, Savanah stood in silence for a moment, as the consequences of what had just been said sunk in. She was feeling a bit numb – a feeling that had become recurrent since she started poking into Colon's mysteries.

As if his previous listing of facts was not enough, or maybe fearing it had been too dry and difficult to digest by a non-academic, Professor Noronha added with a flamboyant twist of his arm, imitating an artist painting the ceiling:

"Do you know what is painted in the ceiling of the Age of Discoveries Room in the Palace of Mafra?"

The formal royal palace is a national monument built in the eighteenth century. The construction of the palace and convent is the background for the story of Baltazar and Blimunda in Saramago's book "Memorial do Convento". In the ceiling of the Age of Discoveries Room, a great hall to commemorate the Portuguese maritime discoveries, are painted the great Portuguese heroes: Gama, Cabral, Henry the Navigator... and a fourth man, naked, in shackles, a suffering expression on the face and a snake near his neck as if preventing him from speaking. Written below this curious figure, is a banner saying 'A Castella y a Leon Nuevo Mundo dio Colon'. The motto used by Colon's descendants.

"Don't you find this extraordinary?", asked Professor Noronha. "Out of so many epic sailors, cosmographers, captains of the Portuguese Maritime Discoveries, the kings of the eighteenth century chose four: Gama, Cabral, Infante Dom Henrique... and Colon!? A Colon in shackles, when he got chained by Bobadilla, as if the most glorious contribution of Colon to the Portuguese nation was exactly the reason he got chained in Spain."

Art is indeed the ultimate bearer of truth, carrying se-

crets that the powerful want to hide. Art carries our collective conscience across the times with impunity, because the
powerful covet it, want to ingratiate themselves as patrons
of the arts. Or otherwise they simply fail to understand
the subtle hidden references. Art is by nature aristocratic,
serving no material immediate purpose, and that aristocratic superiority grants artists the impunity to expose the
most hideous truths. It often serves as 'The Emperor's New
Clothes', exposing the ridicule of the vain and powerful. Desired, praised, admired by the rich and powerful, Art is the
ignoble varnish with which they cover themselves, hoping
its intellectual aristocracy will transfer to them, as if by os-
mosis.

"Oh, and there is more, so much more! Revelations are
like cherries, they come one after the other. Luis de Camões,
the great Portuguese poet, wrote an epic poem of the Portuguese maritime discoveries, 'Os Lusíadas', first published in
1572. Even an American should have heard of it…, right?"

Savanah didn't appreciate the insinuation, but let it
go.

Professor Noronha quoted Canto X, the culmination
of the epic journey, where the sailors are received to a sumptuous feat by the goddesses in the Isle of Love. Tethys, a
Greek Titan, wife of Oceanus and the primeval mother of
the Greek Gods and the nymphs, guides Vasco da Gama to
the summit of human knowledge, revealing to him a vision
of how the universe operates. After describing all the lands
discovered by the Portuguese to the East, Camões then describes the discovery of America in a veiled passage:

"Mas é também razão que, no Ponente, / Dum Lusitano um feito inda vejais, / Que, de seu Rei mostrando-se
agravado, / Caminho há de fazer nunca cuidado... My apolo-
gies, I really wouldn't know how to translate that. But it is
quite clear: 'you will come to see (truth will surface) that

a Lusitano (Portuguese), pretending aggravation by his king (Colon's staged rage against Dom João II), took new paths to the west (discovered America)'. So, there you go, Kings and Lords concealed Colon's identity, but artists have left a trail of clues".

Savanah was speechless. That was, actually, rather strange. All the other things she had listened or read so far were, well, coincidences, contradictions, theories, the stuff of academic debates by dusty old professors. But this was odd... an Italian who discovered America for the Spanish kings, in the ceiling of the Portuguese royal palace, side by side with the three most celebrated Portuguese sailors? Dias, Magellan, Cão... so many other national heroes could have rightly claimed a place of honor in that pantheon of national heroes... but Colon?

And then there was the very basic, hard issue of money. Money makes the world go round and leaves its trail. Colon contributed 500.000 maravedis to the first expedition of his own money, while the Spanish crown contributed with 1.000.000 maravedis Isabella borrowed from Luis de Santangél. Where in hell did a poor Genoese wool-weaver had either the money or the credit to come up with such absurd sum of money?

In any case, Savanah would not give up easily. She was used to the savagery and carnage in Wall Street meeting rooms, so she would not just let go without a fight.

"But what then? If the traditional version we learned at school is just a fantasy, who was this secretive man? And why did such plot remain hidden for 500 years?", asked Savanah.

"Pertinent questions, no doubt. Regarding the first question, the Who?, we start having a fairly decent understanding of Colon's true identity. As for the second question, the Why?, I am afraid it still eludes us. I mean, it would be understandable that Colon and his sons maintained the lies to protect Colon's position, titles and rights. Especially after D Joao II died and D Manuel became king, as he had the opposite policy towards Spain than his antecessor, which risked exposing Colon. It would be understandable that for a few decades the Spanish and Portuguese kingdoms would maintain the farce, to avoid a political scandal. But what is harder to understand is why for 500 years, silence was maintained despite all the evidence. Or why in the nineteenth century the Genoese publish the Racolta and Assereto documents, which are now under deep suspicion as frauds. Or why in the 20th century a Spanish academic wrote to his friend, President of the Portuguese History Society, claiming he had made an extraordinary discovery about Colon but could not talk about it for risk to his life."

"But let's leave aside the speculative Why? and try to focus on the evidence we can gather about the Who?", continued Professor Noronha.

He described an alternative version, published in the mid-twentieth century and silenced at the time, but recovered by Mascarenhas Barreto in 1999, proposing an alternative Columbus born in the Portuguese villa of Cuba, an illegitimate son of Prince Dom Fernando, brother of King Afonso V and nephew of Infante Dom Henrique. Dom Fernando was also the adoptive son of the Infante and his successor as Grand Master of the Order of Christ. This alternative Columbus was born from a youth love affair between Dom Fernando and a daughter of João Gonçalves Zarco, captain of Madeira.

Some academics have also suggested Colon was son of Henry the Navigator himself, although the Infante supposedly died virgin. The A on his cryptic signature could stand for Anriques, just like the Infante used in his own signature, I.D.A. (Infante Dom Anriques), and it would also fit the two Dom Tivisco books who state Colon was "the last sprout of Henrique".

All these theories could justify some mystery around the parenthood of Colon. But at that time, illegitimate sons of nobles, even Popes, were rather common. So none of these theories can justify the deep censorship Colon's true identity has suffered over five centuries...

"I have spent 20 years of my life collecting facts about Colon's life and consulting original documents instead of just trusting third-party accounts.", continued Professor Noronha. "I have found only one person who fits all the known facts of Colon's life before he 'miraculously' comes to life in Seville in 1494. Contrary to what you might expect, what I found is not one single tremendous revelation, a secret hidden for centuries and suddenly revealed. Science is not usually a big bang discovery, but a strenuous hard accumulation of evidence. So, let me present to you Segismundo Anriques, son of Anrique Alemão. Or Henriques, if you prefer the present day form of the name."[20]

First, of course, there is the issue of his signature. The bottom line is composed of 9 letters, like 9 months of pregnancy, and corresponds to his "Earthly" name. The ':Xpoferens' is widely accepted as meaning Christopher Colon, because ':' corresponds to Kolon in Greek. The top part is a cryptic triangular form with 7 letters, 7 being the number of days of the Genesis, and refers to his "Godly" or original name. S.A., Segismundo Anriques. Or Segismundo Alemão, as he was probably known amongst friends, being son of Anrique Alemão.

Then, there are the genealogy books of the two Don Tiviscos. Two books published in the early eighteenth century, by different authors but with the same pseudonym, Dom Tivisco de Nasao Zarco, y Colonna. One of the books was published in Portugal and subject to censorship by the King, who banned the book by royal decree. The other was printed aboard a ship outside any national borders and then circulated in Spain. A lot of trouble around two genealogy books, published 200 years after Colon's death...

The genealogy books contain a reference to Colon that says: "The greatest Portuguese discoverer of all times was the last sprout of Henrique." For many years, this was interpreted as support for the theories that Colon was son of the Infante Dom Henrique or Prince Fernando, nephew and son-in-law of the Infante. But our Segismundo fits the bid even better, "son of Henrique Alemão". Not Infante Dom Henrique, who supposedly lived an ascetic life and died virgin.

If Colon was son of Henrique Alemão and his wife Senhorinha Anes, it would justify two other claims around Colon's life. Henrique Alemão was a Germanic lord who arrived mysteriously in Madeira around 1447/1450. He had spent several years as a pilgrim in the Holy Land, before arriving in Madeira and making name and fortune on the trade with the mainland. Senhorinha Anes was a descendent of the Colonna family from Sicily. So, the chroniclers who tried to conceal his true identity could, without straying much from the truth, claim he was of humble origins (his father lived as a hermit) and of Italian descent (his mother was a Colonna).

"But let's go back to the basics", concluded Professor Noronha, "... pure physical resemblance. Are you familiar with the most widely portrait of Colon, disseminated in schoolbooks the world over?"

"I guess...", answered Savanah, trying to remember her secondary history books. "A man with a tricorn hat..."

"...and a round fat face, tanned skin, hair hidden under the tricorn hat, a bulbous nose and large neck. The portrait is exhibited in the New York Metropolitan Museum of Art and has traditionally been presented as the image of the Admiral. The portrait was painted in 1519 by a Venetian named Sebastiano Luciani. A painting produced by a Venetian who had likely never seen Columbus in real life (Colon died in 1506), became the standard image of the Admiral. Ignoring portraits produced during the Admiral's lifetime by painters who had seen the man in real person! Check out on your Google the title of that painting at the Met..."

Savanah indulged the Professor's request and was astonished when she read "Portrait of a Man".

"There you go. The doubts about the true likeness of the painting are so obvious that the Met changed the legend of the painting! Instead, if you look at paintings produced in Portugal or Spain by Colon's contemporary, who actually saw and knew the Admiral, the image is rather different. The Virgin of the Navigators, painted in Seville Chapel by Alejo Fernandez, shows a more credible Columbus, next to Amerigo Vespucci and the Pinzon brothers. On the other side of the Virgin, King Fernando and Emperor Carlos V of Spain." Professor showed the painting on his phone, pointing to Colon.

Another contemporary painter, Pedro Berruguete, painted a portrait of Columbus before the Admiral's death. Both show a portrait that fits with Fernando Colon's description of his father: "tall and thin, red-blond hair turned white at an early age, pale skin that reddened easily under the sun, blue eyes and an eagle's nose".

The Venetian painter probably intended to leave some clue, as the supposed Columbus at the Met painting shows his hand on his chest, depicting an intriguing 'M'. Could this be a reference to 'Masonic'? We will never know. But what is extremely probable is that the standard image of Columbus is a deceit, to conceal Colon's true physical resemblance. Columbus replaced Colon, in name and in figure!

"Ok, I see...", answered Savanah, not really seeing the relevance of that besides another obscure confusion around the navigator.

"No, my dear, you don't see. Let me show you another painting. Henrique Alemão built a chapel in the island of Madeira that contained a painting of himself and his wife. This painting is today at the Museum of Religious Art in Funchal, Madeira. Henrique is a tall, broad man, of pale skin, white hair and aquiline nose. The painting depicts Henrique Alemão wearing a peregrine pouch but also golden robes and pearls, as if he was a peregrine noble. Now compare the portrait of Henrique Alemão in Madeira chapel with that of Colon in Berruguete or Alejo Fernandez paintings..."

Professor Noronha showed the two paintings on his phone. Henrique Alemão portrait in the Church of Madalena, Madeira and Colon's image in the Virgin of Navigators, Seville.

"Aahhh...", exclaimed Savanah, not knowing what to make of that. The resemblance was overwhelming.

"Yes, yes... now you see what many have tried to conceal. We are blind people who can see, but do not see."[21]

Colon, who appears out of a smokescreen of mystery in Spain in 1484 with no known recording of his previous life, was definitely a high noble, not the swaggerer, ignorant, uneducated, poor wool weaver fantasy created to conceal his true identity. Most facts of his known life fit this theory: Colon was Segismundo Anriques, son of Henrique Alemão, a noble of Madeira island, and his wife Senhorinha Anes, a familiar of captain Zarco of Madeira and descendant of the Colonna family from Sicily.

Under this light, it makes total sense the marriage of Segismundo, a prince of Madeira, from the Zarco family on his mother side, with Filipa, a noble daughter of the captain of Porto Santo. A 'Jack Nobody' would never reach such a high marriage, 14 years before his expedition that granted him fame and fortune.

"The little things of life are often the most telling", said Professor Noronha. "As you surely know, Colon arrived in Spain in 1484 and his wife Filipa died shortly after. The only known life companion after that is a Spanish lady called Beatriz Henriquez. In his will, he asks his son Diego to take good care of Beatriz and awards her an annual pension. Colon never married Beatriz. But she took the surname Henriquez, 'the wife of Henriques'. Beatriz was the wife of Segismundo Henriques in Spain.

"That is fascinating, Professor.", conceded Savanah, "But why did that take Raven to enter a spiral of conspiracy theories, filling her notebook with cryptic notes about Colon and the Templars, pentagrams, stars and a secret mission?"

"Erhh… well. The truth is, my research had delivered a Columbus, or Segismundo Henriques, that fits most of the proven facts of Colon's life, but two pieces of the puzzle remained outstanding. One, his place of birth. Fernando Colon in 'Historia del Almirante' and Friar Las Casas both state the Colon brothers were from "Terra Ruvia" or "Terra Rubra". I never managed to reconcile this with being born in Madeira. Two, the cover up could be justified by a double agent mission to distract the Spanish monarchs away from the southern route, but it remains unjustifiable the secrecy continuing for 500 years, including books censored in the eighteenth and even twentieth century… something much bigger much be at stake. And then…"

"Then what, Professor?"

"Then, your sister started coming up with crazy theories. For some time, I amused her and entertained those wild conjectures. You don't get much excitement in a History department, you know? Your sister was like a breath of fresh air. But it was just for the fun of it, right? It's easy to come up with all kind of wild conspiracies. I bet you and I could come up with a dozen conspiracies, with all sorts of coded messages and symbols, over a tea and a slice of cake. Well, and then she died. It had nothing to do with her research, surely. But I got so distraught, I ordered the entire department to stop digging around Raven's theories. It was a waste of time. History is what it is, not what it could have been. I decided to retire shortly after."

They had been talking for almost 4 hours now, and it was already dusk when Savanah left Professor Noronha's house. As she exited the main door and said goodbye, she glimpsed on the top of the door a symbol she was rather familiar with: the square and compass engraved in the stone.

As Savanah took the metro back to her attic apartment, details of the conversation with Professor Noronha kept creeping up her mind. "So, Colon was this Segismundo Alemão. Segismundo the German..."

Savanah was climbing up the stairs heading out of the metro station, when the though crossed her mind. She stopped suddenly, a stream of people in the late afternoon rush hour pushing past her up the stairs.

Colon's nickname was "German".

"Leave German Bitch", the threatening message on the piece of paper that had fallen from Raven's notebook. She had always read that note as a race threat, Raven being the German bitch – they were not Germans, but the 'tall, blond hair, blue eyes' stereotype could confuse them as German. Could it be.... not "Leave, German Bitch", but something entirely different, "Leave German, Bitch". A threat to leave Colon alone, stop investigating his secrets.

"Stop making up crazy ideas", Savanah admonished herself. How could an historic investigation about something that had happened 500 years ago be the cause of such aggressive threat like that?

There was another though nagging on her subconscious, though, waiting in line to surface into consciousness. As soon as she managed to put the threatening message behind her mind, another though crept in.

The Freemasons symbol of the square and compass, engraved on top of Professor Noronha door. She knew it well and could not have mistaken it. The trouble is that, as uncle Santiago had shown her over Christmas, the compass and square stand for a pentagram. What was a pentagram doing in Professor Noronha front door? Could the pentagram cuts on Raven wrist that caused her death have anything to do with the Freemasons?

That evening, after a takeaway pizza for dinner, Savanah lied on the sofa trying to focus on a book. But lying on the floor, teasing her, was Raven's notebook. She picked it up and flicked through the pages again, annoyed with herself for not being able to get into her sister's mind, and annoyed with her sister for not letting her in.

"Oh, Christ, what a load of crap. Raven, sis... you lost your senses, spending too long in the library. Your mind wrinkled like the wizened pages of those dusty old books."

LISBON, JANUARY 2019

*"Sometimes people don't want to hear the truth because
they don't want their illusions destroyed."*
FRIEDRICH NIETZSCHE

T he day after Professor Noronha presentations, Savanah returned to the university to start her work.
Pedro received her politely and provided a monotone
and uninspiring, but detailed and factual, talk about the
Columbus controversies and the Portuguese origins theories Raven had been researching. Plus, a pile of books enough
for two months reading, even for a fast ex-Harvard MBA student.

"So, you see", concluded Professor Pedro flatly, "all
this is a bit unsubstantiated, we only have third-party accounts and lots of contradictions. For sure, Columbus lived
in Portugal several years, where he learned or improved his
sailing and cosmography skills, before appearing in Seville
in 1484. It's certain he had a Portuguese wife Filipa and a
son Diogo. He may even have received detailed information
about land west of the Azores from Portuguese sailors, or
seen it in maps from his father-in-law, Bartolomeu Perestrelo, captain of Porto Santo. We are fairly certain Columbus was not the first European to reach America and he may
even have simply "rediscovered" the lands already known
by the Portuguese. But History is not about facts, it is about
impact. The Vikings, the Portuguese, maybe even the Phoe-
nicians had been to North America before Columbus. We
will probably never know the truth about Colon's life before

showing up in Seville in 1484. And so what? His "life", as far as history is concerned, starts then. The impact on the course of history started with the 1492 expedition and the colonization process that ensued. Before that, well… it is just speculation. It doesn't matter because it didn't have an impact."

Was Pedro dismissing Raven's work as futile and irrelevant? As the whim of a spoiled rich American girl, nothing more than interesting soundbites to entertain dinner-party guests?

To be fair, she had herself silently felt a bit like that, too, but refused to allow the feeling to grow into a complete, formed though. Ignoring the feeling didn't mean it wasn't there, though, at least on some cynical remote part of her mind, fiercely reprehended by the rest of her brain, out of a sense of loyalty towards her sister. Like a filthy, abject, unworthy pre-though, prohibited from forming by majority vote of the synapsis in the parliament of her brain.

Considering the lack of solid information, absence of first-hand credible documents and 500 years of lies and forgeries, the search for the true identity of the navigator was probably futile. Columbus (or whatever his true name was) "appeared" on the world stage in 1484, with a foggy past… but what matters for the course of history is what he did afterwards!

The Portuguese already had plenty of bragging rights for their endeavours in the fifteenth and sixteenth century, they didn't need to get embroidered in a nasty web of rumours around Columbus. Over almost 200 years, the Dynasty of Aviz ruled the country, from 1385 to 1580. During that period of time, starting with the conquest of Ceuta in North Africa in 1415, the Portuguese caravels pushed relentlessly into the Ocean Sea, destroying myths and legends centuries old: explored both coasts and large inland rivers of Africa, reached North America in 1473, discovered the passage to the Indic and reached India in 1498, officially discovered Brazil in 1500, reached Malaysia in 1509, Thailand in 1511, Indonesia in 1512, China in 1513, Vietnam in 1516 and Japan in 1543. A Portuguese sailor, Fernão de Magalhães (Ferdinand Magellan) launched the circumnavigation of the globe in 1518.

The world became a global village, for the first time, under the vision and curatorship of the House of Aviz, bringing to Europe a flurry of new cultures, colours and languages that definitely put an end to the Middle Ages and laid the foundation of the global economy. A country of less than one million people moved itself from the periphery of Europe into the centre of the world, a maritime empire of planetary reach that immodestly and presumptuously took what it considered its God-given right: gold and slaves from Guinea and Brazil, pepper and precious stones from India, cinnamon from Sri Lanka, clove from Indonesia and intricate jewels from China. It set in motion the forces of globalization and 500 years of western violently imposed supremacy.

Pedro wasn't denying the mysteries around Columbus. Just questioning the relevance of stirring the past. And yet...

"There is a lot of myth-making PR around Columbus", added Professor Pedro, with a sly smirk. "He has been glorified, turned into a symbol of the New World. Colon is the second most recognizable name in the world, after Jesus Christ, and probably one of the personalities about whom most has been written. There are more than 100 monuments to Colon in the world. The mystery around his identity and origins, the rags to riches novella, it all contributed to elevate Colon's to global stardom: the myth of a man who, by strength of character, vision, genius and courage, fought the 'fossilized' middle ages 'flat Earth' cosmography of the church and found the New World. That is pure non sense, I hope you realize..."

"...you mean?! Sorry, I got lost. That Columbus disproved the flat Earth vision?"

"He didn't, that's what I was saying! That's just a myth created during the 17th century by the Protestants against the Catholic Church and popularized by 19th century atheist books trying to escalate a conflict between science and religion [22]. There have been conflicts between science and religion, granted, mainly around Galileo's heliocentrism and Darwin's evolutionism. But the myth that the church ever defended the Earth to be flat is a misconception. The view of a spherical Earth has been established since the fifth century B.C., accepted by Ptolomeu and never contested by the main scholars of the Middle Ages. In Colon's time, belief in a flat planet amongst educated Europeans was virtually non-existent, and there was scarcely a Catholic scholar who did not acknowledge sphericity and even know the approximate circumference of the Earth."

Ok. So much for Colon's myth-breaking! In any case, Savanah thought, some people become symbols or an era, attracting popular conscience.

After three hours jammed with information and discussion, Savanah sighted and headed alone to the bar for a quick lunch. On the corridor, though, Ndunduma caught up with her and invited her for lunch outside.

"It is such a lovely day, isn't it?" Duma said, more a statement than a question.

"Yes, beautiful. Thanks for inviting me out, by the way. I was needing some sun and fresh air, after three hours stuck with Pedro. He is a bit...erhh...

"Gloomy and boring?", interrupted Duma, with a

119

broad smile. "Yes he is! He scares me out a bit too. But I think he is a good guy. You know, I suspect they had something going on, Pedro and Raven. Nothing too obvious. In fact, I only thought about it later on. Pedro doesn't talk much, but he left a few hints escape... I reckon they were dating or something, seating together in a separate table at the canteen over lunch, leaving together in the evening as if they were going somewhere together, stuff like that. I suppose Pedro had a big crush on your sister. He was desolate after her death, shaved off his beard, let his hair grow and started dressing... well, differently, as you can see. No more jeans and t-shirts but very neat, sharply-ironed trousers and shirts buttoned all up. He started looking like a seminarist!"

Savanah felt her batteries charging up with the midday winter sun, as they walked over the Portuguese-style sidewalk, with black and white small cobblestones polished by centuries of footsteps.

Duma's reference to a love affair was a surprise, because Raven had not mentioned a 'boyfriend' in Lisbon. Not that it would be the first time Raven had failed to tell her sister about some lover. No, what would be surprising was if Raven had had an affair that lasted more than a couple of nights, a few weeks at most. Her sister had always taken a liberal view of relationships, no strings attached. And it was also a bit odd Raven had taken a boyfriend, because since her late teens she had assumed herself as gay, but eii... if someone could have changed her mind about sexual preferences or assumed bisexuality, it was Raven.

"Lovely sidewalk pattern", commented Savanah, "but I wouldn't like to run on these polished cobblestones on a rainy day."

"You are quite right, dear", replied Duma laughing enjoyably, her big bosom shaking madly. "Especially in high heels! Aahh, your sister was always running from one place to the other, so full of life. Unlike most of the other self-conscious posh girls we usually have around, your sister cared little for appearances. Once she arrived at the university with her jeans covered in mud… she was running from the metro to the university under a downpour of rain and skidded on these polished cobblestones, landing on a puddle. Oh, I loved your sister! So bright, hard-working, always polite even when she asked me for endless impossible queries to research. She was on to something, Raven was."

"What do you mean?", asked Savanah, catching the hint that something odd might have been going on.

"Well, Raven was researching into some strange stuff, she never wanted to discuss it with me 'for my own sake' she had said, but the things she asked me to dig up, old books on the Templars and always insisting on going straight to the original sources instead of the revision papers most PhD students use. She travelled to Rio de Janeiro, Seville and Genoa to look at the original documents. I don't know. In the end she was a bit out of her mind…After her return from Paris, though, she was really in a craze."

They walked together in silence for a few minutes until they reached a small local restaurant and took a table on the outside terrace. "Not a fancy place, but much better food than the cafeteria", said Duma, greeting warmly the waiter and briskly ordering for the two of them, not even allowing Savanah the opportunity to see the menu. "I just ordered for both of us, you will love it". Savanah smiled inwardly, recalling her grandmother who had a similar way of always acting as if she knew what's best for everyone. True enough, the cod cakes starters and the grilled sardines with salad and skin-boiled potatoes were lovely.

"So", asked Savanah, unable to stop her curiosity. "Ndunduma is an African name, right?"

"Angolan, yes. In fact, a Bantu name that means thunderstorm. My son says it is quite appropriate for me", Duma replied, laughing heartedly again. "I was born there, daughter of the foreman at Professor Noronha coffee plantation in Kwanza Sul. He was a professor at the Luanda University and the family came to the plantation only during the university holidays, so the plantation was basically run by my father. In the colonial era, life of the black population was quite tough, still very much dominated by remnants of the old slave-and-master ties. Although the white owners did some effort to avoid the harshest slavery practices, everyone knew each other's place."

"Ah, so, that is how you came to be Professor Noronha goddaughter?"

Duma smiled, in a soft, awkward way which seemed intertwined with several different feelings. "It is a bit more complicated than that, but basically, yes, I guess."

Duma quickly became a key support and friend to Savanah. Pedro was helpful, keeping her busy with all the immense literature he continued to pile on Savanah's lap every time she came to the university. But he was sombre, always a bit gloomy, whereas Duma had a sunny talkative manner and Savanah enjoyed their lunchtime breaks at the university cafeteria. The place was agreeable and the food decent, although a bit greasy with too much carbo-hydrates. Savanah was trying to keep her NY healthy diet habits, but between the canteen lunches and the splendid dinners in many of the city restaurants, she was finding it difficult to keep the waistline – she was no longer 20 and food was unforgiving. Anyway, the morning runs helped to keep everything in balance, or at least she tried to convince herself of that.

As it turned out, Savanah found later, the story of how Duma came to be Professor Noronha goddaughter and research assistant was not as straightforward as Duma made it sound on their first encounter. Ndunduma family lived and worked on Professor Noronha coffee plantation, her father running the 'fazenda' while the Noronha family was in Luanda. She had been promised in marriage by her father to a wealthy merchant, son of the head of the local Ovimbundo ethic tribe. At the age of 15, Duma was soon to become the second wife of this man, who was almost 20 years older than her. This was in the early 70s and Duma's father had used his position as foreman of a large plantation to ensure a good marriage for the family. However, a few months before the arranged marriage, Duma´s belly started growing. She was pregnant. Her son was born in early spring, with light brown skin. Although no-one talked about it, everyone in the plantation knew the boy had been fathered by one of the white masters.

As Duma confided to Savanah during a cold winter Friday afternoon, over a tea and custard pie, she had been raped by the son of Professor Noronha, during one of the family's stays. In those times, a girl, especially a black girl, had very few rights, if not legally at least in practice. So she just accepted the fact. The marriage her father had arranged for her had obviously been cancelled. Angola at the time was already in the middle of a nasty independence war. In November 1975, about a year after the Portuguese democratic revolution, Angola achieved its Independence. Facing a hostile environment, the Noronha family hastily left the country, fleeing to Lisbon. Shortly afterwards, as Angola descended into a nasty civil war, one of the many proxy USA/USSR wars that tormented Africa for decades, and facing the prospect of raising her son as a single mother and shunned as a ´whites' whore' by the neighbours, she decided to plead to Mrs Noronha to take her to Lisbon. She was turning 19 with a 3-year old son and decided to try to start a new life in Lisbon. Professor Noronha and his wife responded to her letter by sending her money for the boat ticket and a job declaration stating she was Professor's Noronha personal research assistant in Lisbon.

What she lacked in formal education, she compensated with a ferociously hardworking and determined attitude, ignoring the racism in the former imperial metropolis and affirming herself, by her own merit, as the research assistant of Professor Noronha at the Lisbon university. Many people probably suspected, not always silently (especially when she was promoted over other women) that she had an affair with Professor Noronha and the son was his. Duma ignored those comments with a mixture of resignation and contempt. It was with special satisfaction and pride that she received her graduation degree in 1990. She had come a long way from a destiny as a second-wife of a local merchant or a "whites' whore" to a well-respected position as university research assistant.

MARCHENA, 1467

Letter from Frei Antonio Marchena
to King Afonso V of Portugal

"To the great and victorious Lord Alfonsus, by grace of God king of Portugal, the Algarves and overseas domains in Africa, from his devoted friend and servant in Palos.

I write to you from the offices you provide in this village of Marchena, near Seville. Maintaining this villa and accommodating your agents when they come to meet me and do their business in Seville is a high cost a friar would be unable to afford, and I depend to do so on your regular payments. This is a necessary precaution, to meet your agents in secrecy, away from my Monastery of La Rabida where the Spanish monarchs have many eyes.

My lord, as you know, for many years I have conducted my astrological studies and religious duties in the Monastery of La Rabida, in Palos [23], where I can observe not only the night sky and the winds but also the comings and goings of the Spanish ships as they depart and return to Sanlúcar de Barrameda, on the mouth of the Guadalquivir, from where they reach Seville. Of all these movements of the Spanish ships I have kept you aware.

I have just returned from Segovia, where I spent two weeks with princes Isabel and Afonso, instructing them in mathematics and astrology. The news I send you today are most disturbing, as they confirm the suspicion I have held from my previous stays with the princes.

Princess Isabel is bright and I have always enjoyed our theological and cosmographic discussions. Besides the arts and readings considered appropriate for the education of a princess, I have also tried her with some of the mysteries of the mathematical and astrological sciences, which she finds fascinating. She shows interest on these subjects, which surely her tutors have always kept away from the young woman, and for this she has grown some affection and respect towards me. She confides with me on matters of science and cosmography which her preceptors do not think adequate for a noble lady. I find she has a rather restless and ambitious disposition, prone to action and control, instead of the passive and contemplative spirit suitable for a princess. This is probably also a reflection of her mother's attacks of madness the princess has witnessed, and the difficult and tense relationship with her half-brother, King Henrique.

She resents her half-brother, first born son from her father's first marriage, for taking away the position and dignity she feels are deserved by her mother and herself. Her rage, resentment and sense of indignation create a fertile ground for the hypocritical moralities and self-righteousness of that Torquemada. The priest is always around the princess, instructing and counseling her while at the same time impregnating her mind with his vile visions of a vengeful and spiteful God. I've overheard their conversations, the priest claims the Spanish are the new Chosen People, elected by God to lead the Christians to destroy Islam. He compares the escape of the Visigoths from the Moors invasions of the Peninsula to the Jews escape from Egypt. He eludes the Infanta, saying she is an instrument of God to fulfil the prophecies of doomsday, instilling her with the fear of the final judgement. Torquemada is astute. His perfidy is turning Isabel into a beatific radical, convinced she has a mission to eradicate the Moors and prepare for the next coming of Christ! By doing so, Torquemada is making the princess an instrument of his own power. Princess Isabel talks as if she is God's messenger on Earth, with a mission to clean Spain of the infidels, not just the Moors but also the Jews. She treats any deviation from the strict observance of the Pope's doctrine as heretic.

I have overheard Torquemada telling the young and impressionable princess that she is an angel sent by God to prepare for the next coming of Christ!

Torquemada and the church have the princess on their hands. I fear they will scheme against the interests of Portugal. There are already movements from the nobles opposing the succession of princess Joana to the Spanish throne when King Henrique dies. Rumors are being spread that the King is impotent and cannot father children, so princess Joana is a bastard. The union of Iberia under a single Portuguese king has long been planned, but alas... You married Isabel of Portugal to King João II of Castella but his first born with her first wife took precedence. Now the daughter of Joana of Portugal and King Henrique risks seeing her claims to the Spanish throne overthrown by princess Isabel.

Isabel is now 16 and the King is desperately trying to marry her off to a Portuguese or French prince to keep Isabel away from a succession battle with his daughter Joana, but Isabel and her supporters have so far maneuvered to escape. Instead, they are scheming to marry her with prince Fernando of Aragão, which would unite Castella and Aragão kingdoms. This is a solution that seems to please Torquemada and the Pope. They believe Fernando is weak and Isabel is a pious puppet on their hands and so are ready to make a blind eye to the fact they are cousins and provide a special authorization for their wedding.

The nobles in this country are too distracted with the politics of unification and the war to reconquer Granada. As the Pope is in the only supra-national authority able to bless these territorial disputes, the politics of unification depend of Rome. So the nobles and royal families are all trying to please Rome, ignoring the winds of change blowing from the Atlantic thanks to the discoveries and scientific advancements brought by the great maritime enterprise of Portugal. The nobles here are rude and ignorant. Rome has absolute power over the minds. How nice would it be to have a powerful king independent from the vain riches of Rome, like your majesty, to rule all of the peninsula and send these false priests back to their churches, away from the palaces.

When I learn anything certain or remarkable I shall send you word by letter or by your agents in Seville. I am and always will be faithful to your case.

Written in Marchena on 21 June 1469.

J.P."

SAGRES, 1472

(Columbus)

I am 21 and anxious to get to sea, impatient for an opportunity to prove my skills and achieve the command of
my own expedition, to look for fame and fortune. Cadamosto once told us in Sagres that "each sailor has only one
great voyage in him", and I feel a burning pull to go further
than those old sailors who walk around the Fortaleza in
Sagres. What if some other man reaches it first? The passage
to the Indic, the sea-route to India, the trading outposts in
China or Cipango? Or the new lands to the west, that sailors
have hinted about from their long arched courses on the return from Africa? Or the contact with the heirs of the Templars in the new continent on the west... I cannot wait and
risk arriving late. Every year the Portuguese Caravelas push
further south.

Prince João is coming to Sagres to watch our final test.
A few of the boys who have taken the vows five years ago
as Initiated will have the privilege to become 'Senhores',
Knights of the Order of Christ. Last year, Prince João, son of
King Afonso V and grand-nephew of the Infante D. Henrique,
was armed a Knight in the battle of Asilah in North Africa. His father, King Afonso, is increasingly focused on the
clashes with Castella in the succession war, defending the
right to the Spanish throne of his wife Queen Joana in the

succession wars. So the Prince is assuming the reigns of the kingdom. Also last year, the Azorean captain João Vaz Corte-Real sailed in an unconventional route to the North seas, and there are rumors in the inner circles at Sagres that he reached a new land west of Thule at 60º North. I am particularly curious about this northern expedition. As a young boy, my father told me time and time again the adventures of the Norther Knights who departed from Scotland to the new land on the West with a most valuable treasure.

I don't want to spend the afternoon paying pleasantries to the courtly procession and even less waste my time in irrelevant talk with the ladies and priests who will come with the Prince to watch the Confirmation. This should be a private affair, witnessed only by the knights of the Order. The Initiated, as they prepare for the final test, should be allowed to meditate and ponder. It should be a moment of honor and valor, as the new Knights are chosen – not a public jest for the entertainment of the court. Like the roman games or the tournaments... No, I don't want to witness that unfortunate show, confounding my mind with the color of ladies' dresses, the shy flirting looks of the girls, the vain twirl of the nobles with their laughs, each talking louder than the others to catch the Prince's eye.

So we leave early afternoon, me and Dias, riding hard on our horses so that the wind can blow away the anxiety of tomorrow's test. We don't know what to expect.

On our way back, we cross over the wind rose circle marked on the ground outside the Fortaleza. A stand is being finalized on the west side of the circle, supported against the wall of the Fortress, from where the noble guests will watch the Confirmation proofs.

Alas, fate and fortune have a strange way to disturb the best laid plans. At supper, I see her. Filipa. She laughs softly, talks lightly without needing to impose her presence, for her beauty is enough to command the room. She seats at the high table, the Prince's table. I have seen her a few times before, at court in Lisbon or in the All Saints Church.

About a year ago, during one of the monthly audiences in Lisbon, my friend Diogo Cão whiskered me aside with a mocking smile at the end of lunch to hand me a rose-scented paper with the line: "If you aim to meet an angel, all angels wait for you in the rose garden". Early afternoon, helped by the Lisbon sun which forced most of the palace to retreat to the cool shades, I left the Paço to enter surreptitiously in the All Saints Church. Indeed, an angel awaited me. It was just a slight brushing of her cheek in mine as she walked away with her chaperone maid. Dias, Cão and Covilhã mocked my aspirations, but my heart had set the target. She was a "Dona" of the All Saints Convent, one of the nine high-noble ladies who by birth right live at the Convent, part of the Santiago Order. Prince João is the Master of the Santiago Order in Portugal, and thus he would have to approve the wedding of any Dona of the All Saints. What a tall order I had set myself...

This evening, Filipa is wearing a pale rose dress and her hair is done high, dotted with tiny fragrant roses. We cross eyes briefly... no one can know of that stolen kiss on the shadows the All Saints in Lisbon, not before I can formalize my pretension to the Prince.

The young men sat, waiting on the closed central library. One at a time, their names were called.

Dias was called. He rose to his feet, a short solid man, with a firm decided face. He had large furry brows and a high forefront that accented that fierce determination and stubbornness. His eyes were covered before he was taken out to the outer courtyard, walked to the center of the wind rose. The Orders' knights closed a circle around the wind rose. Dias was turned 32 times around the central steel rod, the measuring stick, and then ordered to walk 100 steps. Understanding downed on him, as he realized what this was. He was on the wind rose, outside the Fortress in the open promontory. 100 steps in the wrong direction would take him to plunge from the cliffs into the churning waves. He could hear the chanting of the knights, their horses trotting on a closed circle. Dias stepped back, recovering is balance. With eyes covered, he could not judge direction by the sun or by the shape of the clouds. The only route was East – Northeast, away from the Fortress at the West and the deadly cliffs North and South. He could feel the wind on his face. There are eight types of winds, Dias knew them better than his soul. He knew how each felt, the smells each carried, the way each touched the skin. This was a dry wind, warm. A wind that had run the arid deserts of North Africa before reaching the Mediterranean and being forced upwards. The Nortada was a fierce, continuous wind close to the ground. This was the southern wind, a soft silky wind, lighter on the feet than on the hair. Confidently, Dias turned the right side of his body to the wind, rotated about 20º against it, and walked on. He made it, received by cries of joy saying "We have a knight of the Seas".

The second man to succeed was Pero da Covilhã. He didn't have Dias sense of the sea, but he was cunning. His travels and dealings with untrustworthy merchants at his father side had made him resourceful. He always seemed to have a Plan B, a hidden card under the sleeve. He rested motionless for a long while, absorbing the situation and thinking. Then a rueful smile came to his lips. He kneeled and cleared a surface in the gravel, took the piece of silk he used wrapped around his fist and laid it in the ground. He then removed his cape and from it, blindfolded, took the metallic pin used to clip the cape around the neck. He ripped a portion of his cape and wrapped it in a tight knot around the little eye of the needle. Once satisfied he could difference the two sides of the pin, Pero started scrubbing the pointy end of the pin with his wool cape, to magnetize the tip. He did this for a couple *of minutes, uninterrupted. He then laid the pin carefully on top of the silk. The point jumped northwards, attracted by the polarity of the world magnetic field. He had just improvised a basic compass, even without the lodestone typically used to magnetize the needle. Carefully, he rose, turned about 70º to his right and walked in a straight line to the joy of the knights. "We have a knight of the Seas".*

The third to pass the test was Cão, which was not a surprise – if anyone could endure the most trying trials, it was Diogo Cão. He used a quite basic and practical approach to the situation. He cried as loud as he could, scaring the gulls that always roamed the Fortress. As he listened to the cries of the seagulls flying seaways for protection, he could perceive the diminishing sound as the gulls flew away. So he had to go the other side. Not trusting his first instincts, he took four pebbles from the ground and threw each on a cardinal point, listening intently to the crash of the pebble. It crashed into water to north and south, ricocheted off a wooden wall to the east and landed on gravel to the west. The course to take was thus clear. "We have a knight of the Seas".

Almost all of my class has already been called. In the closed central library, silence is heavy, as none of us knows what is going on... I am called, blindfolded, taken to the center of the wind rose and turned on the spot 32 times. "Walk 100 steps", a harsh voice tells me. A whirlwind of thoughts crosses my mind, as my future lies uncertain on the thin path of the choice ahead.

In my mind, I recall the Old Man saying "in the high seas with no visible shores, in the midst of a dark storm, sky black as pitch and waves pounding the ship, you will not have the pole star nor the sun or the pattern of clouds to guide you. You must learn the winds, the smell of the sea, the cries of the birds, the calling of nature – that's the only way you will find your way on the midst of the storm. Hone your sea senses." Yes, I can feel the warm wind on my face, uncertain, in brief gusts. This could be the southerlies or the eastern winds. Waves pounded all around, it seems there is only one side without the sound of waves, but the trotting of the horses and yells of the knights makes it impossible to be certain. I start walking towards the wind, hoping this is east, landwards. But after a few steps, a scent... the scent of roses, wild roses. That must be Filipa! A slight but clear scent of roses, like the ones she was wearing on her hair. Remember! Where was that stand being put up, when I returned from my ride yesterday evening? It was against the wall of the Forte. So I must walk away from this scent. The wind is not east; it is the southern. Saved by the rose. By an angel rose. I turn around and walk on, to be received by acclaims of "We have a knight of the Seas".

SAGRES, 1472

(Columbus)

Four have been chosen. Dias, Covilhã, Cão and myself. We are the new Knights of the Order of Christ, sworn into secrecy and heirs to the Templar legacy. What a pity the Old Man is not here, how proud I would be to kneel in front of the Infante as the grand master of the Order to receive my Confirmation. But it doesn't matter. I carry the secret mission he and my father have bestowed on my shoulders and will pursue it with honor. Both are now death, but I carry their secret with me.

The ceremony is brief and plain, like the spirit of the Order. Immediately we pass to the central room in council with Prince João. Long face, black beard with a drooping moustache, quiet eyes and a grave melancholic expression as if disdaining from all around, the Prince commands authority. He is a few years younger than me, barely seventeen, but already a knight tried in battle in Asilah, an influent counselor of his father Afonso V and a married man. The Prince shows a stern interest in the issues of the kingdom, listens calmly and speaks wisely. He speaks to each of the new knights, listening intently and asking about the scientific, cosmographic and technical developments of navigation. Seated next to him is Father Fernão Martins, a priest, good friend and counselor for many years of King Afonso and now of the Prince as well.

As the thirty-odd knights of the Order seat around the central room of the Fortress, the Prince addresses us. The issue is the possible existence of a vast new land to the west, suggested by signs accumulated during the preliminary exploration voyages. The proper place for such a discussion would usually be the Paço, in Lisbon, but I suspect the Prince unusual presence in this ceremony is a ruse to speak to the trusted knights away from the intrigues of the palace.

"My Lords, as my great-uncle Dom Henrique used to say, God gave us a small country as a cradle and the entire world as a grave. No man can escape the turning wheels of fortune – but we choose how to face it: willingly, or as cowards. And so, yet again, a decision must be made, and a swift one. What we decide may impact the future of the kingdom and our rule of the seas. Whatever we decide must be executed in absolute secrecy. We are a small nation and do not have the means to control all the lands we now reach, so we must use deceit and cunning to make our enemies desire what we do not want and hide from them what we do desire."

The Prince seats back and listens as the discussion unfolds.

The expeditions down the African coast continue at an unstoppable pace. The commerce of pepper and slaves from the Guinea coast south of Sierra Leone is growing, bringing the first visible profits from the Infante Dom Henrique endeavors over the previous decades. Portuguese sailors have just discovered Mina, reaching the African gold routes, so far monopolies of the Arabs. From there, they travel to the delta of the Niger. João Santarem named a wide lagoon in Benin region the Lagoa de Lagos [25] and Fernão Pó explored river Wouri which he named Rio dos Camarões [26].

To protect the expanding trade routes and Portuguese dominions over these lands, King João has tightened even more the policy of secrecy and the Mare Clausum. The Pope granted the Portuguese exclusivity to sail south of the Canary Islands and King João established the death penalty to any men found in Portuguese waters without the crown permission or to anyone who disclosures secrets, maps or navigation routes to foreigners.

A very different expedition led by João Vaz Corte-Real and Martins Homem recently returned from an exploratory voyage in the Northern seas. They have sailed west from the island of seven cities [27] maintaining parallel 62º North, passing south of Thule and sailing always west.

I know from the teachings of my father that the secret books of the Templars indicate this was the route followed by Prince Henry Sinclair when taking the Rose Line to safety.

Corte-Real and Martins Homem are present at the meeting and tell us in vivid voice they have found land, which they named Terra Nova, Newfoundland. They failed to reach contact with European settlers, but as they explored the coast they found signs of civilization, including what might be Templar monuments with inscriptions.

We also know for many years that on the westernmost isles of the Azores, sailors sometimes see driftwood (some claim also carved wood), carried by currents from the west, which is a ponderous sign of civilization to the west. Islands have been sighted southwest of the Sargasso Sea.

Further south, beyond the Equator, our pilots also suspect a land mass to the west, because of the cloud formations. More importantly, the cartographers have mapped the wind currents of the Atlantic: the wind blows from North on the east coast of Africa, but further west it blows from south. The pilots know this pattern well, as the Caravels descend Africa by the coast but then to return home they make a wide circle to take the southern winds. Cartographers suggest this wind pattern could mean a large landmass, the size of Africa, lies to the west. The Atlantic would then be sided by two large continents, with a circular wind pattern from North to the South in the east and South to North in the west.

Our navigators and explorers, by royal command, have been for decades accumulating measurements of the shadow of the Stick, steel rods exact replicas of the one at the center of the wind rose outside this Fortress. We now have measurements of several places at similar latitude, taken at the same time on the same day: Azores and Lisbon; Madeira and Tangier; Canarias and Azamor; Cabo Verde in the African coast and the Cape Verde islands; two places wide apart in the Guinea coast. Our royal cosmographer Zacuto has estimated the latitude circumference of the world by measuring the length the Stick shade in different places at the same latitude, at the same hour of a reference point, concluding the planet is about 25.000 true miles near the Equator. Each longitude degree is worth 1/360 of this distance at the Equator, which is 69 true miles. This is more than the Ptolomeu calculation. Using the same method at different latitudes, we now had a cross check of the distance at the north-south longitude through the poles, the equatorial circumference and the circumference at different latitudes.

My mind is trying to comprehend all its implications. Well, at least the Earth is not an egg! It is almost the same size at the Equator as on the North-South arch.

But there was a most relevant consequence to all this. The route to the spices has to be south, around Africa. The westwards route is not only much longer than suggested by Ptolomeu, but also it may be blocked by a large landmass.

Prince João ponders in silence, pacing the room as discussion goes on around him. Sometimes, when he listens to something that arises his interest, he asks the person to elaborate, and he nods thoughtfully. Only after long hours of listening does he speak again, having reached a ponderous conclusion that accepts no counter-arguments. A decision has been made.

"This information can be extremely useful. Firstly, I order that the chronicles of the Corte-Real and Martins Homem expedition be changed, to the fact that the expedition met disaster and never returned." He looks at the two commanders. "I am sorry my friends, you will be rewarded. But this must be done. Your deed must remain a secret and our enemies believe you failed, at least until the appropriate time comes to divulge those lands to the world. We are not ready yet. The Antilles islands and Newfoundland are all north of the Canary Islands latitude, so they would fall on Spanish domain according to Alcaçobas Treaty."

"Secondly, we will accept the invitation of the Danish king to sail the northern seas. We will have a strong and experienced commander to make sure we steer the fleet away from Newfoundland and push it towards Thule. In that expedition, Alemão will serve as a common sailor." The Prince looks at me meaningfully "You understand their language, so listen intently to what the Danish folk say about those lands. This will give you valuable information to later sail your own ships and complete the mission. It must be you to establish contact with the Rose Line, so that they recognize your mark. We shall endeavor to complete the promise made to the Templar brothers who helped the founding of this nation."

"Thirdly, it must be our absolute priority to keep pushing south. The Spanish may soon stop their internal squabbles and unite against the Moors, and when that happens and the Reconquista ends, they will turn to the Atlantic. We will also need spies to reach overland to Egypt and Ethiopia to find out the way to India, where to trade spices, where to replenish the ships and how to hire translators and pilots who can sail the Indian sea. We need spies who can speak Arabic, who are used to their costumes and manners.

Covilhã should be ready for that task."

"And finally, we need to set in motion a plan to confound our enemies with tales and deceptions. I believe there are reputable philosophers throughout Europe who defend the western route to the spice islands. Let us engage in discussions with this Italian Toscanelli and also that German map maker Benhaim, foster their theories of a "smaller world" with a single sea between Europe and Asia. If the Portuguese are seen to be interested on those theories and ingratiate Toscanelli, even pay him an annuity for his counsels, it will reinforce his credibility to other nations. So we can use this to our advantage by maintaining our secret knowledge of the size of the world and the probable existence of a new continent to the west."

Father Fernão Martins has been corresponding with Paolo Toscanelli, feeding him filtered information about the discoveries, to lead him towards conclusions that fit our purposes. I've heard Toscanelli is even proposing to King Afonso an expedition to reach India through a western route. Basic math proves such enterprise would be condemned to failure, even if the Antilles are just islands and not a full continent preventing passage. The distance is too long, the crew would perish of hunger on the way. But it seems people are ready to believe what they want to believe, looking for fame and sponsorship.

Prince João concludes the meeting. The orders were given, the wheels are in motion. But I guess not all has been said. As the new knights of the Sagres School raise to depart, Prince João turned to Father Fernão Martins, as if continuing a previous dialogue between the two. He says something I catch only in passing: "For the plan to succeed, we need a person of high standing, educated in the classics, able to speak and convince kings, daring and tough, experienced in the nautical sciences, and of our absolute trust."

The words stick in my mind. Of course, whatever the mission, the elite knights of the Order of Christ have the attributes the Prince mentioned, which the Sagres School would complement with the nautical and scientific knowledge. My adventurer spirit is enthralled, fueled with the prospect of a perilous mission, that would require moral fiber, noble character and personal sacrifice.

My mind races wildly. I will finally set to sail, prepare the achieve my mission. The mood during dinner is joyful but sober. I escape towards the inner courtyard to see the stars, and talk alone to the moon.

Instead of the moon, I see the most brilliant star, my Filipa. She is giggling in the company of some of her maids of company. One of the girls calls my name, no hint of shame or malice, to complement me on my performance in the wind rose.

As I walk towards the small group of ladies, I pluck a red rose blossoming in the inner courtyard, and offer it to Filipa. "This afternoon I was saved by a rose. Doña, please accept this rose in gratitude. It is the wind rose of the sailors, red as the fiery sun of the south".

LISBON, FEBRUARY 2019

S avanah needed to get some colour on the dry facts and speculative theories she had spent the weekend reading. Professor Noronha had not seemed very keen on unveiling whatever Raven had truly discovered or suspected... if he knew what it was at all. So, Savanah decided to try talking to Pedro. Maybe he would be more forthcoming, despite his cold attitude towards her so far.

Now she came to think about it, his coldness could be some kind of protective carapace. If Duma's suspicions were correct, Pedro had been Raven's direct supervisor and, apparently, kind of boyfriend. At least as far as Raven did 'boyfriend'.

The conversation with Pedro had been disappointing, though. He was perhaps even more nebulous about Raven's research than Professor Noronha. It seemed everyone was keen was putting her off Raven's scent.

Pedro agreed that the Italian wool-weaver merchant fairy tale had indeed many inconsistencies and based on fabricated documents, namely the Mayorazgo. However, he put that down to a greedy merchant trying to exploit the similitude between the Latinized version of Colon's name, in order to claim the rich inheritance and titles of the Admiral. At the time the Spanish court dismissed the claims as unfounded, but the story stuck for the lack of a better one. Later, the city of Genoa simply tried to take advantage of the tale to get the credit for the origin of the famous navigator. But there was nothing more to it. All the conspiracy theories were, in

Pedro's view, just a diversion. Speculations for dinner party conversations. The fact is: there are no facts. Colon chose to hide his true origins and we can but speculate.

"The Portuguese theory does fit most of the few known facts of Colon's life and is much more believable than the Genoese version.", stated Pedro in his calm professorial tone, "However, these Portuguese theories Raven was so excited can be rather dangerous. Once you discard as lies or forgeries the most obvious and literal documents where Colon is identified or hinted as Italian, then you open the door to all type of wild speculation. You get in very muddy terrain, fertile ground for all sorts of conspiracy theories. And the link to the Templars is even more dangerous. There is already enough speculation about the Templars and the Grail, we don't need to join Columbus into the gung-ho party."

Each era has its own mystic heroes, representations of the limits of the human body: The Greek had the Olympic athletes, the Romans had the gladiators, the Middle Ages had the Templar Crusaders, Portugal had the Discoverers and Spain the Conquistadores... 'today, we have the fitness sculptured bodies, I guess', though Savanah, lost in her own lateral thoughts. She could often do that, keep two conversations in parallel, one outwards and another inside her head. It was quite tiring, but she did it without even realizing. The trick took her through many boring Wall Street meetings. The collective conscience of the times is projected and amplified into those heroes, so their stories cannot be taken at face value, but as the enlarged fears and hopes of the times that created them.

"Yeah, more Templar lore...", said Savanah aloud. "We get plenty of speculation in the US as well, you know, George Washington a Freemason, Area 51 aliens, Elvis is alive, Trump an alien scout ahead of full invasion..."

Pedro was taken wrong-footed by the comment, turning his eyes from staring at the wall behind Savanah to looking to her, maybe pondering if he was being jested. Then he returned the stare to the dot on the wall. Savanah decided to add a politer comment.

"But are you not concerned the traditional view is just a fairy tale, a massive lie hiding some much deeper secret? Why has it been kept secret for so..."

"...oh, don't go there. Historians hate void, and feel in the blank spaces with the available information. Theories about Colon's true identity are a penny a dozen! Genoa, Cataluña, Galicia, Ibiza, Madeira, Greece... all have been advanced as his birthplace. Which simply demonstrates how well the secret was hurdled. For instance, it has been suggested Colon was an illegitimate son of the pope Martinho V, whose birth name was Otto Colonna. There are plenty of alternative theories, but we simply don't have facts to irrefutably prove one or the other."

Pedro looked at her again for some instants, with a conciliatory expression. "Look, if you want a reasonable alternative for the traditional view, there is no need to go looking for fancy, esoteric conspiracy theories. One of the best documented 'alternative theories' was advanced by Professors Serpa and Ferreira in 1930. At the time it was discredited, but was later recovered and defended by Mascarenhas Barreto in 1999. It fits many known facts and safely places Colon's childhood in Madeira. His true name may have been Salvador Fernandes Zarco, a bastard son of Dom Fernando, brother of King Afonso V, with Isabel Zarco, daughter of João Gonçalves Zarco."

Pedro explained with some detail this version of the story, which was less esoteric than the version of Colon as a secret Templar and more like a Mexican novella.

Salvador Fernandes Zarco was supposedly born in the Herdade de Columbaes, near the villa of Cuba in Alentejo, around 1449. At the time, the Duke of Beja was Dom Fernando, brother of King Afonso V and nephew of Henry the Navigator. Dom Fernando would eventually marry his cousin Beatriz, daughter of the future King João II. Beatriz would give Dom Fernando nine children, including Leonor (who would become queen by marrying her cousin Dom João II) and Manuel (who would become king after Dom João II death). However, Dom Fernando, Duke of Beja, had an affair with Isabel da Câmara Zarco, daughter of João Gonçalves Zarco, captain of Madeira. Although they lived in Madeira, there is evidence of Zarco family links with Cuba, near Beja, where a tombstone with the inscription Zarco was found. This tombstone is in the Convent of Santa Clara in Beja, which later originated the Convent of Santa Clara in Funchal, Madeira, founded by João Gonçalves Zarco, probably to install his daughter Isabel and her illegitimate son, the would-be navigator.

So, Isabel Zarco was in Cuba, near Beja, with close relatives, gets pregnant of Infante Dom Fernando and Salvador is born. Being a bastard, he received the mother's surname Zarco, although retaining Fernandes, which means ´son of Fernando´. As son of Dom Fernando, Colon would be cousin and brother in law of the future King João II.

This theory also fits into the statement contained in the 18th century genealogy books of Dom Tivisco, claiming that Colon was "the last sprout of Henrique". Dom Fernando was nephew and the chosen heir (adopted son) of the Infante Dom Henrique as Grand Master of the Order of Christ.

In 1492 Colon discovered "the most beautiful place in the world", according to his journey logbook, and named it the island of Cuba. The official name was Juana, in honor of the Spanish princess, but he always referred to the island as Cuba, and the name stuck.

In a less obvious passage of the "Historia del Almirante", unlikely to have been adulterated by the Italians translators, Fernando refers to the Colon brothers coming from Tierra Rubia. Vila Ruiva (Rubia, in Latin) is an ancient Portuguese village a few kilometers from Cuba, in Alentejo.

Pedro moved to the shelf and opened a book "His signature ´: Xpo Ferens. / ´, where many see cabalistic symbology, may be a simple codification of his true name. Colon needs to hide is true name because he was a bastard of the Portuguese royal family. Xpo means Christ, the Savior, or Salvador in Portuguese. Ferens is a normal abbreviation in the Middles Ages for Fernandes. And the symbol ´./´ at the end of the name is a connector symbol, like the semi-colon, which in Hebrew is a Zarqa. There you go, Salvador Fernandes Zarco. Also, the monogram the navigator often used on the side of his cryptic signature is composed of the three initials S F Z, the navigator's true name."

Salvador Fernandes Zarco

Professor Pedro was clearly satisfied with his own performance. As if delivering the final checkmate, he concluded: "Finally, you have to consider Colon's toponymy, the names he attributed to the discovered lands. In 1492, when he arrived at the Bahamas archipelago, the first island at which the fleet anchored was named St. Salvador, supposedly after Christ the Savior. But the fact remains: he baptized the first island with his own name, Salvador. To the second island he gave the name Fernandina, apparently in honor of king Fernando of Spain, although it is rather strange he would choose Fernando ahead of Isabella, who was more powerful (as Queen of Castella and Leon) and more supportive of Colon's expeditions. Incidentally, this second island is also named after himself (Fernandes) or his father (Fernando). Only to the third island he gave the name Isabella.

Now, was this in honor of the Spanish Queen, or his mother, Isabel da Câmara Zarco? The fourth island he names Juana, in honor of the Spanish monarchs' son, Prince Juan... or was it king João II of Portugal, where his true loyalties laid? In any case, it seems king João II was concerned the ruse could be discovered and in Vale do Paraíso asked Colon to change the name of the island. Colon maintained the original name of Juana, but started calling the island by a different name, Cuba, supposedly derived from the name used by the natives... or was it a reference to his true place of birth, the villa of Cuba in Alentejo?

"Humm... interesting", agreed Savanah. "Colon really seems to be mocking us, laughing from his grave at all the mess he created."

For the first time, Savanah saw a brief smile on Pedro's lips.

HONDURAS COAST, JULY 1502

(Fernando)

> "From a very early age I started navigating the sea, and continued doing so until today. For forty years I have been sailing. All that until this date was navigated, I have travelled. I had contacts and discussions with wise people, clergy and secular, Latin, Greeks, Jews and Muslims and others of other beliefs."
>
> CHRISTOPHER COLON, 1501

The respite from the storm did not last long. For another two weeks, during the beginning of July 1502, the fleet was relentlessly fustigated by one storm after another. On 14 July we departed, aiming for the safer waters of the southwestern side of Hispaniola, in the province of Xaraguá ▫. The promontory extending to the southwestern side of Hispaniola is a serene expanse of thick vegetation, bordered by a beach of glistening white sand, with great strategic value for those looking for shelter as it is 60 leagues away from Santo Domingo and the sails of approaching ships can be seen from far away in the flat open waters.

But Father was reluctant to take refuge in those beaches. The calmness had proven deceptive in the past, as Xaraguá had served as base of rebellions by local Taínos against the Spanish occupation and also as refuge for Francisco Roldan's mutiny against the three Colon brothers during 1497/98.

As we approached the western promontory, we ran into such a flat weather that we could not hold course, carried by the currents. At risk of being drawn into some of the many beautiful but hazardous coral reefs of the area, we took anchor. To me, we were at the doors of paradise.

As we waited, Friar Bartolomeu de las Casas [29], who had sailed with Father in his second expedition, told me about the beautiful Anacoana. The name means Golden Flower in the native's language. She was the Taíno chief of Xaraguá since her brother Bohechio death in 1500, and also a singer and poet of legendary beauty and wisdom. Since succeeding her brother, she had promoted some appeasement between the Taínos and the Spaniards, reducing the tension and attempting coexistence with the settlers. She was the first Indian to learn to speak and write Castilian. Friar Bartolomé praised the Xaraguá Indians for their fluency of speech and politeness, and Anacoana for treating the "rude, rapacious Spaniards" of wicked and dissolute behavior with "civility, and by delivering them from the evident and apparent danger of death, did a great service to Castella". Her keen mind and ability for interpersonal relations made Anacoana a true diplomat, looking for a pacific coexistence between the two cultures and even contributing decisively, in some occasions, to appease squabbles and rebellions amongst the settlers.

Anacoana was the sister of Bohechio, the cacique who consolidated power over all of Xaraguá, and wife of Caonabo, the cacique of Maguana [30] who was arrested by Columbus in his second voyage, accused of destroying the Fort of La Natividad. After her husband's arrest, she had returned to Xaraguá and to the side of her brother Bohecio. Caonabo was shipped to Spain, but died during the journey.

During 1496/97, Bohechio harbored the rebellious Francisco Roldan, who fired up the natives' revolt against the Adelantado, my uncle Bartholomeu Columbus. In 1498

Batholomeu arrived in Xaraguá with his troops to quell the Indian rebellion and subdue Bohecio, who avoided a probable massacre by recognizing the sovereignty of Spain.

Finally finding wind again, and after a brief stop in Cuba to replenish stocks, we departed on a south-southwest route. We were embarking into what would become Father's most extensive recognition of the shores of the new continent. We didn't know at the time this was a new continent and still hoped to find passage between the Caribbean islands to reach Cipango and the Indies. Although, looking back, I now realize Father was certainly aware we were a long way from the true India, almost halfway in fact, and therefore he never truly aimed at reaching the true India.

We travelled parts of the world never before seen by Christians, lands that were not yet in any maps. On July 30 we arrived at a small island with many waterways running through it and a dense pine forest. We called it Isla de los Pinos [31]. The island's warm, clear waters support an extensive and treacherous coral reef. My uncle Bartholomeu went ashore with two skiffs. We came across a canoe "as long as a galley", with twenty-five paddlers. I marveled at this, because it had no joints or nails, having been built from the hollowed trunk of a single giant tree. This long canoe like boat was very agile and maneuverable, with a palm-leaf awning which provided protection against rain and waves. Under this awning were the children and women and all the merchandise. The natives, unlike those in the islands previously discovered by the Admiral, were not naked, but wore colorful clothes and large gold ornaments [32]. "They also had thick quilted overcoats, like breastplates, that were sufficient protection against their darts and even withstood some blows from our swords."

This suggested we had stumbled upon a remarkable, advanced civilization, indicating we should be getting close to the great civilizations described by Marco Polo. An elder we took on board told us of horses and swordsmen and people living inland with "ships and bombards, bows and arrows, swords and armor". This was all rather difficult to ascertain, because the translators we had brought from Hispaniola did not understand the local language and so we were communicating mainly by gestures. Still, this exchange allowed Father to claim we were "only a ten days' journey from the river Ganges."

The people on the canoe offered no resistance as we approached them. The cargo transported in the vessel was like nothing previously seen in these islands: "cotton mantles and sleeveless shirts embroidered and painted in different designs and colors, breechclouts of the same design and cloth as the shawls worn by women on the canoe, being like the shawls worn by the Moorish women of Granada; long wooden swords with a groove on each side where the edge should be, in which were fastened cord and pitch; flint knives that cut like steel; hatchets resembling the stone hatchets used by the other Indians, but made of good copper."

They seem to place a great value on a type of dark, large, dried bean, with a very fragrant and pleasant smell. As we approached the vessel, the elders in the canoe took purses of these beans, as if taking coin in preparation for trading. As a few beans fell to the floor of the canoe, "all the Indians squatted down to pick them up as if they had something of great value – ignoring the feelings of terror and danger at finding themselves in the hands of such strange and ferocious men as we must have seemed to be."

This was, as I remember it, the first time I saw cacao beans. As we came to understand, this was a valuable commodity in their culture, believing it was an offer from the Gods. They called it Ka'kau, from where our word cacao is derived. The roasted beans were mixed with spices and water and heated until producing a bitter silky smooth brew the Mayas call chocol'ha, a highly prized drink reserved for the wealthy. The Indians consider it to have medicinal and spiritual powers. We brought the beans to Spain but the concoction did not attract much enthusiasm. Despite its bitterness, it is a "divine drink which builds up resistance and fights fatigue. A cup of this precious drink permits a man to walk for a whole day without food."

Father was thrilled by the encounter with the remarkable people on the canoe and their merchandise. The signs were clear. Even if it certainly was not India, perhaps we had finally found a land of "great wealth, civilization and industry" that would appease the Spanish monarchs and reinstate Father's titles and rights.

We continued our journey and approached the mainland, in a point the Admiral named Caxinas. We continued to look for the passage, the doorway into the southern seas of Cipango and India.

After assessing the friendliness of the natives, we went ashore on Sunday August 14 and celebrated Mass. Three days later, Bartholomew went ashore again, with a significant number of sailors, to take formal possession of the land. "More than a hundred Indians bearing food came down to the shore; as soon as the skiffs reached the beach, they offered the gifts to the Adelantado, who ordered them repaid with hawk's bells, beads and other baubles." The Indians here looked very wild, with pierced holes in their ears the size of a chicken egg. Father called the region Costa de la Oreja (coast of the ear).

We pushed further on, but as land turned eastwards we had to struggle against contrary winds, which delayed the fleet considerably. All elements in nature were conspiring to prevent the Admiral moving forward. It is as if we were on the last step of a religious revelation, at the doors of paradise, crossing the purgatory, a final long passage to test our valor, skills and devotion.

The entry on Father's diary reveals our mental state in the face of those probations. "I found myself going against the wind and terrible contrary currents. Against them I struggled for sixty days, after which I managed to cover a little over seventy leagues. In all this time I did not enter any port, nor could I, nor did the storm leave me; rain, tremendous thunder and lightning came continuously so that it seemed like the end of the world (...) Other storms had been experienced, but none ever lasted as long or had been as frightening."

We languished on that forsaken shore, away from everything, losing hope at each passing interminable day. Life on board at the open sea, away from land, is an unimaginable probation. The air in the officers' private cabins becomes nauseating, almost unbreathable, with a foetid smell of rotten wood, body odour and mice droppings. But nights are infinitely worse for the others: ranked sailors in the forecastle, skilled artisans and gunmen under the bridge, convicts out on deck. No-one washed for months. Clothes became perpetually wet, stiff with salt. In stormy weather, every task is a life threat, sailors hanging from the rigging to adjust the heavy soaked sails, above roaring waves that threaten to devour the ship whole. Days are marked by the change of the watch, turning of the glass and the hours of meals. We ate hard unfermented biscuits, little salted meat or fish, oil and vinegar, beans. As the weeks pass, the biscuits become full of worms until they turn into a foul nasty looking porridge.

The truth is, food is never the key concern. We would run short of drinkable water much sooner, as it quickly becomes foul due to the pitch lining the barrels, and has to be mixed with vinegar. And if not the drinking water, then diseases: malaria, dysentery or scurvy. In the Dark Ocean, the clock is always ticking, relentless, merciless, marked by the three sailor banes: ravaging storms, undrinkable water and disease.

Albeit terrible life on-board during those first months looked, they were nothing compared to what we would face later.

Father insisted we keep morning and evening prayers, to maintain a minimum of human dignity. The skies were sometimes so dark and the sea so rough that we lost sight of some of the other ships. In the barrage of rain and wind, communication to the other ships often became impossible. When a ship was gone for days, we never knew if she disappeared by its own accord, in a mutinous disobedience of the Admiral's orders, or got pushed away by the strong winds and currents, or drowned under the waves and all lives lost. These moments when a ship disappeared were always a cause of much anguish for Father. I guess he feared for his crew, brother and friends, but I suspect he was also anxious, fearing one of the other captains would claim new lands or the passage to Cipango.

Father had trusted loyalists commanding the ships. La Capitana, where me and Father travelled, was captained by Diego Tristán, with the Sanchéz brothers as master and pilot. La Gallega also had a trustable crew, with Pedro de Terreros as captain, a loyal man who had sailed with Father in all four voyages.

Santiago de Palos, nicknamed Bermuda after her owner, Francisco Bermudez, was trickier. The formal captain was Francisco Porras. His brother Diego Porras acted as the crown's representative and treasurer. Father had tried to avoid the Porras brothers, but they were imposed by Alonso de Castile, the crown's coin master. To keep them under close control, uncle Bartholomew sailed on the Bermuda. His imposing figure and position as the Adelantado, made him the in fact captain of the ship.

The true motivations and plans of the captain of Vizcaína, the smallest ship, were harder to assess and was cause of much anxiety to Father. She was commanded by Bartolomeo Fieschi, from a renowned Genoese family, and her crew included several other Italians. Father was so concerned about the allegiances and motivations of the Vizcaína commander that he bought the ship from her owner after we departed Cadiz.

Father lied in his small cabin, crippled in his sickbed. I was often tempted to give the Admiral some of that concoction alchemists use to calm delusional people. It is made of poppy seeds from the orient and mother smuggled some into my pocket before we left Cadiz, making me promise to keep the Admiral sane and prevent his madness to lead us astray. But how can I truly believe he is mad, if so often during this expedition he is the only one to keep us safe, with his unique instinct of the sea and the winds?

He continues to keep records on his double log books – one I understand is for the kings and the public, the other only for himself, God and who knows who else. In extreme circumstances, the Admiral jumps from his sickbed and blasts orders, commanding the respect of all and revealing skills beyond the competencies of our best sailors. Extreme circumstances focus his senses and sharpen his mind. But outside those moments, without the thrill of the challenge, he falls into periods of delusional hallucinations. During these periods I try to keep him inside the small cabin, as he is prone to blasphemy against King and God. That might get him killed, if that diabolic Torquemada hears about this.

"Fernando, you must believe me. I will reconquer our titles and wealth. I will leave you mother a wealthy woman. My true-born son Diego is a spoiled young man, although smart and brave. He does not know the true reason I abandoned him and his mother Filipa, so he is sometimes resentful. It is you that must complete my deed. Look after my books, Fernando, look after my books and keep them safe. I took my most precious treasure from Madeira to Seville after my first voyage, and then to my house in Hispaniola. I have sent it back to Seville in that cursed armada that left Hispaniola in the eye of the storm. What a disaster if it sinks! We must recover the treasure, the Wind Rose. Keep the book safe until you are old enough to understand its meaning. Then you will know what to do. Look for the counsel of Friar Antonio Marchena in Palos."

"Father, you must rest." I try to sooth his pain, which is perhaps more spiritual than physical. "Do not worry, I will take care of everything. You will, in fact. You will take us back to Spain in safety, with more land explored, and recover your honours. They are rightfully yours."

But my words seem to be just distant echoes, bouncing back from the walls of his obsessions. Father continues – but he talks to himself, I just stand there witnessing his mental delusions. "I am condemned by men, but praised by God. Even when I had to be cruel... Greatness is not easy or pleasant, it required all my energy and uncompromising dedication. Even those nasty things I'm accused of, I had no alternative. I must confess my crimes, and they are so many! I have deceived, lied, tortured and killed Spaniards and Taínos alike, submitting all around me to my whims! All in the name of keeping the farce, the charade... and for what? It seems all I've done was still not enough to complete the mission."

"I killed to silence them. First it was that poor Italian in the dungeons, in 1484. Then Pinzón, on the return from the first expedition, to ensure his silence. And also Miguel Muliarte, you know? Yes, yes, the husband of my sister in law, Briolanda Moniz Perestrelo, sister of Filipa. The man participated in my second expedition, he probably thought just because he was my brother in law I would facilitate and accommodate him. But the bastard joined a mutiny. I caught a letter from a French missionary, Frei Juan Francés, that Muliarte translated to Spanish and intended to deliver to the monarchs. The letter accused me of brutality against the Spaniards and denied the riches of the Indies. The ungrateful. I killed him right there, with my bare hands."

"So much abnegated effort, for what? They took me everything. My titles, but mostly my dignity and pride. I am a king! A king of two worlds, the world of men and the world of God. The Spanish dog Bobadilla took me in chains, in front of my men, and they all stood there, mocking. Oh, I know why they mock. They could not accept a foreigner ordering them around. They accused me of tyranny and violent manners. How else could I deal with this scum? I had to control the new lands with iron fist, otherwise the Spanish would first rob me and then massacre the natives. The Spaniards are lazy, rude, greedy, untrustworthy... but above all, ignorant! I can't stand ignorance! The Portuguese sailors are rough, but at least they know what to do on sea. I never had any trouble with my crews in the Portuguese ships to Africa or Newfoundland. And that expedition was harsh, when us and the Danish tried to pass into the sea of Cipango by rounding Newfoundland through the North. This scum complains, but they don't know what real peril is. In 1476-77, our boats faced artic ices, massive tides and turbulent waters in truly uncharted territory."

"The Portuguese abandoned me as well, after all I did for the Infante and King João II. That greedy King Manuel does not understand the larger purpose of what the Infante started. For him it's all just riches and spices and gold. He abandoned me. Now what am I to do, without the Infante and without King João? The 'hidalgos' suspect the trickery and only Queen Isabella keeps the vultures at bay. I must conquer new lands, find the centre passage and reclaim my honours. That is the only way to achieve the final mission."

Then Father started rambling non-sense. "The book, the book, save the book and take it to the Promised Land. If we survive the storms, you must promise me to keep my library complete and safe, do not touch or sell any of it, and reach the Templars of the first route to establish the reconnection. They will know what to look for amongst my belongings."

He was sweating despite the cold windy night, restless between fits of sleep. Father slept very little, if at all. He pretended to lie still, but I could see his open eyes when our ship was struck by lightning. I know he was torn between loyalty to the kings who stripped him of his achievements and a sense of the mission, a mission I sensed but failed to understand.

SHORES OF COSTA RICA, SEPTEMBER 1502

(Fernando)

A t the end of September, we arrived at the island named Cariay ™. "The land was high and abounded with rivers and great trees, and the island itself very green, with many groves of palm trees and a great number of Indians, many armed with bows and arrows or spears black as pitch and hard as bone and tipped with fish teeth, and still others with clubs (…) determined to resist us." There we stopped to repair the ships as best we could, although we lacked the necessary instruments and materials.

We offered our trinkets to the Indians, to sooth them, but strangely, later that day, they returned all our gifts. Were they offended by being offered worthless baubles? Or was this a sign of mistrust? The first encounter between peoples of worlds so far apart in costumes and beliefs is always fascinating but unpredictable.

Bartholomew went ashore with a retinue of protection and a scribe. However, the moment they saw the pen drawing on paper, the Indians became very agitated. They were probably afraid of being bewitched by the magical pen, as if its symbols worked like voodoo dolls. "On approaching the Christians, they scattered a powder in the air and also burned this powder in censers and with these censers caused the smoke to go towards the Christians."

A few days later, on Sunday October 2, my uncle went

ashore again. The sailors were marveled to find a wooden crypt containing several tombs and dried and embalmed corpses, with no bad smell. The following day, a delegation of Indians presented us with "two native wild boars [34], (...) small but very savage."

I had become fascinated with a playful, agile cat-like creature captured in the forest by one of the crossbowmen. This bizarre cat was very bold and naughty, "the size of a small greyhound, but with a longer tail, so strong that if one coils it about something, it holds it as tightly as if it were fastened with a rope (...) These animals move about in the trees like squirrels, leaping from tree to tree and grasping the branches not only with their hands but also with their tails, by which they often hang for rest or sport [35]. (...The crew) had the cat and the boar thrown together, whereupon the cat coiled its tail around the pig's snout, seized it by the neck with its remaining fore claw and bit the pig so hard that it grunted with fear."

For two months we had been exploring the coast [36], always under very foul weather, looking for the passage to the southern seas, before arriving in Almirante Bay [37] on October 16.

The following day the Admiral sent boats ashore at the Chiriqui Lagoon, where they were met by a hundred Indians "brandishing spears, blowing horns, beating a drum, splashing water toward the Christians and squirting toward them the juice of some herb they were chewing." Despite the threatening episode, the Admiral and the captains were very pleased, because they traded with the Indians for mirrors of pure gold. This further assured us we were indeed in rich and civilized lands.

At the beginning of November we reached a "very large, beautiful, bay, thickly populated and surrounded by cultivated country", which my Father called Puerto

Bello [38]. The land was cultivated and everywhere around we could see fields of tall cane-like plants with long leaves and a soft brown bristle, like a tuft of hair or wiry strains of beard. The humid, hot tropical region and fertile land should yield two crops a year. The bearded plants were still growing, several months to go until harvest, but the natives showed us elongated yellow-red cobs, which the natives use in many different ways, namely to produce a yellowish sweet flour. We stayed in the harbor for a week, enduring the continuing rain, before resuming eastward to contour the land.

We came to rest in a cove where Indians were fishing. The natives got very scared at the sight of our large vessels and swam ashore, as some of the sailors chased them in the rowboats for fun. The Indians "would dive like a waterfowl and come up a bowshot or two further away. It was really funny to see the boat giving chase and the rowers wearing themselves out in vain, for they finally had to return empty-handed."

On November 26 we squeezed into a tiny harbor, where we stayed for nine days, repairing ships and mending casks to take fresh water. In this harbor we saw many giant lizards, which Father called crocodiles for there are similar beasts in Africa. These lizards "came out to sleep ashore and gave out an odor as strong as if all the musk in the world were collected together. (...) They are so ravenous and cruel that if they catch a man they will drag him into the water to eat him, but they are cowardly and flee when attacked."

The following months would prove to be the worst test of survival and resilience I ever experienced. For eighty-eight days, the storms abated over the ships, relentlessly, preventing the pilots from seeing sun or stars to act as guide. We faced a near-death experience, as if Heavens were probing us before opening the doors of paradise, or punishing us for daring to go beyond the limits of the realm of men. The fleet was devastated. We lost rigging, cables and anchors, as well as many of the skiffs and most of the food. Sails were ripped. The wood of the hulls was infested with wood-worms and resembled honeycombs, with thick holes that threatened to sink us. The ships were barely seaworthy.

Finally, on December 5, Father reluctantly accepted the demands of the crew to initiate the return voyage. We had not found the crossing to the china seas, but discovered many new lands for the Spanish sovereigns and clear signs of a rich civilization with whom to trade.

Father surely felt this as a failure nonetheless, unable to find a central passage to Cipango and India.

PANAMA, DECEMBER 1502

(Fernando)

*"Is it the prophet's thought I speak, or am I raving? / What do
I know of life? What of myself? / I know not even my own
work, past or present; / Dim, ever shifting guesses of it spread
before me, / Of newer, better worlds, their mighty partur-
ition, / Mocking, perplexing me."*
WALT WHITMAN, "PRAYER OF COLUMBUS", 1872

Although we were supposedly on the way back, Father still kept stubbornly eastwards along the coast. The other pilots considered we ought to turn north, but Father insisted that if we were to find our way back to Hispaniola, the fleet had to keep going east for many miles, before turning north. Looking at the maps today, he was right of course, but at the time I suspected he hanged to a last desperate hope of finding the straight to the west.

The weather remained unsettled, the mighty Lord continuing to probe and test us. The wind whipped the ships, like an enraged master, driving us back and forth. My memory of those days is clouded, storms merging together into a single one, as if the endless storm kept chasing us, like a wild animal chasing its prey.

In his journal, Father wrote that "for nine days I was as one lost, without hope of life. Eyes never saw the sea so angry, so high, so seething with foam. The wind not only prevented our progress, but offered no opportunity to run behind any headland for shelter. I was stranded in an ocean turned blood, boiling like a cauldron on a hot fire. Never did the sky look more terrible; for one whole day and night it blazed like a furnace, and the lightning broke with such violence that each time I wondered if it had carried off my spars and sails; the flashes came with such terrifying fury that we all thought the ship would be blasted. All this time the water never ceased to fall from the sky; I do not say it rained, for it was like another Deluge. The crew were now so worn out that they longed for death to end their martyrdom.[39]"

But the Heavens were not satisfied yet... they had yet another phenomenon to throw at us, as if we were toys in the hands of a vicious, whimsical infant God. What cosmic forces or powerful sorcerers were at play, to conjure that water vortex? It was 13 December. A deathly current of churning water passed between the ships, raising "the water up in a column thicker than a water spout, twisting it about like a whirlwind (...) Had the sailors not dissolved it by reciting the Gospel according to St. John, it would surely have swallowed anything it struck."

As soon as a menace passed, another loomed on the horizon, an unending succession of probations, like the penance labors inflicted by the Greek Gods on Hercules.

If the storms and the woodworm were not enough, we were then surrounded and chased by 'tiburones', terrifying sharks cutting through the surface of the waters. "These beasts seize a person's leg or arm with their teeth and cut it off as clean as with a knife, because they have two rows of saw like teeth." They are a bad omen, preying on vulnerable ships like sea vultures. Still, we killed as many as possible, as they provided valuable meat. So ravenous are these beasts that "out of a shark's belly I saw a turtle taken, that afterwards lived on the ship."

On December 17, the sharks left behind, we met another marvel, entering Puerto Gordo [40]. This is an "harbor, resembling a great channel", where the native "people lived in the tops of trees, like birds, their cabins built over frames of poles placed across branches." We stopped only briefly on that harbor, as the unnatural behavior of its people made everyone edgy and anxious.

The new year of 1503 seemed to bring us better fortune. At least, so it seemed on the fine morning at the beginning of January, when the fleet entered the mouth of a river Father named Rio Belem. We were in the region of Veragua, where we had previously found natives wearing large gold rings and earrings on the outwards journey. Looking for the source of the gold, we entered the bar and continued upriver. Thousands of Indians met the fleet from the shores, astonished by the sight of the large vessels. On the third day, uncle Bartholomew took the skiffs to row upriver, heading for the village of Quibian, which was the name the Indians gave to their king.

This was a most friendly and civilized exchange, "each giving the other the things he most prized". We stayed there about three weeks, feeling safe and much relieved. The Indians of Veragua "had a habit of constantly chewing an herb, which was probably the cause of their rotten teeth".[41]

But those peaceful and restful weeks amongst civilized and friendly natives would prove to be just a lull in our ordeal. A sudden storm broke on January 24 and Rio Belem quickly overflowed. "Before we could prepare, (...) the fury of the flood water struck La Capitana with such violence that (...) she broke its cables and drove against La Galega, with such a force that the blow broke the mizzen. (...) Then, entangled in one another, they drifted in great peril".

By God's intervention or the Admiral's cosmic powers, the two ships disentangled and floated down the river to the sea. It was nothing short of a miracle, like many others I witnessed during that outlandish and most admirable expedition.

After all such perils, I expected Father would swiftly proceed with the home-bound journey. However, now the Admiral and his captains had seen the mirage of the gold mines of Veragua, they would not let go easily. At the beginning of February 1503, just days after so gravelly facing a near death experience, Father defied destiny once again. Despite his illness that kept him stranded in his cabin most of the time, my father Cristobal Colon remained as temerarious and confident as ever.

And so it was that on 6 February my uncle led sixty-eight men in rowboats into the mouth of the river Veragua and upriver until Quibian's village, venturing far inland in search of the source of gold. Here he saw the stone buildings of the Mayas, which was considered as proof of a more advanced and civilized culture than that of other Indians.

By the end of the month, after uncle Bartholomew's return, we were all convinced we had finally found the region of the gold mines. We thus set upon establishing the first Christian settlement on the territory. We now suspected we were not in an island but in Terra Firma, a new continent stretching all the way from Newfoundland to Veracruz... we had failed to find a central passage, and the southern passage around Veracruz was also proving illusive for the Portuguese.

At the banks of river Belem, we built twelve houses of timber and thatched roofs made of palm trees leaves, a signal to all that the Conquistadores were there to stay. As we finished the small settlement, we found ourselves trapped inside the bar of the river. The rain had finally stopped, but this quickly reduced the water level and closed the mouth of the river with sand. The relationship with the Indians, which had started so amicably, was also turning sour. The Indians resented us settling on their territory, and the sailors' dissolute and rude manners, robbing and raping in the villages despite the Adelantado strict orders against such behavior, further strained the relations.

By the end of March, uncle Bartholomew was restless to settle the disputes with the natives and assert the superiority of our Christian God. That usually meant, as I would sadly come to realize, a bloodbath on which two peoples, both God's creation, killed and massacred each other, like brothers competing to call the attention of a tyrannical father. In the case of the Indians, it was more like a brute older boy, a bully, going into a rampage of abuse and violence against a smaller, weaker boy, shamelessly and unapologetically, convinced of full impunity, as if God was either not looking at those distant forgotten corners of the world, or turned His eyes away in a silent approval.

The Adelantado arranged an ambush to take chief Quibián hostage and force the subjugation of the natives to the Spanish power. This was an unnecessary folly, I now realize. Friar Bartolomé las Casas resolutely condemned these hasty and violent measures that would poison the relationships between local natives and the Spaniards forever.

As my uncle returned downriver with the prisoners, chief Quibián managed to escape, jumping overboard and swimming ashore, but his wives, children and relatives remained prisoners, kept underdeck in the Caravels. The deed caused deep wounds in the local population against the invaders, and the Indians would soon retaliate.

At the beginning of April, Bartholomew presented the Admiral with "about 300 ducats worth of booty in gold mirrors and eagles, gold twists that the Indians wear around the arms and legs, and gold cords that they wear about their heads." The local villages were deserted, a grim sign of the sacking. We separated the 1/5 owed to the king and "divided the rest among the crew, giving the Adelantado one of the crowns as a sign of his victory".

As rains returned and water levels rose again, the Admiral was finally able to take the flagship La Capitana out to the sea. La Gallega would stay behind, with the Adelantado, with supplies for the new settlement.

However, as soon as "the Indians and Quibián saw that the caravels had sailed and we could not help the men left behind, they attacked the Christian settlement. The dense woods allowed the Indians to remain undercover until within fifty feet of the huts. Then, they attacked with loud cries, throwing darts at every Christian." The Adelantado men, taken by surprise, managed to fight back and drive the Indians away, who retreated into the woods "by the edge of the sword and by a dog who pursued them furiously".

I was at sea at La Capitana with father and did not present the clash. Later, as Friar las Casas told me of those events, he fumed with rage at the barbaric and atrocious behavior of the "conquistadores". "As ever, it is the poor naked and defenseless Indians who come off the worse while the Spaniards are free to butcher them with their swords, lopping off their legs and harms, ripping open their bellies, and decapitating them, and then setting their dogs to hunt down the remaining survivors and tear them to shreds."

In the settlement, there were few casualties: one dead and seven wounded, including my uncle Bartholomew. Unfortunately, the bodies of many others lied spattered in the forest or washed downriver, taken by the Indians darts. They were men who had been outside the settlement at the time of the attack or who had tried to flee the Indian attackers in canoes.

Despite the violence of the Christian's response to the Indian attack, my uncle and his men had no choice but to flee the settlement before the Indians returned to complete their revenge. But they were stranded again, unable to take the ship to the open sea due to the onset of bad weather, not even send a rowboat to alert the Admiral of what had happened. They waited, as vultures and crows circled overhead, "all of them croaking and wheeling about", feasting on the corpses of our killed companions.

We left the deserted settlement behind on Easter night, April 16, after gathering the surviving victims of the massacre. We had to leave la Gallega behind and would soon abandon Viscaína as well, for they were no longer seaworthy. "That left us only two ships, in not much better conditions, without skiffs or provisions, to cross 2.000 leagues of sea and water".

Only two vessels remained, Bermuda and La Capitana. The wives and children of Quibián, the cacique who had escaped Bartholomew's ambush, remained prisoners in the stinking hold of the Bermuda. Desperate, without hope of regaining their freedom and facing the unknown and inhospitable seas, they hanged themselves "bending their knees because they had not enough headroom to hang themselves properly".

We sailed east along the shore before crossing the sea northbound to Hispaniola. At the beginning of May we arrived on a cape we named Tiburon [42] and finally turned northbound. On May 10, we passed a group of small islands breaming with turtles, and named them Las Tortugas [43].

The two ships were taking in water from the holes of the wood worms and the crew was working the pump day and night to keep the ships afloat. It is ironical, nevertheless: we survived the storms of the mighty Gods to succumb to those miniature creatures that pierced our ships to death. We were starving, with nothing else to eat but nauseating biscuits covered with larvae and fungus. On May 13, we were approaching Cuba, hoping the ships could stand to make it to Hispaniola.

It took us much longer than expected, slowed by the desperate state of the ships and the rough seas. As we tried to cross the last few leagues from Cuba to Hispaniola, we were paralyzed by easterly winds and westerly currents. Unable to make it to either Cuba or Hispaniola, we were forced south. The ships were no more than ghostly floating wraiths. We hanged to our lives, sustained by whatever dregs of humanity remained in our souls.

After fifteen months at sea, without proper instruments or materials to repair them, the ships were in such a state that we could not avoid the water level rising, even operating the pumps all day and night. "The water in our ship rose so high that it was almost up to the deck".

Those desperate days lost at sea, waiting to drown at any moment, are deeply engraved in my soul. Over little more than a year, I had grown from a boy to a man.

Through the endless nights, I stayed with my Father at his cabin, keeping company to his insomnia, while we languished like pariahs forgotten by God. I feared falling asleep but my stubborn eyes closed down and I doze off in the stormy night.

Fernando dreams of threatening Indians jumping from their treetop houses, with painted bodies and ears pierced with fist-sized holes, terrible crocodiles, sharks and chopped heads in a swirl of red sea.

Christopher Colon lies next to him, touching the silver bullet he carries on a chain around his neck, close to his chest.

"I will make it. I am strong, the chosen one to discover these new lands and bring them to God. Has He not again and again delivered me from the worst dangers? It will not be a little king or Ovando or Torquemada to break me. I will find the passage to the western sea and regain my titles. That should leave my sons well off and Fernando's mother a respectable woman. Then com-

mission my own secret expedition to the northern lands of this new world to find the Rose Line, fulfil my duty. And finally return to Hispaniola, my lovely Hispaniola, for the rest of my days. All I want is to get my mind to stop whirling around. I am Colon, reborn once and if need be, I will reborn again. The House of Colon will rule these Indies, my Indies. They will not rob them of me. Filipa... I wish you had used that silver bullet to take my life, as I told you, so that we could depart to the Heavens together."

His thoughts start again, in endless circle, as if he is falling down a water well. Endless, obsessive thoughts. He feels his mind floating in the air, looking down at his earthly body carrying on the theatre of life, trapped on the same old scenery. He is stuck in repeat, playing the same scene again and again. The mind looks at the life that was, the life that is, the life that will be, and finds no resting place. The circle starts, an endless loop of repetitive thoughts he cannot escape, trying to take full control of life but in doing so, losing the flow of life.

"*Find the passage. Recover my titles. Finance the secret voyage to fulfil the mission. Rest in peace until Filipa calls me to her side... That's easy, Alemão. Now go to sleep. Find the passage. Recover my titles. Finance the secret voyage to fulfil the mission. Rest in peace until Filipa calls me to her side. Yes, I know. Sleep, you must be alert to achieve these goals. Find the passage. Recover my titles. Finance the secret voyage to fulfil the mission. Rest in peace until Filipa calls me to her side.*" His mind floats, looking from above at the crippled, alien body in bed. "*That is not my body, wrinkled, weak, defeated, is it? Can I skip directly to the end? Why go through all the motions of this pathetic theatre?*"

Colon raises from his bed, silently not to wake up Fernando who sleeps on the floor. He takes is gun and fills the barrel with the single silver bullet on his neck chain and rolls the chamber. He points it to his head. "*The thoughts must end, the endless obsessive devils screaming in my mind. Stop these thoughts going round and round and round again... Shut up, devils.*" He presses the trigger, but the shot is empty. Again. "*God, why do you play* with me? Let me go!"

The silver bullet is the one he had offered to Filipa, many years ago on that Sunday morning at the All Saints Convent in Lisbon. Alemão had looked deep into her serene eyes and proclaimed in the excitement of youth. "This bullet is my life I give to you, Filipa, it is yours to save or to destroy – kill me if you need, but do not abandon me". She had abandoned him without killing him, she died without taking him away too. From that moment, he never found serenity and calm again.

When Filipa died, he had asked his friend Dias to send the bullet to him. In those months he spent in delirium at the Monastery of Santa Maria de las Cuevas, having lost the last remaining thread that linked him to his past life, to his real identity before the theatre started, he tried to kill himself several times, but each time the shot was empty. How cruel God was.

LISBON, FEBRUARY 2019

(Savanah)

Days turned into weeks, and I had not yet discovered anything particularly outlandish in all the reading material Professor Pedro kept giving me. Except for the still incongruous ramblings in Raven's notebook, which I still failed to understand, there was nothing that I could consider a likely reason for murder. It was all quite interesting, yes, but mainly dry academic debates about the birthplace of a man 500 years ago. History would not be changed whether Columbus true name was Colon or whether he was Jewish or a poor Genoese or a Portuguese noble.

I was getting a bit disappointed. And I hadn´t managed either to get any leads from the Policia Judiciária, the investigative branch of the Portuguese police force, who were dragging their feet replying to my request to consult the investigation material. There were better ways of spending my days, taking some real holidays instead of spending my time reading until my eyes ached.

"Bota a dobrar que ela só come metade". Twice the portion as she only eats half, the guy was saying to the waiter.

I turned around with a smile to meet Sergio, the Brazilian Visiting Professor who was spending a year teaching in Lisbon on the subject of Brazilian declaration of independence from Portugal by Dom Pedro in 1822, who self-proclaimed himself emperor of Brazil. I had been lost in my own thoughts in the canteen line and failed to see Sergio approaching. This had become a common joke of him, teasing me for always leaving my meal half eaten. The portions were huge and I continued to fight with my diet. Anyway, I enjoyed Sergio's company and we had taken to have lunch together quite often, myself, Pedro and Duma. They were both fun and I enjoyed their company. Sergio was a tall, thin man in his early thirties, who used his olive black hair long, always tied in a knot at the top of his head, kind of samurai-style. It suited him, with Amazon Indian features. He was not what you would call handsome, but his good natured spirit and light-hearted style was impossible not to like. He talked in the singing intonation only the Brazilians have and walked in a jingly fashion, like a long limbed articulated puppet.

We walked together to seat with Duma on a round table near the window.

"So, Savanah, is Professor Twilight keeping you busy?", Sergio teased me. It had become an insider's joke between the three of us, referring to Pedro as Professor Twilight. I could see where Sergio had gotten the nickname from... Pedro did look a bit like a vampire, not only due to his sickly white skin and perpetual deep dark circles under his eyes, but also because his gloomy mood managed to suck all happiness away from people around him.

"Oh, don't be mean", I replied with a slightly telling off tone. "Pedro is being quite helpful. It is very interesting in fact."

"Yeah, Savanah, it is all quite interesting. But you have found nothing that Duma here couldn't have summarized to you in a couple of days, right?"

Duma nodded in agreement, mouth full with pasta.

"Actually", Sergio continued unfazed, "I have a present for you. Why don't we go out for lunch tomorrow and talk a bit about something that I have been meaning to tell you for a while now?"

This time Duma jumped up, smiling broadly. "Oh, slow down your horses, cowboy. Savanah is a married woman, you know?? I am the one unmarried lady here, so how come I never received that invitation?"

I guess I was getting a bit blushed on my face. Sergio was always on the flirting side, that was just his style, but this was the first time he seemed to be really hitting on me.

Wanting to move the conversation away, I said lunch would be lovely but I had already planned a trip to Sintra that weekend. Which was not entirely false as I had been intending to go to Sintra for a while.

"Ei, I am seating here with the two most beautiful ladies at the university, so...", replied Sergio turning to Duma and jesting with her. "Let's make a threesome then. Please make me the happiest man in Lisbon and come both for lunch tomorrow."

"Ah, don't you dare", replied Duma. "If we are going for a lunch together, then it's my invitation. I'm the elder here, so respect me! I will make a great chicken muamba that will make you two weaklings jump to the roof with your taste buds on fire". Muamba is a traditional Angolan dish, a spicy chicken casserole with mandioca flour. "I use real jindungo hot sauce I prepare myself, that makes Mexican jalapeno sauce a child's play."

Inviting as it was, I did not want to retreat easily from the previous white lie and said noncommittedly we could postpone to the following weekend.

At that point, Pedro approached and asked if he could join our table. Although he was not the best lunch companion, I quickly said yes, putting an end to the conversation.

"Pedro, it is always a pleasure to have lunch with you", Sergio addressed him as he sat down. "Can I get you some spicy tomato juice to go with your meal? They make a really good one here."

"Why would I want a tomato juice, Sergio?" said Pedro with an uncomprehending expression, as Duma made an ill-disguised effort not to laugh.

We made small talk for the rest of the short meal and cleared our trays away. The three of them headed for the elevator and I took the stairs, as I always do. I was climbing up to the second floor when Sergio came running up to catch up with me.

"I left the elevator on the first floor pretending to go to the library, but I wanted to talk to you. Look, there is really something we should talk about sooner rather than later. Come on, come for lunch tomorrow. We will have a great time and get to taste Duma's muamba", he said.

My face must have shown some discomfort as I fumbled awkwardly for something to say. I am married and almost 10 years older than the guy, the last thing I wanted was for Sergio to start hitting on me and risking our friendship. Seeing me looking for some excuse, he quickly added "Ohh, for God's sake, just because I am a Brazilian doesn't mean I want to bed every woman I invite for lunch....". Unable to stop himself, he smiled broadly in his gingerly manner and added teasingly "Not that I would mind sleeping with you, mind you."

I was quite embarrassed by the remark, mainly because the invitation had all come suddenly and never before had Sergio broached the subject. For the past few weeks since we met, our conversations had only been good friendly chats at the cafeteria or over the coffee machine.

"Honestly, Savanah. I do have something to tell you about all the time you are wasting on those books Pedro keeps feeding you. The though came to my mind a few days ago when I saw the list of readings Duma was preparing for you on Pedro's request. We go to Duma's and have a friendly conversation. Promise – no second intentions."

So that was it. I was quite trapped. But what the hell, it would be nice to see Duma's place and try the muamba, so I accepted.

LISBON, 1476

The Italian arrived in Lisbon on a stormy January afternoon. He entered the grim, cheap tavern and asked for some bread and wine. It was the only thing he could afford, but at least it was warm inside. It would have to do at least for the next few weeks, as he established himself in the city. Cristóbal Colombo was a small merchant from Genoa, son of a wood weaver and trader, who aspired for more. He descended from an honorable family of small merchants, traders of wool and silk, respected members of the cloth and tailor guild. His father, Gianfranco Piccione ", was president of the guild, which amplified even more the embarrassment and shame for the son's petty scams. Cristóbal was removed from the family's inheritance and forced to leave Genoa. That was for the best, anyway, the family inheritance was just hindering his movements and that city was choking his artistic and adventurer spirit.

Lisboa fitted him better. A new city, growing, full of opportunities for enterprising spirits. The future was in the Atlantic, not the Mediterranean. The Mediterranean routes were controlled by the powerful families and there were no opportunities for men like him. He would get rich and famous, and he couldn't care less about the family he had left behind. To turn a new page on his life, he had shed his family name Piccione (derived from "pigeon" in Italian) and fashioned himself as Colombo (derived from Colomba, "dove" in Italian). He liked the ring of his new name, Cristóbal Colombo.

No-one does business with a beggar, so he had come up with a tale to explain his origins and current condition.

To open doors in this city of adventurers and navigators, you had to have a story who could entreat you to the right people. So he fashioned himself as the Italian bastard son of Guillaume de Casenove Coulon, the infamous French corsair and terror of the Mediterranean. The pirate was well known for his attacks on Venetian, Genoese and Castilian ships. Shortly after arriving in Lisbon, Cristóbal had heard of a large sea battle in the south coast of the country, an attack of the French pirate against Flemish and Genoese ships [45]. So, he came up with the idea of saying he was a son of the French pirate, having lived with his mother in Genoa until the age of 14, when he joined his father's fleet. He had sailed in the English Channel to Rotterdam, Provence and north of Spain and in the Mediterranean to Venice and Genoa. In a skirmish with African pirates he had been captured and so learned their language (Colombo though this added an exotic touch to his story and he did speak a little Arab), sailing with the pirates for two years in the galleys from Tunis and Algiers. The African galleys had joined Coulon on that attack against the Flemish and Genoese ships, but in the midst of battle, his ship had been hit and he swam 6 miles to coast, washing ashore, exhausted. He had almost drawn at sea and then almost starved in land. The battle had been an act of God to release him from captivity, the exhausting ordeal was a trial of his valor and the arrival to the Portuguese beach a message he should devout his strength to serve the kingdom of Portugal. Or so the story went...

This had the side advantage of providing him with seafaring credentials, which should improve his opportunities in a city like Lisbon. So here he was, a land Pigeon turned into a sea Dove.

Colombo was magnificent: tall, broad, blue eyes, tanned and long dark hair, with the rough looks of an adventurer. The build of a bear, an intriguing look that was at the same time cute and fluffy as well as threatening and imposing. He was used to get away with his tricks and scams just by holding his powerful gaze and talking smoothly. He had a good hear for languages, so he managed to pick up a bit of Portuguese quite quickly. He intended to play the Genoa card, a city of respected mapmakers, together with his little knowledge of sailing and Arabic to find his way into the profitable business of painting and trading in maps, portolans and books.

Lisbon was full of sailors ready to trade a secret of Portuguese navigation (often fantasized, as common sailors rarely knew what lands they had reached or the routes or locations, which remained secret to only the elite of the kingdom) for some food and wine, as well as charlatans ready to peddle the maps to foreign states. The profits of copying and trading Portuguese state secrets were high, as were the risks. There was a tight policy of secrecy that had been imposed by the Infante Dom Henrique and reinforced by the royal decree of Dom Afonso V prohibiting the copy of maps and punishing with death anyone who spoke about Portuguese maritime secrets to foreigners. But the risks were worth it, especially if you traded fantasies and inventions.

So it was that Colombo managed to establish a promising business in just a few months. A large part of his success was the mysterious old man who had contacted him some weeks after his arrival in Lisbon. The man was in the tavern with a bunch of sailors, each of them drinking heavily except the somber elder dressed in black who paid the rounds of wine and prompted the boastful sailors. Colombo sat nearby, paying attention to the talk. It appeared the sailors had just arrived from the Guinea coast with slaves and gold and claimed the passage to the indies through a big river was within reach. Colombo gapped as he saw a map surreptitiously exchanging hands, acquired by the old man for a purse of coin. The sailors were in good spirits. One of them joyfully invited Colombo to join their table and share the food and wine. It was his opportunity. He offered his tale and told about the Italian mapmakers who claimed the Indies could be reached westwards in a much shorter voyage than the Infante's route around Africa. And with less perils. The sailors joined in a chorus of improprieties against Dom Henrique, how stubborn he had been, the Old Man and all his kin. The king and this new Prince continued to send valiant sailors to terrible deaths in the southern seas. One in three ships didn't return. In a Caravela of 200 men, there were at most 50 qualified seamen, the rest were convicts or young boys. And they didn't even pay proper salaries, 40.000 réis per year for an experienced sailor, who risked leaving widow and orphans unprotected.

The old man returned the following day, enquiring Colombo about his past and those theories of a western route. His back curved by the weight of old age, snow white hair and baggy grey eyes. He presented himself only as Dom Fernando, a noble concerned with the useless maritime expenses that deviated the kingdom from the honorable mission of a Christian: to fight the Moors in military combat, where the nobles of the kingdom could prove their military skills and conquer lands. He saw the crown taken hostage by the Italian and French banks who financed the expeditions. Lisbon was under siege by the scum: Jews, Arabs, sailors of dubious origins, adventurers and fortune-seekers. This illusion of maritime discoveries was ill-fated, the sooner it finished, the better.

Dom Fernando came weekly and sat with Colombo in a dark corner of the tavern. He brought news and sketches, which Colombo draw into beautiful maps. The man paid handsomely and praised the work. He said they would both get rich using his sources and Colombo's skills. To further promote Colombo's name, which would help their trade, it was important to introduce him to the right people, the people who counselled the big houses and the kings – that was the way for them to move from the shadowy taverns to the palaces of the powerful.

So, Dom Fernando started promoting correspondence of Colombo with cartographers and cosmographers from Italy, Spain and Germany. Toscanelli, the Italian cosmographer whom Dom Pedro, the brother of Infante Dom Henrique and King Dom Duarte, had met during his voyages through Europe, was gaining fame and prestige. Colombo corresponded with him and used wisely the connection to affirm his own credentials. Dom Fernando worked behind the scenes, ensuring an introductory letter was sent from some noble from the court presenting Colombo. He tutored Colombo in writing the letters and counselled him to do so in Latin, which was "more erudite".

This strategy also served well to pass information to Toscanelli that Prince João wanted to spread to other kingdoms. What is at stake is too high and the Spanish kingdoms are stirring its head towards the Atlantic. When they take Granada from the Moors, and if Castella and Aragão unite, the Spanish could become a real threat to Portuguese interests in the Atlantic. If the fake information was written by Portuguese cosmographers, the foreign kings would look at it with suspicion. It was much more credible if foreign agents conveyed the information.

And thus, over the course of just a few years, the poor Piccione, son of Gianfranco Piccione the Genoese wool trader, became the respectable Colombo, an experienced sailor and versed on the theories of the most prominent European scholars.

In his private chamber at Castelo de S. Jorge, Prince João sat alone in private counsel with a curved old man, white hair and baggy grey eyes. He had known the wrinkled and somber face of Fernão Martins, minister of the church of

Lisbon, since he could remember.

"Father Martins, one last thing before you retire to a well-deserved rest. How is that fellow Colombo behaving?"

"All according to the plan, my Lord. He knows not who I am and trusts the ruse of the grumpy and disillusioned old man. The foreign spies have noticed him and start approaching this Colombo, so we will soon be able to feed our tales to foreign monarchs through the Genoese."

"Good, good. Fortune has blessed us, this fellow looks so much like Alemão."

"If you allow me, my Prince, there is one way we could further this Italian's credibility to our enemies and lure them to the trap."

"Speak, Father Martins. You know how I value your opinion. Nothing would give me more pleasure than to trap those Castilian kings into the empty lands of the western Atlantic, while our ships push forward towards India."

"Then, my Prince, allow me to arrange a royal invitation for this Colombo to be received in audience at full court by your father King Afonso. All the little birds the Spanish court keeps in Lisbon will know of the audience and report to the Castilians."

"Also", continued Father Martins, "there is this matter of the letter and map the Florentine Toscanelli wrote to me just two years ago, proposing to your father the western route. He is well regarded in the Medici's court and we should foster his claims. Let me fake Toscanelli's letter as if it was addressed to Colombo, and give it to him. He will surely sell the secret to the highest bidder. The best way to enhance the name of Colombo and give credibility to the western route is to make it known that the Portuguese crown is actually considering it as reliable."

"Your mind is astute, Father Martins. Indeed, let's do

as you propose. Is the Italian spreading the news we passed him about the Antilles?"

"Very much so. Our friends in the Vatican tell me Toscanelli wrote a letter to Pope Pio II clearly mentioning the Antilles islands in a straight line to the west of Lisbon[46]."

"Very well." Concluded Prince Dom João. "The plan is in motion. But we need to plan ahead, to the moment we are ready to send our agent to Castella. He needs to be credible in knowing the Portuguese ocean secrets but also with a strong motive to depart our kingdom and go sell the western route to the Spanish monarchs. This Colombo will be a perfect disguise for Alemão to set the plot. Whisper to the Genoese the Toscanelli theories, but being uneducated as he is, I am sure you can trick him into a wrong measure of the Earth's degree. Lead him to grossly underestimate the length and time of this western route, and ensure he writes that in his letters to foreign agents. In all our documents we use a secret metric of halving the true leagues. This will help lead the foreign spies in the wrong direction. But this fellow Colombo needs to believe it is all his idea. When he is ready, invite him for a second audience at the palace. All the chronicles are to record and disseminate such meeting. It should be known in Castella that there is this Italian discussing the roundness of the globe and the details of a western route in the Portuguese court."

LABRADOR SEA, 1477

(Columbus)

We live extraordinary times. The first truly multi-national expedition set sail less than a year ago, from Denmark. The expedition is sponsored by the Portuguese king, Dom Afonso V, and the king of Denmark and Norway, Christian I. Besides Danes and Portuguese, such as myself and captain Corte-Real, the crew also includes Norwegians like the pilot Jan Skolp and Englishmen like Sebastian Cabot.

The fleet set a course around 60ºN latitude, heading towards Newfoundland and Thule [47], to explore the region and attempt a northwestern Atlantic passage to Cipango [48] and India. Considering the length of such voyage, it would be critical to find suitable conditions for settlement in the northwestern Atlantic, as a basis to resupply the ships on the way to Asia. If there is no passage or conditions for settlement prove difficult, the western route becomes inviable.

This expedition brings together the knowledge and experience of great sea nations. The Portuguese discovered and mapped Newfoundland in 1473, during the expeditions of the Azorean captains João Corte-Real and Martins Homem. The Nordic peoples have a centuries-old knowledge of Thule, having reached and circun-navigated the huge island during the 2nd century and colonized it around the 9th century.

Alas, we have failed to find a northern passage [49]. The

185

seas are treacherous, with enormous tides, unpredictable and dangerous frozen islets, which could also be floating blocks of ice. And we have also witnessed avalanches from the mountains hitting the sea with a thunderous sound, creating massive waves. If the ship is caught in one of these "sea-quakes", she would be engulfed and sink without any chance of escape.

But not all is lost. From Thule, we continued westwards and reached a new land, which we call Tile [50]. It is a barren and frozen wasteland and difficult to imagine a stable settlement here to support trade routes. We sailed "in the year of 1477, in the month of February, 100 leagues beyond the island of Tile (...) and this island is not within the western line of Ptolomeu, but much more to the west (...). The sea is not frozen, but the tides are so high they can reach 26 fathoms."

Finding it impossible to continue sailing on those cold northern extreme waters, we had to turn southwest, crossing dark and treacherous waters [51] to reach land again. Captain Corte-Real recognizes the area as Newfoundland, which he explored in 1473. The coordinates match his previous expedition.

We are establishing new limits of the known world! Ptolomeu wrote his treaty 'Geographia' in the second century: Thule has since then been the western limit of the world, a point beyond which ships would fall over the edge into an abyss.

I am now 26 years old and part of an extraordinary multinational expedition to break myths 13-centuries old!

We have anchored the ships for a few days on a bay in Newfoundland, to rest, hunt for meat to replenish the stocks and take fresh water before heading back. I have taken to play cards with the Norseman. My father was Germanic and taught me a bit of the language. The words are different, but

I was able to gain some basic understanding of the Danes and Norwegians. I am the only one on the Portuguese side who can communicate with them in their native language. The officials speak Latin or French, but not the common sailors.

The sailors use cards with strange characters. They say it is an old Viking game using an ancient alphabet. I have discussed this with captain Corte-Real and he got very excited when he saw the cards. He says the symbols are similar to the inscriptions carved on the base of a large stone statue found by the first settlers in the tiny islet of Corvo, in the Azores! They call the statue the Raven Knight [52].

Apparently, this large statue on the mountains of the tiny islet of Corvo island was there before the first settlers. It portrays a knight with a cape, in an unsaddled horse. His right arm is outstretched and the fingers of the right hand curled, except the index finger which is extended... pointing westwards!

How extraordinary! A statue in a tiny mid-Atlantic islet, preceding the first settlers and with an extended finger pointing westwards, pointing the way! The larger islands of the archipelago are known since early 15th century and started being colonized in 1431, but the tiny Corvo island was only discovered around 1450.

And a knight! This could only be the work of voyagers coming from the western lands, reaching out to show the way. According to captain Corte-Real, Corvo island is 41ºN latitude. I have insisted we must push further south and reach those lands! I cannot talk to him about my mission to reunite the Templar northern and southern paths... But I am sure this is a beacon left by the Scottish Templars of Henry Sinclair, to show the way.

Did my Father and Infante Dom Henrique know about the Raven Knight??!

LISBON, SEPTEMBER 1483

(Columbus)

For five years me and Filipa have now been married, with a young son, Diogo. The expedition with the Danes was a success and Prince João extremely pleased with my contribution for the discovery of the ancient Nordic dialect in the inscriptions of the Raven Knight statue. Partial copies of the inscription were sent out separately to scholars in the Nordic countries for translation and we now have a full translation of the message.

The expedition proved my worth as a knight of the kingdom and allowed me to put forward my intentions regarding Filipa. King Afonso V, who was my father's best man at his wedding, was very pleased and Prince João, as Grand Master of Santiago, granted the authorization. It makes sense to unite the houses of Câmara Zarco, from my mother side, and Perestrelo, on Filipa's father, thus combining the great captaincies of Madeira and Porto Santo.

On our wedding night, I offered Filipa a silver bullet, as a symbol that my life shall forever be in her hands, to love or to destroy.

Domestic contentment is a bliss which I can enjoy only briefly. My restless mind craves the dangers of the sea and the new worlds to uncover in faraway lands. I am treated as a grand Lord. João is now king and he too knows the secret of my father, my royal bloodline and the mission I have been charged with my father and the Infante.

I returned from Setubal at the beginning of June with the king and his entourage, where the military experiment has proven successful. The idea is elegant and simple, but can create a highly flexible and fast mortal vessel on the seas: we are experimenting with small, fast boats with powerful canons firing in a straight line just inches above the water level, instead of the standard huge fighting galleons that fire bombards from the deck, showering enemy boats but missing most hits. Firing in a straight line, these small vessels can accurately hit enemy vessels in the hull line, causing water to flood in and irreparably condemning the boat to sink. If the gun is fired sufficiently low, close to the water line, the cannon balls can be made to bounce off the water, greatly increasing their range. What we have seen in Setubal was basically a deadly floating cannon, small to make it hard to hit, fast to circle around enemy vessels and with a destructive fire line.

Soon after we arrived, the King departed for Évora. He has been there for the past 22 days, presiding over the judgement of Fernando, Duque of Braganza. A conspiracy to kill the king has been uncovered, from correspondence between Fernando and Queen Isabella of Spain.

King João is proving a masterful king as he was as a Prince, but his strong will is prone to create enemies. In 1479, still a Prince, he convinced his Father to forego the war with Spain in defense of his wife, and true heir to the throne of Castella, Joana (whom the Spaniards insult by calling her Beltraneja). In exchange for recognizing the usurper Isabella as queen of Castella, Prince João negotiated the Treaty of Alcaçobas that protects for the Portuguese all new lands south of the Canary Islands. João, as a prince or as a king, has always been rather sanguinary about protecting the maritime secrets – at least for him, there is no doubt a vast new world remains unclaimed. The future of Portugal lays on those new lands and not on the old rivalries within

European kingdoms.

He ruled that any foreign sailor or ship found south of the canaries is to be shot and death, accepting no prisoners.

We passed Cape Non many years ago and sailed south of the Equator, proving the ships can sail back upwards despite the curvature of the globe. However, King João II continues to spread the false belief that only the Portuguese Caravelas with lateen sails – triangular sails with the main mast at 2/3 of the deck, so that the ship can rotate over water – are able to do so. He even ordered a fleet of square sails to go south of Cape Non and there be burned to ashes, so as to maintain the rumor that square sails can't sail beyond Cape Non.

More than 700kg of gold reaches Lisbon each year, coming from Gana and Mina in the African coast. This is enough to build and fit ten Caravelas. Extraordinary times we live in, extraordinary indeed, but strange. A Caravela fitted for an expedition, with food and a crew of 200 men, costs about as much as 700 African slaves. That is 100 grams of gold each. How little is a man's life worth: black men traded as merchandise, white men burning on spikes, and all, black and white, sent in sea expeditions where most will perish an agonizing death.

Queen Isabella is known to be plotting against the Portuguese king, unhappy with the bargain she conceded in Alcaçobas. Ohh, and she is not one to forget. Surely she still holds a grudge against the Portuguese kings for defending the claim of her half-sister Joana to the throne. King João harsh manners, concentrating power in the crown, is also sparkling discontent amongst the high nobles, which Isabella is just too happy to stir.

So, it is not surprising some nobles of the kingdom have been secretly plotting, with the support and incentive of Isabella, against the king. But Dom João knows to bid his time... He is not a man to vacillate or allow his power to be questioned, but he is also wise and deceitful. The talk of conspiracy has been going on for a while, but the King has been pretending to know nothing of it, waited to exchange his son for Isabella's daughter, reversing the safeguard agreed in 1478 to ensure both sides complied with the Alcaçobas treaty. And only then he marched to Évora.

There, by his own hands, he imprisoned Dom Fernando, the third Duque of Braganza, and then called 21 nobles to be juries in the judgement. Now it will become obvious on which side each of those 21 judges stand! The Duque was condemned and beheaded in the public square.

Meanwhile, Dom João of Braganza, Marquiz of Montemor [53] - Fernando's brother and my brother in law by marriage – run away to Castella. He was also condemned for plotting with his brother against the king. The King ordered a stone statue of the Marquis to be carved and then beheaded in the public square of Abrantes.

King João is strong and cunning. Legend has it that King Afonso V returned from a hunt in the summer of 1454 and entered the apartments of Queen Isabel, his first wife. There, he took her with such passion that he broke the emerald of her ring when he threw her on to the bed. Seeing that, the king exclaimed: 'Take it as a good omen, my Lady, and may it please our Lord that you will conceive a son that you will esteem more than all the emeralds in the world' [54]. King João II was born nine months later, in March 1455.

King João is opening the way to India, which will bring to this kingdom the most precious emeralds in the world, fulfilling his father's omen.

LISBON, FEBRUARY 2019

(Savanah's letter to uncle Santiago)

Dear Uncle,

Lisbon is a lovely city and I would be enjoying myself immensely, were it not for the discipline I have imposed myself on keep looking for what Raven might have uncovered here and make sense of the strange notes on her notebook.

I still can't quite put my finger on it, but I have this strange sense the notebook is not entirely random. Some of the drawings and sentences in there start looking familiar and somehow linked to what I've been reading, although this is still just a nebulous fog. And for some reason, I feel you know more than you told me over Christmas.

In any case, it seems you were right (as usual...☺). There are a lot of contradictions in Colon's life that could have lead Raven to suspect there was a hidden mystery or secret mission. I start to understand why Raven was fascinated about the subject and her obsession with Colon.

There is, of course, his cryptic signature, which we discussed. I must confess that for some time I didn't think much of it. I though Colon was just zesting with everyone or playing the intellectual, using a cabalistic signature to create an aura of mystery around him. The man was surely a great actor!

But after all the reading I have been doing, something

jumped to my attention: there are absolutely no written references to Colon or Columbus prior to 1487! The first reference to the Admiral appears in the log of payments of Pedro Diaz de Toledo, in 1487, who refers to him as "the Portuguese".

It's as if the man was a ghost, and suddenly materialized, conveniently with a complete biography to tell the world... as if this Colon had been conjured from the depths of the sea, like a triton, for a specific purpose – which that might be, I don't know.

There is a very detailed account of his life from 1487 onwards, since he arrived in Spain, with logbooks, letters written by and about him, official records... but absolutely nothing before that. This was a man who sat on the counsel of the king of Portugal, corresponded with known scientists, married a "fidalga" of royal lineage... but there is no record whatsoever before 1487. As if his previous existence until arriving in Spain had been wiped out... or entirely fabricated.

In 1500, he was arrested by Bobadilla in Hispaniola and sent back to Spain in shackles, accused of preparing a rebellion to establish his own kingdom. By this time, Vasco da Gama had already reached the true India and returned with the ship full of spices and precious stones, making it plain obvious Columbus had delivered to Spain a false India. And he killed, mistreated and committed unspeakable atrocities against his crew, including nobles... You would expect that, on arrival to Spain, he would be subject to trial and beheaded. But instead, the Queen sets him free, allows him to maintain his titles and rights and even approves a fourth expedition in 1502! He must have been a noble of very high lineage to get away with all this...

Colon supposedly ran from Portugal after the conspiracy to kill Dom João II, persecuted by the Portuguese and fearing for his life. The arm of Dom Joao II reached wide and he had a long memory: other conspirators who fled the kingdom seeking refuge elsewhere ended killed or jailed. Dom Lopo de Albuquerque, Colon's nephew, was imprisoned in 1488 in the Tower of London, at the request of Dom João II. Another traitor of the 1484 conspiracy, Fernão da Silveira, was killed in France by Portuguese agents. Other plotters of the 1484 conspiracy were relentlessly persecuted by Dom João II, imprisoned or killed. But not Columbus!

Instead, the King – who supposedly was his sworn enemy – continued protecting and receiving him like a friend. Colon visited Portugal at least 5 times after he fled the country accused of conspiracy, and all these times he was received as a loyal friend at the service of the Portuguese crown.

Even after 7 tiring years trying to convince the Spanish monarchs, and despite having letters from England and France to back his expedition, still Colon stubbornly insisted that the great expedition was reserved only for the Spanish kings. Why was it so important to take the Spanish to look west?

To finance his expedition, Luis de Santangél contributed with a loan on behalf of the Spanish Queen, but Colon agreed to invest from his own money half a million maravedis! This from the poor and uneducated child of a poor family of Genoese wool weavers!

The signs of the special friendship and mutual respect between Colon and King Joao II are plenty. The King sent him the Tables of Solar Declination, a valuable scientific tool for navigation, just before Colon's departure for the first expedition in 1492.

In March 1488, as King Joao II was waiting for the return of Bartolomeu Dias from his expedition to round the Cape of Good Hope and pave the way to India, the King writes a most intriguing letter that contradicts the fable of the Italian who ran away from Portugal persecuted for treason. This letter, currently in the Archive of the Indies in Seville, is not an indirect source written by someone else based on "hear say", but a letter signed by El-Rey himself. The King addressed the letter to "Xpovam Colon, our special friend in Seville". How amazing! In the letter, the King addresses Colon in a respectful and friendly manner and clearly states that Colon is "in our service", ie, Colon was in the service of the Portuguese crown. It further states that the King has matters to which the "industrious efforts and ingenuity" of Colon are necessary, and for his services he shall be rewarded "to Colon's contentment". You must wonder why was Colon still being paid by the Portuguese crown, being at its service, four years after fleeing the country accused of treason.

This letter is the ultimate proof of the special bonds between King Dom João II and his special agent Colon, a valuable ally and not a traitor as the traditional theory holds. This makes a strong argument to defend that the treason that led Colon to flee to Spain and his hate against Dom João II were simply a simulation to deceive the Spanish and allow Colon to infiltrate.

Astonishingly, after Dias's return, the India Project mysteriously stopped! Dias expedition was one of the most significant journeys in the history of the discoveries, a turning point sought for decades, immortalized in Camões epic poem as the symbolic victory over Adamastor, a giant who commanded formidable forces of nature to keep humans away from the domains of the gods… but it went ostensibly ignored, just marginal notes on maps and fleeting references in the chronicles of the time. The silence from the Portuguese about Dias success is deafening!!

After decades of a resilient and constant effort to push down the coast of Africa, year after year in a persistent effort to find the passage into the Indic ocean, when Dias finally paves the way for the ultimate prize – the route to India – suddenly everything stops! You would expect that, being a stone throw away from the final goal, the King would immediately launch another expedition to complete the journey. But instead, suddenly, the expeditions stop, for almost ten years, between 1488 (Dias return) and 1497 (Gama departure to India). Even Brazil, which multiple evidence suggests was known by the Portuguese since at least 1488, had to wait until 1500 to be (re)discovered. Dom João was waiting... waiting for Colon to finally convince the Spanish kings, (re)discover the Antilles, offer them to the Spanish monarchs as the Indies, leading them to wish for a new Treaty: The Tordesillas Treaty, brokered by the Spanish Alexandre VI, dividing the globe between Spain (west) and Portugal (East). Tordesillas finally protected the Portuguese eastern route to India, while reserving for the Portuguese a large chunk of the south-western Atlantic (Vera Cruz, now Brazil) and north-western Atlantic (Thule, now Greenland), thus closing a potential northern and southern western passage around America to the true India. King Dom João II and his "special friend in Seville" played masterfully this political game. Like in a chess game, they executed a "queen's gambit", sacrificing a piece (America) in order to win the main game (the trade of spices, silk and precious stones with the East).

In fact, contrary to all the Portuguese expeditions previously that had been kept under an iron Rule of Silence, Colon's success was publicized to the four winds and spread throughout Europe. The news was communicated in the famous letter to Luis de Santangél, written by Colon in Lisbon where he went to meet King João on his return journey, before he even sat foot in Spain. This propaganda letter was so quickly disseminated that less than a month later there were already 11 editions published in Spain, Italy, France, Switzerland, Holland... The same king who had kept Dias achievement in silence, now spread the news of Colon discovery to the world – making the discovery of India by Colon a "fait accompli" and cornering the Spanish into accepting the success of the expedition, despite the little Colon had to offer as proof of the riches he supposedly had discovered.

Is it possible that the Portuguese king, aware the country was too small and could not defend by military force such a vast empire, consciously abdicated of the western continent (at the time little populated and with little evidence of gold or spices), to protect what he perceived as more valuable trade routes to the far east?

It's quite revealing that Colon's first port of landing after returning from his first voyage was Lisbon. He wrote to Isabella and Fernando claiming that when he was already approaching the shores of Castella, a powerful southeast wind pounded the fleet so hard they were pushed north and had to seek refuge in Lisbon. A fantasy! From is personal sailing log, it is quite obvious when he left the Azores islands he set a straight route to Lisbon, keeping east, and correcting to that route when contrarian winds stirred them away. He intended to go to Lisbon and nowhere else! On their arrival, the Nina anchored next to the war vessel São Cristovão. Based on the ship diaries, the captain of São Cristovão, instead of arresting a wanted traitor, came onboard with a music band to celebrate Colon's arrival. He spent two weeks in Portugal, conferring with the King in Vale do Paraíso and then visiting the Queen before returning to Lisbon.

The level of deceit in this first expedition was well prepared by all counts. While in Hispaniola during the first expedition, a Portuguese sailor, who sailed in the ship captained by Martin Alonso Pinzon, came to his captain to give him a few sticks of cinnamon. The sailor claimed that as he roamed the island hunting he came across a native who carried a large bunch of the valuable spice. Well, that was probably the first and last cinnamon found in the Caribbean islands and surely it had been taken in secret by Columbus, or his associates. They knew beforehand what they would (not) find and prepared for it.

The claims that Colon was often lost at sea, could not use navigation instruments or grossly underestimated the size of the globe are also unsustainable. Sometimes, Colon seems to be totally lost regarding location at sea and measurements – but only when that serves his purposes! When trying to convince the Spanish court to support his voyage, he uses a measure of the degree at the equator of 56,66 miles, underestimating the true size of the equatorial circumference by 20%. But the calculations on his personal logbook demonstrate he had a pretty good idea of the globe's true size, erring by only ~5%. And during the moon eclipse in Saone, an islet on the eastern tip of Hispaniola, he wrote in his personal diary an estimate of 5h (just 83º) west of Cape Saint Vincent in Portugal, whereas India was 15h (225º) west! Colon knew perfectly well he was still more than 140º from the true India! Despite recording on his personal logbooks the correct 5 hours' longitude difference from Cape Saint Vincent to Hispaniola, he changed to 10 hours in the letter he wrote to the Pope. The impunity of such blatant lie to the Pope can only indicate the extent of Colon's deceit and his contempt for the church of Rome, despite all the courtesies.

Colon looks like a child unable to use basic navigational tools – there is an episode described in the log books where he measures latitude in the island of Cuba and says to his pilot they are 42º North, which is a gross error (Cuba is at 21º). He then shakes the Quadrant as if it was broken and casts it aside. As if shaking an instrument which is basically a 90º quarter circle with a pending plumb line would cause malfunctioning! He was just confounding his pilots about their true location. In fact, in his personal ship logs, he measures location and distances with extreme accuracy.

There are plenty of other examples... Colon writes to the Kings claiming to be in Canary Islands when his personal log book shows he was in the Azores. In his third voyage, Colon takes an unusual detour to Madeira island, writing to the Spanish kings that the detour was caused by the threat of a French pirate, whereas the logbook shows the pirate fleet was nowhere near their route.

The Portuguese and Colon knew already there was a massive continent west of the Azores, but Colon stuck with the islands, always clearing away from Terra Firma! Only on his third expedition did he go to "Terra Firma". Why? On 24 April 1498, King Manuel I of Portugal, having married the Spanish princess, is sworn the heir of the Castella y Leon throne, in Toledo. A month later, 30 May, Colon departs to his third expedition. After five years entertaining the Spanish monarchs island hoping in the Caribbean, he finally decides to explore the continent, when it was expected Castella would be ruled by the Portuguese king.

Another telltale fact is that the three Italian brothers (Christopher, Bartolomé and Diego) never wrote between themselves in Italian, but in Spanish or Latin! The letters written by Colon to the Italian cosmographer Toscanelli, to his Italian friend at Las Cuevas Monastery Friar Gaspar Gorricio and to the Genoese Bank of Saint George, were written in Spanish or in Latin, never in Italian. All his letters and documents, even the exhaustive side notes he used to make on his books, are in Spanish or Latin. And writings in Spanish are laden with 'portuguesismos', the Spanish-like adaptation of Portuguese words, as if the Admiral, when at a loss for the appropriate Spanish word, fell back to his original Portuguese native tongue [55]. On the very few instances he tries to write in Italian, he shows a total ineptitude, not even able to use the write form of "I": he uses the Spanish "Yo" instead of the Italian "Io".

Colon and the powerful people around him never wanted his true origins and mission to be known to the world! At least this surely is consensual. His son Fernando Colon writes these blatant words in his "Historia del Almirante": "He wanted to be unknown and uncertain his origin and homeland".

Raven lists many of these contradictions and deceptions in her notebook, which Professor Noronha affectionately calls the "Little book of lies".

Despite finding all this quite interesting, I have so far failed to understand what took Raven to start going into conspiracy theories and a secret mission that somehow involves the Templars, coded cyphers and Saunière. Gosh! In the summer of 2006 the Da Vinci Code movie was making the headlines... did Tom Hanks and all that Priory of Sion stuff fill Raven's mind with a sudden esoteric craze?

The human brain, as you know, sees patterns everywhere – that is a huge evolutionary advantage, as it allows split-second decisions based on incomplete information. We automatically categorize and generalize groups based on specific characteristics. That's a way of coping with reality and the overload of information. The flipside is that we tend to stereotype and find spurious connections everywhere.

Also, common sense throws away the details that do not fit in the global image, in order to speed up the thought process. That was very efficient when our primate brains needed to decide in nanoseconds to "fight or flee" a lion in the African plains. Better take an imperfect decision fast and survive, than the perfect decision and die. The brain is a "probability machine" that instantly computes all the complex calculations and physics needed to hit a moving tennis ball or simply to get a spoonful of soup into your mouth, even if sometimes you hit the net or spill the soup.

This means we naturally overlook some facts and instinctively invent others in order to "smooth out the wrinkles" of reality, fitting the world into our preconceptions.

So, I don't want to entertain wild conspiracy theories. But one thing has been nagging me, and I would not be at rest if I didn't mention this to you. I found a Freemason square and compass carved at the entrance stone in Professor Noronha house. This is just... but you know the symbol forms a pentagram. I cannot stop wondering about the pentagram cuts on Raven's wrist and whether something really obscure and nasty may have happened. Raven may have touched on deep secrets some people could go to great lengths to keep hidden. I am probably just seeing ghosts here. But I thought I should let you know. I would like to hear your opinion on this.

Huge kisses

S.

PS: I am going to write a similar letter to mum and dad but omitting the last paragraphs. Please don't mention it to them, no need to get them to dwell on these speculations.

LISBON, FEBRUARY 2019

After her morning run, Savanah took a long shower and sat on the attic balcony with a comfy sweater. She took Raven's notebook but in the end cast it aside, spending a nice couple of hours reading the latest João Tordo novel, a Portuguese writer she had recently discovered and quite enjoyed.

As Savanah was leaving her rented room at quarter past twelve on Saturday to head to Duma's house, she did a double take and on a sudden decision grabbed Raven's notebook and put it in her handbag.

Lunch had been quite fun. Savanah found the chicken muamba a bit too heavy, but Sergio literally gorged on it, methodically making its way through three helpings. Duma made a bit of a fuss about showing off to the American girl some Portuguese language music, going from Angolan Kizomba to Cape Verde Mornas to Portuguese Fado and inevitably to Brazilian Samba and Funk. Lunch had ended up with a hilarious demonstration by Duma, a plump 60-year-old short woman, of Kizomba dancing. Sergio joined happily but Savanah refrained from it, a bit self-conscious of the sexy Latin rhythms.

"Come on, Savanah", Duma pushed her, while dancing joyfully. "I used to take your sister to clubs to dance. She loved the Kizomba and the Funk, shaking her body as if possessed by a wild demon. Quite easy, just shake your goodies!"

Savanah though she would never be able to shake her bum and breasts like that. At least not without some heavy psychedelics. You need to have a certain at ease with your body that she lacked.

She enjoyed the Morna but found the Kizomba and Funk dancing a bit sexist, the women displaying her "goodies" out for the men. A simpler world, really, where the animal spirit could reign free, the male peacock displaying his feathers as a show of his genetic material and the females competing for the best sex partner. No bullshit. The feathers nowadays were the number of zeros on the Swiss bank account and the goodies touched up with silicone, but we are not that far away from the same basic animal instincts as the peacock and peahen.

Finally, they all sat down, panting.

Duma patted Savanah's leg as she got up, saying "Raven was so full of energy and life! She loved all types of music and dance. She was into a rock band, used to play Fridays and Saturdays on a rock bar, called The Goat if I remember correctly."

"Yeah, I know... She had a band at high school as well. Bit of heavy stuff, not my type. 'Every day I count wasted in which there has been no dancing' – she used to quote Nietzsche when mum pressed her to stay home and study."

Duma headed for the kitchen to make a pot of strong coffee, while Sergio moved the music to some cool Brazilian Bossa Nova on his Spotify. Carlos Jobin was streaming from his iPhone, filling the room with cool jazzy tones overimposed by Latin warm rhythms. Everyone knows this one, "The Girl from Ipanema".

As Duma fussed around in the small kitchen to get the coffee ready, Sergio noted how a countries music reflects the national soul: "Have you listened to Fado? Give me a break, the Portuguese traditional music mirrors the national 'coitadinho' mind set. You know, a person doomed by its faith, a tragic conception the Portuguese have of themselves, a lost empire that left little behind except the ´saudade´, that nostalgic feeling of longing for happier times that will never return. Come off it! We Brazilians are blessed by rich natural resources, football wizards, lousy and corrupt politicians and a happy samba-dancing people."

Duma came into the room with coffee and the inevitable custard pies, the "pastéis de Belém". Does everything in this country circle around food and football? Salazar, the country fascist dictator until 1968, had put it quite right: Football, Fado and Fatima. Fatima being a reference to Our Lady of Fatima and the conservative religious customs of the country. As religion dwindled and fado came out of fashion, this was being replaced, at least amongst the young and hipster, by Football, Food and Fuck.

Anyway… coffee was being served and a lovely aroma filled the room.

"It's a pity I don't have the pure Robusta beans from Professor Noronha plantation in Kwanza. In my childhood, mother used to roast the beans on an open fire pit, then grinded them fresh to make the loveliest coffee in the world", Duma stated with a barely disguised longing for a world long gone.

"Does Professor Noronha still own the family business in Angola?", Savanah asked, more out of politeness than real interest.

"Oh, no", Duma replied matter of factly. "They lost everything after the independence. The family fled the country with nothing but the clothes they were wearing. Professor Noronha did quite well, getting a teaching position at the university of Lisbon. But most 'retornados' came back and had to start all over again".

The country is, in a way, still coming to terms with the end of the empire, living in the shadows of its former self. Duma recalled an evening Raven had come for dinner and her son, after asking about her job, said in a cool superior tone that Portugal's prime time had passed and now this was just a small country of small people with small minds, lucky enough to be in Europe and surviving from selling sun and port wine to the tourists. "Gosh, Raven response was ice cold...", said Duma. "She told him off. 'Cynicism is easy, the best excuse to do nothing', she said".

The Bossa Nova cool swing filled the room as they sat, sipping the coffee in silence. Then Sergio picked himself up, saying "ok, ladies. As I said, I do have something to discuss with Savanah here". He moved from the sofa to fetch a bag he had left in the entry hall, producing a wrapped package, which he offered to Savanah. She opened it to find a copy of an enormous book by Mascarenhas Barreto, entitled "The Portuguese Columbus".

"What I have meaning to say, Savanah, is... well, it occurred to me a few days ago. I thing Professor Twilight is just wasting your time."

"What do you mean?", answered Savanah, politely flipping through the book and thinking "just what I needed, two guys competing to drown me in literature".

"Look. I know for you this whole thesis of the Portuguese Columbus may look like a novelty", Sergio continued. "Professor Twilight has been keeping you busy with a mountain of source books to make you go through the motions of uncovering what you would think is a secret plot by the Portuguese king and Columbus to trick the Spanish away from route to the Indies, blah blah blah. The fact is... that is old news, really. This book was published in 1999. It will take you a solid week's reading but gets you up to speed with all that. Trust me, the vampire is just taking you for a run."

"Ok, but that is what my sister was researching back in 2006, right?", asked Savanah, unfazed.

"Actually, not quite, dear", interjected Duma in a quiet

whisper. "I guess Sergio has a point. Raven was on to something... much bigger. This Portuguese Columbus theory and his links to the Templars were her starting point, not the subject of her research. Based on all the contradictions and forgeries uncovered since the turn of the century, Raven wanted to take the next step. Her starting point was that a much bigger mystery ought to be at play to justify 500 years of cover up."

At some point, Raven came across the meaning of the enigmatic scrolls discovered by Saunière at the Church of Mary Magdalene in Rennes-le-Chateaux, a small French village in the Pyrenees, at the end of the nineteenth century. The earlier scroll dates from the thirteenth century and refers to a Templar treasure hidden in the Pyrenees. Raven linked this all up and came up with the hypothesis of a secret Templar treasure taken west from Jerusalem to the Pyrenees and Colon's mission to hide such treasure further west, in a new Promised Land: Avalon... America.

"But I guess she went too far. Maybe her ideas could be... dangerous. So, Professor Noronha ordered Raven to stop researching on her ideas", noted Duma.

"Professor Noronha ordered her to stop digging?", asked Savanah, thinking about the Freemason symbol on the Professor's entry door and pondering if he could actually have been perpetuating the cover up of a supposedly dangerous secret.

"Right. But she didn't. She was very smart and energetic. In the end, she apparently found 'the missing link' about Columbus, that justified why kings and popes have for so long hidden Colon's true identity and mission. She told me about a Polish book she had found and would be the final revelation, but she was still working on its translation... and then she died. I never knew what this 'final revelation' was."

"Then Professor Noronha retired.", continued Duma.

"I found it strange at the time, because the university was his life. But I think in the end it was Pedro who forced Noronha to abandon everything." Duma's voice trailed off. "Some more coffee?"

"What do you mean, Pedro forced him to abandon what?". Savanah did not want to let this comment go un-noticed, prodding Duma to continue. The morning bright blue sky was turning grey and a winter storm seemed to be forming. She should have brought an umbrella.

"Well... Pedro was quite shaken by Raven's death. In a way, he considered Noronha responsible. He though those conspiracy theories had in some way put Raven in danger.", Duma confided, putting her coffee cup down on the table. "I don't want complications. But the day after Raven was found death, I witnessed a discussion between Professor Noronha and Pedro. The walls are not thick enough, you know, and I could hear them yelling. Noronha was saying 'How dare you? Get out of my office, I don't want to hear from you again'. I couldn't hear Pedro's answer. He was keeping his voice down. But as I entered the room to say my goodbyes for the day, I could see Professor Noronha was wildly upset, like a madman, his usually kind eyes set with blood. Pedro left the room shortly after, saying as he trailed off 'Think about the proposal. It is for the greater good'. At the time, I expected Pedro to be fired or something. But to my surprise, Pedro was promoted from Assistant Professor to Associate Professor and quickly reached his Aggregation. This was like 3 or 4 years ago, so he should be 39 or 40 max, a rather young age to reach Aggregation. Pedro had a very quick climb through the academic ladder after Professor Noronha left. And also..."

"Also...", Savanah prompted her, not wanting the conversation to tail off.

"Well, it is probably nothing, but shortly after

Pedro's promotion, Professor Noronha bough his mansion in Restelo and retired, leaving the department to the leadership of Professor Pedro."

There was an undeniable hint of accusation on Duma's voice and Savanah made a mental note to arrange an informal meeting with Professor Noronha to check how he had afforded his mansion in Restelo on a university teacher's salary.

Jobin's Bossa Nova had ended in Sergio's Spotify and an ominous silence descended upon the room.

Duma raised from her chair, silently, to clear the table and the coffee cups to the washing machine. Savanah followed her to the kitchen.

"Duma, I know this might be difficult", Savanah said, when they were alone in the small kitchen. "But I need to know. Is there anything suspicious you remember about my sister's research back then, before her death?"

Duma placed the dishes in the washing machine as if in auto pilot and stored the leftover of the muamba in the fridge. When they came back to the living room, Sergio was at the window, smoking.

"Savanah, it was a long time ago. Better leave it alone.", Duma said as she sat on the sofa next to Savanah. "I was quite fond of your sister and I respect Professor Noronha very much, despite, erhhhh... what his son did to me. Raven was a bright imaginative young mind. I remember her and Professor Noronha seating on his office with closed doors, which was uncommon for Professor Noronha. For ages after Raven's assassination, I searched my brain trying to locate some hints of what could have happened, but they were quite secretive, so I didn't listen or see much. There is this recurrent image that still comes to my mind sometimes, of them stop talking after realizing I had entered the room with some tea. Raven seemed agitated. From what I overheard, they were talking gibberish, really, I could never make any sense of it. Something about 'Rome's secret was hidden by the Templars in the Love Chapel of Tomar´. It's nonsense, right? Maybe it is just my silly mind playing tricks."

Sergio had stopped mid-breath and smoke caught in his throat. He started coughing in fists. "What...what did..." Sergio was coughing and trying to speak at the same time, while gasping for air and trying to clear the smoke that had gone down the wrong path on his throat. His eyes were glared with tears. "Sorry, Duma... erhhhh... what did you say?"

"Calm down, Sergio. I was just telling Savanah about a conversation I overheard between Raven and Professor Noronha, days before her death, something nonsensical about a Love Chapel in Tomar", Duma explained.

"you mean, Capela do Amor in Tomar?", Sergio asked, after regaining his breath and drinking some water. "That's the Portuguese translation for 'Love Chapel'."

"Well, what of it?", Savanah asked, confused.

"Oh... quite a lot, actually. AMOR is ROMA spelled backwards. ROMA means Rome and symbolizes the Catholic church, the vast hierarchy of cardinals and bishops that swayed immense power in the spiritual and political life of the Middle Ages. The Fedeli d'Amore, meaning Faithful to Love or Unfaithful to Rome, was an intellectual community that rejected this absolute power of Rome. A brotherhood whose best known member is Dante Alighieri. Supposedly, the Portuguese king Don Dinis, who harboured the Templars after their extinction, was also a member of the Fedeli d'Amore. AMOR means to "turn Rome around", reform the church. Much like Bernard of Clairvaux, founder of the Templars, also intended."

Savanah got closer. "You are saying Raven meant this

Capela do Amor, an anti-Rome chapel in Tomar, where a 'Rome's secret' was hidden?"

"I guess. It's possible" Sergio continued. "You know, those were turbulent times. The change was not painless, and the Church fought back fiercely to keep its power. So, these reformist movements were, at the beginning, veiled, restricted to a community of insiders."

Sergio sat down at the table and grabbed a pencil, writing on the back page of the book he had just offered to Savanah. He pencilled down

LOVE CHAPPEL: CAPELA DO AMOR (Anti-Rome Chapel)

TOMAR: ROMA TEMPLARIA (New Templar Rome)

"But there is more. If you move the T and R in TOMAR, you get ROMA T" Sergio concluded, looking at Savanah. As she blinked back vacantly, he pressed on.

"Roma Templaria, a "new" Rome under the Templar principles. The Templars set their headquarters in Tomar, the "new" Rome, as if they planned to replace Rome's world order by a new Templar order."

"Actually", added Duma excitedly, "What Raven and Professor Noronha talked about was 'Rome's Treason' hidden in the Love Chapel in Tomar. ROMA T could mean Rome's Treason. God, I really thought they were just talking gibberish".

"Well...", Savanah added a bit discouraged after an instant of silence. "It seems we now only have to find out what this ´Love Chapel´ is..."

"Right", responded Sergio. "I have visited and studied Tomar and never heard of a Love Chapel. Raven could be using a codename."

"Tomar is a charming city near Santarém", Sergio continued, trying to recall what he knew about the Templar city. "The charola of the Covent of Tomar has a circular shape, a rather unusual design in Europe, probably inspired on the mother church built by Emperor Constantino over the Holy Sepulchre in Jerusalem. Legend has it that the Templar Knights entered the temple church charola on horseback. The Grand Master of the Order, Dom Gualdim Pais, started the construction of the Castle and Convent of Tomar in 1160. Shortly after the Templars were forced to flee Jerusalem when it was reconquered by Saladin in 1187."

"Convento de Cristo has so many intriguing features and esoteric references", said Sergio, thinking out loud more to himself than to the others "a Love Chapel could refer to the winery, the large vaulted space which is said to have been the place of the Templars initiation rites. On its ceilings are feminine symbols related to the cult of the Holy Mother, roses and shells of Santiago. There is a hidden tunnel that goes from this winery directly into the Seven Hills Forest. There are seven stairs that ascend from this room, and these stairs are out of proportion: the height of each stair increases as you ascend, as if symbolizing the increasing demands of reaching the upper mysteries of the Order. Another possibility is the round church charola with paintings depicting the Passion and Resurrection of Christ. Or..." Sergio held his breath, gathering his thoughts.

"Oh, Gosh, the Love Chapel!" Sergio got up excitedly, tapping furiously on his iPhone. "I just remembered. It is highly symbolic. There is this little room on the Church of St John the Baptist in Tomar, at the left of the main door. The baptistery, it is not usually open to the public but I managed to convince the sacristan to let me take a look, thanks to my academic credentials. It is a quite simple room, but I remember a very delicate tryptic painting in the baptistery, depicting three scenes of the life of Christ – the Baptism of Christ, at the central panel; the Temptation by the Devil on the right side; and the Wedding of Canaan on the left side. I remember looking it up afterwards. As it were, the tryptic was lost or hidden for centuries and only rediscovered in the early 20ᵗʰ century, when a heavily damaged painting was being prepared for restauration. Wait, let me check... here it is. Professor Luciano Freire, also nicknamed "the Invisible Painter", worked on the restauration. As he was pulling out the painting, he noticed that hidden behind the painting, there was another one. The central piece of the tryptic was discovered in the main altar. Look here, there is a photo on this blog of the tryptic after restauration."

"So, you are suggesting this could be the Love Chapel?", concluded Savanah, impressed. "Could be, I mean: the angelical and pure nature of true love symbolized by the baptism, the carnal sexual temptations represented by the devil and the socially accepted institutionalization of love through marriage. I've seen worse definitions of Love. Maybe Raven went to Tomar, on the eve of her assassination, looking for this secret or treasure she believed might be hidden there."

Then she added, almost as an afterthought "Could this Canaan Wedding actually be Christ's wedding?"

"Oh, Savanah... five hundred years ago you would have burnt at the fires of the Inquisition for that thought", said Duma.

LISBON, FEBRUARY 2019

"We are blind, Blind but seeing, Blind people who can see,
but do not see"
JOSÉ SARAMAGO, BLINDNESS

Duma insisted on driving Savanah home at the end of their meeting. It was already dark, a clouded, moonless winter night. As they parked in the narrow street in Lapa near Savanah's building, Duma turned to Savanah, in a concerned voice:

"Savanah, there is something else I didn't mention... When Sergio talked about that master who restored the tryptic, the "Invisible Painter"?... Well, I remembered something Raven said that didn't make much sense at the time. I now realize might mean something... Raven was quite intrigued by three paintings she discovered during her research. I didn't relate it until this afternoon. I had lent her a book from my favourite writer, José Saramago, Blindness... She returned it to me a couple of weeks later. In the first page she had stick a post-it with a message: "The Invisible Painter. The Invisible Book. The Invisible Crown. Will we ever see or forever be blinded?"

"Hummm, and what do you think it means?"

"Not sure, really. I recall Raven asking me to accompany her on a visit to what she called 'The house of the Invisible Painter', because she might need some help with translation. She was always a bit cryptic, so I didn't ask. Anyway, we went to this house in Oeiras, a nice old house with two huge Camellia trees in the front. A middle aged woman received us, quite nice and welcoming. We had tea and biscuits together. Raven asked several questions about a painting of the Canaan Wedding and a part of the original painting that had been covered up. Apparently, Raven had discovered an obscure biography of the 'Invisible Painter' hinting he had been forced to cover up part of the original painting. At the time the restauration was concluded in 1930, Portugal was ruled by Salazar's Estado Novo and the fascist censorship was starting to force its grip on journalists, artists, you know... the usual. The woman, who I gathered was a granddaughter of the restorer, seemed oblivious to the entire thing. Even a bit annoyed at the suggestion that her grandfather had covered up part of the original painting."

"The extraordinary thing happened as we were leaving. An old lady, who had spent the entire time in silence in a sofa at the corner of the room, staring into nothingness, said out of the blue: 'Blindness is a blessing. A blind person can see beyond what they want you to see'. Our host smiled dryly as she opened the door of the living room, making it clear the conversation was over. She whispered something in a low voice, so that the old blind woman couldn't listen: 'Don't mind her, my mother lives in her own fantasy world. Poor silly old woman'."

"But Raven turned back and asked, in a very rough Portuguese 'Are you Luciano Freire's daughter? What can you see that we don't?' The old lady stared at her empty world and said something remarkable: 'Blind people can't see, so we are the memory of the world. They forced my father to do it. He became consumed by angst, never painted again. Started calling himself 'The Invisible Painter'. At the back of the Canaan Wedding, on the base of the St John Baptist image that had been turned back and hidden for centuries, there was an inscription: 'Protect the Queen and the Book of Canaan'."

Duma looked at Savanah expectantly. After a short dense silence, Savanah said: "It can only mean one thing... the Queen of the Canaan Wedding can only be Christ's bride. But what is the Book of Canaan?"

"It made no sense to me, but Raven got very excited.", acknowledged Duma. "We returned to the office and Raven showed me copies of two other paintings."

Duma looked up on the web and showed Savanah an image of a painting now at the Religious Art Museum of Funchal. It was originally at the chapel constructed by Henrique Alemão, and depicted a noble, richly dressed man with his wife, Senhorinha Anes. Despite the rich clothing and pearls, the man in the painting also carries a pilgrim's pouch.

Savanah knew the theory about Henrique Alemão as Colon's father, but failed to see the link with the Canaan painting in Tomar. Then Duma enlarged a part of the image on the screen, the pilgrim pouch.

"A pilgrim pouch ought to be rounded at the bottom, from the weight of its contents, coins, shells and stuff, and its neck closed by the strings. But in this case..."

"...it's flimsy at the corners but with a bulging square in the middle", completed Savanah, "as if it contains... a book!"

"The Invisible Book", concluded Duma.

Then Duma moved to another painting on her screen, The Virgin of Navigators, painted in the early 16th century and exposed in the Seville Cathedral where the tomb of Columbus is. Duma pressed Savanah's attention to the robes of Columbus, a gold coloured intricate embroidery with patterns of pomegranate trios. Duma enlarged the sleeve of Columbus arm, and Savanah gasped...

"A crown!"

"The Invisible Crown".

The Invisible Painter. The Invisible Book. The Invisible Crown.

This started to look like an entangled ball of thread without ends. Every time Savanah though she had found a threat, several others appeared.

RETURN FROM CONGO, DECEMBER 1483

(Columbus)

My friend Diogo Cão returned from his expedition. He reached river Congo [x], planted two stone pillars topped with a cross to claim the newfound lands and climbed 150km upriver until the Yellala falls. The memorial Cão left engraved in the stones on the riverbanks of the Yellala falls is the most poignant mark of his sense of mission and a proof of endurance and outright stubbornness. Cão was only stopped by the unsurpassable falls and unable to proceed inland due to the hostility of the local populations. To get there, the fleet had to sail or row upstream passing swamps and dense forests, facing an increasingly ferocious current until they reached the falls, a thunderous torrent of water born at the heart of the wild continent.

The intention was to test the old Arab maps that show wide rivers crossing Africa, linking the Atlantic to the Nile and the Indian Ocean, while at the same time try to find the mythic kingdom of Prester João, a Christian King in the east (supposedly Ethiopia), in the backs of the Moors, who could join the European kingdoms against the Arabs and Ottomans.

In any case, King João is increasingly confident of success and rewarded Cão an annual pension and elevation to nobility. He deserves it, no doubt. Of the four knights chosen in 1472 in Sagres, only I was a noble by birth right. Dias,

Cão and Covilhã all have humble origins, but by cunning, bravery and loyalty are now knights of the Order of Christ. I'm sure Dias and Covilhã will also achieve nobility titles. Covilhã is doing an extraordinary job as a diplomat and spy in Italy and Egypt. Dias will lead the next expedition and attempt the turning of Africa – if any man can do it, it's him.

Diogo Cão brings news that the coast of Africa starts bending eastwards, suggesting the Portuguese are close to finding the passage between the Atlantic and the Indic, which would disprove Ptolomeu, who assumed the Indic sea was closed.

"My dear friends", King João proclaims as the high council comes together to listen to Diogo Cão account, "again, I must insist with everyone to keep absolute secrecy about our discoveries, at the cost of our own life. We are a small country, with just 1 million souls. If we exclude women, elders and children, we are barely 250.000 men to protect the kingdom and our growing overseas empire. We cannot protect the kingdom or our foreign interests by force, so we must use cunning. The only way we can protect our interests down the coast of Africa and elsewhere is by keeping those routes secret. We must continue to feed our competitors with false maps and measurements, rumors of African cannibalism, legends of sea monsters, ships catching fire in the boiling waters near the Equator or falling into hell from a cliff. But that is not enough. Granada will soon fall and Isabella will turn her serpent's head towards the Atlantic. I will, soon enough, ask some of you, my friends, the ultimate sacrifice. When the time comes, do not judge me too harshly, I beg you..."

João looks at me and makes a barely perceptible nod. For too long I have been stranded inland, I am ready to go. However much the prospective of leaving Filipa and Diogo saddens me, I must become a man my son looks up to. To arrive, I must depart. I only exist through my deeds and only by departing and becoming do I gain the right to return and be. Only by becoming what I am meant to be, can I hope to finally achieve some peace for my restless soul...

LISBON, APRIL 1484

"The man of knowledge must be able not only to love his
enemies but also to hate his friends."
FRIEDRICH NIETZSCHE

The royal guard called at Alemão and Filipa´s home as the sun set over the ocean sea, reflecting silver droplets of light on the still waters of the Tagus river. Their young son was taken to his chambers by the servants, as the guards escorted Alemão to the dungeons of St Jorge Castle. There had been no fight. Other knights of the Order of Christ were also taken to the dungeons, including Alemão's friends Bartolomeu Dias and Diogo Cão.

It was surely a mistake. Still, Filipa grew nervous. These were uncertain times in Lisbon, as the plots against King João by factions of Portuguese nobility thickened. João had become king in 1481, after the death of his father Afonso. Since taking the crown, João had started concentrating power on himself and away from the aristocracy. The year before, in 1483, the clerk of the royal hunting palace in Vila Viçosa had delivered to the king correspondence from Fernando, duke of Bragança, to the Catholic monarchs of Spain, complaining against D. João and plotting to regain the throne for the house of Bragança [57]. The compromising correspondence was found hidden in the chimney of the fireplace in the chambers Dom Fernando kept in the palace. The new King himself arrested the Duke of Bragança, who was tried for 22 days in Évora by 21 judges. The vote took two days and ended with Fernando being sentenced to death.

Fernando, duke of Bragança, was publicly executed on June 20, 1483.

Alemão was locked in a cell, without knowing what was going on.

"What has happened? I am Alemão, a knight of the Order of Christ. Always served the king honorably. There must be a mistake. Let me speak to Dom Diogo, the master of the Order, and this misunderstanding shall all be explained."

"Save your breath, young man. Dom Diogo is in chains as well, he is no use to us." – This was the voice of an aged man, who sat at the darkest corner of the room with his head covered. "This is the doing of that usurper, João. The House of Aviz has indebted the kingdom with the folly of the maritime expeditions, neglected the true mission of a Christian king to fight the Moors in north Africa and is now clinging to power. But do not fear, the Spanish kings this time will not allow us to meet the same fate as befell Dom Fernando of Bragança last year. The plot is in motion and soon Dom Diogo will take the crown."

"Shut your filthy mouth! I served under Infante Henrique, navigated the north Atlantic on the service of Prince João. He is the most perfect prince this kingdom ever saw and with him, the mission started by the Order almost a century ago will finally be accomplished."

All night, the old man cursed against the King, mumbling at the corner of the cell or in shouting ramparts of rage. "The usurper intends to cast away all the Jews from Portugal to endear him with the Pope and save the wars with Spain. For the sake of the Conversos, he must be deposed."

"You lie. If they released me of these shackles, I would shut you up with my own hands.", answered Alemão, desperate for his own situation as much as for not knowing what conspiracies were going on in the Paço.

The entries to the Palace had all been closed. Early morning, King João summoned the Duke of Viseu, Dom Diogo, his cousin and brother of Queen Dona Leonor, as well as Grand Master of the Order of Christ. Dom Diogo and other prisoners were brought to the center of the crown room, heavy tapestries draping the windows and closing the room in ominous shadows. João raised himself, walked towards Diogo looking straight into his eyes, and stabbed him right there, in the middle of the room, in front of everyone. The Duke had conspired to kill the King on the beach in Setubal, as the sovereign returned to Lisbon. Advised of the plot, the King travelled by land, unmasking the conspiracy.

"Dom Manuel, come forth". The middle of the floor was dark red, a pool of blood in the naked stones, staining the robes of the King. Dom Manuel was one of the brothers of the deceased Dom Diogo, grandson of King Dom Duarte and cousin of King Dom João. "Dom Manuel, your brother plotted to kill me, but I trust you were not part of this conspiracy. I hereby ordain you as the Grand Master of the Order of Christ, to make right your brother's wrongs. The Houses of Viseu and Aviz should be united in this moment of our history, as our country becomes more powerful than our forefathers could ever imagine. To finally end the squabbles between our two Houses, I pledge, in front of all the nobles here present, that if by any ill-fate my son Prince Afonso dies before becoming King, you, Dom Manuel, shall be my heir as King of Portugal".

Of the several other men who stand in the middle of the room, imprisoned on last night cull, Dom João called several names, satisfied of their loyalty. The others were to be taken to their cells and wait trial. Filipa, standing on the front row of the group of noble ladies, felt her knees tremble. Where was Alemão? Why was he not here and what was happening to her husband?

Over the following weeks, more than 80 people were persecuted on suspicion of involvement in this conspiracy. Several were executed, murdered or fled to Castella.

LISBON, MAY 1484

Bartoloméu Dias had come, to convey the terrible news. Her husband stand accused of treason and would be executed on the public square in front of the Paço, together with several other traitors. Filipa had visited Alemão the previous evening, in the dungeons of the Castle of St Jorge. She was inconsolable, but Alemão seemed relaxed, accepting his fate.

"Never stop believing me, Filipa.", her husband said. "Whatever they say, whatever may the appearances seem to be, never stop believing me. I promise our pain will be overcome. Please, promise me that tomorrow you will not watch the execution. Go to those flower banks near the river we enjoy so much, on the road to Santarém. Look at the flowers and think how much I love you, always have and always will. We cannot argue against our fate, but willingly take it as further as we bear to endure."

The day raised calm, as if the terror was not about to abate over her life. She could not heed Alemão's request not to watch. How could she? The prisoners were taken to the public square, head shaven and in shackles. The gallows were set. The noise of the crowd was deafening, but Filipa's mind drifted away, into some state of numbness where nothing was real, just a foggy and messy blur of faces. Then she saw him.

Alemão was brought forward, tall and broad, his blue eyes downcast, torn clothes and shaven head, in shackles.

He was walking on bare feet, five toes on each foot. But...
this was not her husband! He did not have the mark. Some
trickery was at play! In a flash of realization, she darted out
of the square and run in a craze towards the eastern exit, by
the flower beds near the Tagus river banks on the road to
Santarém. My God, that man was so similar to her husband,
with a shaved head Alemão's fair blond hair was undistinguishable. How could she have been so stupid? Of course
Alemão was not involved in any conspiracy, his family had
the strongest of all bonds with the Aviz dynasty.

She arrived and stumbled, looking everywhere as if
possessed by a demon. The sound of a galloping horse came
up the dusty road. Covered with a hood over his head, the
knight stopped by her side just briefly and handed her a red
rose: the symbol of the wind rose of the sailors. Red as the
fiery sun of the south.

This was her husband!

LISBON, MAY 1484

In the course of just a few weeks, his life had changed dramatically. He had been arrested at the beginning of April and for weeks stand in the dungeons, accused of treason, not really knowing what intrigues were going on in the Palace. The old man in his cell almost drove him nuts, with his constant ramblings against King João and the Infante. Alemão was now on horseback, crossing the border to Spain near Ayamonte, on his way to Huelva. But he was no longer Segismundo Alemão. He no longer had red-bold hair. That brief instant in Santarém, saying goodbye to Filipa, had almost shattered his resolve... But he had to be strong. Honor and valor demanded this ultimate sacrifice.

More than a week after their imprisonment, the King, escorted by his guards, descended to the dungeons accompanied by an old man with baggy greyish eyes and white hair. The king summoned Dias, Covilhã and Cão, who had also been imprisoned the week before. They then entered the cell where Alemão was retained. The King took Alemão by the shoulders and helped him raise.

"My friends, you must forgive me for this treatment. But I had to be sure. Father Fernão Martins", he said, nodding to the white-haired old man, "has tested you to the limit. The four of you proved loyal beyond doubt. In these turbulent times, there are few people I can trust... but at least this ordeal has served to sift through the appearances and fakeness of the intriguers, allowing me to see more clearly who stands at my side. Alas, it is to the most loyal and brave I must ask for the highest sacrifices."

It was there, in the shadowy tiny cell, barren of all commodities worthy of the high deeds being planned, away from the luxury and hears of the court, that the grand plan that would culminate the Age of Discoveries was sketched by the King and his advisor Father Martins.

The war of succession in Castile had raged for four years after King Henrique IV death in 1474, but finally ended in 1479, with the victory of Isabella. The rightful heir of Henrique's throne would be his daughter, Joanna. But the Castilians were plotting against her. Shortly after Henrique's death, King Afonso of Portugal invaded Castile and married Joanna, his niece, vowing to protect her claim and betting on becoming king of a unified Portugal and Castile. The Spanish nobles schemed against that, saying Joanna was not Henrique's true daughter (the king was said to be impotent, despite several claims by Segovian prostitutes asserting the Kings virility), but a bastard fathered by Beltran de la Cueva. So, Joanna la Beltraneja claim was disputed, with another claimant put forward: Isabella, her half-aunt, supported by Aragon. The war had finished in 1479 and the kingdoms of Castile and Aragon were now joined through the marriage of Isabella and Fernando. The attentions of the now unified Spain would fall into Granada, the last Muslim State in Iberia for the past two centuries! The Emirate would soon fall.

Isabella and Fernando were ready to finish the Reconquista. Granada was crippled by internal disputes and economic decline, in an almost constant climate of succession struggles. Isabella and Fernando launched the campaign against Granada in 1482 and the city should soon fall [58]. Once that happens, the unified Spain would have no expansion alternative but to look to Africa and the Atlantic, putting at risk the Portuguese rule of the ocean.

So, the plan had to be put in motion without delay.

Diogo Cão had just returned from his explorations

in the coast of Africa, unable to cross the vast continent through a river route. The kingdom would sponsor another fleet to attempt again a river crossing of the continent, but the hopes the continent could be crossed by river were dim [59]. Cão is to return to Africa, continuing his push south [60] and taking with him the German cosmographer Martin Behaim, a faithful servant of King Dom João and member of the Junta dos Matemáticos. Behaim was erring on a much smaller size for the world, following Toscanelli theories, which would prove advantageous for the king's plot [61]. Behaim could still be of great use, completing the bait to entice the Spanish kings. However, Cão was not, under any circumstances, to make the Passage rounding Africa. Not with a German cosmographer aboard.

Three Portuguese spies [62] had recently been sent on a land expedition through Egypt and Ethiopia, to explore the eastern coast of Africa. Pero da Covilhã is to follow them, to familiarize himself with the manners and languages of the Moors. He would set out overland, disguised as an Arab merchant, to the east of Africa and Arabia, to find out and report on where could caravels be replenished and pilots found in the Indian ocean. The caravels, unlike the Mediterranean galleys or the large carracks, are small boats to improve tacking and speed, so they need to stop often to replenish water and food.

Bartolomeu Dias would follow Cão and push forward, resting only when a Passage around the south of Africa could be reached. But once the Passage had been found, he should not make it to India. For one, they needed the information Pêro da Covilhã would try to raise, in order to improve the odds of success in the Indian sea. Secondly, the final leg of the voyage would have to wait until the Portuguese rights in the Indian ocean were protected. For this, the King needed to lead the Spanish kings to revise the Alcáçobas Treaty. In order to achieve that, Portugal would need to put the Spanish on the route of something they would want to protect, away from the true India.

That final piece of the puzzle would lay on Alemão's shoulders.

"Of you, my noble and special friend, I must request the most demanding sacrifice. I am sorry to put such a task on your shoulders. But I know this is pivotal to protect the interests of Portugal. I will ask you to forfeit your life, wife and son, and become another man, whose proposals for a western route have been rejected by me, a cast away on the run accused of taking part on the conspiracy we just unmasked. This new man will take refuge in the Castella. There you will plot to take the Spanish monarchs towards the western route and deliver to them the Antilles, as if they were Castilian discoveries. We must do this so that they feel compelled to protect their dominions over the west Atlantic, thus demanding a new Treaty. We must protect the southern route and the Indian ocean from Spain – there is no way we can fight them in open war, so we must use deceit and cunning to make them want what we are willing to forfeit, while protecting what we truly want. Alas, if I was King of a large and populous country, I would risk taking claim to all these new lands. But as it is, we must make choices."

Alemão looked at his King, astonished.

"My Lord. I am ready to do as you ask. But will the Spanish fall for such a scheme? Surely their cartographers and cosmographers will never back up a plan to reach the Indies by a western route. That voyage is impossible. It would take much longer than any armada can sustain and the fleet would be decimated by sickness or famine. They have read Ptolomeu."

"Alemão, we know that. But the Spanish are anxious to step on our advances, they may be gullible enough to believe whatever they are fed, under the promises of riches and conquest. Isabella has pawned her own crown jewels to finance the succession war against her niece and now against Granada. She will be desperate for a miracle, and she is so pious she may well believe God has sent her a messenger to deliver that miracle. It is your job to confuse them and make them believe other kingdoms are ready to back your plan. That will make them at least mistrust old Ptolomeu, not wanting to risk missing an opportunity to beat us to India.", concluded the King.

Father Martins added "You will count with the support of influential people in the Spanish court, who are our agents or inclined to favor us against the excesses of Isabella and Fernando. Men of science, merchants, Jews, even some priests who mistrust the Catholic Kings. Their excessive proximity to Rome and extreme views have brought them many enemies."

"When you cross the border, ride swiftly to the Monastery of la Rabida in Palos. Frei João Peres, a Portuguese Franciscan, has long lived there. He has the confidence of Queen Isabella on astrological and scientific matters, so he will be a great help. When Frei João Peres took his vows, he took the name of the Saint Anthony. Since arriving in La Rabida, he has kept a villa in the small town of Marchena, near Seville, under cover of his parents living there. The congregation has thus taken to calling him Anthony of Marchena. Take care to use the name he uses in Spain, Frei Antonio Marchena."

Alemão was aghast with the perspective of abandoning Filipa and his son Diogo. But surely, they could take disguise and join him in Seville shortly after he established himself. And also... indeed, that was the opportunity to complete his task. That was the card King João was playing with him. That was why he had chosen him. While playing the farce to distract the Spanish monarchs on a wild goose chase westward, he would have the chance to complete the task his father and the Infante had encumbered him so many years ago. As Governor of the Antilles he would be able to establish a strong base from where to send exploratory expeditions looking for the heirs of Henry Sinclair. That was the path to finally take the Wind Rose, the treasure his family had been entrusted with, to the Rose Line.

"One last thing, Alemão", concluded the King, showing the conversation was over, "It is best that you keep a foreign identity. When Isabel and Fernando find out they have been ambushed into a fantasy, if they know you are Portuguese, there would be hell on earth and no way to avoid war between the two countries. They will surely suspect, but as long as there is no evidence, they will prefer to maintain the charade than recognize they were tricked."

Alemão looked sternly into the eyes of his King. That man was four years younger than him, but so well versed in the ways of men. In just one year, he had got rid of two threats, the House of Bragança and the House of Viseu: first by killing the plotters, then by playing to their interests. He now had a large noble house aligned with him, both by marriage with Dona Leonor and by the prospect of Dom Manuel becoming king.

Both men knew there was more at stake than just the words that had been spoken. "You honor me with such task, my king.", said Alemão, as the King left the dungeons.

Dias went to convey the terrible news to Filipa.

JAMAICA, JULY 1503

(Fernando)

"A batter'd, wreck'd old man, / Thrown on this savage shore, far, far from home, / Pent by the sea, and dark rebellious brows, twelve dreary months, / Sore, stiff with many toils, sicken'd, and night to death, / I take my way along the island's edge, / Venting a heavy heart..."
WALT WHITMAN, "PRAYER OF COLUMBUS", 1872

We languished, desperate and with no hope left, until we washed out in Jamaica on June 24, at a port named Puerto Bueno. We strained one more day eastwards along Jamaica's north coast, trying to locate a place with fresh water where we could land. We found deliverance on a shallow bay the Admiral called Santa Gloria. "Since we were no longer able to keep the ships afloat, we ran them ashore as far as we could, grounding them both close together and shoring them up on both sides."

The place was a marvel. I could smell and see ebony, rosewood, cedar wood, palm trees, coconut trees and many other trees not known in Europe. Chirping birds and colorful parrots flying around, playful and carefree. We were stranded in paradise.

Fearing the rogue manners of the sailors, desperate for food and women, would lead to another confrontation with local Indians, Father imposed strict rules – which many men considered tyrannical, but ensured at least for some time a peaceful co-existence with the Indians. We thus managed to settle into the stranded ships as our fortresses, trading water and food with the Indians for our colored beads, lace and hawk's bells. The Admiral justified his stern rules because "our people, being disrespectful by nature, no punishment or order could have stopped them from running about the country and into the Indian's huts to steal what they found and commit outrages to their wives and daughters, which would have caused disputes and quarrels that would make them our enemies."

We were stuck in the island. Our Caravels had suffered heavy damages and lied on their sides, like fish expelled by the sea and left to rot on the beach as the tide recedes, one frozen eye staring blankly at the sky and the other buried on the sand. There was no chance of escape or getting help.

What drove Father to push the ships so hard, relentlessly? He stubbornly refused to turn back or pause to repair the ships, until it was obvious the fleet could stand no more. He acted like a maniac, looking for the passage into the southern seas. But the way he kept going back and forth along those shores, apparently at random, tells me something else was going on. Father seemed to be looking for someone or something he believed should be there. Only the threat of mutiny forced Father to retreat, heading back to Hispaniola. We barely made it to Jamaica. The ships were beyond repair.

The men discussed how to proceed, the prevailing opinion being that our only hope was to fetch canoes from the Indians and try to reach Cuba or Hispaniola. Father looked dubious, continuing to look to the other side, towards west, collecting driftwood from the beach as if he was expecting some secret message from a lost tribe in the western lands. He seemed to be bidding his time, making us stay there longer than necessary. Surely, I thought, with a few strong canoes we could make the crossing to Hispaniola and call for rescue. But Father was dragging his feet, which was not at all like him.

The Admiral's authority was again at risk, and in fact we were living in two camps. The small group faithful to the Captain held the remains of La Capitana and Bermuda as our fortress, whereas most of the rowdier sailors had moved ashore. Despite Fathers' orders to maintain peace with the natives, the men were restless and had been robbing and raping in the villages. We faced a dangerous situation, as the natives had grown defensive and refused to trade or bring us food. This had been caused mainly by the acts of hostility to the Indians, but many sailors again blamed Father for the food shortage. The natives, on whom we depended for water and food, had run away into the forest and refused to help us.

Father spent his days writing in his logbook, describing in some detail our extraordinary voyage. He was probably thinking we would die in this forsaken paradise and wanted to leave his final legacy for posterity. And yet, he remained... duplicitous.

Even then, as we seemed near the end, Father continued to shows himself with multiple personas, varying his accounts depending on the recipient. I read the letter he wrote to the Spanish kings, which contained many true things, but one episode was notably omitted... our stop in Asilah, near Tangier, to fight the moors and rescue to Portuguese soldiers stranded there. It could have been just a lapse of memory, but the fact is his other letter to friar Gorriccio described that episode in some detail.

At the beginning of July, I could finally witness some action. Father and uncle Bartholomew were plotting something with Diego Mendéz. I could see them secretly talking in Father's cabin and strained my ears to try to understand what was going on.

"None of the men realize the peril we face", I heard Father confiding to the two friends. "We are too few, these savage Indians are too many, and their mood can change. One day, when the mood strikes them, they may come and burn us here in these two ships." At least they were planning to do something. Father was convincing Mendéz to make the crossing to Hispaniola with a canoe, and return with a ship to Jamaica to rescue us all. Bartholomew would in normal circumstances be the one to do the deed, keen as he always was to acts of heroism and bravery, but this time Father needed him to stay behind and protect the makeshift fortress. If uncle Bartholomew left, I guess the Indians would be the last of our concerns, as the other sailors would soon rebel and kill the Admiral.

Two canoes were equipped with a simple sail, keels for additional stability and some planks nailed to the prow and stern to prevent water coming inside. Still, they were no more than fragile nutshells. The canoes were set to depart, each taking six Spaniards and several Indian paddlers under the command of Diego Méndez. The crossing was demanding in a canoe, about 125 miles from Jamaica to Santo Domingo in Hispaniola, where Méndez could hope to get a ship to rescue us.

As Diego Mendez took his leave from us all, Father approached him and embraced the man with his wide, once strong arms. He looked deeply into Méndez eyes, who couldn't stand the deep penetrating eyes for long and turned his gaze down. Father then did something utterly unexpected... He took the chain with the silver bullet, his precious silver bullet, from his neck and placed it on Diego Méndez neck. "They will ask you for the proof.", I heard Father saying between gritted teeth, as he departed from his only remaining memory of Filipa.

Méndez departed at the beginning of July 1503.

How long would we have to wait until Diego Méndez

returned with help, assuming he would return at all? Idleness is for the mind the equivalent of woodworms for the ships... It corrodes from inside, a hidden threat always lurking and ready to attack the weakest. Morale degraded fast in that corner of paradise, as we waited for deliverance. Myself and Father found ourselves almost prisoners in our own cabin at the wreck of La Capitana. As we waited, I could witness Father's mental state deteriorating. He was anxious, with obsessive demons roaring inside his mind.

Seven months passed, which should have been time enough to make the crossing and return with ships. Méndez had probably failed. Meanwhile, the situation on the forsaken island was deteriorating dangerously.

The crew increasingly doubted the sanity of the Admiral and resented his rigid discipline, accusing him of devilish plans to avoid returning to Spain. On 2 January, 1504, a mutiny started, raised by the Porras brothers. Father had had good reason not to trust them, Francisco (the captain of La Bermuda) and his brother Diego (the crown's treasurer representative). About 50 men joined the insubordination and confiscated the canoes to attempt the crossing by themselves.

As they were 4 or 5 leagues out of the coast, contrary winds and high waves threatened to end the mutiny even faster than it had started. Terrified and trying to get rid of some excess weight, the deserters threw overboard the Indians they had taken as paddlers. They killed 18 in this dishonourable manner.

Three times the deserters made out to sea, but every time they were forced back by the elements, their own cowardice and lack of skills or leadership. The sea disgorged them, refusing to take the scum. For more than a month the deserters toiled in this fashion, establishing a makeshift base in an Indian village, stealing from the Indians. The atrocities they committed deeply aggravated the already sour state of relations between the Christians and the Indians.

JAMAICA, JANUARY 1504

(Columbus)

Forgive me God, if my thoughts are sinful. I have seen the true Book, what others call the forbidden Book. Why should truth be sinful? When I first realized the meaning of the treasure my father and the Old Man passed on to me, I too was confused. How not to be, when you realize the very core of our world is founded on a lie, kept hidden for centuries to preserve... to preserve what? Not You, really, only the church that lies in Your name to protect itself.

All creation myths are a rite of passage, men and women robbing the fire of knowledge from the divinity. Reaching out for our own divinity. Those who dare to seek beyond the darkness, driven by curiosity and progress, are always portrayed as castaways from paradise, ignoble creatures who confronted God and are punished by You. Prometheus was chained to a mountain and condemned to have his guts pecked everyday by birds, for robbing the fire of knowledge from the gods. Eve was cast away from paradise for tasting God's forbidden fruit of curiosity. Is knowledge a murdering of God? Ignorance is the shield of the old gods and knowledge an inevitable harbinger of those gods. So many crimes committed under Your name! Those who dare to seek knowledge are punished by You. No, not by you. By your church, as if You were playing and teasing us... why would You give men curiosity if not to prod and ask and move forward?

Is this what it is? We are stranded here, in this forsaken

islands, as a test to prove we are worth of receiving the fire of knowledge? This island is our hell, a passage we must struggle through in order to bring a new era for humanity. I will endure it, if that is what it takes, to end centuries of moral and intellectual slavery and free my mind, our minds, from the terrible lie!

I am not one, but many. My mind struggles between conflicting loyalties, multiple identities, opposing objectives.

But I have seen the true Book, and the truth is... liberating! The humanity of Christ and the divinity of Men breaks the false dogmas that have for too long imprisoned men's spirit, intellect and freedom. Once the shackles are broken, we will finally enter the Age of Enlightenment! Not without pain, not without pain, because the old gods and their churches will try to hold on to the power, like stingy scrooges.

So Father, if this is the probation we must endure, another rite of passage for mankind to evolve to its next stage, so be it! Our catharsis, the trial of passage into the new Promised Land.

This is blasphemy. Is it? My mind is confused. We live in confusing times. But truth is what it is, no matter how confusing it may be. We are forever condemned to choose between the boredom of stillness or the anguish of struggle, never able to live at peace.

JAMAICA, FEBRUARY 1504

(Fernando)

February was drawing to its end. We were reduced to a band of vagabonds. In extreme times, even the most honourable man resorts to violence and stealing, in a desperate fight for survival. We were back to our most primitive and barbaric instincts. The mutiny had aggravated the divisions and sowed the seeds of mistrust of the Indians against us, who vanished and refused to trade with us. Without them, we were starving to a slow, agonizing death. As the Indians "are people who don't work enough to cultivate extensive fields, and we consume more in a day then them in twenty, having them lost interest in our baubles and trinkets, (...) they no longer care to bring us the food and water we need, for what we found ourselves in serious trouble".

I wanted to trust father's immense skills and instinct, but I thought we were beyond even the Admiral's superhuman capabilities. He had been closed in his cabin for the last couple of days, barely eating, just taking his measurements and scribbling in his notebook. He studied the Almanac Perpetuum created by Zacuto, the great astrologist and mathematician.

On the morning of 29 February, the Admiral sent word summoning the caciques of the region for a feast on the beach at sundown.

"He told the Indians that we are Christians and believe in the true God (..., who) rewards the good and punishes the bad, as he had punished the mutineers by not allowing them to cross over to Hispaniola, as He allowed Méndez (...), and by causing them to suffer trials and dangers (...). God was very angry with them for neglecting to bring us food even when we pay them by barter, and would punish them with famine and pestilence."

This my Father said, to the unbelieving and scornful Indians, who burst out laughing at him. That was a humiliation. But Father continued, unfazed. He admonished the Indians that "God would that night send them a token of the punishment they were about to be inflicted. They should attend the rising of the moon for it would arise inflamed with wrath" and then vanish, turning the starry clear night into pitch black darkness.

No-one knew what the Admiral's plans were, but the men grew restless as we faced ourselves surrounded by hundreds of tribespeople, not looking very friendly. We didn't have enough guns or swords to ambush them, and firing the ship's cannon at her state would be madness.

The night came, calm and warm, with a large full moon bright in the sky. We would usually be lighting fires to prepare dinner, but it was pointless as we had no food whatsoever.

It was the silence that called my attention... The noisy crowd fell into a hush, eyes towards the tall rock at the eastern tip of the beach. A man was standing there, tall, immense, a massive figure with broad shoulders, pointy nose and long reddish-white hair. Was that Father? It could not be, I had always known Father as dark haired, although for the past months he had kept his hair short and hidden under a hat or headscarf. But his figure was unmistakable. Clad in black rags, with a long black cape around his shoulders and the halo of the full moon over his head, he could be Poseidon, the God of the Seas himself. He raised his arms, looking towards the night sky, and then spoke like thunder, a strong and angry voice you would not expect in such an old and sick man. What divine source of energy he kept calling upon, surprising everyone when all thought him about to give up, remains a mystery to me.

"God is angry with you! We are His sailors, commanded by Him to spread the true faith to these distant lands and bring you to kingdom of Heaven. The Spaniards are the chosen people of God! And how do you treat us? You refuse to help us build ships to cross to Hispaniola and now you refuse us, the chosen people of God, the water and food that is rightly ours, Lords of all these western lands? The fury of God shall be shown tonight, and those who do not repent will be punished by His fires."

The natives probably did not understand all of what Father was saying, but the meaning was plain enough, as he talked angrily, pointing to the skies as if commanding them. Father was superb, his immense power of persuasion convincing Indians and sailors he was a sorcerer who not only commands the winds and the seas but also the celestial bodies.

The sound started as a deep sight that seemed to rise directly from the depths of the earth. A long gasp for air as the dozens of people assembled on the beach froze in incomprehension. How could it be, what witchcraft was at play in the heavens? A shadow, dark and ominous, consumed the moon. In a matter of minutes, the bight starry night illuminated by the large full moon became dark, a hole of nothingness that threatened to engulf the human souls lost on that beach. Natives and sailors alike were shocked into silence, as minds tried to process the situation. But the silence lasted a few instants only, replaced by screams of fear from the native women and children, prayers from the sailors now fallen to their knees and loud cries of panic everywhere.

How could Father have mustered the disappearance of

the moon? Natives were perplexed, restless and fearful. The cacique, leader of the tribe, threw himself on Father's feet and promised to bring us the food and water we needed.

After some pondering, Father said he would intercede and ask God to forgive them, but if they ever failed again to obey him, the people of the island would be consumed by God's wrath. He retreated to his cabin, alone.

Most sailors and tribespeople were scared to death. A few sceptical may have seen this as just another fit of his hallucinations, an elusive show of a madman suffering from dehydration, pain, scurvy and near blindness. But the fact remains, for anyone to see: the moon had vanished at the command of the Admiral!

I suspected what was going on, although I remained unsure. Father was probably consulting Zacuto's astrological tables and measuring time with the hourglass, timing the end of the celestial phenomenon. Then, "when the Admiral estimated the crescent phase of the eclipse was finishing and that the moon would soon shine bright again, he emerges from his cabin and says he had prayed for the Indians and promised Him in their name that henceforth they would be good and treat the Christians well, (...) bringing provisions and all else we need." [91]

The moon eclipse did not last long. By then, I had no real sense of time. How long had it been? Seconds, hours...? The bright round disk of the full moon slowly returned, as the shadow drifted away from the face of the moon. Father was at the bow of our wrecked ship, silent and spectral, arms stretched to the sky.

Most natives had fled, awestruck and terrified. But later in the evening, the cacique, accompanied by a group of Indians, came to Father, bringing many offerings of food and a tangy tasting fire water that the natives brew from sugar cane, which we now call rum. The chief offered some dry leaves, aged brown but still moisty, which he rolled and pressed into small balls and gently placed in a stone cup, over some embers he took from the fire. This must have been a much valued gift by the natives, as it was offered with great ceremony. Father and the other captains seemed to have already seen the leaves before, because they reacted with much joy and appreciation. The smoke had a delicious pungent scent, which was most satisfying to breath [92].

I now understand the magical phenomenon was a moon eclipse predicted by Father based on his cosmographic knowledge and deep study of the Almanach Perpetuum compiled in 1496 by the Portuguese Jewish astrologer Zacuto as well the Ephemerides Astronomicae published in 1474 by the German astrologer Regiomontanus. Science and cunning saved us. "From that moment forward, (the Indians) were diligent in providing us with all we needed and were loud in praise of the Christian God." We had been stranded in Jamaica for eight months, and had it not been for that mystic show Father pretended to play, we would probably have starved or been killed by the natives.

After the events of that evening, natives (and most sailors actually) believed Father to be some type of deity, powerful to command the elements or to talk directly to God. Father has actually fed these rumours during the last years of his life, writing those demented Prophecies. I now know that the events of that night in Jamaica, Father's entire life actually, were a tremendous farce, a well-orchestrated ploy. The best way to take people's attention away from something, is to draw their attention to something else. People are gullible, the human mind wants to believe in the fantastic and improbable even when a simpler and more logic explanation is at hand.

In fact, Father was maybe the first to put into practice the idea of using a lunar eclipse to determine geographical longitude. A moon eclipse is visible across the globe. Everyone sees it begin and end at the same moment, but at different local times. The difference between one's local time and the time predicted in the Almanac for a certain place equals the difference in geographical longitude, by 15 degrees per hour (360 degrees divided by 24 hours).

The Admiral observed the lunar eclipses of 15 September 1494 near Hispaniola and 29 February 1504 from Jamaica. His capacity to accurately predict the time difference to the start of the eclipse is a powerful indication Father knew exactly where he was on the globe, his longitude position, and therefore he was certainly aware we were still many time zones away from the India he "sold" to the Spanish monarchs.

At that time, as a young and impressionable boy, I was at the same time honoured and ashamed by the genial madness of the Admiral of the Ocean Sea, my Father Christopher Colon.

It was that night, after the episode of the moon eclipse in Jamaica, that I came to know Father's true identity.

The mysterious events of the evening were incomprehensible. I had seen, with my own eyes, the moon consumed by apocalyptic shadows and then miraculously returning to a calm and bright night, at the command of the Admiral.

It was late. Everyone had retired to get some rest from the emotions of the evening. I approached the Captain's cabin in the shipwreck and entered cautiously, to avoid the risk of one of Father's bursts of rage and violence.

But he was calm, organizing the books and papers on which he had been working for the previous weeks.

"Fernando, come in. Do you have a question?"

"I have two questions, if I may, Father... First, what has happened to the moon in the skies? Second, how has your dark hair turned, uhh, reddish-white?".

"The first question is easy and you will learn for your-self, by studying my books on cosmography and maths. The books are the most valuable treasure I own. What you know, you owe no-one. I just hope that madman Ovando has not brought doom to by library... I told him a storm was coming, but he insisted on sending the fleet from Hispaniola, including a ship with my belongings he was so keen to get rid of. I just hope the fleet has survived the storm and my books arrive in Castile safe. Our most valuable treasure is amongst those books."

"You mean, a book with a treasure map? Is that why you keep all the secrets and mystery, allowing all sorts of lies to be told about you? To protect a map?"

"The Book is not a treasure map, Fernando. The Book is the treasure. But we carry away of ourselves. I shall answer your second question. It is time you know the true origins of our family. My hair has not suddenly turned white... I was born with a fiery reddish-blond hair, which soon turned a shade of white, and so remained for 33 years, until in 1484 I started to dye it black. Over the last few months I simply could not dye it for lack of my ointments, which got lost in the shipwreck, and have been covering it with my hat pretending to shield from the sun.

The fiery hair comes from your grandfather, Henrique Alemão, 'the German'. He fled the Germanic kingdoms to take refuge in the westernmost edge of Europe, the island of Madeira, protecting an ancient treasure the Templars found in the Temple of Solomon.

The Church of Rome has always been suspicious that some daunting truth has been discovered in Jerusalem, something so powerful that could undermine the Catholic faith and the power of the church. In 1307, the Templar Order was extinct by the French Pope Clement V, shortly before he established the seat of the Papacy in Avignon. The Templar knights were humiliated, arrested and tortured. So, they fled France and scattered to the edges of Christendom, protecting the secrets.

The Northern Path of Henry Sinclair took the Rose Line to the North, hiding in Scotland. Around 1400, Henry Sinclair sailed west, taking the Rose Line to Nova Scotia.

The Southern Path took the Wind Rose to seek refuge with the Teutonic Knights, a sister order of the Templars, in the German Holy Roman Empire.

Others fled to Portugal, a country the Templars had helped to create, preparing for a new Crusade to find a Promised Land to the west, where the Northern and Southern Paths could reunite in safety – Jerusalem is forever lost, a new Jerusalem must be found to the west.

Sixty years ago, the Teutonic knights saw the Templar secret of the Southern Path was at risk. The German Holy Roman Empire was under pressure from the Turks and weakened by internal infights between factions. It was at risk of falling to the hands of the Habsburgs, a dynasty aligned with Rome – which in fact happened when in 1452, Frederick III became the first Habsburg emperor. With the fall of the German Empire to the hands of the Habsburgs, the secret of the Wind Rose that our family has sworn to protect would land straight on the lap of the Roman Pope.

So, your grandfather sacrificed everything, riches and titles, to take the Wind Rose to safety. A kingdom was lost, but the secret endured. He became a pilgrim in the Holy Land, then a hermit in the Pyrenees mountains and finally took refuge in Madeira island, which was and remains property of the Order of Christ. In Madeira island my father became known as Henrique Alemão, Henry the German.

For those paying attention, though, this poor hermit and pilgrim was more then met the eye, for he was given vast land in the island and soon married my mother, a noble lady of Sicilian ancestors and a member of the Gonçalves Zarco family, the captain of the island. King Afonso V was my father's best man at the wedding! Although my father kept his identity secret, the high Lords of Portugal were fully aware of his true identity and probably his mission.

I was born in 1951, in Madeira. A strong, tall boy, pale skinned, strange reddish-blonde hair... and the mark of our family, six fingers on each foot, like my father. From ten years of age, I trained in the School of Sagres. For 33 years I was called 'o Alemão' after my father, and so remained until in 1484 I left wife and son behind in Portugal to be reborn in Spain as Christopher Colon.

But for all the sacrifice of your grandfather, the Wind Rose is not safe yet. Europe remains under threat. From the south and east, the Moors. From the east, the Turks. And most perilous of all, from inside, the insatiable beast of the Inquisition. The forbidden Book must be taken away and protected, reunited with the Rose Line in the new western Promised Land."

LISBON, FEBRUARY 2019

(Savanah)

The afternoon at Duma's has been quite revealing. Since yesterday evening I have been struggling with the idea of giving Sergio and Duma a copy of the notebook. I had put it into the bag on a whim before leaving for the lunch yesterday, but in the end have not dared to share it. The last thing I need is Sergio and Duma to take a ride with me to fantasyland. But the truth is... I know very little of this mystical symbology Raven was investigating, maybe I do need some help. I have not moved much closer to understanding Raven's murder or even what she was investigating, and yesterday conversation with Sergio and Duma has been the closest thing to a breakthrough I have had since landing in Lisbon 5 weeks ago.

I pushed hard during my ritual morning run, stretching my legs and mind furiously. By 8.30, I was back at the rented loft and after a quick bath called Professor Noronha to invite him for a coffee. He had a lot of explaining to do.

It was a grey morning and it started to rain by the time I left my attic flat. What a difference from yesterday's crisp sunny weather. Not the heavy pouring rain that soaks you to the bones, just a drizzle. I took the metro at around 11.00, looking forward to meeting Professor Noronha. We had agreed to meet at the bat of the Altis Belém hotel, a neutral meeting place with tourists around to make me feel safe.

When Professor Noronha arrived, I skipped through the usual niceties and went straight to business, although keeping to a diplomatic and concealed tone. "Pedro has been quite helpful, but, well, you know… it has been 5 weeks now and there is nothing I find that could remotely justify the murder of my sister or all the mystery. There must have been something else going on. I know Raven had been talking to you about a Love Chapel in Tomar where a Rome's Secret or Rome's Treason was hidden. Can you tell me about it, Professor?"

He became livid, unable to find a suitable response for a few minutes. I saw him raising his hand to the waiter, as if wanting to gain some time to collect his thoughts as he ordered two cappuccinos and croissants.

"I haven't had breakfast yet, and at my age I do need to get some coffee into my brain to start working, you know", professor Noronha said, looking out of the window to the grey coloured Tagus. "I come to this cafe quite often, now I'm a retired useless old man. It's near my house and I can just seat here watching the river on its inevitable, unstoppable path towards the sea, reminiscing about the past. The Padrão dos Descobrimentos is just 5 minutes away, you can see it from outside."

"I know, I run every day along the riverside path, passing the MAAT towards Belém and then back. It is lovely, indeed". The MAAT is a modern building constructed on a former electric central with a sleek rooftop in the form of a wave, which was always packed with skateboarders, descending from the wave-styled rooftop at great speed. Here is something Savanah would surely never try.

Professor regained some composure as he sipped through his cappuccino. Addressing Savanah in a whisper, he noted:

"Savanah, you are stepping on dangerous grounds. Some stones are best left unturned. Please, leave it alone."

"But you have to tell me something, Professor. What

were you and Raven researching, what have you found?"

"Well, Raven had some wild theories. At the time, it looked worth exploring. You know, I had been a history professor for, what? Oh God, too long. I saw the opportunity of an interesting breakthrough. But after Raven's death, I let it go. As time passed, I have concluded it was nothing but a bunch of well-intentioned but delusional theories Raven was after. There is nothing to support it. So I left it alone. Look, even if there once was this treasure hidden in Tomar, the Convent of Christ has gone through so many changes it would surely have been found. The place was literally dissected during Dom Manuel I time, who reconstructed the place turning it into a royal palace. Coincidence or not, many documents harboured in Tomar Castle and Monastery were burned in the Inquisition fires. During this time all the tombs of Templar masters in Tomar were desecrated and the bodies exhumed. So, you see, Savanah... there was plenty of opportunities for the Church of Rome to search, remove or destroy any secret treasure, if ever there was one. Tomar is a lovely place, full of history and prone to wake up the imagination of young minds. But like Fernando Pessoa poem 'Mensagem', it is all a lost dream of a bygone era. Portugal was once the centre of the world, but nowadays...that is past."

I was not convinced. Professor Noronha was hiding something. As we walked out of the door, bracing ourselves for the rain, now a heavy downpour, I motioned towards the metro hinting we would part here.

"Well, thanks for the cappuccino, it was great" I mentioned. "I hope to see you again at the university soon... This looks like an expensive area, it is a nice place to retire, right?"

"Oh, yes. I keep to my garden these days, no more classes. You are right, it is an expensive area. My family had a big coffee plantation in Angola, so I inherited a fair bit of money. When I retired, I could finally sell off my flat near the university and buy a beautiful house here in Restelo. You should come over for dinner. I will set it up, invite Duma as well. Gosh, it has been ages, I do miss her."

As I walked towards the metro fighting off the wind and rain with a useless umbrella, my mind wrestled with an uncontrollable flow of thoughts. I could not quite put my finger into it.

It occurred to me as I entered the rented rooftop loft and shook the water off my hair. A tired face stared back at me from the mirror, hair glued to my head running down with water and clothes soaked. "Gosh...". I looked at the drained face staring at me in disbelief, then picked up my mobile and called Duma.

"Hi Duma. Listen, you remember what you told me about Professor Noronha fleeing Angola after the independence?... Did they get to sell the coffee plantation?"

"What are you talking about, Savanah? They were 'retornados', they fled the country with nothing but the clothes they were wearing. They got nothing for it, the plantation was taken over by the local people. Professor Noronha lost everything and had to start over in Lisbon... What is this all about, silly woman?"

There it was then. Professor Noronha had lied straight to my face. He was hiding something.

LISBON, FEBRUARY 2019

Time was running out. Just reading all those books would lead her nowhere. Whatever Raven had found was somewhere else.

Savanah thus decided she needed to share the notebook with someone who might help her deciphering its secrets. She texted Sergio and Duma asking them to meet the following day at lunchtime, some place outside the university. Duma called almost instantly, checking if everything was fine and what was it she had found that could not be discussed on the cafeteria. A lovely woman, but she could not steer away from a gossip.

"Well, Duma. It's just... I have a copy of a notebook I want you and Sergio to look at. But better not to talk about it over the phone"

"Oh girl, you are starting to sound like your sister. Ok then, see you tomorrow."

After hanging up, Savanah could not bring herself to continue watching the Netflix series, but was also too tired to work. The drizzly weather outside made her feel glum and melancholic. She changed to comfortable pyjamas and was getting to bed at 9.30pm, hoping she would just crash out. But as often happened to her, no matter how tired she was, the moment she turned off the lights her mind just started buzzing around. It was exhausting. The more she tried to stop the whirlwind of thoughts, the more her mind would get stuck into the dark well, spinning round and round into a bottomless pit... lying in bed surrounded by darkness, trying to block the world away, waiting for sleep to come, but unable to switch off. So, she just let the thoughts come and go, a strategy she got used to playing with her mind. If you free the mind to come and go, it will eventually stop and rest...

In the morning, with barely four hours sleep, Savanah picked up Raven´s notebook and went off to a nearby copy shop, not wanting to use university photocopy machines.

She arrived early at the agreed place near the university and looked for a table at the back where they could talk. Luckily the weather was still a bit gloomy, otherwise the place would have been packed with tourists and people from university. Duma arrived shortly after, her chubby body and big umbrella dragging chairs as she pushed her way to Savanah´s table.

"So, what's up?", she said, while calling the waiter for some sparkling water and two codfish cakes "to share while we wait."

"Well, I would like you and Sergio to look at something, but I'll explain when he arrives. Do you know anything about...erhhh, mystical symbols, cryptic messages, you know..."

"Hang on, you are not going to pull out a deck of Tarot for a divination session to ask the spirits what happened to Raven?", Duma interjected, half-jokingly. "I´m a God fearing woman, I will have nothing to do with dark magic and stuff."

"No, that's not... well, not exactly that, more like hidden messages and cult sects, the freemasons and stuff.", explained Savanah.

"I don't know about that, but well... you know, where there is light, there is darkness. People have always tried to gain some sense of control over the implausibility of life's randomness by resorting to the mystic, the occult, the religious. I believe in God, go to Church most Sundays. I was taught that way and never given it much thought. The church provides healthy moral standards and spiritual references to guide one's life in a clean and safe way. As to all that, you know, tarot, voodoo, astrology and zodiac signs... I don't pay too much attention, although, well, better be safe than sorry.", Duma laughed heartedly.

Savanah felt they were entering personal-beliefs territory and therefore off limits. She herself believed religion was indeed an "aspirin for the people". The Church had sanctioned the atrocities of colonization and slavery, providing spiritual comfort for masters and slaves alike: the "conquistadores" were spreading the "only true religion" and to the poor and explored it offered a hope of paradise. Slavery and colonialism. You can't change history, but you have to acknowledge it and keep it well alive in our collective consciousness, to make sure those atrocities are not repeated. Anyway, these were her personal thoughts and she had to respect other views, so she usually preferred to avoid theological discussions.

The two women fell briefly in silence as the waiter placed on the table the water and the cod cakes. "Thank you, great. You should try, Savanah, they make it very well here, proper salty dry cod with a lot of parsley. Now, about those occult arts... I've seen and heard many stories about black magic. During my childhood in Angola but also here in Lisbon too. You know, when people are poor, they resort to whatever means they can to try to get some control over their lives..."

Savanah spotted Sergio at the entrance and waved to him.

"So, beautiful ladies, what do I owe the pleasure of

your company?", said Sergio brightly as he sat down.

Savanah smiled. Sergio was not handsome, with a bony mousy face covered in teenage pimple marks and thinning hair. But he was spirited and good humoured, his eyes always shining as if spreading the sun around.

She took Raven's notebook and placed it on the table. As Sergio flipped through the pages, with Duma hanging over his harm to look at it as well, Savanah briefly explained what the notebook was.

"Columbus apparently lost his mind towards the end of his life, writing his undecipherable Book of Prophecies, which seem nothing more than the ramblings of a madman. But... what if there is indeed some kind of hidden message, something that many have tried to conceal by rewriting the history books into that tale of a poor Genoese wood weaver?"

Sergio was lost into the ciphers and codes of the notebook. "There is plenty of stuff here, that's true. Can I take this with me? I would like to look at it carefully."

"Actually", said Savanah taking from her bag the two packs of copied pages, wrapped in brown paper and secured with an elastic band, "I have made copies for both of you. I guess you can reflect on this for a few days and we meet on Friday to discuss, how's that?"

"Of course Savanah.", answered Duma. "I mean, I don't like this esoteric stuff. I find it either a sham, a hoax to extort money or otherwise just outright nutcases. Mind you, it is very real in the sense that people believe in it and are ready to go to great lengths for it. If this can bring some light into Raven's death, you can count me in."

SEVILLE, JUNE 1484

Monastery of Santa Maria
de las Cuevas

(Columbus)

"And all must be in secret, so that no-one ever suspects"
CHRISTOPHER COLUMBUS

I crossed the border in Ayamonte and headed to the Monastery of La Rabida, in Palos, where I met Friar Antonio Marchena. As Father Fernão Martins indicated, Marchena is well aware of the plot laid out by King João, of my true identity and motives. We met and discussed for a week, honing the details of the plan, but now need time and patience to put the wheels in motion. Like at sea, the waiting is the worst part.

I have thus moved to Seville, where I must be to meet the nobles and the financiers whose support I will need to convince the Spanish monarchs. Many of the Portuguese nobles who fled Portugal after the curtailed conspiracies to kill Dom João II have taken refuge in Seville and enjoy in this town a privileged treatment by Queen Isabella and the Castilian 'hidalgos'. There is a large Portuguese community here. The Feitoria of Andalucía, a trading post over the river Guadalquivir, conducts intense trade with the Algarve and serves as base to supply the Portuguese possessions in North Africa.

I am currently living in La Cartuja, at the Monastery

of Santa Maria de las Cuevas, where Friar Gaspar Gorricio has sheltered me. News of my decapitation are grossly exaggerated, but have nevertheless reached Castella even faster than me... Alemão is death at the hands of Dom João and I arrive in Seville as the Italian Cristobal Colon, taking the place of the poor Genoese sacrificed at the dungeons.

I have been seating here at the window of my cell for days now, allowing the dust to settle while Frei Gorricio widens the net of the plot. Las Cuevas is a place with strong Portuguese influence. In this Monastery, built in an islet in the middle of the river Guadalquivir near Seville, King Afonso V met with King Henrique of Spain on his return from Ceuta to arrange the marriage of the Spanish princess Joana with the Portuguese prince João. The high altar was commissioned by King Afonso V and at the ceiling of the main nave is engraved the Portuguese royal coat of arms.

I seat for endless hours, thinking of my Filipa alone in Lisbon, probably suspecting what's going on but not knowing for sure. I seat looking at the Guadalquivir river from the window of my cell at las Cuevas. The Mediterranean is just a stretch down the river, entering the Gulf of Cadiz at its mouth in Sanlucar de Barrameda. That is where my expedition will depart, as soon as I convince Castella to support the western route. The wait is the worst part. Like at sea, during the lulls with no wind, the wait is the worst part.

My father talked highly of Friar Gaspar Gorricio. He was the priest who helped him hide in the Pyrenees as an eremite for two years, covering up his true identity and the Book, until moving to Madeira. Friar Gorricio knows the last secret of the Templars.

The Monastery of las Cuevas is where the caterpillar turned into the butterfly. Segismundo Alemão died in Lisbon a few weeks ago, and was reborn as Cristobal Colon in las Cuevas.

The show off trial at the Castle of those involved in the plot to assassinate Dom João II was the perfect cover up. My cousins were accused and have fled the country, I was imprisoned in everyone's sight, so I became, to the eyes of the world, part of the assassination conspiracy. Which makes me an enemy of the King of Portugal.

The night before my execution, the Italian was arrested in a bar brawl accused of bragging about his maps and secret information. The Italian was brought in and his hair shaven, like mine. The exchange was swift. We are quite similar in body and looks, except his hair was black and mine is fair, but no-one could tell with shaved heads. I ran away on horseback while the Italian was executed in my stead in front of all the Spanish spies. God save his soul. But it had to be done.

Now we need to convince the high Lords of Castella that I am who I am, a Portuguese insurgent noble part of the plot against Dom João, intimate of the Portuguese navigational and scientific secrets, that took the cover of the poor Italian to escape the king's wrath. The Spanish would never listen to a poor uneducated pirate, no matter the maps and letters Father Fernão has put into his hands. Friar Gorricio and Antonio Marchena are whispering my secret identity to the little birds of Queen Isabella, playing the plot to perfection.

The name is quite fortunate. I am not going to take Colombo's name, but adapt it to Colom. It is similar enough to confound everyone, but has a totally different meaning. Colombo is Latin for dove. Kolon is Greek for Member. Cristoferans Kolon: member of the Order of Christ.

Officially, I am no longer the high Portuguese noble member of the Order of Christ and faithful to the king, but a poor Italian adventurer in search of fame, who can claim to have seen the Portuguese secrets, had correspondence with

Toscanelli and received in audience by King Dom João II to present his western project but rebutted.

I cannot imagine what a mess this will create for the years to come!

For now, I seat and wait, bidding my time to resurface. The waiting is the worst part. Like on the sea, the waiting is the worst part.

And so it was that Christopher Colon was born in 1484 from the blood of a forfeited conspiracy to assassinate Dom Joao II and on the grave of the lowlife Genoese wool-weaver and pirate Cristóbal Piccione-Colombo... At las Cuevas Monastery started Colon's tiring 7-year journey to convince the Spanish kings to support a western exploration route. It is no surprise we find no reference to Colon or Colombo prior to 1484 in any Portuguese or Spanish documents. Even the marriage documents of Dona Filipa, a high noble of All Saints convent, have disappeared. Colon was born in 1484 with a complete fake identity.

SEVILLE, JUNE 1484

"If I don't write to you in more detail about what is happening, it is because these things cannot be put to paper."
CHRISTOPHER COLUMBUS, LETTER TO GASPAR GORRICIO

"**F**riar Gorricio, are you sure you are comfortable doing this?", asked Colon to his friend as they approached the brothel. Friar Gaspar Gorricio was wearing a richly ornamented blue and plum silk robe and Arabic turban, which looked displaced but served the purpose of disguising him. Colon was likewise richly dressed in magnificent black silks with a red velvet cape and shiny gold rings.

"Oh, believe me. I have been to worst places. You cannot imagine the dens of sin Spaniards are capable of imagining. Not more than the French or Italians, mind you, but anyway."

The two men entered the expensive looking establishment and took to the cards gaming room, a large oval place with rich rugs of geometric patterns hanging in the walls. The entire place had a Moorish feeling, lending it an exotic air. Scantily dressed ladies dotted the room, prodding their patron's as they drank and played. Colon and his friend sat at the table, producing a large purse of gold maravedis. The eyes looked inquisitively. Who were these two strangers with foreign looks who arrived suddenly at Seville with money to spend?

"My name is Cristobal Colon, I am an Italian merchant

and map maker who has been at the Portuguese court for many years. I have been presenting my promising exploration project to the hardheaded Portuguese king but he fails to understand it. So I am coming to Castella to present my project to the illustrious catholic kings, who will surely understand and back this most promising and lucrative enterprise."

Colon and Gorricio simulated becoming drunk, playing increasingly higher stakes and calling the attention of the girls. After significant amounts of wine were liberally offered by the two strangers around the table, Colon caused a row with a big, fat and mousy figure, accusing him of cheating. The table became quite excited, heavy with expectation and nervous. The fat man raised to his feet and slammed his potato-like fist on the table, yelling he would not take offence from foreigners, by their looks probably a Jew and a Muslim. Colon remained composed, with a mockingly superior smile that further ignited the Spaniards wrath. As the fat man stormed towards Colon, his companion jumped to his feet to interpose himself.

"Now, now, gents...", he said, in a very decent imitation of the dragged drawl of a drunk. "Do you know who you are talking with? Don't be deceived by the appearances. Dom Colon is a high Portuguese noble, lord of Madeira and captain of the seas. He fled the country..."

"...Hush, are you mad? Hold your tongue. Or do you want that tyrannical King Dom João to find where we are? You know damn well what the man is capable of, he killed his wife's brother with his bare hands!", intervened Colon, dragging the apparently drunk Friar Gorricio away from the brothel.

As they approached the Monastery of las Cuevas in La Cartuja, Friar Gaspar Gorricio took off his robes, keeping his Friar's habit underneath, laughing heartedly.

"So, Friar Gaspar", asked Colon, "Do you think they fell for it?"

"Oh, of course, my son, of course. There is nothing better to get the pulses running wild than a good intrigue. Tomorrow, I assure you, Isabella's little birds will have already told her about your true identity and the disguise you are using to conceal yourself from King João. Do you know how Isabella calls the Portuguese king? She despises and fears him in equal measure, referring to him only as 'the Man'."

True enough, the news soon disseminated through the grapevine and arrived to the court in Valladolid, where Isabel was staying.

"So, you tell me that this Cristobal Colon is in fact Dom Alemão, cousin of the Portuguese conspirators who plotted to kill the King. He took the skin of an Italian mapmaker, whom his accomplices managed to exchange in prison. But why has Dom Alemão felt necessary to change his name, does he not feel secure in Castella?", the Queen asked, furious that the plot to kill the Portuguese king had failed. The House of Aviz had supported Princess Joanna, the bastard who would have succeed the Spanish throne if she had not taken the place of her younger cousin. She was destined to rule and do God's work on Earth, her legitimacy emanated from the heavens, was not subject to earthly rules. Torquemada said so.

"Your majesty, taking the place of the Italian mapmaker allowed him to escape the death sentence in Portugal and remain undercover. The Portuguese king is vengeful and has a long harm. By using the skin of the Genoese, Don Colon can talk to your majesty about his exploration plans without arising suspicion in Lisbon, as the Italian is known to have been at least twice in audience at the Portuguese court and been refused. Don Colon is resentful against the

Portuguese king and ready to offer his navigation skills to the Queen of Castella."

"Well, we shall see", concluded Queen Isabel. "Tell him to come pledge his allegiance to me and present me his coat of arms. If that Don Colon can't even kill that wretched Man, how can I ever trust him to lead our overseas expansion? Anyway, let the Portuguese waste time and money finding the new lands, then we will just take them by force."

By the end of June, Gorricio confirmed to Colon that the ruse had played to perfection. "The Spaniards believe you have managed to escape from the dungeons, a runaway persecuted by the Portuguese king, and taken this Italian disguise to conceal your identity and cover up proposals to navigate at the service of the Spanish monarchs. Those who matter know your true identity and thus are aware of your extensive knowledge of the Portuguese maritime secrets, which makes your decapitated self of much interest for the Castilian court, even under the disguise of a poor uneducated Italian pirate."

Colon was received with all the courtesies of his noble condition and granted access both by the high nobles of Castella and equally by the Jews, cosmographers and merchants who wanted to undermine Isabella. These court games were uncomfortable, Colon was much more at ease facing sea monsters than courtly well-mannered duplicitous lords. At least with the monsters you know what you are fighting. Colon was starting to feel a bit annoyed with the tiresome charade, paraded around like a poor quality minstrel pretending to know tricks he did not. But the deceit had to go on. They were all lining up, coveting to speak to him about the Portuguese maritime secrets, sniffing like salivating dogs waiting for the opportunity to join in or to run away, following the prevailing mood and disposition at court.

COPENHAGEN, DECEMBER 2005

Raven had decided to attend the conference in Copenhagen, on the pre-Columbian explorations of North America, mainly because of a panel about the Luso-Danish expedition of 1476/77, which supposedly reached Iceland (Tile), Greenland (Thule) and Newfoundland in Canada. Christopher Colon claimed to have participated in such expedition. She was already familiar with the well-publicized signs of early European settlers in North America from the 8th century onwards. The Kensington Runestone, probably Viking. The Newport Tower and the Westford Knight, probably Templar. The Dighton Rock, most certainly Portuguese. What she was looking for were new ideas and theories, gossip about the research projects of her academic colleagues that could open new avenues of investigation.

If there was a secret mission behind Colon's expeditions, a secret powerful enough to justify 500 years on conspiracy and lies, could it be related with the westwards quest of the Templars? As Jerusalem in the East was definitely lost to Saladin in 1187, less than 100 years after the first crusade, the Templars had turned west, looking for a New Jerusalem. Several legends talk of the quest to the west. The tales of King Arthur echo a Templar quest for the Grail in a lost island to the west, the Promised Land of Avalon. The ancient myth of Atlantis refers to a mythic island to the west. Saint Brendan, a legendary Irish monk of the sixth century, sailed west in search of a new Promised Land. The legend of Rosslyn Chapel in Scotland suggest that, as the Templars faced extermination in the early fourteenth century, a grand Templar secret (supposedly, the bloodline of Christ) was taken to protection by the Norwegian-Scottish nobleman Henry Sinclair, Earl of Orkney and Roslyn. The bloodline, the Rose Line, was hidden in his lands of Roslyn, where later the Rosslyn Chapel was built. One century before the Luso-Danish expedition, Henry Sinclair sailed westwards, taking the Rose Line to a new garden where it could flourish in safety, a new Promised Land to the west.

At the end of the fifteenth century, the Portuguese, besides their continuous push south to round Africa and reach India, seemed obsessed with North America: Nova Scotia, Newfoundland, Labrador Sea. In 1473, the João Vaz Corte-Real expedition to Newfoundland. In 1476/77, the Luso-Danish expedition to Greenland. In 1498, João Lavrador explored the Labrador Sea. In 1500 and 1501, the Gaspar Corte-real expeditions to Newfoundland and Nova Scotia. In 1502, Miguel Corte-Real joined his brother in Newfoundland and never returned, inscribing the Dighton Rock engravings in 1511... What were the Portuguese Caravelas of the Order of Christ, with the Templar Cross proudly displayed on their sails, so persistently looking for in North America?

And then suddenly... it all stopped. As if the mission had been completed. North America was left alone for more than 100 years, until the Mayflower arrived in 1620 with 102 Pilgrims to settle in the new Promised Land to the west where they could freely practice their religion.

The conference dinner had been a boring thing, with forgettable people, unremarkable food and unremarkable conversation. As a PhD student she had been allocated to one of the graduates tables, far from the big shots. The main topic of conversation at her table had been the draw for the groups stage of the 2006 world championship, which would take place the following year in Germany. The draw had been during the day, defining the groups for the playoffs. Europeans do love their football, so the graduate students table turned into a live proxy match, with each punter defending the national colours on behalf of their team.

Dinner had lowered her spirits a bit, so she decided to lounge at the hotel bar for a drink. December temperatures in Copenhagen discouraged the most avid club-goers, and she had an early flight tomorrow anyway. The hotel was depressing, a standard 5-star conference hotel, equal and undistinguishable from many others around the world. Seated in the designer-sofa at the bar of the international hotel chain, she could have been anywhere, Copenhagen, Moscow, Rio...

She felt tempted to go up to her room and fetch the novel she was reading, but her drink had already arrived and if she left the table, the over-zealous waiter would most likely take it away. So, she let herself be, playing with her mobile.

"Have you seen the ancient Scandinavian runes in your iPhone?". The question was coming from of a pair of skinny long legs in tight blue jeans. Gosh, how dupe can a guy be to have a line like that?

"Yeah, I've seen the Bluetooth symbol.", she responded dryly to the pair of legs in jeans.

But the legs were stubborn and didn't go away, keeping their ground. She reconsidered and briefly held up her head, facing first a white t-shirt of stretch-cotton, as tight as the jeans, and then a nice-looking square face framed by a mane of curly iridescent blond hair. "I know the Futhark runes...", she briefly lowered her eyes on a down-left diagonal towards the name tag clipped to the right-side pocket of the blue jeans, then back up to the square face, "... Erik".

Erik smiled and sat down, uninvited.

"Gosh, no, I'm not in the mood to babysit an over-confident self-imposing asshole", though Raven, grinding her teeth and closing her eyes with a sight. Raven was used to these unsolicited attacks and was unintimidated by them. On the other hand, she had nothing better to do anyway.

"That's impressive!", the guy said. "Raven, not a common name..."

She regretted wearing the nametag, but smiled mildly. Not a broad inviting smile, but a brief uplift of the lips, checking where this would go. "I'm not a common woman. About the impressive, I'm not so sure, though. Has that pick up line ever worked?"

"Well, Raven, it just did, right? I'm seating here talking with you."

Ok, fair point. 1-1.

Erik was Swedish and a PhD student working on the Vikings period. When Raven mentioned she worked in Lisbon researching on the first expeditions to America (she omitted the specific interest on Columbus), Erik came up with a weird story. Was he picking on her or still flirting?

The story was, nevertheless, too outlandish and detailed to be made up on the spot.

"There is a story amongst Viking scholars about a 'Raven Knight', a stone statue in the Corvo Island in the middle of the Atlantic. That's an island named after you!", he said, looking directly at her with no hint of shyness. "Corvo means Raven, in Portuguese. So, this stone statue in the island with your name, portrays a knight riding a horse, with his right arm extended, the index finger pointing westwards. Corvo island is situated at 39ºN latitude, almost the same as Newport Tower in Rhode Island. The intriguing thing is that the Portuguese chronicles of the time state the statue was found there by the first settlers, as if it had been placed in the tiny island on purpose beforehand, pointing the way westwards. And the statue disappeared after 1500: either it was taken down, or it was a fable and had never existed. As the story goes, an inscription was carved on the pedestal of the stone statue, bearing some strange symbols. During the 1476/77 Luso-Danish expedition a fellow (some claim Columbus) noticed the strange ancient runic symbols used by the Nordic sailors. The inscription was indeed Futhark runes and was sent by the Portuguese king to several scholars in Scandinavia to decipher it. The meaning has been lost, but the runes survived."

Erik picked up the napkin and asked the waiter for a pen "and a Grey Goose with tonic please". He drew four symbols on the napkin:

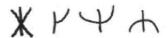

Raven translated the runes: "H K M R".

Erik laid down the pen, saying "You do know Futhark... impressive, I thought you were just pulling my leg... So, a beautiful 21st century Raven following the path of a pre-15th century Raven Knight of the first expeditions to North America", he concluded with a victorious but engaging smile.

"What does it mean? H K M R?", asked Raven, staring at the napkin.

"Well, the meaning has been lost – if ever it was deciphered, in fact. But I have my own theory...". Erik paused for impact. His vodka tonic arrived, a perfect timing as if it was all a pre-agreed staging. He raised the glass in a friendly salute and both took a sip of their drinks. Raven was having a beer, crisp and clean tasting with a brilliant golden color.

"So...?"

"So... you just put it all together. They stand not for

letters, but for a drawing. If we overlay the four runes on top of the Templar square cross, you get... this. Sorry, I don't draw very well, but you get the idea."

"Huumm...", mumbled Raven, a bit disappointed.

With a slight smile, as if he had been waiting for this all along, Erik picked up the napkin again and joined together the open ends of the pictogram. The resulting image caused cold shivers up Raven's spine:

"Uaauuu. Now, that's impressive!", exclaimed Raven. "That's the..."

"...the Templar cross carried on the sails of the Portuguese Caravelas that launched the Age of Discoveries, spanning the globe from Brazil to Japan. Yep."

"But hold on. The Templar cross was used in the sails of the Portuguese Caravelas long before the 1476/77 expedition that allowed the mysterious Raven Knight inscriptions to be decoded."

"Yep. But it is still extraordinary. As if the same Templar symbology was pushing across the Ocean Sea, one from the East (Portugal) and one from the West (America), looking for each other, and meeting in a tiny island in the middle of the Atlantic.

Raven became thoughtful. This was extraordinary indeed, and she suspected the four symbols had another meaning. But she would need to think about it with a clean head, in the morning.

They had sex that night, of course. But they didn't sleep together, because Raven had an early flight, and she liked her life tidy. There was too much mess in her mind already.

In the airplane back to Lisbon, Raven though back to the symbols inscribed in the Raven Knight. She took the napkin from her briefcase and stared at it for a long while, just letting her mind go.

She realized two intriguing things.

Firstly, if you take the four runes and the Templar square cross, you get 5 symbols which can be used to build two very meaningful images, which then overlap to form the cross on the sails of the Portuguese Caravelas.

The H and K runes together with the square cross form an image that looks like a wind rose, used by sailors to mark cardinal points on maps or to check where the wind is blowing from.

A slight knot caught on her stomach as she recognized the design. It was embossed on uncle Santiago's gold ring. She pushed the though aside.

The wind rose invokes the search for the right path. There is a massive, enigmatic, wind rose construction on the Fortaleza de Sagres, the headquarters of the naval school founded by Henry the Navigator. Sagres was and still is a mystical place, an isolated fortress on a steep promontory, battered by the Atlantic waves on the south-western tip of Europe, as the Mediterranean opens to the wide expanse of the Atlantic. The mega wind rose or sun dial in the Sagres Fortress was excavated by archaeologists at the beginning of last century, a huge circumference composed of 32 lines made of rocks, to form a circumference with 40 meters' diameter and close to 140 meters' perimeter. Its uses remain unknown. If it had mere utilitarian purposes, like a compass or wind rose or sun clock, its size would make it cumbersome. So it probably had some mystical and symbolic value.

The other two runes, the M and R, formed two chalices, one upwards and another downwards.

The chalice is the symbolic Holy Grail, the cup used by Christ in the last supper. But it is typically associated, in pagan mythology, with the woman's womb, and thus a symbol of the feminine and motherhood.

The wind rose and the chalice engraved in the Raven Knight, constructed with ancient Nordic symbols, may well have been used by the Norwegian/Scottish Earl Henry Sinclair, sailing from their new base in North America, to place a beacon in the miniscule island on the middle of the Atlantic to indicate the way towards the chalice. To signal to the bearers of the Wind Rose the way to the Chalice, the Rose Line. As if the Raven Knight was saying, his index finger outstretched towards the west: "The Chalice waits for the Wind Rose, this way".

The second intriguing thing that caught Raven's attention as she stared at the napkin, was that the overlap of the runes formed the Templar cross, but with one little detail that was missing from the cross on the sails of the Caravelas: the little wiggle at the top right arm. The hook on the northeastern arm of the wind cross.

JAMAICA, MARCH 1504

(Fernando)

*"If we cannot live entirely like human beings, at least let us
do everything in our power not to live entirely like animals."*
JOSÉ SARAMAGO, BLINDNESS

A sail appeared on the horizon. It was late March 1504.
The small Caravela anchored close to the shipwrecks of La Capitana and Bermuda. The captain of
the Caravela, Diego de Escobar, came ashore and informed
Father he had been sent by Nicolás de Ovando, the Governor
of Hispaniola, after hearing of our ordeal from Diego Méndez. The rescue canoes of Diego Mendez had left nine months
before! We had lost faith they could have made the crossing.

Regretfully, Diego de Escobar informed the Admiral,
the Governor had no ship large enough to rescue all the crew,
but hoped to send one soon. As a token of good will, Escobar
left the Admiral a "barrel of wine and a slab of salt pork." He
then returned to his ship and immediately sailed away.

The all episode was utterly astonishing. Ovando was
probably just spying on the Admiral and had no intentions
of rescuing us, instead plotting to leave us rotting and let
the Admiral die on that forsaken island, because he "feared
the Admiral's return to Castella", having discovered so many
new lands and the gold mines of Veragua, could lead the
monarchs to "restore the Admiral to his office and deprive
Ovando of his post".

The short visit of Escobar's ship, instead of providing

hope, further depressed our spirits, for we feared Méndez had sailed forth to Spain without saving us, and Ovando had no intentions of doing so. This again fuelled the renegade mutineers. Everyone was in a deranged mental state, to the point Francisco Porras claimed the ship had been just a ghost, "a phantasm conjured by the magic arts of which the Admiral is a master", just like a month before he had hidden the moon.

The rebels occupied a nearby Indian village, preparing an assault on the remains of the shipwrecks and kill the Admiral and his loyalist. On May 17, a fierce battle amongst Christians took place, which Father's loyalists won, capturing the Porras brothers and hurting or killing many of the rebels.

The anniversary of our arrival to the island came and passed. For more than a year we had been stranded on that beach, castaways in a paradise now tinged by the blood of our own.

Finally, at the end of June 1504, Diego Méndez caravel arrived, to end our martyrdom.

After dropping anchor at the bay, Diego Méndez came ashore on the row boat. Upon disembarking, he walked up the beach to where Father was standing. I was next to Father as Méndez took the chain from his chest, with a bullet swinging at the end, and handed it to Father. For the first and only time in my life, I saw Father crying, thick, silent tears. He took the chain and embraced Méndez.

"Is it done?", Father asks.

"It is done, my Lord", Méndez answers.

That evening, as Father lied on his cabin, he sighed with relief.

"Fernando, it is done. The mission has succeeded."

"You mean, reaching Hispaniola to get help?"

"Yes, yes, Fernando. That too."

After so many probations and struggles, we all "embarked in this ship, friends and enemies alike". It was 28 June 1504.

Something had happened that Father did not want to discuss. His spirits had improved. A few days later, I realized the bullet was not the same. The bullet Méndez returned to Father was not the silver bullet Father gave him a year ago. It was a lead bullet.

JAMAICA TO HISPANIOLA, JULY 1504

(Fernando)

> "The desert is what it is, it surrounds us, in some ways
> protects us, but when it comes to giving, it gives us nothing,
> it simply looks on, and when the sun suddenly clouds over,
> so that we find ourselves thinking, 'The sky mirrors our sor-
> row', we are being foolish, because the sky is quite impartial
> and neither rejoices in our happiness nor is cast down by our
> grief."
>
> JOSÉ SARAMAGO, THE GOSPEL ACCORDING TO JESUS CHRIST

Contrary winds and currents delayed us throughout the crossing from Jamaica to Santo Domingo, where we arrived only on August 13, 1504. It took us longer to cover the distance from Jamaica to Santo Domingo than it had taken us in 1502 to travel from the Canary Islands to Hispaniola...

I cannot avoid thinking history might have taken an entirely different path, if not for the permanent easterly winds that prevail in this region. There are two main regions of trade winds in the Atlantic Ocean. Near the tropics, they run constantly east-west. Further away from the equator, the winds circle back on a west-east course. This means the Europeans, as soon as they gathered courage to make it into the Atlantic, were inevitably pushed towards those new lands, which we call the Indies.

The civilizations we encountered during this fourth

voyage were ancient and proud, with a spiritual and scientific understanding of the world we failed to understand or accept. They were nimble navigators with highly manoeuvrable ships, very effective for the region.

If the winds had been fashioned the other way around, blowing westerly, maybe we, the Europeans, would be the ones stranded shore-bound to our coasts. What might have happened if, centuries ago, at the might of those western civilizations we unapologetically destroyed, they had travelled east, pushed by favourable winds, to meet the Europeans? Harassed by the Moors to the south, the Turks to the east and by these newcomers from the west, entangled in many internal and external wars, maybe we would be the ones called "New World", condemned to exploitation and dominion by the "Old World" civilizations that circled us and which were, at the time, more advanced than the tiny, fragile Europeans.

During the lengthy crossing, Father spent much time talking with Diego Méndez. I witnessed some of those long conversations, when Méndez confided to Father what he had seen and heard during the seven months he and his men had spent in Hispaniola.

The rescue canoes had paddled swiftly in the calm waters and breezy air. In just four days, they reached Cape San Miguel, the south-western point of Hispaniola, on the province of Xaraguá. As it happens, Nicolas the Ovando was in Xaraguá, crushing the Indian rebellion. Shortly after becoming Governor, replacing Bobadilla, Ovando defined as his priority to squash the rebellion. He ordered a great number of Taínos Indians to be closed in their huts, and then set the huts on fire.

During the months they were stranded in Xaraguá, prevented by Ovando from moving forward to Santo Domingo, Méndez witnessed many atrocities and brutality. "He burned or hanged eighty-four ruling caciques, (including) Anacoana, the greatest chieftain of the island, who was obeyed and served by all the others". Ovando invited her and other caciques to a banquet, which was an ambush. When the caciques were gathered in the meeting hut, Ovando's men set fire to it. They arrested Anacoana and other caciques who escaped the fire and hanged them all.

Another month we toiled in Santo Domingo, delayed by Nicolas de Ovando. Father used his funds to charter two ships to take us back to Spain. We were by then 110 survivors of the initial 147 that had sailed from Cádiz with the Admiral. Thirty-eight decided to stay behind in Hispaniola. The rest of us departed on 13 September 1504, heading for Spain.

I had grown during those two and a half years, no longer the boy with a head full of stories of knights and conquests. I felt grateful Father had taken me on the expedition and chosen me to complete his mission, a bastard born of a relationship of Colon with my mother Beatriz Henriquez, out of wedlock. His firstborn son, Diego, had remained in Seville at the care of his aunt Briolanda. Father probably thought the boy too spoiled to face the rough life at sea.

Nothing Father did was ever by chance. He was consumed by the demons on his mind, forced to juggle contradictory objectives and loyalties. In a confusing world of shifting seas, Father's life was itself engulfed in chaos and mystery... but a singular mission, a path plotted many years ago, was always a constant, the solid and resilient rock at the core of all his actions.

As the expedition approached its end, I was starting to realize Father was part of the most amazing conspiracy and lie ever created, for the sake of something greater than the petty skirmishes between kingdoms or lords.

A masterful plan of deceit, where my Father has played the central role throughout his life. This is a global game and victories are not made in single moves. Father offered the Western Indies to the Catholic Monarchs, entertaining them and the Spanish Pope with a child's play in those beautiful islands of naked Indians and colourful birds, leading them to sign the Tordesillas Treaty, in effect protecting the Portuguese monopoly of the Indic ocean.

But there was something grander behind Father's actions. Still as we returned from that extraordinary expedition, Father insisted on continuing what he called his "true mission". Had he not done enough? What else was he looking for?

CÁDIZ, NOVEMBER 1504

(Fernando)

"The journey never ends. Only the travelers end (…) The end of a journey is just the beginning of another (…). A journey needs to be restarted. Always."
JOSÉ SARAMAGO, JOURNEY TO PORTUGAL

We sailed back home, finally arriving in Sanlúcar de Barrameda, Cádiz, on November 7, 1504, two and a half years after departing to what was, I am convinced, the most extraordinary of Father's four expeditions. For more than a year we had been castaways in that beach in Jamaica, a merciless illusion of paradise that saved us from drowning just to keep testing us. Who could believe what had happened during this final voyage of the Admiral? As Father reported to the monarchs, "in this letter, I have reported but a hundredth of what happened. Those who were with me can bear witness to it."

As we sailed up river Guadalquivir to Seville, I sat with Father in his cabin.

He looked finally at peace. Sure enough, it was a relief to be back home, alleviated from the dangers and probations we had endured. But there was something more. Whatever Diego Mendez did during the twelve months he had been away, it surely appeased Father's anxiety. His eyes looked clear as I had not seen them in a long time, as if a shadow had lifted. Only later would I come to understand why.

"Whatever happens, my son, you must keep what you promised me before our departure from Cádiz two and a half years ago.", Father told me. "You must do everything in your power, take all resources I shall leave you, to recover my books. Alas, if Ovando's foolish decision to send the Caravels with the Spanish treasure and all my belongings in front of the hurricane has not thrown everything to waste."

"I remember, Father. And I shall keep my word. I will recover your books and add to the collection, building a large library that will be the envy of European intellectuals. I will not let your name disappear in vain."

"Indeed, Fernando, indeed. A great secret, a most valuable treasure, is amongst those books. Protect the books and keep them safe from that madman Torquemada. The church has already extinguished the Templars looking for the forbidden Book, but it escaped between their fingers because they were looking in the wrong place. All this time, the guardian of the Book was the German Holy Roman Empire. My Father abandoned his lands and titles to protect the secret and hide the Book. Now it is your honour and duty to protect the secret. Torquemada and his Holy Inquisition are burning books, heretics and Jews in equal measure, desperately in search of the Book... You cannot imagine what they would do to get hold of the Book. I fear they will burn all libraries in big "Autos de Fé" in search of the Book."

"But how can I protect something if I do not know what it is?"

"It is better this way. You, like me, are a son of Kings. Keep my signature alive. It is a message for future generations, until the time is ready for the secret to be revealed. They will try to destroy me and push me aside to forgetfulness. Keep the signature alive."

Father pulled one of his logbooks and opened it on the first page. At the bottom was inscribed his mysterious signature, which I had often seen in many letters and scripts.

: Xpoferens ./

"Can you decipher the code, Fernando? You must become familiar with the code, for I do not know how long I will live"

"Xpoferen is a Latinised version of Chistopher. The ":" comes from the Greek rhetoric term 'kôlon'. This reads your name, Christopher Colon."

"Yes, yes, true. The eyes see only what they want to see. I have taken to use that name, and so people read it in the signature. But look deeper, Fernando. Always look deeper."

"Well, Xpo is an abbreviation for Christ. And "colon" in Latin means 'member' or 'limb'. You are Christ's limb, walking with Christ, doing His work on earth, finding new lands for His glory."

"But the colon is more than that. The eyes see only what they expect to see. Think of your Latin, what is the other meaning of 'colon'?"

"uhh... 'member' not as a limb but as belonging to group. Aahhh... Member of the Order of Christ!"

"Well done, my son. What about the scribble at the end, beneath the ': Xpoferens ./'?"

"Isn't that just a scribble?"

"Look at me. Nothing I do is just a scribble. Nothing is left to chance. How do you think I survived more than 15 years of deceit, coning the Catholic Kings? Nothing I do is by chance, even when I look insane and lost. Men like to feel powerful, and the best way to trick them is to flatter their snobbery. That way they let the guard down and become easy prey to deception."

Realization downed on me. The scribble was in fact an S. Segismundo. Father's true name, hidden there, in plain sight. Father never signed "Christopher Colon", although he tricked everyone into reading that name into his signature.

"Segismundo, Member of the Order of Christ".

Father lied down and closed his eyes. "Protect the books and hold the signature. I shall not be confounded forever."

LISBON, FEBRUARY 2019

"The Portuguese Empire is one of the biggest enigmas of History"

SANJAY SUBRAHMANYAM

T he three met at Duma's place, on a cold and cloudy Friday afternoon at the beginning of February. Duma's apartment would henceforth become a kind of unstated headquarters for their meetings to discuss Raven's notebook.

"I bet you haven't figured this one out!", stated Duma as soon as they were installed around the table. Duma had gone straight to the middle pages of the notebook, which contained some strange symbols that Savanah had vaguely recognized as ancient Viking runes, from her childhood games, but failed to understand what the heck were Viking runes doing on a research about Colon.

"That's…. well, it looks like a spider. The central body plus 8 legs". Savanah threw her head back, hands holding up her long hair on a ponytail at the top of the head. She felt a mix of desperation and amusement.

Duma pulled the page towards her and picked the pen.

With a slight smile, she joined together the open ends of the pictogram.

Sergio and Savanah exclaimed simultaneously, although choosing different terminology:

"Oh Fuck!", exclaimed Sergio, at the same time Savanah said "Oh God".

The Templar cross carried on the sails of the Portuguese Caravelas!

"Raven showed this to me. The connection between the Templar cross on the sails of the Caravelas and ancient Nordic runes is actually what started her thinking about the connection between a Templar southern path (the Portuguese discoveries) and a northern path (Henry Sinclair and Rosslyn Chapel in Scotland). Earl Henry Sinclair, a Templar knight and Norwegian/Scottish noble, supposedly took a portentous secret into hiding in Nova Scotia. In the early twelfth century, when the Templars were born the runes had been replaced by the Latin alphabet and cast away into shadowy corners of medieval magic, so it would be perfect for a secret order to convey a message amongst their members."

"Amazing", conceded Savanah. "Still, what the fuck are Viking runes doing in the fifteenth century Portuguese Caravelas? What have the Vikings to do with Columbus?"

"Well, there is a link, I guess", said Duma. "It is well known that the Vikings reached and settled Greenland and maybe Canada before the tenth century, almost 500 years before Columbus reached America. The Portuguese sailors had plenty of opportunity to contact American peoples many years before Columbus. The 1473 Corte-Real and

1476/77 Luso-Danish expeditions explored Nova Scotia and Newfoundland. The map of Pizzigano, dated 1424, already shows what the Portuguese had named the Antilles (meaning, "ante as ilhas", in front of the Azores islands), corresponding to the current Nova Scotia and Newfoundland in the Pizzigano map."

Savanah sat in silence, lost in her own thoughts, not really listening to Duma. She tried to focus her mind on connections between the tons of facts bombarding it. Her subconscious mind was following some line of thought, but not yet ready to raise to the conscious level.

"Extraordinary, the cross in the Portuguese Caravelas constructed from ancient Nordic runes...", said Savanah, staring at the symbol that had eluded her so far.

"It just misses the wiggle...", noted Duma in a whisper.

"The what?", asked Savanah, still in a trance.

"The little wiggle at the top right arm. That kind of hook on the north-eastern arm of the wind cross."

Savanah realized what Duma was referring to. The Templar cross on the Caravels was missing the little hook.

LISBON, FEBRUARY 2019

When she returned to her attic flat that evening, Savanah felt tired to the bones, with the threat of a headache at the back of her mind. She managed to take a shower and mix a stir fry of vegetables and some chicken leftovers. She ate on the balcony, enjoying the cold windy evening.

Savanah could barely focus on the Netflix series playing on her iPad. She had been distracted all evening since returning from Duma's apartment, her mind whizzing uncontrolled between the fabulous story of an anti-Rome conspiracy at the heart of the Templars, catching Professor Noronha lie about the source of his wealth and this afternoon's revelation of ancient Nordic runes embedded into the Templar cross of the Portuguese Caravelas.

She was lying on the couch staring at the screen, firmly trying to ignore Raven's notebook lying provocatively on the floor near the feet of the sofa. But it was pointless.

A heavily marked sentence in the notebook, which she had ignored so far, acquired a new meaning. It read:

"Professor found Sauniere's treasure, but refuses to share.

The church of Blue Apples protected the Ark, hidden from the devils. The Ark that conceals God's secret is in Arcadia, with the Shepherdess."

It was, of course, indecipherable. But Noronha found a

'*treasure*'… Was this treasure the source of the sudden riches that paid for the Restelo mansion? And, if she remembered correctly, this Saunière guy was somehow related to the legend of the Holy Grail. As was the Scottish Henry Sinclair, who had unexpectedly appeared that afternoon, through the ancient Nordic runes, connected to the Portuguese Caravelas.

"Ohh, all right. I guess I'm just postponing the inevitable, so better get going with it."

She got up and took her iPad, preparing for several hours of research on Saunière and Henry Sinclair. As it turned out, both were a kind of movie stars in Templar lore.

The Order of the Temple of Solomon was formed in Jerusalem after it was captured by Christians in 1099, during the first Crusade. The Order's was formed supposedly to protect the peregrines to the Holy Land, but that was only the fronting for its true objective: protect a tremendous secret discovered in the ruins of the Salomon Temple in Mount Zion, hidden in Hagia Maria Sion, the Mother of All Churches constructed on the site where Christ died and ascended into heaven.

A restricted brotherhood within the Templars kept the sacred vow to protect the secret: the royal bloodline of Christ. The Grail, the Chalice of eternal life. The bloodline was dangerous for the Church's doctrine and would fatally undermine the Pope's power and wealth as the delegate of God on Earth. Royal Blood is Sang Royal in French, Sang Real in Spanish. This tremendous secret discovered by the Templars in the Temple of Solomon has been known by many names: Sangreal, San Greal, Saint Graal, Holy Grail.

Mary Magdalene fled to the south of France with her child after Jesus crucifixion. Her descendants were the Merovingian kings who ruled large parts of France, Germany and Poland until the eighth century. The German Holy Roman

Empire later ruled many of those regions, refusing to recognize the authority of the Pope of Rome on Earthly or political matters.

At the beginning of the thirteenth century, facing political unrest and anticipating the threat from the French king and the Pope, the Templars took their treasure to a new safe place. According to legend, Earl Henry Sinclair escaped through Norway, crossed to Scotland where the bloodline of Mary Magdalene and Christ was hidden, in the lands where later the Rosslyn Chapel would be built. Before the end of the century, Sinclair sailed to Nova Scotia, the western legendary lands of Avalon (America), taking the Sang Real to protection.

In the nineteenth century, the French priest François-Bérenger Saunière was sent to run a church dedicated to Mary Magdalene in the Pyrenees village of Rennes-le-Chateaux. There, Saunière became suddenly very rich. Between 1898 and 1905 he amassed a large estate, including a magnificent palace, Villa Bethania.

Rennes-le-Chateaux is located close to the family estate of Lord Godfrey de Blancheford, whose youngest son Bertrand de Blancheford was the sixth Grand Master of the Knights Templar from 1156 until his death in 1169.

So, it is natural that rumours around Saunière started running wild: he had stumbled upon a great secret and discovered a Templar treasure hidden by Blancheford in the Mary Magdalene church. Saunière's sudden enrichment, together with the vicinity to a Templar Grand Master ancestral home and the holy site of Virgin Mary of Lourdes nearby contributed to generate a wave of superstition and mysticism around Rennes-le-Chateaux.

The supernatural attraction of the place was such that, during the second world war, Nazi soldiers conducted deep excavations in the area. The Nazi were most likely looking for the Holy Grail, a supreme power which the Merovingian kings of the ancient Germanic Holy Roman Empire had kept secret for centuries. In fact, the German composer Richard Wagner composed his opera Parsifal shortly after visiting Rennes-le-Chateaux, based on the medieval Grail quest of Avalon. Parsifal, or Perceval, was one of King Arthur's knights of the Round Table. Curiously, Perceval is a derivation of "par cheval", the French for "by horse", which can be a hidden reference to the Order's whose symbol was two knights riding a horse: The Templars.

Savanah put two and two together. This guy Saunière found some secret treasure in a church near the castle of a Templar Grand Master and became suddenly rich. Taking Raven's note at face value, Professor Noronha had found Saunière's treasure and refused to share it... was this the source of his sudden wealth, to pay for his mansion in Restelo?

She fell asleep on top of the duvet, still dressed, but woke up just a few hours later. It was still dark outside, but it was useless to try to go back to sleep. She got up, yesterday's headache threat now turned into a migraine. This was probably her rational, ordered brain recoiled in protest against all the wild guesses and esoteric non sense it was being subject to.

SEVILLE, 1485

Monastery of Santa Maria
de las Cuevas

(Friar Gaspar Gorricio)

"There is always some madness in love. But there is also always some reason in madness."
FRIEDRICH NIETZSCHE

Colon is restless. I see him lingering here in the Monastery, reading endlessly and taking copious notes. I am certain he feels he is wasting valuable time he should be using to take part in the epic discoveries going on. But we must persevere. The task is too important. Colon knows his name will never be associated with a grand discovery as he is bound to lead Isabella and Fernando to those western islands and the wasteland beyond, which has in the first explorations failed to provide any sign of civilization or gold or any valuable merchandise.

I fear there is more to his restlessness, though. He tells me he has been having dreadful nightmares about Filipa, as if a premonition of something wrong. I tell him to rest, Filipa is surely being well taken care of. But he feels something is amiss. I try not to give much thought to his dreams, but they are disturbing. If only he could get his mind soothed with plans of preparing an expedition... Las Cuevas library is well stoked, but by God, there is only so much a man can read!

Thankfully, Colon's restless mind got some well

needed respite from the obsessive machinations it tends to fall into, when not focused on work. King João II invited him to join the audition of the cosmographer José Vizinho, just returned from Guiné to take measurements of the sun. It is of the utmost importance to develop tables with accurate sun altitude on the equator at different times of the year, so that sailors can estimate latitude in the high seas without depending solely on the evening star. I guess it was odd for him, returning to Portugal. This was his first visit to Lisbon after the exile in Spain. All had to be secret, of course, but upon his return he told me excitedly about the developments. It must have been rather extraordinary to take part in the discussions amongst the great scientists of the 'Junta dos Matemáticos' assembled in Lisbon to receive Vizinho's news. But the secret trip to Lisbon also played a heavy toll on his soul. Colon met Filipa in secret, and he is convinced she is not well. It distraught him to see his beautiful and noble wife willing the days away in the All Saints Monastery. He fears for her life. And I fear for his mental sanity.

The dreams were an ill-fated premonition. I received a letter from Father Fernão Martins, private councilor of King João, just weeks after Colon's return from the Vizinho's council. I read Father Martins' letter in disbelief, as he passed me the news of Filipa's death. I strained, unable to muster the courage to break the terrible news to Colon. Oh, words are pointless, nothing but noise unable to penetrate the complex layers of conflicting thoughts that must be going around my friend's mind. I knew his father well, when he took refuge in the Pyrenees, living like a hermit for two years before moving to Madeira island. Colon is like a son to me.

I don't know what to do, though. Since hearing the news about his wife, Colon shut himself in a cell in spiritual deluge, eating only bread and water. He won't talk to me, but at least I see he is writing like a maniac. Probably an internal dialogue with God, going through his own catharsis. The death of Filipa severs the last link to his previous life. I hope Colon will be able to pull himself together, morphing into a new person. Like a caterpillar, Colon shut himself inside his cell, his very own cocoon. The grief must be eating its way through his soul, destroying the last vestiges of his previous existence. But he is strong. I pray for him. I pray he will be able to clutch to the strongest threads of his mission, feeding on the raw energy left being in the void of his previous self, and hatch from the cocoon. I pray he is strong enough to leave Segismundo Alemão definitely behind and fill the empty space in his life as Cristobal Colon.

I have to refrain from interfering in his catharsis. It is risky to disturb a caterpillar inside its cocoon during the metamorphosis process, any outside interference may adulterate the whole process and leave him a ghostly zombie. This is an internal process Colon needs to go through himself. I just stand by him, waiting until he is strong enough to sail again.

Colon asked his friends in Lisbon to send him the silver bullet that Filipa kept in a neckless. He now clings to it, carrying it at his chest. He tells me that in the hardest moments, he clings to the bullet and dreams of dying and meeting Filipa in the afterlife. This concerns me significantly. I saw Colon yesterday putting the single silver bullet in the chamber of his pistol, spinning the chamber, and firing the pistol to his head. I tried to take the pistol away from him, but he just looked at me with those supernatural blue eyes, in a crazed fury. I had no alternative but to leave him be. The only thing I can do is to stand by him and be there when he is ready.

Filipa's grave is kept at the Chapel of Piety in the Carmo Monastery in Lisbon, the majestic gothic monastery founded by the Portuguese hero and saint Constable Dom Nuno Alvares Pereira, in the hill frontal to the St. Jorge Castle. This befits her status and noble position.

SEVILLE, 1487

(Columbus)

The wait again… the never ending wait! I must get to the sea again. This quotidian life kills me, with its succession of never ending sameness, tomorrow the same as today the same as yesterday. At least on the sea we face storms, winds, unknown – the real dangers on which I know how to excel. Not this… the little court games, the domestic problems, the endless list of small things to do. God, how I would give everything for my life to be a constant swirl of being, instead of this lull of nothingness.

Lorenzo di Berardi arrived in Seville. He is the father of my personal secretary here in Seville, Juanoto Berardi. These visits from Portuguese friends and agents are a welcome change to the boredom of Seville. I crave the seas, but am stuck with the power games and gallantry I am forced to play here, allaying the suspicions of the Spaniards. I met Juanoto and his father in Lisbon, after my confirmation as a knight, during the preparations for the several African expeditions I participated. Lorenzo di Berardi was already at the time a very expedite merchant in the African routes, thanks to a trade privilege he received from the King Dom Afonso V. Juanoto is astute and hard worker like his father, but more philosophical. He prefers the subtleties of court politics than the rudeness of business and commerce. Juanoto worked closely with me all those years in Portugal and joined me in Seville shortly after I left Portugal. He is also the fiscal of Dom João II in Seville to charge the fifth part of the profits owed to the King of Portugal by the ships licensed to operate in Guinea. He is a good friend and great company during these times of loneliness and wait.

Lorenzo bought me an extraordinary letter from Lisbon, signed by the Italian cosmographer Toscanelli. It is addressed to me, signed by Toscanelli and dated 1481, before the man's death, although this is the first time I see the letter. It is a wonderful forgery. Toscanelli had already underestimated the size of the globe, but the calculations shown in this letter are even more deceiving than the original. I shall use the letter in the audience with Isabel and Fernando to support my claims. Lorenzo says it is copied directly from the original letter received in 1474 by Father Fernão Martins, which remains in the secret archives of King Dom João. The date had to be changed to be after the arrival of the Italian fellow Colombo in Lisbon and before Toscanelli's death.

Also, Pero da Covilhã is in Florence, on his way to Egypt and Ethiopia, to strengthen the cooperation with the Medici. He is spreading rumors of a vast correspondence exchanged from 1476 to 1481 between Toscanelli and a Genoese trader in Lisbon named Christopher Colon. Pero's letters also suggest Lorenzo di Medici promised to send Amerigo Vespucci, a reputable and industrious official who should warrant no mistrust from the Spaniards, to support and participate in the enterprise of the western indies.

Perhaps even more extraordinary are the news brought by Lorenzo Berardi of the latest feats from the Portuguese scientists.

I am keen to discuss these developments with Friar Antonio Marchena. The Queen trusts him in cosmographic matters and he shall make this Toscanelli's letters known to her. Hopefully he will also be able to secretly bring me a copy of those Zacuto's Tables of Solar Declination, now perfected after José Vizinho's calculations.

LISBON, DECEMBER 1488

(Columbus)

T he letter from El-Rey summoning me to this private Council arrived in Seville 9 months ago, in March. It was signed by El-Rey's own hand and addressed to "Xpovan Collon, our special friend in Seville": [141]

"We, Dom João II, by the grace of God king of Portugal and the Algarves, of overseas lands in Africa, Lord of Guinea, send you our deepest regards. We have seen the letter you wrote us, which shows your good will and affection for being at my service. We thank you for your devotion and loyalty. Regarding your visit to Lisbon, for the reasons you mention and also the other matters for which we need your industrious diligence and ingenuity, we will be very pleased to receive you and provide your dues in a way that you should be pleased. And to avoid any apprehension, we, by this letter, ensure your safe coming, stay and return, ordering you shall not be arrested, detained, or accused for any matters. By this manner, we request and pray you come swiftly, for which we shall thank you and take in good service.

Written in Avis, twentieth of March 1488.

EL-REY"

I was very pleased with the letter. Pity I cannot show it to Beatriz, as she sometimes doubts my standing. I can hardly blame her, considering how my proposal to sail west is much scorned by everyone at the Spanish court. My coat of arms ensures our social position and they keep consulting and paying me, eager to peek on the Portuguese maritime secrets I slow feed them. I guess they fear there might be some reason in my proposal and miss an opportunity, but also they fear being mocked and ridiculed for taking such mad enterprise.

Dias's return was expected much sooner. The letter from El-Rey in March was a summons to the council, to be held after Dias return, which was expected shortly. But he took much longer. Some feared the fleet had wrecked and his mission failed.

So I waited yet nine more months until Dias fleet was seen approaching the Algarve and heading to Lisbon. December was already high when I received the news and travelled fast to Lisbon.

Bartolomeu Dias has finally returned, victorious, 16 months after departing Lisbon in August 1487. Seventy years of a continuous and persistent national project to reach the southernmost tip of Africa, turn into the Indic and reach India, is finally a stone throw away. Dias crossed the illusive cape many though did not exist - Cape Diab, as it was named in the Venetian Fra Mauro's map, commissioned 30 years ago by King Afonso.

Dias voyage took 480 days! He discovered 360 leagues of new coast from the point Diogo Cão previously reached, and opened the passage into the Indic. The strategy set by King João twenty years ago proved right: the shortest ocean route to India is by contouring the south of Africa.

This is a tremendous achievement by Dias and a momentous time for the Portuguese ambitions to rule the seas. The southern tip of Africa has proven a hard challenge, claiming many lives and requiring fierce determination. Dias honored the heroes of this grand national project by naming the Cape of Storms, in remembrance of all who perished to fight the turbulent waters and deadly winds. But King Dom João II wants to rename it as Cape of Good Hope. This is the beginning, not the end of Portuguese achievements.

The reports of Dias are inspiring. The fleet was small and agile, only two caravels and a supply ship. But what they lacked in size, they compensated in skill, with some of the Portuguese leading pilots. The fleet passed the last stone pillars left by Diogo Cão on the west coast of Africa. They carried Portuguese speaking Africans who they landed at several points along the way, ambassadors to collect information about the Arab routes, whom they would recover on the way back (unfortunately, few did).

At the beginning of 1488, the little fleet was almost at 30º South, after more than five months struggling against contrary winds and currents, tacking in a zig zag course. Then, Dias took a counterintuitive and inspired decision: he stopped tacking, giving up the battle against the winds. Instead, they took sails to half-mast and turned the ships away from the shore, sailing out to the west, the opposite direction they aimed to reach. The maneuver makes sense, inspired by the wide loop westwards into the middle of the Atlantic that the ships returning home from the coast of Africa make, to use the trade winds. For thirteen days they got carried southwest into the vast and cold ocean. At 38º south, they were already in the ice cold Antarctic regions. Then, the maneuver paid off. Winds became more variable, allowing an eastern course. Dias turned the ships east and sailed for several days, no land in sight, until turning back north.

At the end of January, finally, they spied high mountains in the horizon. On 3 February 1488 they touched land, having rounded the Cape without seeing it, after 4 weeks in the open sea. They saw a large herd of cows guarded by men with wooly hair, like those of Guinea. Dias named the spot Angra de São Brás [64], nicknamed Cowherds Bay. They continued upwards for a few days until Rio do Infante [65], where they turned back after leaving the last stone pillar. On the return journey Dias could sail close to shore and sighted Cape Needles and, in May, the Cape of Storms, now renamed Cape of Good Hope by the King.

Rounded the cape, the sea is the same! Another mythic giant fallen, the fear conquered.

I am happy for my friend Dias, although this puts additional pressure on me to achieve my mission of taking the Spanish kings to commit to a western route, protecting the Portuguese southern route to India. The king wants to stop everything until we are certain the Spanish kings will leave the southern route alone. This means Dias achievement shall remain secret and the preparations for the next expedition to reach India will have to wait until I convince Isabella and Fernando to sail west, tricking them into demanding for a new Treaty to protect their new lands, these Antilles I shall serve them disguised as the Indies. Portugal is a small country with not enough men to protect the empire by force. Cunning and diplomacy are the only weapons the politicians can use to protect what the science, wit and courage of our cosmographers and sailors discover. Only a new Treaty can protect the southern route for the Portuguese king.

I have travelled fast from Seville as soon as I had word of Dias' return, answering the King's summons. I carry the King's letter with me, as a safe conduct. The ruse created to justify my departure from Portugal and make the Spanish believe I hate the King requires that everyone thinks I am a persecuted man in Portugal.

As I wait in my chambers to be called for the council, I read again those friendly lines El-Rey wrote me, his 'special friend in Seville'. Oh, it is such a lonely and frustrating position, to stand aside peddling a lie while others get covered in glory. An ungrateful mission, but a critical one nevertheless. I must remind myself that I will never make a truly new discovery. I am simply to rediscover for the Spanish the lands of the Antilles already known for decades – but that is a critical mission and the King could only bestow it on a knight of his great trust. And then there is also the ultimate goal, the final mission that must remain secret. Secrecy is the only way to protect the Wind Rose and the Rose Line from the greedy tentacles of Rome.

The king is in the courtyard, despite the cold December afternoon. He seems in a very foul mood. He is cracking nuts open with his bare knuckles, a pile of hard shells in front of him on the wooden table.

"Dias, what do you think you were doing?", Dom João exclaimed as we entered the courtyard, without any of the usual preliminary courtesies. "Your orders were clear, were they not? To pass the cape, map the currents and winds, and TURN BACK! Instead, what do you do? You keep sailing north, like a leisurely Sunday cruise, up to this River of the Infante [66]. You reached barely a day's distance from Sofala. You know damn well the Arabs trade down the Indic coast of Africa and Sofala shows in several Arab maps. What if they saw you, or the locals got scared of the big Caravelas, so different from the Arab vessels, and then start telling stories?"

He crushes another nut with his knuckles, a loud cracking sound filling the courtyard, as if the King was crushing skulls instead of nuts.

"God, you know what would happen if the world finds out we cornered the south of Africa, proving there is a passage from the Atlantic to the Indic? Soon we would have Spanish, French, Flemings, English, Italians... all lining up to take the route and circumvent the Arabs monopoly on the spices and silk trade."

Then the King turns to me and punches the table hard with his right hand, sending nut shells showering all around.

"What about you, Colon?! What are you waiting for? Almost five years you have been in Spain, I have provided you all the support and allies in the court to conquer the trust of the devil woman. How hard can it be? Like all courts in Europe, Isabella and Fernando crave our maritime knowledge and secrets to reach the Indies. You have to make that pious beatified queen wet herself just by dreaming of fleets full of the riches from the Indies."

"I even got you two letters, from the English and French kings, delivered to your brother Bartolomé committing to back your enterprise to sail west. This should allay the Spanish fears, make you coveted and disputed by the great European powers. How long more, Colon? We need a new Treaty. The Alcaçobas line is based on the Canary Islands latitude. We find the passage, reach India and China, but then these lands are North of the Alcaçobas line and... for Christ's sake, the Spaniards keep it! We need a new Treaty based on a meridian, protecting the east for us!"

"My Lord", I answer humbly but firmly. The King is not being reasonable and he should know that. "The expedition we want the Spanish to undertake is just foam in the water, it dissolves in the hands of reason. Even Dias journey proves the west route would be too long to undertake. He has travelled 3.100 leagues, which is 1.550 leagues each way. Lisbon is 38º North latitude and Cape of Good Hope is 33º South, which means Dias travelled just 20% of the circumference.

That should be enough to scare the Spanish. Lisbon to India, on Ptolomeu's maps, is 9 hours or 135 degrees traveling east, which means 225 degrees travelling west. That would be almost 19.000 miles on a rough inference based on Dias journey. Even if the Spaniards are not famil...."

"God almighty, Alemão. I don't need a geography lesson. I don't take the Spanish kings for fools, I take them for greedy!", exploded the King.

There was nothing more to say, really. But the King was right. I knew from the start this would be a difficult and trying mission, which would require great cunning. I have struggled for almost 5 years now to convince Spain to back my expedition. "Never, in all this time, has it been found a pilot, sailor or philosopher or man of any other science that would say my enterprise was not false." [67]

The King continued rattling, hammering the table repeatedly with his fist and spreading nut shells around the floor.

"Alemão, I don't care how you do it! If reason and faith don't make it, then you...you get into the queen's bed, make her scream for redemption with your cock between her legs until you convince her! That woman has probably never had the weight of a proper man on top of her, that's why she prays so much. I bet she gets wet in her legs as she listens to your tales of conquering new lands and submitting infidels to Christ. With your blue eyes and long hair, she probably thinks you are some kind of angel, with that air of mysticism you exude."

LISBON, FEBRUARY 2019

S avanah was struggling with another question, which she wanted to discuss with Duma. But alone. So she had to keep the question nagging on her mind still a bit longer, seating at her desk and pretending to read, to kill some time until she could get hold of Duma.

She had to wait a couple of hours until Pedro left to teach one of his classes. Then, she took the opportunity to approach Duma's desk and ask her:

"Duma, there is something else I've been wanting to ask you. Does the name Saunière mean anything to you? I mean, Saunière's treasure…"

Duma looked at Savanah as if she was from another planet. Well, indeed, a New Yorker investment banker was probably as far away from the world of fifteenth century historical academic research as a Martian from Earth.

"Of course", she answered. "Professor Noronha dwelled into Saunière's parchments for a long while, he was convinced they were somehow related with Henrique Alemão, Colon's father. And Raven did as well."

Duma told Savanah the details of Saunière and his church in the French Pyrenees, pretty much in line with what she had read online some nights before.

However, the story did not end there. In 1982, Michael Baigent, Richard Leigh and Henry Lincoln published a book entitled "The Holy Blood and the Holy Grail". It revealed evidence that about a century earlier, Saunière had discovered four parchments in sealed wooden tubes. Saunière had sup-posedly found these parchments when he had the altar stone removed in 1891, during reconstruction works at the Church.

Those parchments have since been subject to scien-tific dating tests – the earliest one was dated from 1244 (so, 75 years after Blancheford death) and the two latest were dated from 1780. They looked like Latin texts but made no sense, suggesting some type of coded message. These parch-ments are very real and were in fact part of several documen-taries by the BBC.

It took a while to decipher the code in the parch-ments. The key is to read the letters in the order created by the movement of a Knight on a chessboard... rather ap-propriate, for a Templar coded message. Even this is not straightforward, as on every "letter", the Knight can make four possible moves. The simplest form is to take the 8x8 chess board and mark only the squares where knights can land, and use that as a grid for the text.

"So...", Savanah prompted her friend. "What do the parchments reveal?"

"At the time when Professor was working on this, it was all rather hush hush. Now, it is all online." Duma's fingers flew over the keyboard on her desk and an image filled the screen:

"Right... that's gibberish, looks like someone was playing a prank on all the Templar maniacs out there...", sighted Savanah, tired of all the codes and conspiracy theories. Why can't people just say what they have to say, for fuck's sake? Does it make them feel more important, if they pretend to have some secret message only unveiled to the worthy...??!

"My thoughts, exactly! I told so to Professor Noronha and Raven, they should focus on proper historic work instead of poking around into this non sense that just feeds wild and dangerous theories. Anyway, in case you are curious – here are the translated messages using that 'knight on the chessboard' algorithm.

The first parchment, of the thirteenth century, reads:

'A Dagobert II ROI et a Sion est ce tresor et il est la mort'.

This translates to: 'To King Dagobert II and to Sion belongs this treasure and He is there dead.'

Or alternatively, 'To King Dagobert II and to Sion belongs this treasure and it is Death.'

The second parchment, dated of the eighteenth century, reads:

'Bergere pas de tentation, que Poussin Teniers gardent la clef, Pax DCLXXX1. Par la croix et ce cheval de dieu, j'acheve ce daemon de gardien a midi. Pommes Bleues'.

This translates to something like: 'Shepherdess no temptation, Poussin, Teniers hold the key. Peace 681. By the cross and this horse of God, I make this Demon Guardian. At midday Blue Apples.'"

"Ok. And you call that deciphering the code? That's still nonsense.", said Savanah, rolling up her eyes in disbelief.

"Well, that's where Professor Noronha comes in. He proposed a meaning for the first parchment. This was 2006. I remember that time quite vividly. Your sister had just arrived. His interpretation for the first Rennes-le-Chateaux parchment establishes the link between Colon and the parchments in the Pyrenees: In 1444, the Germanic Holy Roman Empire went to battle in Varna, Bulgaria, trying to stop the advance of the Muslim armies from the east. The army was decimated. Shortly after emerges in Madeira, around 1450, a mysterious Germanic pilgrim and Knight of Mount Sinai, Henrique Alemão, who marries an elite noble lady, daughter of the Captain of Porto Santo."

"I'm lost, Duma... What has all this to do with the parchment... oohhhh" understanding downed on her mind. Of course.

The Rennes-le-Chateaux church in the French Pyrenees, dedicated to Mary Magdalene. A thirteenth century parchment in the Pyrenees talking about a Templar treasure. A Germanic pilgrim to the Holy Land who then takes a secret identity in Madeira, painted with a secret Book hidden in his pilgrim's pouch. A Templar's treasure carried into hiding in the western limits of the known world, Madeira island. Colon as the son of this secretive pilgrim who carries the treasure to... to do what?

"I see", gaped Savanah, her eyes wide open. "The Templar treasure belongs to the Merovingian kings and to Sion. Dagobert II was a Merovingian king who ruled regions of France and Austria and considered a martyr. Sion refers to the Templars, founded on Mount Sion. So the treasure belongs to the Merovingian kings, whom legend portrays as descendants of Mary Magdalene royal lineage, and to the Templars who protected the bloodline. That explains the first part 'To King Dagobert II and to Sion belongs this treasure'. But what does the second part mean 'and it is Death´?"

"Well done", said Duma. "That was Professor Noronha interpretation as well. The second part is trickier. I remember Raven and Professor Noronha discussing it. One version was that the treasure is Death itself, the opposite of the Holy Grail legend who was supposed to grant eternal life. The true treasure is not to live eternally but the inevitability of Death that rejuvenates all things. The other version is that the translation means 'and He is dead'. Someone who was supposed to be eternal but this treasure proves is dead..."

"You mean... Jesus Christ?"

"Let's stop here, Savanah. This is where we enter speculative territory."

"Hold on, but what happened next? What did Noronha and Raven do about this? Did they publish their interpretation?", asked Raven.

"I'm afraid things turned quite weird at that point", said Duma. "One day, Professor Noronha arrived in the office and ordered everyone to destroy all documents about the Saunière transcripts. He forbade PhD students to even mention them. He sounded maniac. I remember vividly Raven discussions with him about this. He said it was dangerous, she should drop it. Well, and then..."

"Then...??"

"Then she left to go to Paris on her own. She said it was a short holiday, but Professor Noronha went ballistic when he found out."

Gosh. This was relevant information. The potential implications could be quite daunting.

On one hand, it seemed to alleviate Savanah's concerns about the first part of Raven's note. Professor found the hidden message in Saunière's parchments, but refused to share, i.e., publish them.

On the other hand, the second sentence strongly suggested Raven had not taken the Professor's order to drop the research but carried on digging into the meaning of the second parchment.

What was she looking for in Paris? And what secret was Professor Noronha hiding, or protecting?

"Professor found Saunière's treasure, but refuses to share.

The church of Blue Apples protected the Ark, hidden from the devils. The Ark that conceals God's secret is in Arcadia, with the Shepherdess."

PARIS, APRIL 2006

T he short break in Paris was a cover for her true purpose. But anyway, as Raven left the hotel on Saturday morning, she could not help feeling in a holiday mood. She took the long way towards the Seine, doing a detour to reach the river and then strolled by its margins. The cafés, the sumptuous bridges, the magnificent neoclassical buildings, it all looked so... dignified, as if the all city was stuck in another epoch where time moved at a slower pace, without the rush of movement that characterized modern cities. In a way, this was a blessing. The world moved too fast nowadays, not allowing time for the minds to assimilate the deep meaning of things.

In a way, that's what attracted Raven to historic research. The long tide of human history was marked by deep, constant forces, so different from the ephemeral movements of stock markets or fashion or pop stars. The web of history provided solid references to understand the forces shaping the world, unlike the transitory fast paced modernity.

Raven stopped in a boulangerie and sat in one of the outdoor iron tables watching elegant women and men walking past, baguettes under their armpits. She took her time savouring the croissant and cappuccino, enjoying the pleasure of anticipation. Her destination was the Louvre museum, but she was not in a rush. She wanted to allow her mind to wander freely so that it could see the hidden patterns. If you focus too much, you will only see what your brain expects, not the unexpected.

What had Professor Noronha found? Had he discovered the hidden meaning of the second parchment, and if so what could it be that had so much scared him? Anyway, she didn't care if the secret put herself under some kind of risk. She just wanted to understand.

She stepped into the great glass pyramid that since 1989 serves as the main entrance of the Louvre, taking a brief instant to absorb the symbolism of the structure. The pyramid was commissioned by French president François Mitterrand and designed by Chinese-American architect I. M. Pei. The structure was arguably intended to have a rather pragmatic function, with multiple stairways and a central court top distribute the millions of visitors through a multitude of underground corridors, dispersing the crowd which the previous entrance was unable to hold.

Nevertheless, the Louvre pyramid soon attracted attention and proved a fertile ground to esoteric and symbolic interpretations.

Completed 100 years after the Eiffel Tower, the Louvre glass pyramid is a massive structure above the main courtyard of the Louvre Palace. A short distance away, there is the Pyramid Inversée, a glass inverted pyramid in the Carrousel du Louvre, the underground shopping mall right in front of the Louvre pyramid.

The two glass structures, the pyramid and the inverted pyramid, are symbolic representations of the male and female unity and thus fertility and descendancy.

Overlapping the two pyramids forms a six-pointed star, the Seal of Salomon (also called the Star of David). Also, the two pyramids standing on top of each other, touching just the tips, form vertically the Greek symbol of infinity.

Moreover, the two pyramids stand as symbolic representations of the square and compass, the most well-known symbol of Freemasonry. The square and compass are architect tools, emblem of the Great Architect, and often embed a "G" letter in the middle (standing for 'Geometry' or 'God').

Of course, this can all be just hocus pocus. Why would you place an esoteric symbol in the middle of Paris?

But the conspiracy theories took flight when the official brochure about the new Louvre pyramid published in the 1980s stated that the glass pyramid would contain 666 glass panels. Speculation ran wild ever since. 666 is the number of the beast. The two glass pyramids form a six-pointed hexagram, the Seal of Salomon. The 666 glass panels were later denied. The Louvre museum stated, after completion, that the structure includes 673 glass panels (603 rhombi and 70 triangles). The architect I.M. Pei office stated the structure contains 689 glass pieces [68].

Raven, for her part, believed there is no smoke without fire. In any case, after seeing the translation of Saunière's second parchment, she started having a troubling suspicion.

As she descended into the main concourse, Raven wondered if the truth was in between the 673 glass panels claimed by the museum and the 689 claimed by the architect... 681 glass pieces. Could that be a coincidence? The second Saunière parchment contained the expression "Pax 681".

She had to keep her mind open to follow the signs and information without pre conceived ideas.

Raven walked down the corridors, passing the exhibitions and taking the opportunity to admire the art. She roamed the early Picasso works, astonished. At the age of eight, he painted his first oil painting. At thirteen he was accepted into the Barcelona Academy of Arts after completing a nude drawing in a day that accomplished artists took a month to do. If you paint like that at such young age, what could you do later? Picasso paints those cubes and scribbles because he wants. If I draw scribbles is just because I couldn't do anything else. That's why his scribbles are genius, and mine are just scribbles. Because he chose to do them when he could have done anything else.

Raven tried to force herself to take a slow pace, but she could feel the growing impatience to reach her destination. As she approached room 14 on the second floor of the Richelieu wing, her heart was pounding.

The first part of the Saunière's second parchment read "Shepherdess no temptation, Poussin, Teniers holds the key". Her idea was that this referred to two well-known paintings, "The Arcadian Shepherds" by seventeenth century French painter Nicolas Poussin, and "The Temptations of Saint Anthony" by seventeenth century Flemish painter David Teniers the younger. Poussin's painting was in the Louvre, and the reason for Raven to be here. Tenier's, unfortunately, was in the MIA in Minneapolis, but she had managed to get a picture of the painting sent to her by the museum curator.

Poussin's "The Arcadian Shepherds" depicts a pastoral scene of an idyllic setting from the classical antiquity, with three shepherds and a woman, possibly a shepherdess, gathered around a tomb. Poussin in fact painted two versions of the scene, one in 1627 (held at Chatsworth House) and the other in 1637/38 (held at the Louvre).

However, what makes both Poussin paintings world famous is the enigmatic inscription in the tombs of each painting, which the shepherds contemplate:

"Et in Arcadia Ego"

The inscription has been interpreted by art experts as a reference to the inevitability of Death. It is usually translated as "Even in Arcadia, I am". Arcadia is a region in central Greece, often used in art as a representation of a nostalgic utopia, a rustic and bucolic classical paradise. So, the inscription would remind the viewer that death is forever present, even in the blissful and idyllic Arcadia.

But the reference to Poussin's painting in the enigmatic Saunière parchments suggested there might be a deeper hidden meaning. Raven contemplated the painting, trying to perceive other meanings.

Unlike the three shepherds, who seem to be receiving the message in the tomb for the first time, the shepherdess does not seem surprised, but rather showing the inscription to the others, as if announcing the message. The inscription, quite literally, means that the tomb, the ark, is in Arcadia.

Raven eyes smiled as she contemplated the possibility that Arcadia referred in the seventeenth century paintings was not the nostalgic pastoral region in Greece, but the New Arcadia. Could it be that Poussin had hidden such a tremendous message in plain light, to the eyes of everyone, and yet it remained hidden for almost 400 years? All art experts took the literal reference to the Greek Arcadia, whereas Poussin could be referring to a totally different Arcadia.

As Raven allowed her eyes to soak in the scene, her brain started unconsciously to play with the letters in the tomb, like she used to do in the teenage games with uncle Santiago. The fourteen letters moved in her mind's eye. Then she gasped, in shock. She stood there, unmoving, trying to make sense of what her brain had just conjured.

She got pulled back to reality as a tourist pushed her aside, passing by to the next painting, oblivious to what had just happened. Raven pulled a pen and paper from her bag and moved to the side, writing the anagram of the fourteen letters in Poussin's painting:

"I Tego Arcana Dei"

"I conceal the secrets of God". Or "God's secret". Was she doing this right? There was no doubt. There it was, plain and clear.

The ark, the tomb that conceals God's secret, is in Arcadia.

The "Et..." in the inscription suggested a sense of completing a long sought achievement. As if, after a long time and effort, the ark was finally in Arcadia.

If Poussin provided a lead for a response, Teniers raised a troubling question. The parchment states "Teniers holds the key". On Teniers "Temptations", the treasure St Anthony is protecting against the demons is a Book. It's as if the parchments, by referring to the two paintings, were saying that the Ark was finally in its final destination in Arcadia, the New World, reunited with the bloodline Henry Sinclair had taken to Newfoundland in the fourteenth century. But the key, the final secret, was still under threat by the demons, in Europe. Is it possible that the Templar secret the first parchment refers is not one but two: The Ark and a Book?

Colon secret mission, for which his life had been hidden for five centuries, may have been to take the Book further west, to Arcadia, to reunite it with the bloodline of the northern path. The Book his father had brought to Madeira and depicted in Henrique Alemão's painting, veiled inside his pilgrim's pouch.

But he never made it there. Colon never made it to North America. So, the Book must still be in Europe, in the safe place where Henrique Alemão hid it. Colon's son, Fernando, amassed the largest private library in Europe of his time. Why? Was he trying to hide a secret Book in his massive library, to save it from the claws of the Inquisition fires?

Raven couldn't still make the connection between the Church of Mary Magdalene in the Pyrenees and Colon. But if there is still a lost Templar secret, a Book, hidden somewhere, there is only one place it could be hidden in the tumultuous European fifteenth century: Port-du-Graal, Portugal. In the Covent of Christ, the last bastion of the Templars.

Colon's ultimate, secret mission could well have been – beyond all the other motivations in the political stratagems of the Age of Discoveries – to complete the last Templar mission and take this secret Book to Arcadia, the New World. All the other mysteries in Colon's life are insufficient to justify 500 years of deep conspiracies and lies to hide colon's true identity and mission. Only a massive, dangerous secret could justify the five centuries of relentless efforts by kings and Popes to hide Colon's life.

The discovery Raven made that afternoon in the Louvre was tremendously exciting, and yet she had no one to share it with. Professor Noronha had explicitly told everyone to stop any research on the meaning of the transcripts. She had dinner alone in a nice bistro by the opera house, a delicious steak au poivre with a glass of Cote du Rhone red wine. She was in a celebratory mood.

While enjoying a second glass of Cote du Rhone, she took the image of the "Temptations of Saint Anthony" the MIA curator had emailed her.

Several things called Raven's attention, although she could not yet tell if they were relevant or not. The Tenier's painting depicted the hermit Saint in a grotto or cavern, harassed by a crowd of beaked beasts, a toad, a dwarf riding an animal skeleton and other absurd creatures that surround a horned devil. Disguised as a pimp, the devil tempts the Saint with the pleasures of a woman, while the Saint struggles to protect a Cross, a Book and a Skull. The theme of Death appeared again, represented by the skull, similar to the tomb in Poussin's painting. In the 1627 version of Poussin's painting there was also a skull painted on top of the tomb. Finally, the second Saunière parchment clearly stated "no temptations". As if the Ark "finally in Arcadia" next to the Shepherdess was now guarded against the devils, unlike the Book.

The third glass of Cotes du Rhone was now having its effect. Raven felt ideas started to get mixed up and confused, so she decided to force herself to walk back to the hotel to wear the alcohol off and sleep.

Sunday morning was spent walking leisurely around Paris, sightseeing like a normal tourist, waiting for her 6pm flight to Toulouse, from where she had planned to rent a car and visit Lourdes and Rennes-le-Château church. Not sure if that was wise, but her mind was set on going all the way with this mystery.

During the flight, she took the opportunity to write

down some notes about what she though could explain the reference "Pax 681" in the parchment. If her intuition was correct, it referred to the Third Council of Constantinople, an ecumenical council that intended to end the Monothelite controversy of early Christianity. On 7 March 681, the Third Council of Constantinople adopted the decision previously taken on a synod in Rome presided by Pope Agathus, which had condemned Monothelitism. The doctrinal conclusions were later promulgated in September 681.

Throughout the first centuries of Christianity, the Catholic church faced debates about the nature of Jesus Christ. Monothelitism is the "doctrine of one will", which views Christ as having only one nature, simultaneously human and divine. This is opposite to the Dyothelitism which considers Christ embodies two different natures: the human and the divine are and remain distinct. If Christ has two natures and two wills, then God's will can remain superior and impose itself over the human will. The death of Christ is only the death of his human nature, and the Assumption of Christ returns his material body to the sphere of the divine from where it was initially separated.

Monothelitism is dangerous: each person carries the flame of the divine and is simultaneously human and divine, with free will unrestrained by the boundaries of a frail and limited human nature. The priests and bishops, as interpreters of God's will, would no longer have the monopoly of the souls.

If the Ark containing God's secret was, as she suspected, the mortal remains of Christ, that meant Christ's divinity was inseparable of His humanity. The unity of Christ's divine and human nature could not be separated into a resurrection and ascension.

All this was very interesting, but so far Raven failed to understand how it related to the rest of the message. And how the Pyrenees church was linked with Colon.

The next bit of the parchment she could understand. "By the cross and this horse of God, I make this Demon Guardian". In French it became easier to understand: "Par la Croix and per cheval". Percheval is Parsifal, a Knight of the Round Table of King Arthur who departs in quest for the Grail. He can be seen as a representation of the Templars, whose seal shows two knights on a horse (by horse, per cheval). So, this would mean something like "In name of God, the Templar knights build this Guardian of demons". Would this be a kind of fortress? Or a church? To protect the Templar treasure (Poussin's Ark and Tenier's Book), which held God's secret (Poussin's anagram in the Ark) from Tenier's devils, until they could be reunited with the Shepherdess.

Raven's biggest surprise was yet to come, though. The anagram in Poussin's tomb had fired up her imagination, but she still had no clue about the meaning of the blue apples in Saunière's parchment.

So, it was with a sense of expectation that on Monday morning she entered the church of Mary Magdalene in the hilltop village of Rennes-le-Chateau. She roamed the small church, astonished by the multitude of symbolic references that had for many years attracted occult aficionados. Right above the entrance to the churchyard there was a skull and crossbones. Above the church entrance there was a Latin inscription that read "Terribilis est locus iste", meaning "This place is terrible".

The holy water stoup features four female angels, each with their right hand in a point of the sign of the cross, with the inscription below "Par ce signe tu le vaincras". Below the inscription stand two basilisks above the sculpture of the horned demon Asmodeus.

How much of this was already in the original church and what was installed by Saunière in his renovation works?

In fact, surviving receipts and account books indicate Sau-nière's renovation works cost 11,065 francs over a ten-year period between 1887 and 1897, the equivalent to 4.5 million euros today. That is an absurd amount of money for a small town church.

As fascinating as all this was, Raven could not find anything that would help put all the pieces of the puzzle together. Although not a religious person, she sat on the benches, contemplating the colourful and strange church around her. The main altar featured a beautiful stained glass set in deep blue arch. Above the lateral alter with the bass relief of Mary Magdalene was also a stained glass set within an abode of blue sky with a myriad of white dots... blue apples!!

No way... Raven rushed to the altar of Mary Magdalene. There they were. The midday sun entered the stained glass in the church, creating a luminous pattern of circles in the blue sky above Mary Magdalene.

It was difficult to take all this in. But the message was rather clear. The church of Blue Apples was a bastion to protect the treasure.

Why was Professor Noronha so afraid? She felt thrilled, not afraid. The hidden message could be so... liberating. Centuries of a tremendous lie to deny the unity of the human and the divine, an entire dogma to keep human spirits fearful of an all-powerful external God. No wonder secret orders had gone to great lengths to protect the bloodline and the tomb against the devils.

As understanding downed on her mind, she took her notepad and wrote:

"Professor found Sauniere's treasure, but refuses to share.

The church of Blue Apples protected the Ark,

hidden from the devils. The Ark that conceals God's secret is in Arcadia, with the Shepherdess."

SANTA FÉ, SEPTEMBER 1491

(Columbus)

F rei Antonio Marchena has succeeded! After 6 years, when all seemed lost, Frei Antonio Marchena managed to get a new audience with the Spanish kings to reconsider my expedition. We had used all means of persuasion, including two letters from the English and French kings concocted by Dom João, committing their support to my enterprise as a way to stir pride and jealousy from the Spanish kings. Nothing seemed to work, so obvious is the fallacy of the project. But Frei Antonio, who was a tutor to the Queen since a young age and has great credibility in the court, has managed to get us another audience.

Frei Antonio and I met in Palos in July. He wrote to the Queen directly, insisting with her to authorize the expedition. Not two weeks had passed when she returned his message, accepting to meet him.

The kings have set up camp in Santa Fé, for what is hoped to be the last siege of Granada. There, Friar Antonio met the monarchs and convinced them to reconsider my proposition. After hearing the Friar, Queen Isabella sent 20.000 maravedis ordering Diego Prieto, mayor of the villa of Palos, to deliver them to me, for the expenses of the journey and to prepare appropriately for the audience with Her Highness [69]. We met the monarchs at the beginning of September. Both myself and Friar Antonio presented the most fervours defence of the expedition.

The mood is changing, I feel, and at long last there

seems to be some hope. Two factors probably softened the Queen's mind. Firstly, Granada will soon fall, completing the Reconquista and expelling the Moors from the territory. This will release resources and attentions to the sea as the only route for expansion. Secondly, prince Afonso of Portugal, son of King João II, died mysteriously in July, probably poisoned. The death of prince Afonso paves the way for Dom Manuel to be the next king of Portugal, and he is much more agreeable to the Spanish monarchs than Dom João II. He is plotting to marry the Catholic Kings' daughter and is ready to satisfy the Queen's demands to achieve that.

But this is just a small part of the great plan. However critical the role of Frei Antonio Marchena, several other agents of the king of Portugal are plotting on the side lines. The Order of Christ is gently prodding the Catholic Kings from the background, using the long harm of King João.

The Germanic cartographer Martin Behaim [70] , from Nuremberg, has created a spherical mapa mundi, a Globe. I have not yet seen it, but Father Fernando de Talavera, confessor of Queen Isabel, says it is a wonder. My good friend Antonio Marchena confirmed that in Behaim's globe half the globe is missing, grossly underestimating the true size of the planet. It also dislocates India several degrees east, making it closer to Azores and omitting the Antilles, the new western lands that may block the way. I bet there is a hand of King João II involved in this. Martin Behaim took part in Diogo Cão expedition to Congo, has been knighted by King João II as member of the Order of Christ and is part of the elite Junta dos Matemáticos. He has lived for many years in the Azores and married Joana de Macedo, daughter of the Jew João Huerter, first donatary captain of Faial and Pico.

Behaim's globe should reinforce the theories of the Florentine Paolo Toscanelli, instilling Queen Isabel with the hope my enterprise is doable. Toscanelli wrote to King João in 1474, a letter addressed to Father Fernando Martins in Lisbon. The original remains in the secret archives of King Dom João. However, a copy addressed to me and dated 1481 has been produced. After the 1487 mission of Pêro de Covilhã to the Medici, on his way to Egypt and Ethiopia, other letters addressed directly to me have come to my possession... although the Florentine died in 1482! These forged letters provide credibility to my claims. Indeed, any maps or theories supporting my proposal, if made by Portuguese, would be discounted as a bait by the advisors of Isabella and Fernando, who are of course suspicions. But documents from Germans and Italians can prove much more relevant in seducing the Spanish monarchs.

A Gutenberg's incunabula of the Imago Mundi, from Cardinal Pierre d'Ailly [71], has just been printed in Leuven and is circulating in Spain. I have secured a copy and am using it to sanction the estimates of the circumference that sustain the expedition.

My conviction that the Portuguese king is pulling the strings in a last push to convince Isabel and Fernando is further confirmed by the petition of another German, Jerónimo Munzer. Munzer arrived a few months ago from Nuremberg, where Behaim globe was produced, travelling Spain and Portugal. He wrote a letter to the Portuguese king presenting a proposal from Maximiliano I for a joint expedition to reach the Indies by a western route. His petition to the Portuguese king has been widely talked about by the Spanish spies!!

How extraordinary that just as me and Marchena make a last desperate hope to convince Isabel, after so many rejections, these two Germanic cosmographers appear in Spain, providing credibility to my claims! I strongly suspect both Behaim and Munzer are agents of King João, who recently signed a treaty of cooperation with his cousin, the Germanic emperor Maximiliano I.

The relations between Portugal, France and Germany

encircle the Spanish monarchs like pincers. Dom Pedro, great-uncle of King João II, set the solid foundations of the relationship with the Germanic kings, battling side by side with Emperor Segismundo of Bohemia-Bulgaria against the Turks in Hungary and then in Moravia in 1424. The two families have since established a strong relation.

But the trap being set by the Portuguese king and his agents do not involve only Germans. Since Dias returned from Cape of Good Hope, Dom João II is pressing me to convince Queen Isabel and pulling the strings of his wide network around Europe. My brother Bartolomé was sent in 1488 to the courts of England and France, where he brought with him two amazing letters of the kings purporting they are ready to support and finance my expedition. This must have left Isabella ravening mad!

While in France, my brother was hosted by Madame de Bourbon, regent of France, who suggested and facilitated discussions with the Italian Amerigo Vespucci [72], whom she knows well from the years he spent in her father's Louis XI court. Lorenzo de Medici, honouring the agreements with Pero da Covilhã during his mission in Florence, has sent Vespucci to Seville. He has been working here since 1489 with my secretary Juanoto Berardi, as agent of King João II.

There are several other Italians playing their part here in Seville, Huelva and Cordoba. Lorenzo Berardi, father of Juanoto Berardi, who benefitted greatly from the licences granted by the Portuguese king to trade in Guinea. Ando also, I suspect, Bartolomé Marchioni, Luis de Oria, Francisco de Bardi, Francesco Carduchi, …

Will I finally be able to set sail, more than seven years after giving up my former life in Lisbon and arriving in Palos?

SANTA FÉ, APRIL 1492

I n January 1492, Granada was finally taken by the Catholic Kings.

Shortly after, Isabel signed the royal decree to expel the Jews from Spain. The mad woman is taken by a sense of divine mission. So be it! Me and Friar Marchena are using this missionary impetus to push them to support the expedition and accept my terms. We were received by the royal council, but Hernando de Talavera continued to oppose my plans, calling them implausible. Stubborn man!

Many forces have been at play. Greed and fear, as ever, were the ultimate factors convincing the Queen: greed for glory and fear I sail for France or Portugal.

The Jew Luis de Santángel, treasurer of the Santa Hermandad, has been whispering to her hear and promising to contribute with large part of the financing – that must have been the tipping point to make up Isabella's mind! Becoming the greatest Queen in Christendom and someone else paying for it... that surely appealed to the prophetical destiny she believes for herself.

Between January and April, Friar Antonio Marchena, as my representative, has been leading the negotiations with Juan de Coloma, representative of the crown, to establish the terms of the expedition.

And finally the monarchs capitulated to all my demands. They "ennobled me so that henceforth I may call myself Grand Admiral of the Ocean Sea and Viceroy and

Perpetual Governor of all the islands and mainland that I should discover or win (...) My eldest son will succeed me, and thus from generation to generation, forever". This was a hard bargain because King Fernando's maternal family have until now the only title of Admiral of the Seas in all Spanish kingdoms.

I will also be entitled to ten per cent of profits from "every kind of merchandise, whether pearls, precious stones, gold, silver, spices, and other objects and merchandise whatsoever, of whatever kind, name and sort, which may be bought, bartered, discovered, acquired and obtained within the limits of the said Admiralty". On top of all that, 1/8 of the profits from commerce with those lands.

After signing the Capitulações, Friar Antonio Marchena was also pivotal in overcoming the resistance of the ship owners to support the expedition, convincing Martin Alonso Pinzón to participate with two Caravelas and respective crew. My friend Marchena has been relentless in his support of me and my true mission.

Nicolas de Ovando, in his 'Historia General y Natural de las Indias', asserts that "Friar Antonio Marchena was the sole person in his life to whom Colon confided most of his secrets". Manzano y Manzano stated that Friar Antonio Marchena was the "principal depositary of Colon's great secret".

There is still much debate about who this Friar Antonio Marchena was, and whether he was Portuguese or Spanish. Were Marchena and Friar or João Peres the same person? Fernando Colon and many others call him Juan Peres de Marchena. Bartolomeu de las Casas calls him Antonio Marchena.

The fact is that Colon himself says, in a letter to the catholic Kings: "I never found help from anyone, except Friar

Antonio de Marchena, besides that from God eternal".

LISBON, MARCH 2019

S avanah had spent ten solid weeks going every day to the university campus, reading all the sources Raven mentioned in her notebook. Pedro continued helping to guide her through the labyrinth of information, maps and often contradictory sources. In any case, Savanah had kept the notebook hidden from him.

Sometimes she felt Pedro had a hidden agenda, guiding her in a certain direction, leading her to conclude Raven rumblings were nothing more than that... farfetched theories of a spoiled American girl with nothing better to waist her time and dad's money on, besides flying around between Lisbon, Barcelona, Paris and Genoa trying to get noticed with wild speculations. Maybe he was still traumatized by the sudden death of his girlfriend, if indeed they were dating as Duma suspected.

Besides the university routine, she kept meeting Duma and Sergio every Friday afternoon to discuss and try to decipher Raven's notebook. There was something she had so far omitted from her friends, though. The reference to Professor Noronha having discovered Saunière's treasure, deciphering the hidden message on the parchments, his decision not to publish his findings and insisting with everyone on the team to abandon the investigation of those parchments. And then, his sudden enrichment.

The church of Blue Apples protected the Ark, hidden from the devils. The Ark that conceals God's secret is in Arcadia, with the Shepherdess.

The message in Saunière´s first parchment referred to the treasure of the Merovingian kings and the Priory of Sion, "and the treasure is Death, or is dead". The second parchment mentioned the key was Poussin's Shepherdess and Teniers's Temptations, two well-known paintings by seventeenth century artists. Savanah had been doing her own research on this and found the Arcadian Shepherds painting by Poussin quite disturbing. The inscription in the tomb read "Et in Arcadia Ego". Raven made the same reference in her note, "The ark that conceals God's secret is in Arcadia".

Gosh! What was Washington DC doing in the inscriptions on a coffin in a sevententh century French baroque painting, or on the parchments discovered by a suspicious French priest in a tiny village in the Pyrenees, or by that matter on Raven's notebook?

She had immediately recognized the name, and surely Raven had as well. Uncle Santiago usually referred to Washington DC, when they were alone, as New Arcadia. This was an insiders reference to the Cèllere Codex written by Giovanni da Verrazano to King Francis I of France describing his exploration of the east coast of the United States in 1524. He sailed from Madeira in December 1523 and arrived a month later at what is now North Carolina. His journey covered the east coast from Florida to New York and Newfoundland, before returning to France. In his letter, he describes a region around Chesapeake Bay, probably Worcester county, as "very green and forested, but without harbours". Due to what he called the "beauty of the trees" he named the country Arcadia, reminiscent of the agricultural, bucolic artistic landscape symbolized by the region of Arcadia in central Greece.

This little historic reference is hardly a secret, though. The Arcadia Conference is a landmark of World War II. It was held in Washington DC from December 22, 1941 to January 14, 1942, two weeks after American entry into WW II. It brought together Winston Churchill, Franklin Roosevelt and the top British and American leaders.

What could Raven possibly mean when she wrote that the Ark is in Arcadia??!

After ten weeks of non-stop reading, Savanah's head was throbbing. Despite the piles of information she had accumulated, the same insistent though continued creeping into her mind. What was astonishing about all she had read was not what she had found... but what was missing. How was it possible that there were no documents in Spain or Portugal with the name Colon before 1487, and that the Columbus name only appeared in Portugal in 1504 and was never used in Spain? The silence around Colon before 1484 was almost deafening.

The headache was killing her. She needed a strong expresso. And it was time for lunch anyway – this afternoon she had an appointment at the Policia Judiciária, the investigative branch of the Portuguese police. She had been requesting access to the files of her sister murder investigation for a while. It was a cold case and the police hadn't been very warm to the idea of a foreigner poking around in the files, but her charms had produced some effect. It was an unofficial visit anyway. She would go through the material but would not be allowed any copies or to take it out of the precinct. But what the heck, she could do with some time off those old history books.

She joined Duma at the University canteen for a chicken salad before heading out.

"Savanah, I do hope you find something this afternoon at the Judiciária. I can go with you, if you want, I can skip the afternoon and no-one will ever notice. You know, everyone loved Raven. She was such a driven brilliant young mind, so full of energy. She talked about you to everyone around, all the time..."

"That sounds a bit like Raven, talking about her little sister... You know, that's how she called me, I was born three minutes after her. So, you mean, like...everyone around here knew she had a twin sister?"

"Of course! She even had a photograph at her desk of the two of you. She was so excited before your arrival. She had told everyone you had married and were arriving to Lisbon to spend a few days with her, on a European honeymoon tour. Where on earth did she go on the day of your arrival? She was so much looking forward to spending those days with you. Shortly before... you know, her death... she had said everyone she would be gone for a few days to show her sister around town."

"Is that so? Everyone around here knew I was arriving that day?"

"Oh, certainly."

LISBON, MARCH 2019

Polícia Judiciária

S avanah sat for a couple of hours in the tiny room she was allocated at the Polícia Judiciária, going through the few evidence materials. No more than a couple of briefcases. As Inspector Silva had said, the investigation had provided very little information. There were no fingerprints. The autopsy suggested she had bled to death from the pentagram-shaped cut in her left wrist. Traces of Fentanyl in her respiratory system. No witnesses.

Savanah went through the material one last time. Phone call records, credit card statements, electricity bills and copies of her notebook.

She signalled she was done, and after a few minutes a sleepy Inspector Silva joined her.

"Look, Mrs Clifton", said the officer sternly, using Savanah's married surname. "It is always very difficult to tell the family we found nothing. But this is a cold case. We never found any leads, so it was a difficult case from the beginning. Now, more 13 years later, it is impossible."

"I understand, I am really just trying to understand what she was getting herself into", answered Savanah.

"Sure, yeah... I mean, those satanic images in the notebook and the pentagram wound, they look suspicious. It is for family members to come to terms with loved ones making the wrong choices and getting involved in drugs or stuff like that. The pentagram cuts and the horned-goat pictures look nasty. If I had to guess, I would say this was a drug gang job, or a suicidal pact gone wrong. Or she just cut herself, lonely young women get involved in crazy stuff..."

"That's not what I meant", Savanah looked at him crossly. "I meant what my sister was researching and what historic facts she may have uncovered that might have annoyed some powerful people".

With that, Savanah got up, preparing to leave the PJ offices as empty handed as before, but more annoyed. Then she halted, turning back to Inspector Silva.

"Sorry, I didn't mean to be rude. It just crossed my mind... I don't see here the tape or disk with the emergency call recording. Do you mind I listen to it?"

"Mrs Clifton, it's is stored digitally in the central system, we have not made a tape recording."

"Could we, still...? To put my mind to rest, hear my sister last words..."

"Well, I guess. Ok, fine, come with me."

The officer moved towards a desktop computer in a cramped room behind the reception area. After logging in and inserting his security credentials, he accessed a folder with the case identification number and looked for the file. It took him no more than a couple of minutes, considering the scarcity of the material in the digital folder of Raven's case. He clicked the voice file and Raven's voice streamed from the poor quality speakers, covered by static noise. She sounded rather calm, as if addressing someone she knew well. The words she said, though, were not what Savanah had expected.

Savanah jumped up, covering her mouth with both hands, as she gasped in shock.

What Raven said was not "High Goat, is Satan with you?"

But instead "Hi, Goat. Is Saint Anne with you?"

It was difficult for non-Americans to understand the subtle intonations of English language. Or otherwise, people just listen what they expect to hear.

HUELVA, AUGUST 1492

Palos de la Frontera

(Columbus)

Finally, the ships are sealed. Tomorrow, 3 August 1492, we shall set sail for the Indies, eighty nine men in two caravels and a nau ™ - the Pinta, the Nina and the Santa Maria. The caravels would never be appropriate ships for a journey so far as the true India, into unknown seas. Caravels are small, nimble vessels appropriate for exploring the shoreline of Africa, with a shallow draught to enter river mouths and lateen sails to tack upwind, but unfit for a long ocean journey. The true India would require large, stout carracks with large hulls, high sides, tall after-castle and sturdy square sails able to cope with the battering of unpredictable winds, waves and currents. But the caravels will be perfectly fine for the Indies we are heading. We should make the crossing in less than five weeks from the Canary Islands.

The fleet is well rigged and provisioned. Each ship carries three anchors and sets of rigging, barrels lined with pitch and copper for water, wine and vinegar, provisions of meat, flour, sea biscuit, vegetables and an excess of ammunition, large bombards, gunpowder and cannon balls. We should enter those beaches and salute the natives with a show of strength, to make our intentions clear. This is not a trade expedition. It's a conquest.

Fitting out the ships is expensive. Castella coffers are drained from the Succession war and the Granada war, and expelling the Jews eliminated an important source of financing. But Isabella's grand plans and self-righteousness belief that she is a herald of the new Christ makes her blind – someone else should pay for her grandiose fate! So, the crown forced the city of Palos to provide three ships: Juan de la Cosa advanced with the carrack Santa Maria, under my command, and the city sponsored the two caravels, the Pinta and the Niña, owned and captained by the Pinzon brothers. The crown contribution of 1.000.000 maravedis was loaned by Luis de Santangel from the Santa Hermandad funds. Some say the Queen pawned her jewels as collateral for the loan, but Santagél laughs at that... the Castella crown jewels were already pawned to fund the Granada war. I personally contributed with 500.000 maravedis of my own family money, which would of course be impossible for the son of a poor wool weaver, but there was no way to cover it up. Let's hope no-one pays much attention to that.

On my personal trunk, I carry in secret some Portuguese vinténs and cruzados, coins the natives of the islands have already seen. I also take with me some sticks of cinnamon, which shall be 'discovered' when we arrive at the Indies. The plot must be perfect. And of course the Tables of Solar Declination, written in Hebraic so that the other pilots won't be able to read them, prepared by Samuel Ben Zacuto [74], son of the great master astronomer and physician Abraão Zacuto. This is an updated version, which besides Zacuto's original measurements also include the studies of the Portuguese mathematician José Vizinho, the Jewish cosmographers Samuel and Jehuda and the Arab Aben Ragel, the Alchemist. The Tables are based on dozens of measurements taken during the Portuguese expeditions. This is a most powerful navigational tool, as it derives the height of the sun at the Equator at noon for each day of the year. Based on this, it is possible to measure one's latitude position in plain daylight, instead of having to take measurements only at night from the Polar star, which is invisible south of the Equator.

Contrary to the usual tradition of spending the night in vigil praying at the chapel before moving in procession, captain and crew, into the ships, I strictly ordered the crew to board in advance and stay aboard during the night. No one enters or leaves. The sailors are saying I have tyrannical manners, but they are men of little judgement and do not know what is at stake. Anyway, I managed to keep the complaints at bay by arguing with the ship's captains that I want to sail fast tomorrow and thus did not want to crew to spend the night drinking and whoring in town.

Tonight at midnight is the deadline established by those maniac Catholic Kings Isabella and Fernando to expel de Jews from Spain. The Jews must leave or convert. Who does she think she is, what gives her such pretensions over the lives of thousands? Preparing the second coming of Christ by purifying the land... a fanatic, a little girl playing with the lives of fellow men and women like if they were toys. A maniac whose flames of religious zeal have been fanned by that dangerous wizard Torquemada.

Oh, what do they know? I filled the crew with Jews: sailors, mapmakers, doctors. They will think I ordered the closure of the ships tonight, ahead of the midnight deadline, to protect the Jews in the fleet. They will probably even come up with stories that I myself am a converso, a converted Jew, protecting my fellow friends. So be it. The Secret Rule of the Templars, written by Master Roncelin de

Fos [75], the *Perfecti*, makes no distinctions between creed: "God makes no difference between people, be them Christians, Muslims, Jews, Greeks, Romans, French or Bulgarian, because all men who pray to God shall be saved." That was also the creed of Saint Bernard of Clairvaux, although his diplomatic ways prevented him from being so plain. What matters is that the secret remains hidden from the princes and high priests, who contaminated the faith with their hypocrisy and greed and depraved ways, fighting their petty selfish fights while oppressing millions of God's sons, turning Europe into a new Gomorrah.

The true secret mission of the Templar brothers, set by Grand Master Roncelin in The Book of Baptism of Fire, is "to conquer a New World and establish a united kingdom" ruled by the Holy Spirit and not by earthly princes or popes. The new Promised Land to the west is waiting, to establish this new kingdom of freedom.

The ships are closed. The gossip around the reasons for my decision is favorable – nothing better to divert everyone's attention away from the truth than rumors and intricate conspiracies.

Tomorrow I shall sail to take the Wind Rose to be rejoined with the Northern Path of the Rose Line. It will be safe in a new hiding place, away from these madman of the church and their Inquisition. God, give me strength to fulfil the mission my father and the Old Man bestowed upon my shoulders.

I must keep a detailed record of my actions and thoughts. I write what Isabel and Fernando want to read, convincing them and keeping the farce. "I departed well furnished with very many provisions and many seamen on the third day of the month of August on a Friday, at half an hour before sunrise, and took the route to the Canary Islands (...)

that I might thence take my course and sail until I should reach the Indies, and give the letters of Your Highnesses to those princes, and thus comply with what you had commanded."

We stopped in the Canary Islands to take in supplies. I ordered the replacement of the rigging in the caravel Pinta from lateen sails to square sails. The crew protested much, but what do they know?! I know exactly where we are going, and the winds we will find there. We shall set sail directly to the Antilles. There is no time to waste. King João II is growing impatient. I need to bring the good news quickly to Isabella and Fernando, offering them the new lands and the promise of gold, a dream to feed their pride and greed, the vision of a treasure they will feel compelled to defend.

October 3, 1492. "Some fish that looked like carp and a lot of seaweed, some of it very old, some of it fresh, and it looked like fruit on a bush: no birds appeared; the Admiral thought that the islands depicted on his chart had already been left behind." [76] According to my map and estimates of the course, we should be close to the Antilles, which the Portuguese have known for more than a decade. I fear seven years without sailing have turned me into a land rat and I may have already passed the western islands.

October 11, 1492. "I sailed to the west southwest, and we took more water aboard than at any other time on the voyage." [77] The crew is on the verge of mutiny, fearful and doubtful. This Spaniards are not used to the sea! Just over 30 days ago we sailed from La Gomera, in the Canary Islands, and the crew is already restless, fearing to fall over the edge of the world. Ignorant. We have made good course and should be arriving soon, as long as I can keep the sailors under control.

There are clear signs of land already, so we must be

hours away from the islands. A large flock of sea birds flew overhead, and I steered the ships to follow their course. A reed, a kind of tall and grass-like plant, floated by the Santa Maria. It was still green and hard, meaning it has grown in wetlands nearby.

I am pushing the crew hard, forcing the ships to sail all through the night. The sooner we arrive and complete the farce, the better. I pace the stern castle, scanning the horizon. But, for hours, I could see nothing but the black endless night.

Suddenly, I see a flicker of light in the distance, an omen against the darkness, "like a little wax candle bobbing up and down".

I know my true challenge starts now. No matter how hard it was to convince Isabel and Fernando to commit to this expedition, it will be incredibly harder to maintain their interest. They expect me to reach the great civilizations of China and India, the large cities of the Great Khan with whom to trade silk, gold and spices. Instead, I am about to deliver them these savage islands of naked people and little riches. How long will I be able to maintain the pretense? As much as I can praise the tropical splendor of these cobalt-blue waters, the fertile land and the docile natives, the Spanish are expecting something entirely different. It will be required much more than words to keep the illusion of the Indies. Oh God, forgive me for the atrocities I am about to unleash. Show me another way, if there is one, to complete my mission!

On October 12 at 2 in the morning, two months after departing Huelva, a sailor named Rodrigo de Triana aboard the Pinta, sighted land. The fleet reached the small island of São Salvador [78]. Columbus later asserted he had been the first to sight land, referring to the image of the "little wax candle" written in his diary, to claim for himself the reward Queen Isabel had established for the first man to sight land, of 10.000 maravedis.

They had taken only 33 days to cross the Atlantic from the Canary Islands to the Caribbean, which is a remarkable mark even today. Colon sailed on an almost straight line directly to the Caribbean, as if he knew where he was heading. He explored the Bahamas, Cuba and then Hispaniola (nowadays Dominican Republic and Haiti), before heading back.

Columbus never referred to his destination or to the territories he discovered, as "India", but always as "the Indies".

Although in most languages, people from India as well as the native Americans are referred to as "Indians", in Portuguese there are two separate words: ´Indios´ refer to American natives, whereas ´Indianos´ refer to people of India. The rest of the world remained confused by Columbus deceit, but the two regions were never confused in Portuguese chronicles or by Columbus himself, calling the new lands "Indias" but never "India". Decades later this denomination was also adopted in the Spanish chronicles, referring to the "western indies", to hide Columbus ´mistake´, or forgery.

HAITI, DECEMBER 1492

Natividade Bay, nowadays
Caracol Beach

(Columbus)

W e have been exploring these islands for weeks. As I suspected, there are no signs of riches we can carry to Spain. The natives are simple, walking naked and surviving on fruits, fishing and hunting. "They are people very guileless and unwarlike (...) very modest and not very dark, less so than the natives of the Canary Islands."

The ornaments are simple and I see not much signs of gold or precious metals. The islands have a luxuriant and diverse vegetation, the azure blue waters are a beauty never seen...but these wonders will not substitute for what all expect me to bring: gold and spices. I have not yet found anything worthy we can take to Isabell and Fernando. Not even slaves, I fear, as the natives have a physical built much less fit for heavy labor work than the peoples of west Africa.

In any case, I shall sing the praises of this place. It surely is beautiful and peaceful, with a luxuriant vegetation and many exotic animals. The land should be fertile if we get colons to settle here and farm the land.

At the end of October, we reached a large island I named Joana [79], supposedly after the Spanish princess. We entered a deep river [80] and took anchor, surrounded by "trees all along the river, beautiful and green, and different from ours." We found fishermen huts with "nets of palm fiber and ropes and fish-hooks of horn and bone harpoons", but not natives. The inhabitants of this place have fled. On November 1, I dispatched two scouts, Rodrigo de Xerez and Luis de Torres, to find the island's king. Martin Pinzon has also been fooled by the sticks of cinnamon I brought from Spain and handed to a Portuguese sailor from the Pinta, who pretended to have found them inland while hunting and brought the sticks to his captain. Pinzón is so gullible he already says he can see cinnamon groves!

The scouts returned on November 6 with an extraordinary tale. They have reached the main village, with about fifty tents and a thousand people, who received them with great solemnity. The locals touched and kissed their hands and feet, as if to ascertain they were made of flesh, believing the Spaniards were men from the sky. Men and women, as they go about their businesses, carry in their hands "herbs to drink the smoke thereof" [81], dry leaves which they set on fire and deeply inhale the fumes. When they departed the village, many natives wanted to accompany them, believing they were returning to the sky.

I can see those two jealous courtiers are thrilled with the prospect of humiliating me by demeaning the value of these lands, or even openly contest we arrived to the Indies. Rodrigo Sanchez de Segovia and Rodrigo de Escobedo, treasurer and secretary of the armada, were forced into the crew by King Fernando, to control my doings. But a plan is already in motion. I managed to convince Juan de la Cosa, Master and owner of Santa Maria, to sacrifice her. This took much persuasion and promises of a privileged position in the trade with these new lands. Honor and moral are always for sale, as long as you discover what the person desires.

It's Christmas Eve, 24 December 1492. The fleet sails in calm waters with no wind, approaching the Northeastern point of Hispaniola, so I retire to my cabin to get some sleep. But I rarely sleep... I have been convincing the captains about the importance of establishing a settlement and fortification here, to consolidate Spain's claim on these lands. They correctly argue we miss the proper construction tools. For my side, I have no wish to spend here too long in a lengthy construction project. But an alternative plan has presented itself, which shall solve several issues simultaneously. I have put the nau Santa Maria in front of the armada, although as we approach these shallow waters near the coast it would be wiser to have a smaller, lighter ship sail ahead. During the day I could distinguish a foam line in the water, separating the deep blue choppy ocean sea from the azure calm waters beyond. The birds' deep dives 8 miles from shore and the different color of the water suggest shallow waters rich in fish feeding on the reef. I am most certain there is a reef. We are approaching the cape in high tide, concealing the reefs.

So, it comes with no surprise when the watchman calls, crying the Santa Maria is stranded. I am the first on deck, to make sure I am the one orchestrating the plot. I would never risk her or the crew and food, but our measurements show the difference between high and low tide around here is less than ¼ of the hull. So, if she gets stranded at high tide and is not released quickly, even in low tide it would have ¾ of the hull underwater, even without unloading the cargo. That shall cause no more than a slight inclination, but not enough to take water and sink.

I order Master Juan de la Cosa to cast anchor at the stern and to get some men in the small boats to pull and free Santa Maria. Instead, as we had agreed, Master Juan rows to the caravel Nina, apparently to save himself from inevitable disaster.

Christmas Day has been spent transferring the cargo out of the Santa Maria and then towing her to the beach.

Orders have been given to start building a watch tower and some houses that can serve as settlement. This shall be the first colony in the Indies, which I named Natividade [82]. The natives come and go, suspicious. But no more suspicious than the treasurer and the secretary and many of the higher ranked crewmembers.

A settlement requires a fortification to protect it, and stores of food sufficient until the next fleet returns. I shall give them the fortress.

Meanwhile, we take some days to recover and replenish our water and food stocks. Hunting in these regions is not exciting, mainly birds and small animals, but it will do to get some fresh meat. These days are the time I need to set in motion the wheels of the plan.

I do not want Pedro Gutierrez and Rodrigo de Escobedo to return to Madrid, risking them contradicting my version of the Indies. So I must make them desire to stay here! Men always crave for titles. The prospect of power and riches is too attractive. I am offering them a position as commanders of Natividade, this first settlement in the Indies, with full titles and claims to a share of all future trade that passes here. Sure enough, I must have a man of my trust to control the situation, so I have also invested my loyal Diego de Arana, brother of my companion Beatriz Henriquez [83], as captain of Natividade.

For Natividade to warrant the name of a proper settlement, I have decided to establish a church here, using the big cross and the iron bell of the Santa Maria to stand in the largest building on the beach. It shall impress the natives to hear the sound of the bell.

I'm claiming that the nau Santa Maria is unseaworthy or would need repairs we cannot complete without proper tools. The damage to the hull is not that bad and we could repair it for the return trip, but I want to convince Pedro

Gutierrez and Rodrigo de Escobedo that the ship is irrecoverable and so can be put to a better use by using it as a fortress here in Natividade.

So it is done. On Wednesday, 2 January I call the king and tribespeople to the beach for a show of the Spanish power. The sound of the canon blast and the damage to the Santa Maria hull will surely make a lasting impression on the natives, inspiring the fear of God into them.

Alas. Here is the Fortress of Natividade.

With no delays we depart Natividade, leaving behind a settlement of 40 men with provisions for one year, and a fortress to further strengthen Isabella and Fernando's claims. More importantly, I leave behind those two courtesans, Pedro and Rodrigo, who could be tempted to contradict the version of the Indies I shall present to the court and the kings. All the pilots of the Santa Maria are returning with me, just in case they could repair the ship. Without pilots, even if they repair the ship they will never be able to sail back to Spain.

The iron bell and the huge anchor are the only surviving evidence of the nau Santa Maria. In his letters to the Spanish kings, Colon recounts an entirely different tale of the wreckage of Santa Maria, claiming it had capsized on the reef, 6 miles from the coast. Then, to impress the natives, he ordered a canon to be fired against the Santa Maria, which was doomed anyway, to demonstrate the fire power. However, despite many attempts by treasure hunters and marine archeologists, the Santa Maria has never been found.

When Colon returned on his second expedition, in November 1493, he found Natividade settlement burned down by the natives and all the crew death.

The most likely explanation, considering the improbability of irreparable damage to the Santa Maria from stranding on a reef in calm waters with less than ¼ of the hull exposed at low tide, is that this was yet another lie created by Colon and his associates to protect the deceit of the Western Indies. The Santa Maria did not capsize on the reef, as Colon says, but was stranded on the beach on purpose, where a few days later she was trespassed by a canon shot. A canon shot in those days would never have hit a ship 6 miles away and the demonstration was possible only because Santa Maria was on the beach. This shot, and not the wreckage, made the Santa Maria unseaworthy, and provided the perfect fortress to leave on the beach. On returning to Spain, Colon claimed to have left in Hispaniola a settlement and fortification. Yet, his personal logbooks show they were in Natividade for barely 10 days. It would be impossible to erect a settlement in 10 days. What he left behind was a few feeble thatched houses and the fortification was the nau Santa Maria. The reason her wreckage was never found is because it was burned down by the natives.

In the second expedition, just 11 months later, the crew found the huge 3-meter anchor, which can today be seen in the Haitian national pantheon in Port-au-Prince. This huge and heavy anchor was found on land. Which again demonstrates the Santa Maria had not wrecked 6 miles off the shore.

The massive bell of the Santa Maria was rediscovered, in 1994, in a ship wreck off the coast of Portugal, the São Salvador (interestingly, the name given to the first islet found by Colon). She had wrecked in 1555. The bell was made of iron, surviving the fire and kept in Hispaniola, until it was sent back in 1555.

VALE DO PARAÍSO, MARCH 1493

(Columbus)

W e sailed from Natividad on 16 January 1493. The sailors expect we will return by the same route we arrived here. Instead, I take a north-northeast path, which caused much questioning. I had to force the course by keeping the route secret or by outright brute force against those questioning my will. On the return journey I wrote a document that was signed "by all those that know how to", in which they recognize that we have reached Asia, establishing a penalty of having their tongue cut off and a fine of 10.000 maravedis for whoever contradicted this.

We passed the latitude of Cape San Vincente, where it would be expected to turn east towards the Mediterranean, but I kept the same northeast course we had been consistently following since Natividad. At that time, I had to stifle the potential for another mutiny, as some experienced sailors said I had lost my wits and was lost in the Ocean Sea. Oh, God! Ignorant. I did a splendid course, straight to the Azores islands! It is yet to be born any other captain who could hit the tiny islands in the middle of the Atlantic with such precision.

From the Azores, I wrote a letter to Castella dated 15 February and stating 'written aboard, close to the Canary Islands.' I guess one day the ruse and forgery will be discovered and I will pay a high price for my trickery [84].

Arriving at Santa Maria in the Azores, the captain of the island received me very warmly and sent meat and fresh bread. I had to have a word with him to explain the ruse. To maintain the pretense that I was a fugitive from the wrath of King João, the confused João Castanheira had to stage a turn-face, arresting my crew who had gone on land to pray. The whole scene was a bit of a shambles, but at least it will create some confusion. I exchanged some strong words with João Castanheira in front of the crew, after which he released everyone and allowed us to depart in peace. In any case, I had to stop in the Azores to replenish the ships with food and water before sailing to Lisbon. It had to be done, I just hope the staged arrest convinced the fools.

We sailed from Santa Maria in the Azores on Sunday, 24 February, with good wind to sail east. Monday we kept the eastern route and on Tuesday I corrected the course to northeast. On Wednesday and Thursday, though, we met contrary winds. Only on Friday I was able to correct the course, sailing northeast [85].

Luckily, we met a storm on Sunday, 3 March after sun down, which allowed me to write a letter to the Spanish monarchs saying that, when almost arriving in Spain, a strong wind forced us north against our desires and to seek refuge in Lisbon.

The fact is, on Sunday by sundown, we were already near the shores of Lisbon before the storm broke. Irrespective of the storm, this is where we were heading all along. If anyone comes to study my routes assuming my intentions were to serve the Spanish kings, they will surely conclude I was incompetent, always lost at sea and not knowing where I am. I am not sure if I should laugh or cry at the prospect of being confounded as incompetent!

We anchored in Belém, just next to the war ship São Cristovão. Her captain Álvaro Daman came aboard with a band of music to celebrate my victorious arrival. How ironic, a persecuted and wanted man in Portugal stationed next to a war ship in Lisbon, received with a fanfare! It is laughable, I guess, if anyone believes this... Even if a storm had pushed us away from the Mediterranean, would I ever anchor in Lisbon, a supposed fugitive persecuted by the Portuguese king, instead of just seeking refuge at a less conspicuous bay before returning to Spain after the storm passed? Oh, well, nothing the promise of gold and slaves will not make Isabella forget. Fernando is more suspicious, but he will keep shut, at least for now.

The city has transformed itself over the past decade since I left. A city buzzing with activity and opportunity, exotic products from the shore of Africa traded in the docks: spices, parrots, sugar, gold, slaves. This city has more black slaves than any other place in Europe, I reckon 1 in every 5 inhabitants are African blacks. And Jews, as well, expelled from Spain as I departed last year, have flocked to Lisbon, learned, entrepreneurial people who further add to the cosmopolite dynamism of the city. The market is a marvel: great piles of nuts, large tuna from the Azores, sugar cane from Cape Verde, colorful cloth and copper utensils from Morocco, fiery pepper and tusks of elephants from Guinea, the carcass of a crocodile.

An enormous iron workshop with massive furnaces like the innards of Volcano makes anchors, cannons, breastplates, mortars, hand guns... as if the city is preparing for an invasion! German and Flemish cannon founders and gunners produce the latest artillery instruments.

On 4 March, before setting out to meet the Portuguese King, I sent an extensive letter to Luis de Santangél, the Jew who financed the largest part of the expedition, describing the marvels of Hispaniola - a rich island off the coasts of China, brimming with treasures. I hope they find the description sufficiently enticing to compensate for the absence of spices and pitiful amounts of gold I bring with me. "Hispaniola is a miracle. Mountains and hills, plains and pastures, are both fertile and beautiful ... the harbors are unbelievably good and there are many wide rivers of which the majority contain gold. (...) There are many spices, and great mines of gold and other metals..."

King João retired to Vale do Paraíso to escape the plague epidemic in the city. So, I left the Niña anchored in Lisbon and travelled 50 miles to Vale do Paraíso. Better that way, we will be able to talk away from the prying eyes at the Paço. I paid the sailors, so they should be entertained with the whores and wine of Lisbon not to notice my absence for some time.

King João "sent a reception of nobles to meet me. The King received me with much honors and a splendid welcome, making me seat next to him. He showed much appreciation for the success of the voyage."

We talked for two entire days, discussing the islands discovered to the west. The plan had succeeded thoroughly: I had sailed on a straight line west of the Canary Islands, keeping with the restrictions imposed by the Treaties of Alcaçoba and Toledo which reserved the regions south of the Canary Islands for the Portuguese, but mid-way in the Atlantic, unbeknown to the crew, I started sliding continuously on a west-southwest route, taking the fleet firmly into Portuguese waters. The islands discovered, San Salvador, Cuba and Hispaniola, are all south of the Canary Islands and so King João can claim them.

Dom João was visibly torn by the decision to forsake the new western lands as a way to protect the Indian route to the east. I could tell at some point the King was contemplating the possibility of keeping both, trying to machinate a last minute plan to avoid the stark choice. But it is necessary. It is a hard but necessary choice – give the Spaniards the poor and uncivilized lands to the west to protect the rich routes to the east.

The king will feign interest to claim Portuguese rights over the new lands under the Alcaçoba Treaty, because they are south of the Canary Islands. This should entice Isabella and Fernando to claim for a new Treaty, to replace Alcaço-bas, as if it was their plan! I never fail to admire the deceitful mind of the King, he is a mastermind of political strategy.

During the five days I spent in Vale do Paraíso conferring with the king, I was hosted by the Prior do Crato, Dom Diogo Fernandes de Almeida, "who was the highest ranked man present with the king", whom the king ordered to "treat me very well and in good company". Dom Diogo is also a member of the Junta dos Matemáticos and was very interested to receive by notes and measurements from the western lands.

A reward of twenty gold coins was offered by the king to the pilot Juan de la Cosa, to compensate him for the loss of his ship Santa Maria and helping me to set up the trap in Natividad. The king also provided supplies of food and water to our fleet as we prepared to depart, which may again seem odd to any Spanish paying attention. I trust greed will prevail, as it always does.

Although officially I have been the entire week at Vale do Paraíso, the truth is this time allowed me a detour to Tomar. It took me another two days to cover the 55 miles from Vale do Paraíso to Tomar and back. After eight years, the Book is again with me! I could not risk having it with me in Spain, so the Book was kept by the knights of the Order in Tomar. I am now taking it back with me and prepare the next expedition as soon as possible. I need to establish a secret base in Hispaniola, away from the prying eyes of the Spaniards, in order to launch search missions to the Terra

Firma up to Newfoundland. The Rose Line is there.

The day I was preparing to leave Vale do Paraíso, a messenger arrived from the Portuguese Queen Leonor, "insisting I should not depart before first coming to see her". I thus stopped to pay my respects to the Queen, in the Monastery of Santo Antonio in Vila Franca de Xira.

Almost two weeks after anchoring in Lisbon, I finally departed for Spain.

This should be enough time for the pre-emptive letter I sent to Luis de Santangél, announcing my discoveries, to be spread to the seven winds. When I arrive in Seville, it will already have been read all over Europe. Nothing more powerful than confronting the Spanish monarchs with the 'fait accompli' of my heroic expedition, consummated facts they will have no way to escape.

I stopped two further days in Faro, taking information about the whereabouts of the Pinta and her captain Pinzón. He is a liability and a risk. I must make sure he is silenced before talking to the monarchs.

History books tell a rather different version from the words written by Colon on his private diary. The official version is that Colon, having been forced by a storm to take anchor in Lisbon (why would he go straight into the mouth of the wolf, with so many other smaller bays and ports to take refuge?), only accepted the king's invitation to mock him for the success of an expedition the king had initially refused. The Spanish Bartolomé de Las Casas wrote that "King João II lamented loudly, beating his chest in disgust and angry with himself" and wailing "Oh king of little wisdom, why have you let escape between your fingers an opportunity of this importance?". Dramatic, but totally unsubstantiated.

What important businesses had Colon with the Portuguese King and Queen to delay more than two weeks the return to Castella?

BARCELONA, MAY 1493

(Columbus)

*"And these things I see suddenly – what mean they? / As if
some miracle, some hand divine unseal'd my eyes, / Shadowy, vast shapes, smile through the air and sky, / And on
the distant waves sail countless ships, / And anthems in new
tongues I hear saluting me."*
WALT WHITMAN, "PRAYER OF COLUMBUS", 1872

The Niña arrived in Palos on 15 March. This was a perfect timing, as shortly after the Pinta caravel came
visible in the horizon, commanded by Martin Pinzón.
He is a nuisance. The pilot of the Pinta is on my pay book and
he made sure the caravel meandered all the way to Bayona
in the North of Spain. Pinzón must have been furious... he
probably had hoped to arrive in Seville before me and get
an audience with the monarchs to poison their hears. Tough
luck.

Shortly after their arrival in Palos, Martin Pinzón disappeared. It had to be done. He was a troublesome witness
who could unmask the truth. The forgery is safe, for now.
The most problematic witnesses, high ranked officials loyal
to Spain, are all out of the way, Pedro Gutierrez and Rodrigo
de Escobedo retained in Hispaniola and Pinzón death. I shall
be the sole bearer of the news and no-one will contradict me.
I am now free to sing the wonders of the western lands to the
Spanish monarchs and the Pope, whispering to their hears
to inflame their desire to protect those islands through a re-
vised treaty with Portugal.

I stayed a fortnight in the Monastery of la Rabida, in pray and consulting with Frei Antonio Marchena, preparing for the next stage of the plan and how to lure Isabella and Fernando into it.

The letter I sent to Luis de Santangél upon my arrival in Lisbon on 4 March has spread like a virus. A copy was made to reach Pedro Posa, which printed the letter in Barcelona. At the beginning of April, it reached Italy, where it was translated to Latin and printed in Rome. The letter was copied and disseminated by the Portuguese network throughout Europe, announcing my successful discovery of the Indies. The Spanish kings will have no alternative but to act accordingly – even if they have some suspicions, they will have to play along with the charade, for risk of being exposed to ridicule all over the European courts!

On 30 March, even before setting out to Barcelona to formally offer the new lands to the Spanish monarchs, Queen Isabella wrote to me giving instructions to immediately prepare a second expedition to return to Hispaniola, to increase the population of settlers, subdue the natives and assert the Spanish crown claim on the territories. The rumors Dom João was already preparing and expedition to the western lands was putting the expected pressure on the monarchs.

At the beginning of May, almost two months after arriving in Lisbon and sending the letter broadcasting my heroic return, my reputation now firmly established, I finally entered triumphantly in Barcelona, with all pomp and little substance, to report to the Spanish monarchs.

What a marvel to behold, all the great *hidalgos* and churchmen who once scorned me, now lining up to praise my prowess and looking for some crumbs of the riches of the Indies. What do I have to show? I present myself with six Indians, a few parrots, some gold pieces and pearls. From the rich lands of sapphires and spices, my bounty is ridiculous. A pitiful charade that would convince only those who desperately wanted to be convinced. I compensate in presumption what I lack in evidence! With no-one to contradict me, the letter I wrote from Lisbon created an alternative reality that has now become inevitable, a staged truth everyone wants to believe.

The reception in Barcelona is superb. It is my privilege to ride side by side with King Fernando and his cousin, Enrique de Aragén y Pimentel, regent of Cataluña in the absence of the King. "This privilege was never granted to any other great *hidalgo*". When I went to kneel and "kiss their hands, Dom Fernando and Dona Isabel rose as if they were before a great Lord, (...) inviting me to seat by their side." I was granted the title of knight of the golden spur.

Queen Isabella is also granting an enlarged coat of arms for my house. The royal decree, signed by the Catholic Kings, approves my enhanced coat of arms, which has four quadrants "maintaining in the fourth quadrant the arms I formerly used". For the first and second quarter of the blazon, Isabella and Fernando granted me nothing less than the arms of Castella and León, a castle and a lion, which is a sign of the high esteem the monarchs bestow on me. On the bottom left quadrant, a pattern of sea waves and islands symbolize the new lands, as befits my deeds. The fourth quadrant maintains the ancient coat of arms of my lineage, or better, the adapted version I presented to the monarchs upon my arrival to the Spanish court, which is five gold anchors over a blue field.

Queen Isabella and King Fernando are nervous for me to give them the maps and the exact location of the overseas lands I offered them. On 4 August, the Queen wrote me a letter from Barcelona asking to "send the navigation charts", and concluding with another insistence for me to "remember leaving her the navigation charts". On 5 September, she insisted on another letter requesting – imploring would be a more accurate term – the exact location of the islands "to be able to understand the logbook of the journey, we need to know the coordinate degrees where the islands are located (…). Send the navigation chart you were supposed to have already sent". Tough luck.

I never gave the exact location of the discovered islands to the Spanish monarchs or cartographers. Not even a rough sketch! I remain the only man able to return to Hispaniola. I suspect Isabella and mostly Fernando would love to turn cloaks on me and remove me from the titles and rights they promised. They can't stand that a foreigner rules the Spanish seas. But while they lack the exact location, they will have to keep me. I will inevitably be the Admiral commanding the next expedition! I must prepare their minds that although those lands are not the Indies, they can be a valuable strategic restocking point on the way to Asia. And, who knowns, maybe there is something worthwhile in those lands that may entice the Spaniards attention.

❖ ❖ ❖

The royal decree signed by Queen Isabel and King Fernando in May 1493, granting new arms to Colon's coat of arms, was discovered only in 2006 and published in the Cuadernos de Ayala, by Dr. Félix Martínez Llorente. The document proves beyond the shadow of a doubt that Colon already had a lineage with coat of arms before the new arms were added, as the document states that the fourth quarter of the blazon "maintains your arms that you previously used". Colon's original coat of arms precedes 1493 and showed five golden anchors disposed in the characteristic saltire pattern over a blue background, and below a pattern of gold, blue and red colors.

On the fifteenth century Spanish court, it was not easy to be granted a coat of arms and the right to use it required an in-depth genealogical investigation by the 'armeiro-mor', the keeper of the heraldic arms. On arriving in Spain in 1484, long before setting foot on the Nina, Colon would have been subject to intense scrutiny, having to demonstrate his lineage for his coat of arms to be accepted.

The origin of the confusion about Columbus name – besides the conscious distortions caused by Colon and the Portuguese court – may have started with the First Letter written in March 1493. That letter, describing the epic adventure and the marvels discovered to the west, was sent from Lisbon to Luis de Santangél and probably constitutes the first example of an international press release and political propaganda, in the new globalized world created by the Age of Discoveries!

As it happens, the Admiral's First Letter was later printed in Barcelona and from there reached Rome, where it was translated to Latin and printed. Although Colon in Spanish has nothing to do with the Italian name Colombo (pigeon), in Catalan the word Colom does mean pigeon. When the Barcelona print was translated to Latin in Italy, just two weeks later, the Italian printer mistook the Castilian name Colon for the Catalan word Colom, and translated it as Colombo in Italian – which in Latin is Columbus (pigeon), very different from Colon (member, limb). This Latin version of the letter spread like red-hot wildfire, with 11 editions in 1493 published in Spain, Italy, France, Switzerland and Holland. The misleading form was later adopted by Ruy de Pina, the chronicler of King Dom Manuel I, in 1504.

The Latin name Columbus (pigeon/dove) is Colombo in Italian, Palomo in Spanish, Colom in Catalan, Pombo in Portuguese... but never Kolon or Colon, which means member or limb. The Latinization of Colon would never be Columbus, but Colonus or Colonna.

The many letters written by the Pope to Colon in 1493 are in Latin and address the Admiral as Colon, never Columbus. The Pope surely knew to differentiate Colon (member) from Columbus (pigeon)! And King João II letter from 1488 addresses his "special friend in Seville" as Colon. The Spanish Capitulations of Santa Fé also use the name Colon.

And thus, the Admiral started being known all over the world – except Spain and Portugal – as Columbus! The correct translation to Latin of the March 1493 First Letter should have been Cristoforo Colonus, and not Columbus. By accident, a great monumental confusion started, further adding to the already enormous imbroglio of deceit and conspiracy surrounding Colon. Ruy de Pina, chronicler of King Manuel I, seized the opportunity in 1504 to bog Colon's true identity and mission deeper into the quagmire sands, adopting for the first time in Portugal the name Colombo instead of Colon. Which bears the question: why?

SEVILLE, JULY 1493

(Columbus)

I am preparing the second expedition, but drag my feet to gain some time. It is paramount that I nudge Isabella into signing the new Treaty.

As soon as I arrived from La Hispaniola, after several days conferencing with Dom João in Vale do Paraíso, I wrote to Queen Isabella, urging her to write to the Pope, Alexandre VI, a Spaniard himself, asking him to provide a new dividing line to protect the Spanish interests in the new lands. La Hispaniola stands below the latitude of Canarias and would therefore fall within the Portuguese sphere of influence defined by the Alcaçobas treaty.

Dom João played his part masterfully, feigning to send an expedition to claim his rights on the newfound territories, as to provoke the Queen's fear of losing the overseas islands I had offered her. King João ostensibly fitted out a fleet under the command of Dom Francisco de Almada to claim the western islands. The Spanish monarchs fell to the ruse, and immediately proposed negotiations to revise the Alcaçobas treaty. Oh, I would love to be present in those negotiations! What a charade... the Portuguese envoy, Rui Sanches, is playing irreducible and refusing to renegotiate the terms.

Fear and greed drive all, from the vilest scum to the high lords! Soon after my return, the Spanish monarchs sent the Bishop of Cartagena, Dom Carvajal, to Pope Alexander VI with a protest, and the pope quickly obliged, proposing a new north-south division of the world, 100 leagues west of the Azores. The Church issued five documents, two of them the Bulls entitled Inter Caetera. In their haste to claim the new lands, King Fernando and Queen Isabella failed to notice that the highly publicised fleet of Francisco de Almada was still anchored off Lisbon and had never been fitted to leave the Tagus. It was just a masterful bluff!

Checkmate. The trap is set. Despite all the misgivings and suspicions of the Spanish cosmographers regarding my enterprise, the monarchs cannot be indifferent to these chess games. Fear and greed, as always, are the strongest motivators.

The great success of my expedition was not the nautical feat itself – barely more than a month of straight sailing – but the well-orchestrated propaganda. The letter to Santangél was reprinted all over Europe and read in all civilized courts of the world. Extraordinary. If it had not been for Guttenberg's invention, this could never have been done. And it is not even a great piece of literature! Alas, men are more avid for gold and riches than culture and beauty. They all think gold buys beauty. But I lost my beautiful Filipa for the gold of the Indies... and not even the true India, and of the gold, I've seen nothing but a glimpse of it so far.

The path to achieve the treaty is narrow and treacherous. Any misfortune may alert the Spanish monarchs of the deceit. An ignominious letter was sent to Queen Isabella, by a traitor not even brave enough to sign it. The secret letter cautions Isabella not to trust King João, who it calls an "evil devil, enemy of all good", and about the false trap of the western indies. The letter is dangerous. It forewarns Isabella that "this thing of the western Indies is a hoax and false perfidy of your enemy to deviate (the attention of) Your Highness (...) This (is a) sham and trick from the King of Portugal". Although the traitor sent the letter unsigned, the agents of King João immediately suspected the Count of Penamacor, a traitor who attempted against the King's life in 1484. Did the treacherous bastard expect to escape Dom João's strong and long reaching arm? The man showed up, murdered, soon after the ignominious letter [86]. In the high stakes game we are playing, we can make no compromises. Take no prisoners...

The new treaty shall be a turning point in the balance of power between Portugal and Spain. With the blessing of the Vatican, the treaty protects the false Indies for Spain and ensures the true Indies for Portugal.

But Dom João is not yet satisfied with the line proposed by the Pope. He told me in Vale do Paraíso the exact location of Vera Cruz [87], which is not yet officially announced. Also, the Portuguese have been for decades exploring Thule [88], Newfoundland and Nova Scotia. King João insists I help to negotiate the location of the new dividing line, making the Pope and Queen Isabella believe they are setting the terms of the new treaty whereas the line will fall exactly where King João wants: hold the Northwest Atlantic around Thule and Newfoundland and Vera Cruz at the Southwest Atlantic, preventing a passage to Cipango and India through the north or the south. I must hold the center.

On 25 September, 1493, I sail again with a mighty armed fleet of 17 ships and 1500 men. Without ever having sent the navigation charts or the coordinates to the monarchs or even provided to the captains of the 17 ships where we are heading [89]. This armada is a show of force from the Spanish kings to the Portuguese negotiators of the treaty, showing Spain is putting all its might to protect the western lands. That suits fine for the Portuguese negotiators, revealing the hand of the Spanish monarchs. They are keen to sign the Treaty – they fear Dom João's demand to push the dividing line further west may be a trick, but to the Spanish they think such demand just costs them some leagues of salted water, whereas they are keen to protect the western lands I brought them. All is set. My departure should add additional pressure for the Spanish monarchs to sign the Treaty speedily.

TORDESILLAS, JUNE 1494

As embassies from both countries met again in the ancient town of Tordesillas, to bargain for the world between themselves, the Portuguese negotiators continued to insist for the line to be set 370 leagues west of Cape Verde instead of the Pope's original 100 leagues west of the Azores. This gains for the Portuguese a further 120 leagues of apparently empty sea. The Spanish negotiators were understandably disoriented by this proposal. Because the Portuguese had so far kept Vera Cruz and Newfoundland secret, everyone thought King João was simply being stubborn, insisting on gaining just a vast nothingness of salted water. He must have known, or have strong suspicions, there was land on the Southwest Atlantic. In fact, in 1498 (two years before Cabral (re)discovered Brazil), Colon himself wrote, during his third expedition, when he finally left the Caribbean islands and headed for the mainland, that he "King João of Portugal had told him that to the south there was terra firma (...) and King João had for certain that within his limits (of the Tordesillas Treaty) he would find famous things and lands" on the west Atlantic.

Based on the information they had, the Spanish should gladly accept those terms, but remained suspicious of Dom João's intentions. And they should be. King João would never push the western limit of Portuguese hemisphere, while risking foregoing rich lands at its eastern limit (as would later in fact happen regarding the Molucas islands), if he didn't have a clear idea what he was trading. The 370 leagues line delivered a wide expanse of the new western land, as yet unannounced, firmly under the control of the Portuguese – preventing a northern passage around

Thule and a southern passage around Vera Cruz [90].

Meanwhile, Colon should hold the center, restraining from approaching Terra Firma and entertain the Castilians with the Antilles islands, to avoid risk of a potential central passage. At least until King João controlled the trade routes to India.

Despite the Spanish suspicions, they were bound to accept the proposed terms. After the ruse set by Dom João II and his special friend in Seville, Christopher Colon, Tordesillas was a great diplomatic event with a foretold conclusion...

The main negotiator on the Portuguese side was the experienced and witty diplomat Rui de Sousa, with a sharp mind and sharp tongue. When he met Dom Henrique Henriquez, the most prominent member of the Spanish delegation to Tordesillas, Dom Henriquez enquired when had he arrived. Rui de Sousa, fully aware of the net of Spanish spies following his steps, answered brilliantly: "Dom Henriquez, I arrived exactly when you think I arrived".

This had been the same Rui de Sousa that, amongst several other diplomatic services for the King of Portugal, had negotiated the terms for the agreed marriage between the son of King Dom João II, Prince Afonso, and one of the daughters of Isabella and Fernando. After the arrangement was agreed, Rui de Sousa organized the festivities to celebrate the intended union between the heir of Portugal and the Spanish princess. The festivities were grandiose and went well into the night. Quite late in the evening, Queen Isabella noted to the diplomat: "Dom Rui de Sousa, I must retire, it is already late at night!", to which the diplomat responded "On the contrary, my Lady, look through the window... far in the horizon dawn announced itself, morning is just starting!"

One of the main negotiators for Castella was Dom Rodrigo de Maldonado, who was very influential and for many years a magistrate of the royal council of the King and Queen of Spain. Less known, though, is that since 1483 King Dom João II had been paying the magistrate an annual rent, for his information, advice and influence. This proved a well advised forethought, soothing Maldonado predisposition towards the Portuguese interests.

On 7 June 1494, Portugal and Spain signed the Treaty of Tordesillas, dividing the globe in two spheres of influence.

Only after the Tordesillas Treaty was signed, protecting the southern route around Africa to India, did the preparations for Vasco da Gama's expedition to India finally began, six years after Dias turned the Cape of Good Hope. King João II had finally achieved his goal.

Both sides of the negotiations achieved their goals regarding India: The Queen of Castella kept the path she thought existed, and the King of Portugal kept the path he knew existed.

LISBON, APRIL 2019

The Saints Rock Club

(Savanah)

"I'll bet if we met the devil and he allowed us to open him up, we might be surprised to find God jumping out."
JOSÉ SARAMAGO

It was hard to find it. After leaving the Judiciária, I rushed home and started looking online in a craze. Goat. Saint Anne. Gosh, zillions of hits on google search, but nothing that looked remotely relevant. I repeated the search I had done a few months before, when Duma mentioned Raven used to play in a rock bar called "The Goat". There is no bar or disco or pub called the Goat in Lisbon. Only a performance and rehabilitation centre for athletes, a kind of personalized gym near Campo Grande named The G.O.A.T., standing for Greatest Of All Time.

The link came only when I searched for all of it together. The Goat and Saint Anne, Lisbon 2006. And there it was. A few short entries in obscure blogs which, resorting to google translator, I understood referred to the death, in rather mysterious circumstances, of a guitar player with the artistic name of Saint Sarah, from the satanic rock group 'The Goat and The Saints'. The picture showed a black cladded young woman with a pink tutu, blurred black eyeshadows. But there was no mistake. It was Raven.

How was this possible? There had been some press articles on Raven's death, but referring to her as an American PhD student. The notes on these blogs, which looked to follow the local heavy metal music scene, seemed to refer to a completely different person, as if Raven had been living a double life.

The rock band derived its name from the lead singer, a thin guy with shaved head and featuring a decent sized goatee beard, who called himself the Goat, and the two female guitarists, dressed in black with a pink tutu, who were the Saints: Saint Anne and Saint Sarah.

Another entry some weeks later mentioned that The Goat rock club was changing its name to The Saints rock club, in homage to the death guitar player from the music group. It seems The Goat and The Saints had caused a bit of a furore in Lisbon back then, due to its fusion of Nordic dark metal with African voodoo chants and dances.

That's why I hadn't found The Goat rock bar after Duma mentioned Raven had played gigs there. It was now called The Saints. A rather macabre name for what seemed to be a heavy metal music bar. It was nevertheless suspicious, the name of the bar could have been changed to sever the links with the rock group after Raven's death.

Some further search indicated the owner of the rock club was a bit of a dodgy character and small time crook. He had been in prison a couple of times for possession and trafficking of small quantities of drugs. He had also been a suspect in Raven's death, one of the few interviewed by the police. Savanah had missed the link when reading the transcript of the interviews at the Judiciária, probably because they used his real name, which she still didn't know, and the changed name of the bar, which she didn't recognize. But he was let go because the investigation could never prove his guilt.

Based on what I could gather from the online articles,

he had no alibi, saying he was at home sleeping at the time of death. And he surely had the means, access to the Fentanyl drug. But he didn't have a relevant motive, on the contrary, The Goat and The Saints had been a key attraction and saved the rock club from bankruptcy. Saint Sarah's death was a severe blow for the club. Most importantly, police couldn't figure out how he could have done it. Raven had showed up unannounced, on her street, at 3.30 in the morning. If the guy had been there since the previous evening waiting for her, he would surely have been spotted by some neighbour. He was not a conspicuous character, a bald heavy set guy with a Nirvana shirt and a goatee beard gets noticed in a Lisbon neighbourhood. So, if this really was a murder, the responsible had to know about her movements to place her in that street at that late hour.

I arrive at The Saints rock bar probably a bit too early on Friday evening, the place is still half empty. But still, this gives me the opportunity to look around and take in the feeling of the place. Black and crimson velvets dominate the room, with large plush leather sofas. An awkward mix of bondage instruments, scattered around, mixed with old electric guitars and vinyl recordings hanging here and there, with no apparent order. Several photographs dot the walls, including one of a short, bald man with a goatee beard and a Nirvana black t-shirt, his arms around the hips of two beautiful women in black gear and pink tutus, one on each side of the man. The women bend slightly to kiss him, one on each cheek. I immediately recognize Sarah as one of the girls in tutus. The other must be Anne. And the guy is probably The Goat. The same guy standing behind the counter, staring at me intently (clearly recognizing my twin sister and trying to decide if he is seeing a ghost). His greyish flesh, sagging eyes and flabby skin around the neck and underarms show the cruel signs of an additional decade, mixed with heavy drinking and cigarettes. And he has lost the goatee beard.

The bar actually has a posh narcissistic feeling, more of a fashionable hard-trendy club than a heavy underground place. Urban trendy pretending to play with danger, looking at the dark pit of Satan from a safe distance. I can hear tourists coming in and seating around in the comfortable sofas, confirming the outraged doomsday satanic purity of the old The Goat had probably given way to more commercial considerations...

Suddenly, I hear a muffled cry of surprise next to me.

"Saint Sarah!?..."

"Twin sister, actually", I answer, extending my hand as a way to initiate a conversation that could provide some leads. "I'm Savanah, Rav...errrr, Sarah's sister."

"Oh, sorry, for a second I confused you with...gosh, you are so similar! I didn't know Sarah had a sister!!?"

I glance at the bartender, a sweet looking very bored young girl, and ask for two gin tonics. Hoping this would keep Carminho, my new acquaintance, talking for a while.

As it happens, Carminho had been a huge fan of The Goat and The Saints and knew everything about the band. Well, there wasn't much to know really, considering they had existed and performed for less than a year. Anne and the Goat had been educated at the seminar. Ana, the would be Saint Anne, was going to be a nun and he had just been ordained a priest when they met in a pilgrimage to Fátima.

"I guess carnal love overcame spiritual love.", Carminho said, winking at me. "So, they left the church and came to Lisbon, playing and singing at bars as a couple. According to legend, it was Sarah who originated the name for the band. She started calling the couple 'The Goat and Saint Anne', I guess because he had a goatee beard and she was going to be a nun. The three started playing together, in local gigs, as 'Goat and the Saints'. The Goat was the singer, Ana and Sarah played guitar."

The guy at the bar counter seems to consider my attention was now engaged elsewhere, and takes the chance to leave the bar and move backstage. I follow his back, jeans and a black t-shirt, a solid and muscled guy with shiny bald head.

Carminho keeps going about the rock band. "They became a kind of local cult rock band for a short while, until, well... you know, Sarah departed". The Goat wore satanic t-shirts with goat pentagrams and sang brutal, black lyrics about sin and the devil. This was supposedly a statement of freedom and independence from the shackles of the church he had left behind, against its stodgy moral authority and hypocrite virtues. But I guess it was a branding thing too. The two girls played the guitar, with pink tutus over black outfits. The Saints were really the soul of the band. Hot, horny, liberated, provocative. And their dancing was...free, carnal, as if the devil was in their hips. They sang voodoo chants over the Goat lyrics and danced African and Latin rituals.

When they were playing, this place transformed itself, everyone seemed to be in a trance. Pure ecstasy! Nothing of that satanic sadist bloody mess, but pure sensuality. Their performance was hot and sexy. At the end of the show the two women kissed, tongues in each other's mouth. Then the Goat approached them, his guitar between his legs, pointing upwards like a huge phallus, and put his arms around the two girls. He stooped down to stick his tong on Saint Anne's mouth, then Saint Sara's. "I got so turned on", Carminho concluded. "I used to get out of here with my boyfriend and go straight home for sex. Sometimes didn't get to arrive home, the car would do...

Images flashed in my mind of some of the pagan rituals

I had been reading about, orgies of the senses to abandon the self-control of consciousness and reach a state of ecstasy, closer to the divine. The Barbelites, an early Christian sect, practiced group sex as a praying, the women collecting the ejaculated sperm in their hands and raising them to the heavens, saying, "We offer you this gift, the body of Christ" and the men collecting the blood of menstruating women in their hands and raising them to the heavens, saying "We offer you this gift, the blood of Christ".

I sipped my drink, trying to focus again on what Carminho was saying. "The Goat fucked around quite a bit", Carminho said between high pitched giggles. "He fucked like possessed by the devil, we... yeah, in the toilets over there. Not charming, but hot, so intense, fucking the wrath of God out of your groins! Coming out of the seminar... all the contained energy ready to explode!"

I tried to turn the conversation into another direction. Her talk was actually making me sick.

"Were the Goat and Sarah involved? You know, were they like, dating, or was that tongue thing on stage just for the show?"

"Oh, Goat's girl was Saint Anne! Everyone knew that. But I wouldn't put my hands on fire, he fucked around a lot, so, yeah, he could have made out with Sarah too. To be honest though... I think Sarah was more into Ana. A bit of a love triangle there."

This makes me wonder. Could all the pentagrams dotted around Raven's notebook and the goat image have nothing to do with her research on Columbus, but just Raven's mindless ramblings, doodles on a page that people often draw when lost in thought. She had just been seeing connections where there were none. The pentagram with the goat in the notebook was an outburst of her desire. She had written "The Goat is in my way!" Probably meant the Goat was

Saint Anne boyfriend and in her way from a relationship with her.

Now, could this be a motive? Could the Goat have become violent because his approaches to Sarah were not corresponded, and Sarah was eyeing his girl? But even if it was a motive, it was a rather feeble one. And the issue of how he could have known Raven would arrive at 3.30am on that spot remained tricky.

I would have liked to talk to him. But the guy had disappeared from the bar and never returned, probably left through a back door. I would need to come back another time and get him by surprise.

LISBON, APRIL 2019

The Saints Rock Club

(Savanah)

"I am a forest, and a night of dark trees: but he who is not afraid of my darkness, will find banks full of roses under my cypresses."
FRIEDRICH NIETZSCHE, THUS SPOKE ZARATHUSTRA

I return to The Saints on Saturday evening, determined to have a good talk with the guy from the old photograph with the goatee, who seems to be the owner of the rock club and distinctly avoided me yesterday.

I arrive early again, to have time before the place gets crowded. I seat in a stool at the bar and ask for a soda water with lime. The guy serves me in silence, and as he is pouring the drink I can see an inverted cross tattooed on his left arm. He is wearing a Venom black t-shirt with the cover image of their early 80s debut album "Welcome to Hell", featuring Baphomet in a downward-pointing pentagram (Yeah, I had to bear Raven's punk music and endure the posters plastered in our bedroom throughout my teenage years, until moving out to university).

The guy puts the glass in front of me and then stared straight into my eyes. "So, it is not a coincidence you came here yesterday?", he asks in a deep voice, an accent different from the usual I had got used to in Lisbon. He had a kind of Russian accent but clearly watered down, probably for being out of his country for many years.

"No, I'm afraid not. You clearly recognized me, but you run away."

"No... I didn't run away. It was just too overwhelming, seeing you and remembering Sarah. Savanah, right? I called up Carminho, she is a regular here. I'm Jaros, owner of this place and eternally in love with Saint Anne and Saint Sarah."

"Nice meeting you, Jaros... Is that a Czech name? Hungarian?"

"Polish actually. Jaroslav. Came to Lisbon more than 15 years ago, as an Erasmus interchange student. Loved the city and never left."

"Nice... Look, Jaros, I am trying to understand a bit what my sister was doing back in 2006 and it would be great if we could talk."

"I really don't want to talk about those times. Too painful. I don't need to justify myself. Police interviewed me, as you probably know, but there was nothing. And yes, I did time for dealing with some drugs, but paid my dues and that is long gone. I truly loved working with the Saints, they were gorgeous. Those were amazing times, full of energy. We had a mission! Anyway, the dreams are gone, and with them the hope of doing something meaningful. But we are too weak to give up living, so we carry on, surviving."

There. A hard man playing the sissy. Is he afraid of talking and uncovering old secrets? In any case, it is still quite early and the bar almost empty, so he doesn't have an excuse to escape.

"What are you doing in Lisbon, by the way, Savanah? Doing the tourist round tour of Europe, hoping between main cities for a few days each?", asked Jaros, a sarcastic sneer on his lips.

"Well, Jaros, I don't need to justify myself either.", I

answer. I hate cynical hotshots. But then I softened a bit. I suspect Jaros is not the typical full of shit arrogant bastard I have got used to after almost twenty years in Wall Street, but more of a baffled puppy bearing his teeth, abash for being dug out of his hole. Maybe I'll throw him a bone.

"Fine, I understand. But we both liked Sarah and we should unite forces to understand what happened, no?" I eye him to check his reaction, but his body language is hard to read. "I'm revisiting Sarah's steps here in Lisbon, talking to her old acquaintances, trying to understand… you know where she worked?". Fishing out how much Sarah had told him, how much she had trusted the guy.

"Besides playing the guitar? Yeah, she told me… she was working on her PhD thesis, researching something on Columbus. We talked quite a bit about the Templar knights and…stuff."

Now, that is unexpected. What did a weed head know about Templars?

He probably catches the disbelief in my face. "There is a lot of common ground between the Templar knights and heavy metal music, you know?"

Oh, fuck's sake. Not the conspiracy theories again. The guy can't be serious…

"That's a bit…I heard some satanic bands play in desecrated churches, use an imagery of sexually explicit nuns, horned goats and the anti-Christ. That's way too hard for Templars, no?"

Jaros laughs heartedly and then turns to the young bored looking girl at the counter. "Ei, Maria, can you handle alone for a while? I'm going to take a break." With that, he motions for me to follow him. So I walk behind the guy to the rear of the bar, exiting a small blood-red door into a small outside smoke garden and climb up an iron spiral staircase, entering a large, open plan studio.

"My place, we can talk more privately here, if you don't mind. Do you want something to drink? I'll get myself a coffee."

"No thanks, wouldn't sleep if I drink coffee at this hour."

"Right, right. It's Saturday night, so the bar will stay open late, I need the caffeine." Jaros points to a round table in the area between the small kitchen and the living room. I seat at the table as he kneels to open a door under the TV, taking a bottle of a transparent liquid and pouring generously into his coffee. "Firewater?", he asks. "No thanks", not really wanting to ask what that was. Jaros then returns and joins me at the table. "Sarah was really passionate about everything she did, her work, her music. One of them killed her, I suppose. True to the motto: find what you love and let it kill you."

I am not totally comfortable being here alone at his place, for all I know this dodgy guy may very well be my sister's assassin. But he does look to know more than he has been saying. And the bar downstairs is full of people, if I scream everyone would hear me.

"So, we were saying, yeah, Sarah's research at the university, the Templars and the satanic rock bands... that's a messy melting pot! Risks getting everything confused and get to the wrong conclusions from the right facts..."

"I guess so... I have indeed been fearing mixing things and seeing links where there are just coincidences. But Rav... Sarah was doing just that. She left this notebook where she was writing her thoughts and research, but I can't make sense of it. The pages are full of undecipherable sentences, pentagrams, stars, God knows what. In a page there is a Baphomet goat in a pentagram..."

"...and the police investigators concluded Sarah had been killed by a drugs gang or was a victim of a satanic ritual, right? I know... They questioned me and were going on and on about that, I told them I had stopped doing drugs and Sarah never touched even a joint of "erva", but they had their minds set. Bullshit! Fuck all that prejudice. Preconceptions. The Satanic Bible, heavy metal music is not about... look, evil and good are not absolute, ok?, they are just the expression of our own free will. For centuries, a couple of men in weird tunics and funny hats decided what was "right" and "acceptable". The notion of "good" was institutionalized, which is actually a great way for powerful men to discard themselves of responsibilities. It's wrong to kill and torture, but... just get an authorization from the Pope endorsing the "conversion of the unfaithful", and there you go, free reign to enslave, rape, torture and mass murder millions of people, just because their skin colour is slightly different or they pray to a different God. And today is the same shit. It's ok to kill Iraqis because we want their oil or to destroy the planet because ecology is for communist hippies... mind you, I'm not communist. Communism and religion are just the same – a bunch of guys telling millions what to do, as if they know better!"

"You mean, Satanists are...libertarians, an expression of free will against the institutionalized norms?"

"Yeah, something like that. You know what Sarah used to say? 'We aren't downloaded, we are born!' Human free will vs machine pre-coding, you see? But no matter. The majority likes being told what to do...No matter how loud the Satanists yell their freedom chants, the flock follows and the powerful command. 'Manda quem pode, obedece quem deve ...'. You understand that? Those who can, command. Those who must, obey. It has always been and will always be like that."

"Come on, Jaros, we have evolved from the dark

ages..."

"Sure, and you know why? Because of deviants! Once "good" is institutionalized in a church or a king or a political party, it stops being 'pure good' and becomes just 'rules'. Free will breaks rules, pushing the frontiers. If not for the crazy witches condemned by the mighty – Socrates, Galileo, Copernicus, Turing and millions forgotten by the history books – we would still live in caves obeying the alpha male. Throughout history, what forces change are the indigent, the ignominious. The devil, if you will. Evolution is made by the sinful who don't obey the "accepted good". Through mistakes and error, they push forward, moved by curiosity or simply by a sense of disobedience. Artificial Intelligence will never be intelligent until it can make mistakes and cope with them. That's why quantum computing can be a singularity... for the first time, error is at the core of the machine, instead of just following a pre-programmed algorithm. God creates us to obey, the devil pushes us evolve!"

Jaros lights up a cigarette and walks towards the window, opening it and puffing out. Gosh, who is this bartender philosopher? I'm almost speechless, but can see why Raven could have been attracted by the guy.

"And what does all that have to do with the Templars and the pentagrams Sarah scribbled around her notebook? You have to admit, this looks a bit...fishy, you know, pentagrams, crosses, satanic goats like that on your t-shirt..."

"God, devil, it's all in our heads. Having invented God, we immediately became His slaves. You know who wrote that? Saramago. We have similar minds, but he got the Nobel prize, I got jailed and Sarah's assassin walks free because everyone assumed she was a drugs addict killed by a satanic cult."

That was a bit harsh. But fair enough, you are judged by how you look, not by what you do.

"You look like one of the followers. Sarah was a leader.", Jaros added provocatively.

Silence. Shall I get pissed or keep calm? Funny, the guy complains of being judged by appearances, but he is doing exactly that. Stereotypes go both ways.

"And yet, I'm the one trying to understand what happened. You know, it's all good and nice to change the world and stuff, but someone has to do the housekeeping. Join the middle ground, working within the system, so that the "Impossibilities" the changers crave can become "Possibilities" accepted by common people."

Jaros throws his cigarette out of the window and comes back to the table. "Do you want to fuck?"

I got up instantly, looking towards the door to assess the best course without being blocked by the Goat. "No, I don't want to fuck, I want to know what you did to my sister."

"Well, not much, unfortunately. She was into Saint Anne. A pity, but there you go. That's free will for you, and I respect that. No need to get all worked up, I asked, you answered, not a big deal. If I was a billionaire pop star you would... no, sorry, I see you are upset. Forget it. Years ago, before I met the Saints, I wanted to be a rock music composer, get all the weed and sex in the world, consequence free. That's the shitty thing about free will, right? Consequences... Anyway, I started resorting to artificial creativity enhancers, i.e., drugs. Music is a shit world, ultra-competitive. Either you are the best, or you are nothing."

I cannot make my mind around this guy. I am impressed, but I have learned not to be too surprised.

"So, the pentagram. Come, seat.", Jaros continued. "A lot to say about it. Long before it started being used by metal heads around the world as a symbol of defiance, it was, it is, charged with spiritual meaning. It is a pagan symbol of the balance between the feminine and masculine. The astrological significance of the pentagram is derived from the figure drawn by the planet Venus in the sky during its 8-year cycles. Look here". Jaros pulled his iPhone and googled something to show Savanah a picture of the 8-year cycle designed by Venus around the sun.

"The points of alignment between Venus and Earth in their orbits around the sun, during these 8-year cycles, form the vertices of a pentagram. The pentagram actually shifts a few degrees on every cycle, the last two "south node" alignments, which mark the start of each cycle, occurred in 2004 and 2012."

"You believe that crap??", I ask, probably rolling up my eyes unintentionally. He notices but remains unfazed.

"It does not matter what I believe, but what people have believed through the ages. This pentagram is a symbol of Venus, the Roman goddess of love, desire, fertility and femininity. Venus is the brightest planet in the night sky, describing intriguing cycles in the sky. The short cycle lasts 40-days, similar to a woman's menstrual cycle. The long 8-year cycle aligns with Earth 5 times each cycle, describing a pentagram in the sky. The pentagram of Venus represents the balance between feminine and masculine. You can construct the pentagram as a downwards triangle overlaid with a pointed upwards triangle."

Jaros pulls another cigarette and this time doesn't bother to walk to the window. Instead, he gets a piece of kitchen paper and draws something on it.

"The sexual meaning of that should be straightforward. The downwards triangle stands for the feminine pubic area or the fertility of the woman's womb. The upwards pointed triangle is a phallic representation of the male organ penetrating the female. The pentagram original symbolism is of unity, balance, love and fertility... not Satan, although the church tries to portray the pagan Venus goddess as a symbol of carnal lust and sin! You just add the picture of a goat and, puff!..., you get a satanic symbol."

I look at him, intrigued. Was this a trick to get me to bed?

"Let me just push you a bit more on this pentagram thing. You know Leonardo da Vinci Vitruvian Man, right?"

"Of course, the proportions of the human body."

"I used to talk with Sarah for hours about this stuff. She knew her cabalistic symbols and could see the roses under the cypresses of Nietzsche dark forest. Da Vinci is known to be a Grand Master of the Free Masons, heirs to the Templar tradition... Now, take a look at this.", and he draws again on the kitchen roll paper.

"You are joking, right?"

"Think what you want. Many people have seen these symbols hidden in Da Vinci's drawing. The Pentagram, symbol of the male-female union. And in green, connecting the straight legs with the upstretched arms, the chalice... it is shaped like a woman's womb, symbol of fertility. Or a breast, the source of nourishment for the new-born baby. Some call the chalice the Holy Grail, source of eternal life. The church had to mess everything up into a fog of puritanical outrage, expelled the Templars, relegated the females to a kind of devilish temptresses and forced the free minds into secret societies. The secret symbols of those secret societies are the distant echo of the free minds."

I look in silence at Da Vinci's Vitruvian Man with Jaros' sketched pentagram and chalice.

As I kept silent, Jaros continued.

"The upwards and downwards triangles, touching at the tip, form the X cross. It is often used to mean ´kisses´, right?, but its original symbology is sexual intercourse, the male and female triangles joining together. The cross also stands for the joining and crossing of two worlds, the ethereal and the material, the spiritual and the carnal. The church took the X cross, an ancient symbol of freedom and equilibrium, and transformed it into a symbol of domination. You can also put the two triangles on top of each other...", continued Sergio, drawing on the piece of paper.

"We get a hexagram, the six pointed Star of David. That's amazing!", I exclaim, not really knowing what to think.

"Right. The Star of David, which features in the flag of Israel, or Magen David in Hebrew, literally means "Shield of David". It became a symbol of the Zionist oppression and resistance. However, it has also been used throughout history by other religions. For instance, in Hinduism, it is referred as ´shatkone', the upwards triangle representing Shiva, the masculine side of God, and the downwards triangle representing Shakti, the feminine side of divinity. In masonic symbology it is said to symbolize the union of Heaven and Earth, with God reaching down to men and men reaching up to God. Broadly speaking, it is a representation of balance. This balance has always been embraced by religion: ancient civilizations worship the female ´god of creation ´, with statues of goddesses with huge bosoms and hips. Roman and Greek religions had as many gods as goddesses. For some unknown reason, though, modern religions have all gone chauvinist! Women are treated either as ignorant pious procreation instruments or devilish whores tempting righteous men. Why the fuck have they gone to such lengths to defend the virginity of Mary and the immaculate conception?? Come on, we all know how babies are made..."

There is an awkward silence, during which I just stare blankly. "I could use a bit of that firewater, now".

"Help yourself, dear. But careful, it gives a hell of a headache in the morning..."

I pour myself a glass of the velvety translucent drink. It tastes... I can't quite place it, but I can almost chew the velvety liquid before swallowing. Hell! It fires my insides much more aggressively than whisky or rum. Tears burst unannounced from my eyes and Jaros laughs lightly.

"Americans... I love you guys, but really?! You get more punch from a small shot of this shit than a full pint of beer."

I am still drying my tears and trying to decide whether I love or hate the firewater when Jaros picks up his iPhone again.

"Let me show you something that Sarah was delirious about, when I showed it to her. I told you about astrological path of planet Venus in the night sky, right? That is if you plot the path of Venus and Earth with the Sun at the centre. But also, if you plot the path of Venus on the sky with planet Earth at the centre, instead of the Sun, you get... just a second", he hits some keys on google search in his mobile to show me:

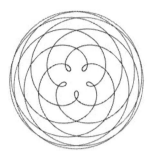

"No way...", I cry, looking stunned at the image. "Gosh...That's...that's the Rose symbol. The Rose Line. The Rose appears in Templar churches and Rosacrux tradition."

"Yeah, that's what Sarah said as well."

Gosh, the guy knows his shit, for an ex-convict drug addict.

"May I?", I say, pulling a cigarette from his pack. He smiles and hand me the lighter. "Sure. I'm hoping when I get to 60 they will have discovered the cure for lung cancer...".

Not the usual charming Latin lover, but he has something about him, no doubt. I force the thought away and move into a new direction.

"Did you have a crush on Sarah? I mean, not artistically, but, did you have sex with her?"

"Uouu, straight to the jugular, eh? Those are two different questions..."

"So, did you?"

"I had a crush, yeah. But every man in this bar 13 years ago had a crush on the Saints! The devils were all converted by the Saints... Not kidding, literally. I think at the time Lisbon was not used to such liberated, frontally sexual, carnal performance. We all, little devils, bowed to the mighty altar of the Saints. But no, we didn't have sex. I think she lusted for Ana, unfortunately."

"And did you and the Saints do drugs?"

"Gosh, you are persistent! I told you. I was never an addict. I passed drugs to get some money, and smoked some weed for inspiration, but was never into heavy drugs. The Saints... were saints, regarding that at least. Neither Sarah nor Ana ever touched drugs, they just played and danced like maniacs and drove everyone crazy. I guess that was their drug."

I don't know what to make of this guy. I extend my hand in farewell, thanking him for the good talk. "Not even a farewell kiss?", he says, with a sly smile.

I walk out towards the door. Jaros stays behind, saying he needed to make a phone call.

ALGARVE, APRIL 2019

Praia do Garrão

(Savanah)

I was excited about spending Easter in the Algarve with Hugh. We haven't been together for almost 4 months, which is the longest span of time away from each other for the past 15 years. Since we started dating in Boston in 2004, we became pretty much inseparable, to the jealousy or scorn of my friends. I never thought it would last so long, but, well, it just happened. Sure, I had my flings and a couple of boyfriends before Hugh, but I guess I had simply been too busy to take a relationship seriously. The two years for the MBA were a break from all the pressure of exams, university and the first years as an analyst at the investment bank. I guess the MBA was truly my late crazy teenage years, with parties and immense confidence in my, our bright future.

Those two years were probably the only period in my adult life I seriously thought about relationships. Before, I had been too busy to think about the boyfriends. After, I have been too busy to think about the marriage. It simply is. We both share the memories of those two years together in Boston, living in an ivory tower of parties, self-confidence and case studies of how we would change the world. Reality ended up a bit different, at least in what regards to changing the world. Lehman Brothers and the Subprime were a cold shower of reality. But the memories of Boston stayed with us, the shared goals, the long walks in the park, the case studies we discussed together and the promises of a great life.

Great life meaning, at the time, a successful life.

Sure, no complaints, Hugh is nice, great in fact, we share similar interests, sex is good. Saturday dinner parties with glamourous friends, jogging in Hyde Park on Sunday mornings, holidays to exotic places every year. We like what we do together. Which is not necessarily the same as liking to be together.

I booked a nice hotel in Garrão, a quiet stretch of sandy beach lined with fabulous sea-view mansions, between the more crowded Vale do Lobo and the somewhat snobbish Quinta do Lago. Duma had recommended the area and after a Saturday afternoon search I had decided for a small boutique hotel & spa in front of the Garrão beach. I was looking forward to the lazy mornings in bed, the afternoon walks on the beach, a gin and tonic by the pool and the warm starry nights inviting the bodies to strip naked and join together. I was craving Hugh's body so much, my groin hurt in anticipation.

Human mind is a funny thing. Hugh had been putting a slight, gentle pressure for me to get pregnant, but I had resisted for fear of... I don't know what, really. All this feminist, equal rights crap just puts additional pressure on women. Now you just don't know what you should aim for. Throughout my twenties and early thirties, everyone expected me to be successful and powerful, a modern super woman. But you get close to forty without two or three children and the world starts looking at you as incomplete. Or perhaps it's just my wired brain that feels the pressure. So... this was going to be it. No protection. Just see what happens.

At the last minute, though, Hugh couldn't make it. A complication had come up in a deal they had been working for months and he had to cancel the Easter break. A long summer trip in June, around Europe, he promised...

"The hotel is booked, so we might as well use it", I said

to Duma after inviting her to spend the three days break in the Algarve with me. After some hesitation about leaving her son alone, she ended up accepting when the son asked (informed) if he could spend the Easter break at a friend's weekend home in Óbidos. The boy was fifteen, at that age when young people just want to get away of the adults and carve out their own space.

We arrived Thursday afternoon, a three hours' drive from Lisbon in a convertible BMW I had booked in advance and the rent-a-car had refused to cancel. The hotel was exactly like the brochure had promised, a small luxury hotel with couples strolling around hand in hand. This might actually have been a mistake, I though, commiserating about Hugh's absence for what should have been a romantic getaway. Is that stupid beautiful VP, Susan, on the deal team? I had seen her eye Hugh more than once in the office Christmas party last year.

I pushed the thoughts away. Duma was fun company. We laughed as Duma made fun of ourselves, two women in a valentine weekend, booking a joint massage in the SPA for Friday morning. At breakfast Duma kept jesting, saying we were a lesbian black & white couple spending the holy weekend of the passion of Christ doing naughty things in the bedroom. "Shut up, Duma, you are just being silly" I said, but unable to control the laughter. No-one cares, really, they are not even looking at us. The other tables, I meant. Although they were, really. I had noticed the furtive glances, stolen away as we passed by. "Silly is good, Savanah... you have been too serious for the past few months. You can do with some silliness."

Duma opted to lounge at the beach while I went for a long walk. An immense 10 miles' expanse of white sand from Quarteira do Faro, part of which along the Ria de Tavira natural reserve park. I walked all the way from Garrão to Faro and back, in the hard wet sand of low tide, the small waves caressing my feet. The dunes carried on for miles and miles of an almost deserted beach, the seagulls and early swallows flying playfully against the clear blue sky. Every 30 minutes or so a plane crossed the sky heading to Faro airport, bringing the discerning English and German upper class tourists to the Quinta do Lago golf courses.

Walking on the beach, alone, whereas Hugh was supposed to be there walking with me, I kept reflecting on our relationship and if we really should have kids. It felt... nice, settled, comfortable. There was no longer the thrill of discovering each other idiosyncrasies, ideas, tastes, desires. At least we were not like those childish couples bickering about every little thing. Still, I missed the emotional rollercoaster, the adrenalin of the chase, the challenge of dazzling and being dazzled. I was looking forward to having children. But somehow this felt like another "project" to do together, a glue to replace the fire.

After a light lunch in a beach shack, we decided to spend the afternoon lounging by the pool. I was used to long runs, but the 10km power walk through the beach in the morning and the swim on the sea, had left me knackered. I didn't feel it at the time, the effect of the sun and sand and salt in my face... until I woke up close to 5pm, stretched in the lounge chair by the pool. I had slept, what? At least 3 hours straight, under the shadow of the large sunshade by the pool, with Lethal White open over my chest, the latest Cormoran Strike novel which I had started the evening before in the balcony.

Saturday was pretty much the same, the lazy passing of the hours with the comfortable certainty that the next hour would be just the same as the prior, sunny, warm, with miles and miles of sand to walk and a languid refreshing sea to swim.

I can't quite remember how me and Duma ended up discussing Columbus and Raven, with a G&T on our hands, on Saturday afternoon. It had been only two days but it felt like two weeks we had been in there.

"There is something I have been meaning to tell you for a while", Duma said. "You need to tread carefully. Your sister just went full blast ahead and… well, I don't know what to think actually. But there are some weird things."

Duma told me a strange story, which sounded like a distant plot made up by over imaginative old academics, as far away from that idyllic Algarve afternoon as the daily grindstone of the office in NY, now long behind me. The warm spring day turned into a mild evening and the pool slowly emptied in preparation for dinner.

I still can't quite make out the meaning of the story Duma told me. In 1928, Ricardo Rózpide, a Spanish historian of the Royal Academy of History and secretary-general of the Royal Geography Society, revealed a portentous secret about Colon to Afonso de Ornelas, the president of the Portuguese History Academy. He had supposedly found these secret documents in a private archive of João da Nova, proving beyond the shadow of any doubt, Colon's identity and nationality. João da Nova was a Spanish sailor who worked for the Portuguese king Dom Manuel I. He was the owner of the ship 'Flor do Mar' used in battles with the moors for control of the spice trade in India. The island Juan da Nova, near Madagascar, was named after the pilot who discovered it in 1501, who died fighting alongside the Portuguese in India, in 1509.

Ricardo Róspide spent his life researching Colon's life. However, when the academic supposedly found an important document, he refrained from publishing it. He confessed to Afonso de Ornelas, in 1928, that if he published what he had found about Colon he would face grave danger. Róspide died shortly after. The document or proof Róspide un-covered was never found. This episode happened during the 41 and 36-years long fascist dictatorships of Salazar in Por-tugal and Franco in Spain, during which press and academics were subject to censorship in both countries.

But the enigmatic roll of censorship around Colon that Duma was unrolling was far from over.

Shortly after, in 1930, António Serpa published his book "Salvador Gonçalves Zarco (Christopher Columbus)". Serpa was an historian, cofounder of the Portuguese History Academy. He had found that secret documents related to the genealogy of Colon, written in Hebrew, had been hidden in the lining of a tapestry at the Convent of Nossa Senhora dos Remédios, in Lisbon, to escape Inquisition and later trans-ferred to a secret compartment in a wall, but they had been discovered and burned in the 17th century. His thesis was quickly silenced by the political power and forgotten.

There were two books published in the early 18th cen-tury by different authors, both using the same pseudonym of Prior Don Tivisco de Nasao Zarco, y Colona. One of the books was named Theatro Genealogico, by Manuel de Carv-alho e Ataíde (father of Marquês de Pombal). The other was Periscope Genealogica, by Jacinto de Sousa. The first was published in Portugal, the second was printed aboard a ship outside territorial waters and circulated in Spain. Although 200 years had passed from Colon's death, the Portuguese king Dom Pedro decided to banish, by royal decree of 1703, the Don Tivisco book, "because the said book is not con-venient to be known nor credited." Both authors wrote in the book that they had written it "with the permission of the superiors" or "with powers given by the superiors". As if, 200 years after Colon, grand masters of some secret order al-lowed the publication of these genealogies to reveal a long kept secret.

Why, in the eighteenth century, had a book that included Colon's genealogy been banned, and other printed outside territorial waters? Why had Colon's genealogy papers been hidden in a tapestry and burned by the Inquisition in the seventeenth century? Why, in the twentieth century, 450 years after Columbus first expedition, had novel research on Colon by credible academics been victim of censorship by the fascist regimens of Portugal and Spain, both with close ties with the Vatican and catholic church?

If Colon was the illegitimate son of a noble or high priest, some secrecy about his parenthood would be expectable, but that was a quite common situation in the 15th century and could not justify so much and continued mystery. The issue must be wider, bigger. What extraordinary danger could Colon's true identity and mission pose to justify continuous censorship all the way into the twentieth century?

"My dear, I'm just a research assistant, but I'm neither blind nor stupid.", Duma continued. "This might be the G&T talking, but now that we are far away from the hears in Lisbon, you should hear me out."

Ruy de Pina, court chronicler of king Manuel I, was the first to adopt Colon's adulterated name of Columbus in Portugal, in a 1504 chronicle guarded in Torre do Tombo [93], the infamous Codex 632. This codex is a turning point in the forgery around Colon, because it is the first ever recorded reference to Colon as "Colonbo ytaliano". The fake Mayorazgo where Columbus claims "I, born in Genoa..." would only appear 80 years later during the inheritance trials. Could Ruy de Pina be under pressure from King Manuel to hide Colon's mission, because it was dangerous to his pretensions of become king of a unified Iberia? He was at the time married to a daughter of the Spanish monarchs. Curiously, even under distress, Ruy de Pina tried to convey some leads over the lie, because he uses Colonbo instead of Colombo.

Also, Ruy de Pina wrote a rather bland and dry description of Colon's visit to Vale do Paraíso on the return from his first journey, transforming the audience with Dom João into nothing more than the crazy Admiral bragging his success in the face of an irate King João… a sad comedy worthy of Abbott and Costello. Notably, all Portuguese authors after Ruy de Pina – Garcia de Resende, João de Barros, Damião de Góis – copied textually, word by word, the description of that visit from the pages of Ruy de Pina. As if wanting to adhere to the official account, for fear of deviating from the official line, but also distancing themselves of the story, as if saying "just transcribing the official version, not necessarily defending it".

By the hand of Dom Manuel, the Inquisition was established in Portugal on 17 December 1531. Besides the human pain, atrocities and assassinations inflicted by the Inquisitorial Court over 350 years, one can only imagine the immense number of books and documents rewritten, adulterated or burned on the Inquisition fires.

On the other side of the border, Carlos V became King of a unified Spain from 1519 to 1556. He named Dom Fernando Colon, the Admiral's bastard son, as his major-cosmographer. On 13 June 1523, Carlos V gave specific orders to Dom Fernando to stop his research about his father's past!

From 1580, three Spanish kings – the Filipes – ruled Portugal for 60 years. At the end of the sixteenth century, exactly when the Colon's Inheritance Trials of 1578-1609 took place, one single political power, The House of Habsburg, ruled over Spain, Portugal and northern Italy. What else would you need to complete the extraordinary cover up? During these years, the House of Habsburg had plenty of time to clean up and remake the Portuguese archives, destroying or copying manuscripts, thus rewriting history at their will. For instance, the marriage certificate with Dona Filipa or the birth certificate of his first son Diogo were never found. In Spain, as well, documents were doctored. The Memorial de Pagos of Isabella's treasurer Pedro de Toledo shows an entry in 1487 of 30 gold coins to a "Portuguese", but the name was later stricken out. Cross referencing this document allowed Spanish investigators to show the "Portuguese" should be Colon... but why has the name been deleted?

At the end of the sixteenth century, when Spain, Portugal and Northern Italy were under Habsburg control, documents never before seen suddenly surfaced during the Inheritance trials, supporting the claim of a Genoese merchant as heir of Colon (then renamed Columbus), including the fake Mayorazgo.

Conveniently, in 1571, Luis Colon (the third Admiral who would die without a direct heir and thus originate the Inheritance Trial) took Fernando Colon's biography of his father, the "Historia del Almirante", to Italy to be translated. The original book disappeared and only the Italian translation survives! This was just before the Inheritance Trial started... how convenient the original biography disappeared and only a copy made under the supervision of the Habsburg controlled Italians survived, referring to Colon's alleged Genoese origins. Luis Colon was, at that time, exiled in North Africa, accused in Spain of keeping two wives simultaneously, and seriously ill. So, how did he manage to get hold of the book, who should have been safely kept at Las Cuevas Monastery in Seville? The exiled and sick Luis, who never cared about his uncle's legacy except for spending the money, was suddenly taken by remorse and travelled to Italy to have the book translated? Luis died in January 1572, months after the Italian version of the "Historia" was published in Italy. This book and the fake Mayorazgo were one of the main evidences presented by the rich Italian merchant Baltazar Colombo to support his claim.

Why all this consistent effort to eliminate or censor

documents, while forcing a bland, innocent (but unrealistic) tale of the Genoese poor wool weaver?

Most of the documents that reached our days are copies, the originals long lost or destroyed. The logbooks of Colon's journeys have pages ripped off or parts cut. The Book of Prophecies, one of the five original Colon's books at the Columbine Library in Seville, is an enigmatic manuscript with 84 pages but 14 have been ripped off. An anonymous note written on the margins of page 77 of the manuscript says "Wrong did who took the missing pages from here, because they were the best part of this book".

The "official" story of a poor Italian with no relevant background started materializing in the early sixteenth century, around Colon's death, with Dom Manuel I and Ruy de Pina. It was then developed during the inheritance trial under Habsburg oversight. And finally established itself, uncontested due to the lack of alternative evidence – precisely because Colon and his sons had been so cautious to always hide the true origin and mission of the Admiral.

Duma's revelations of Saturday evening ruined Easter Sunday. I could not enjoy the charcoal grilled seabass and was glad to leave the Algarve on Sunday afternoon, returning to Lisbon.

In the end, however, I have to recognize it was a nice, relaxing weekend. Not quite what I had expected, a romantic getaway with Hugh, but still rather pleasant in the company of Duma. The talk about all the cover ups around Colon's life and mission was another piece of the gigantic puzzle forming in my mind.

I wonder. Why were emperor Carlos V and the three Filipe kings so concerned about Colon, concealing the Admiral's identity into a fabricated tale? Could Colon and his heirs be somehow a threat to the Habsburgs throne, so long

KARLOS K.

after Colon's death?

LISBON, MAY 2019

The Saints Rock Club

(Savanah)

I returned to The Saints on the weekend after Easter. The night was pleasantly warm, a promise of the hot summer Lisbon nights that lay ahead. As April progressed into May, the anticipation of summer created an increasingly animated night life in the city. The bar was packed.

Stepping into the small smoke garden at the rear, I found Carminho, who immediately walked towards me blowing a cloud of smoke behind her.

"Hi, Sarah's sister!!" She was a bit stoned, I could tell. The air in the garden smelled of moisty grass with undertones of mushrooms and earthy vanilla. Weed or hash, probably. Behind Carminho jostled a tall, thin men with a decently fashionable wavy hair and well-trimmed three-day beard.

Carminho hugged me and kissed my cheeks as if we were old friends. "This place now is posh, nothing harder than weed… you should have seen it back in the day. When the Saints played here. Your sister did a bit of the stuff as well, I bet. I never saw her stoned, but the way they played and danced on stage, I mean, they had to be high, right?! No-one dances like that without some pop in the mind. Right here, where we stand, I was coming out for a smoke and saw her talking to Jaros, you met him, right?, she was saying, I don't know the exact words, but something like 'the shit you gave me yesterday was mind blowing, amazing. Have you got more? Come on, you promised you would bring me more tonight...' Then I started noticing the two of them, you know, he used to stand behind the counter as he always does, even today, just eyeing the clients and flow. Sarah, usually shortly after arriving in the club, came to the counter, they kissed, and he took an envelope from behind the vodka bottles in the bar and give it to her. Wyborowa, he refuses to serve any other vodka, only the original Polish one..."

Could that be true? Carminho crossed her arm with mine and continued. "But then she must have got second thoughts, right Hugo?" She motioned for the man that had so far stand next to us, silent, looking away into the garden.

"This is Hugo, by the way, my boyfriend. Go on, tell her what you told me..."

Luis looked a bit embarrassed and just nodded, taking a sip from his drink. Carminho didn't wait for him to talk and pushed forward.

"We were talking about you looking around Sarah's death, when we recalled... you said it, right, dear? Luis mentioned an episode that I failed to mention to you last night... Luis was in the toilets backstage, when he heard Sarah talking outside. She sounded quite cross, you said it, right, love? She was talking in an undertone, but Luis understood quite clearly behind the toilet door. Sarah was telling him off, yelling in a hushed tone but clearly angry. She said 'No drugs, that was the deal! If I ever catch you again passing drugs in the club, I will stop playing with you and will never set foot in here again. And I will go to the police! Free will means own will, not a fake illusion propped by hallucinogenic.' That was it, right, Luis? Then there was a silence and Luis didn't dare coming out of the toilet. Instants later, the Goat came in and they just exchanged some glances. Luis left, a bit embarrassed, didn't you? But that has stuck with us. At the time we thought about going to the police, after Sarah's death... that looked quite threatening. But, well, we were not 100% clean at the time, so, we just let it go, and then time passed..."

We chatted for a bit and I ended up giving them my mobile number, just in case they remembered anything else that could be relevant. Then I went out. The bar was full with a hipster and noisy crowd, a strange mix of young wannabes and 40-somethings have beens. I waved to the bored looking waitress, who didn't bother to wave back, and exited to the street.

In the taxi back to my attic flat, I ruminated about what had just happened. Based on Carminho's account, the Goat was clearly lying. He had not stopped dealing drugs in the bar.

So, the Goat had no alibi (at home sleeping, no one to confirm it). He had the 'means' (access to the Fentanyl drugs). He also had the 'motive', after all, which had escaped the police investigation (he fancied Sarah but was pissed she fancied Ana, and more importantly Sarah had threatened to expose him to the police for relapsing into passing drugs again). But I was still missing the 'how'. How did he know Sarah would arrive so late in the middle of the night? And again, what had Sarah been doing between 2.14pm when she emailed me, probably when she left Tomar, and 3.30 in the morning?

At least, I now realized all those pentagrams and crosses probably had nothing to do with Columbus research. We had been mixing things up, seeing connections where there were none. Those drawings were more likely related to her artistic life as a guitar player of The Goat and the Saints and not with the Columbus research. The goat inside the pentagram with the sentence next to it 'The Goat is in my way' gained a new meaning. It was not a drug-induced hallucination, but probably just a whining complaint that the Goat was Saint Anne's boyfriend, hampering an intimate relationship between the two women.

LISBON, MAY 2019

I t had been another disappointing week. After the surprise breakthrough at the end of the visit to the Judiciária and the interesting discussions with Jaros and Carminho, she hadn't managed to advance much regarding her sister's murder. And the research continued at a deadend. The feeling remained, insistent: the issue is not what is in all those books and documents, but what isn't there. There must be something relevant in what's missing, but she couldn't quite grasp what it was.

There is no document about Columbus prior to 1484. It's as if the man just... materialized from thin hair, out of nothing, a sudden genius, highly educated, with coat of armour recognized by the Spanish court and married to a high noble lady.

Savanah climbed the stairs to Duma's fourth floor apartment with no elevator, looking forward to the Friday afternoon meeting. They had made some progress with the help of Sergio's expertise on medieval symbology and the history of the maritime discoveries, but these remained loose unconnected facts. Something crucial was missing, the key that would untangle the puzzle making it fall into place.

Sergio was leading their progress, making use of his vast knowledge of medieval history.

"Well", he said after the three of them were sat around the table with the usual coffee and biscuits provided by Duma. "The notebook is dotted with stars, triangles, pentagrams and hexagrams. Unless we assume they are just doodles, Raven must have been rather obsessed with them", continued Sergio, going through the pages. It was quite unnecessary, as the two women had seen all those stars and crosses and wind roses designed all over the notebook.

"Guys, as I told you, it's possible the pentagrams and stars are related to the heavy metal rock band I told you about, more than anything else", answered Savanah. "But still... I think she was after something. The pentagram and rose symbols appear in several Templar churches, in Tomar and the Rosslyn Chapel. They could be signalling something. Why do you have these symbols in two of the most important Templar places, so far apart?"

It was a rhetorical question and Savanah didn't wait for an answer before continuing. "There is an image here... let me see". She flicked the pages in the notebook to find what she was looking for.

"Here, see? She draws a Wind Rose inside the Star of David hexagram and a Rose around the Pentagram. The Rose, the Wind Rose, the Star of David, the Pentagram – they could all be different representations of the same symbology of male-female, fecundity..." (a crazy flash comes to her mind: what if all the symbology actually represents communication signs between two ancient paths looking for each other: the Wind Rose looking to be reunited with the Rose Line?).

Duma interrupted her thoughts, fed up with all the speculation. "Yeah, she curves the corners of the pentagram into a Rose, establishing a half-baked link between Rosslyn Chapel (Chapel of the Rose) and the pentagram in Tomar. And fits the Wind Rose we find in Sagres into the six pointed star. Hints to the bloodline of Christ everywhere, protected by that Priory whatever thingy! Guys, really! This is not proper scientific method, we are just throwing wild theories around.", blasted Duma. "We are getting ourselves caught in the same speculations as Raven did. I don't like this a bit."

"Calm down, Duma", said Savanah, placing a friendly hand in her harm. "This gets us all nervous. We are just trying to follow Raven's line of thought, ok?"

"Actually", interjected Sergio, "it makes sense to find symbols of male-female unity and of Christ's worldly, human nature in Templar temples. The Templars were accused, when the Order was extinct, of the Cathar heresy. The Cathars rejected a separation between the spiritual world of God and the material world of Men, but rather that spirituality, the spark of the divine, is inside each person. They considered Christ as a pure conceptual idea whereas Jesus was a material man and husband of Mary Magdalene. They also rejected the Resurrection of Jesus and the symbol of the Cross. One of the accusations against the Templars is of spitting on the cross during initiation rites. They also believed in the central role of Mary Magdalene as a teacher and spiritual leader, considering her even more important than Saint Peter, the founder of the Catholic church."

The church of Rome had cast women to a secondary role, as dumb and frail, created by God from a man's rib just to keep him company, cook, breed and pray – and when left uncontrolled, these devilish creatures had tempted Adam to take a bite on the Forbidden Fruit, the Apple, and cast humanity out of paradise. Uncle Santiago had said something quite strange "The Church belittled or vilified women. The Templars vowed to protect the Queen and her descendants".

"Oh, I like these guys! If they ruled the church, instead of those chauvinist and sexist priests, maybe I had not become an atheist. Gosh, are you joking?! Adam can't control himself and bites the forbidden apple, but the fault is Eve's for tempting him. It's like the rapist is the victim because the girl was too hot!!", groaned Savanah, half serious, half joking.

"The Cathars also rejected a hierarchical clergy and denounced the ostentatious wealth of the Catholic church. The path to the Light, to God, could be achieved by each person with no need for hordes of prelates and bishops clad in jewels and fine robes. They were a kind of early reformers, but crashed by Rome. As were the Templars!"

"So, Sergio, keep it simple...", interrupted Savanah. "You are saying the Templars, with their links to the Cathars, could do without the power hungry priests and bishops and didn't reject the material male-female world, because the spiritual is an inner experience, not rituals ordained by priests. I was hoping for something more.... saucy, you know, religious sex rites celebrating life and the divinity of the human body."

"Right, Stanley Kubrick did get imaginations all fired up", laughed Sergio. "But this female divinity theme is a constant with the Illuminati. Take Leonardo's painting called "Salvator Mundi", or Saviour of the World, supposedly a portrait of Jesus Christ. Come on!! Either the guy was a lousy painter, or this is a portrait of a woman in a blue dress. A woman, as the saviour of the world. An androgynous Christ? Is he secretly referring to Mary Magdalene, Jesus companion who bore his child? By the way, this painting was bought in 2017 by a Saudi prince for 400 million dollars, the highest price fetched by a painting ever. Ever!"

"You are also surely familiar with the Last Supper painting, a mural on the dining room of Santa Maria delle

Grazie church, in Milan. It has been widely debated who is the person seating to Jesus' right hand. All other figures in the painting are clearly masculine, except Jesus and his companion, both rather androgynous. And note the downwards-pointing triangle formed by the head of Christ and his companion, an old symbol of the feminine."

Duma got up, fed up with all the implied critics to the church those two atheists, Sergio and Savanah, were throwing out. Her church was a local presence who tended for the poor and abandoned. She didn't care much for whatever was going on in distant Rome.

Savanah noticed her friend was irritated. The conversation was bothering Duma and she decided to change course. In fact, this discussion may help them understand the cryptic lines in the final pages, that she had been wondering about.

Savanah moved to the page that showed the three cryptic lines, surrounded by doodles of stars and crosses and flowers.

the X is incomplete

secret mission: find X?

X in America before X !!!

"There is a core message here that has been nagging at me. It seems we can understand most of the symbols individually, but the overall message is still escaping me. And yet, Raven marked it with three exclamation marks, suggesting it is important."

"I guess we kind of have deciphered the meaning of the first line already. In the Templar cross, the X is incomplete. We know that much, because...uhmm", Sergio went back to the draft pages from a few weeks back. "The Wind Rose formed by runes, has this wiggle, or little hook, that is missing in the Templar cross."

"Ok, fair enough.", agreed Savanah. "But why does Raven attach a meaning to that, to the point of writing a specific sentence on the issue? It seems this X means something."

Savanah though aloud as they stared at the image and the three sentences. "In the second sentence I know the initial symbol. Two mirrored Ks joined together, standing for Kristopher Kolumbus. This would then read ´Kristopher Kolumbus secret mission is to find the X?´ Note the question mark though, Raven was uncertain here."

"Gosh, this looks like a treasure map... the X marks the spot!", laughed Sergio, to lighten a bit the environment.

"Actually", said Savanah, "You are not far from it. Look at the last sentence... This does look like a treasure hunt. The X was in America before Kristopher Kolumbus. So, we have: The X in the Templar Cross is incomplete; Columbus mission was to find the X; the X was in America before Columbus; and from our previous discussions, the X may refer to some spiritual quest merging the feminine and masculine"

"Does this make any sense to you?", Savanah continued, exhausted. "Gosh, it seems we have learned a lot of stuff, but still have no clue what we are looking for".

Friday night was depressing, again alone at her attic flat eating take away noodles and zapping between series on Netflix. Savanah woke up on the sofa, well past 3.00am, from a restless sleep and confusing dreams she could not recall. She got up and stretched. The weather outside seemed to be changing, heavy dark clouds covering the stars. She moved to the bed and tried to get back to sleep.

VALLADOLID, MAY 1506

(Columbus)

"I am not the first Admiral of my family. Let them call me whatever they want."
CHRISTOPHER COLUMBUS

I am truly the Last Templar Knight.

The Pope has turned the head around of that sold off King. Dom Manuel craves recognition and acceptance from the European courts. The gold from Brazil, spices from India and slaves from Africa can buy the King the illusion of having a hand at the centuries old political game of old Europe. But it is an illusion. The tiny country will never be accepted as an equal by the blue-blooded, pure-breed, self-satisfied nobility of Italy, France or Spain. They may flatter Manuel´s new palaces, but on his back they all laugh at him as a "nouveau-riche" arrivistic without the pedigree.

But I laugh! Oh, I laugh at all these dogs, playing the same old tricks when the world is changing fast. Do they not sense the winds of change that will tore down their airs of superiority? Even if the old European castles stand, the power within them is moving westwards, to the new continent.

Thirteen! Thirteen kings before Dom Manuel have stood firm against the Papacy tyranny, continuing the mission set by the first Templars. Dom Afonso Henriques, the first king of Portugal, was son of Henri de Bourgogne, a

French Templar knight who came to these lands to help in the wars of Reconquista. Count Henri de Bourgogne brought with him from France the deep Templar roots. He was born in Dijon, in the same city as his niece Friar Bernard of Clairvaux, the abbot who established the monastic rule of the Templar knights. An uncle of Saint Bernard of Clairvaux, cousin of Count Henri, was part of the initial group of 9 crusaders who established the Order of the Temple of Solomon in Jerusalem.

The Templars already owned lands and properties in Portugal as early as 1122, just 3 years after the Order was created in Jerusalem and 7 years before it was recognized by the Pope in 1129. The first King himself, Dom Afonso Henriques, became a Templar knight on 13th March 1129. The destinies and principles of Portugal and the Order of the Temple were always intimately connected.

The same spirit fired the maritime discoveries. Henry the Navigator and King Dom João continued a long tradition of the first 13 Kings of fierce independence, looking outwards to the Atlantic instead of inwards to the other European courts and the Vatican.

But the new King Dom Manuel is forcing a full change on Portuguese policies and alliances. He forgets 350 years of a Kingdom fiercely independent from Rome. It is ironic that as the kingdom of Portugal reaches its highest point, with an empire that stretches from Vera Cruz to Calicut, it bends the knee to the Pope and the European princes, looking anxiously for their approval.

King Manuel craves attention and acceptance by the European Lords. Fool! He expelled the Jews, forcing them to convert, just to please Isabella and obtain consent to marry her daughter. As if one Spanish princess was not enough, 3 years later he married another daughter of Isabella and Fernando, Maria. He dreams of becoming the first King of a united Iberia [94]. He probably comes on his bedsheets, just thinking of it! Only if he knew the Spaniards as I do! Those kings lied to me, they signed the Capitulações de Santa Fé, already intent on not fulfilling their promises.

Manuel usurped the throne through the mysterious death of Infante Afonso, which left King João II without a son. King Manuel is dazzled by his power and this new intimacy with Popes and kings. So he is re-writing history!

My friend Antonio Marchena tells me the King is obsessively covering up and destroying the symbols of the Portuguese links with the Templars. Dom Manuel is covering up 350 years of history, ashamed of his ancestors.

He has started renovation works in Tomar, repainting the frescoes of the main chamber of the Convent, covering up the original Templar paintings. How dares he to silence the voice of his ancestors who made the country great before him? Is he afraid Isabella horde of priests discovers the hidden messages in Tomar? Is he afraid of the Inquisition he himself has invited into the country?

The King's hubris and presumption threatens every sacred Templar treasure in the country. Even the Raven Knight. I am distraught. Manuel ordered the Raven Knight removed! I have seen it myself, the stone statue of a knight riding an unsaddled horse, with his left hand on the horse mane and the right arm extended, pointing westwards, all fingers curled except the index finger.

The Raven Knight is a marvel, a beacon left by the Nova Scotia Templars, to signal they were waiting on the new lands to the west, where the outstretched finger pointed.

I would love to pass all this to Fernando, so that history can be preserved instead of re-written. But I can't. If Fernando knows too much, they will think he knows the whole true and keep chasing down my descendants, looking for the

Book.

The secret shall die with me!

I am comforted though, that the mission has finally been accomplished. The Wind Rose is safe with the Rose Line, in a new land of freedom. As long as they remain secret, unknown and unmolested by the priests – all of them, the Roman Pope, the Jewish Cohen Gadol or the Islamic Imame – all of them! As long as they remain in ignorance, the New Jerusalem is safe, preparing for a new age.

Let them destroy everything. It matters no more. The purpose of all those symbols has been achieved. The statues, the paintings, the cryptic messages hidden in esoteric rites, they were all guiding marks to maintain the memory of the mission. Now the two great treasures found by the Templars in Jerusalem are reunited. Those symbols are now nothing more than memories.

I laugh at all these little ants, running around trying to protect their little world, when an enormous new world is emerging. The Pope conquered King Manuel to his side, ending a line of 13 independent Portuguese kings who continuously protected the Templar mission. The Pope won the battle, but he lost the war!

I shall die in piece. I know I committed many hideous crimes, which I regret. And many more continue being committed in the New World in the name of a savage, tyrannical God. Oh, not God, no... the hypocrite Popes and Kings are the ones committing the atrocities, shielding behind the word of God to appease their conscious. I've looked straight into the abyss of men's soul, and what I saw is nasty. 'Whoever fights monsters should see to it that in the process he does not become a monster. And if you gaze long enough into an abyss, the abyss will gaze back into you'.

Columbus died on 20 May 1506, in Valladolid. Near Tordesillas, the city where the treaty to which he gave a large part of his life was signed. Far away from the sea.

King Dom Manuel I changed dramatically the policy of opposition to Spain, having married two daughters of Isabel and Fernando.

He also conducted extensive renovations at the former headquarters of the Templars, the Castel and Convent of Tomar, including total repainting of the frescoes on the main chamber of the Convent.

In December 1496, he yielded to the pressure of the Catholic Kings and ordered the expulsion of the Jews and Moors, one month after marrying the Spanish princess. In 1515 he requested the Pope the installation of the Inquisition in Portugal, which would happen in 1536. In 1515, the Order of Cluny, the French sister order of the Templars, was extinct in Portugal.

The stone statue of a knight on horseback found by the first settlers when they arrived in Corvo Island, in the Azores, is contested. Some historians dismiss it as a myth, derived from a natural formation on the rocks that mildly resembles a knight on horseback. However, Damião de Góis, a credible historian of the sixteenth century, describes in detail the statue: a knight on an unsaddled horse, pointing westwards with the index finger of his outstretched arm and strange carved letters at the base. He also reports that in 1500, Pero da Fonseca, captain of the islands of Flores and Corvo, ordered an imprint of the inscription to be made. However, there are no references to the statue afterwards. Was it destroyed during the Kingdom of Dom Manuel I? By chance or on purpose?

VALLADOLID, MAY 1509

(Fernando)

F ather died in Valladolid, far away from the sea. The demanding and merciless sea that turned him blind and rheumatic during the last years of his life.

He was a strong, proud man, torn between conflicting allegiances, identities and ends. Father's soul was an immensity, a vastness of wild ocean whose different shores you can never see all at the same time. He contained multitudes and should never be judged by only a part of his life. In the end, the Admiral became consumed by his own internal wars, hallucinating in the madness of his life, of all the lies and atrocities committed in name of his great mission. I hope Father now finally finds relief to his tortured, obstinate soul.

I suspect he sacrificed so much, leaving behind a proud and noble life in Portugal to accept a life of lies and deception. The truth is, he never overcame the memory of his first and only wife, Filipa. She was perhaps the last remaining link to a previous life. Frei Antonio Marchena once told me that when Father received news of Filipa's death, barely one year after leaving Portugal, he became severely ill, demented, in a state of spiritual confusion as if an anchor had broken loose. He shut himself away from the world, delirious, living an austere and eremitical existence in a solitary cell of the monastery of las Cuevas for months.

I guess a man must have some solid anchors in his life, at the risk of just floating around, pushed to wherever the wind is blowing, but without an aim.

After Filipa's death, Father asked his friends in Portugal to send him the silver bullet Filipa carried on her neck, the silver bullet Father had given her as his life, to take or to kill. I've seen him with the silver bullet. He always carried it around his neck, until giving it to Diego Méndez in Jamaica. I know that in the darkest moments of his hallucinations, he inserted it in his pistol, rolled the chamber and fired against his head. I saw him doing it in moments of delirium, during the endless stormy nights of the fourth expedition, as I pretended to sleep in the floor of his cabin. Diego Méndez returned a lead bullet to Father, after returning from his secret detour north in 1504.

Three years after Father's death, king Fernando decided to move the Admiral's remains from Valladolid, where he was buried, to the Monastery of las Cuevas, in Cartuja, near Seville. Now that Father was no longer a threat, it seemed the Spanish wanted to make him into a national hero. Maybe to hide the shameful guilt of being deceived by Colon's fake Indies. They have, in fact, over the course of the past decades since Father died, turned him into a national hero. I guess the best way of hushing someone is to put him in a very high pedestal, where no-one can hear him.

I insisted Father should be buried with the lead bullet around his neck. I know Filipa was one of the few solid anchors in his life. It is also a token of how he gambled his life every day, indifferent to destiny, rolling the dice at every turn, ready to fire the bullet into his head.

The epitaph chosen by Colon for his tomb is ignoble:

"In te, Domine, speravi, non confundar in aeternum". In you, Lord, I trust: I will not be confounded forever. Which can have two opposing interpretations: that Colon recognizes he was confused (wrong) in life about the correct location of the Indies; or that the others were confused (deceived, fooled) about Colon's true identity.

Father was never confused, though. Only when it suited his purposes, to support the farce he was playing for the Spanish monarchs.

Father's epitaph is quite appropriate, indeed: "In you, Lord, I trust, I will not be confounded forever."

I resent but do not mind terribly that he never married my mother, Beatriz Enriquez de Arana, thus making me a bastard. He always treated my mother quite decently and ensured in his will an annuity to make her comfortable. In truth, he did marry Beatriz – she took his name. Beatriz Enriquez, wife of Segismundo Henriques, known as Alemão by his friends and as Christopher Colon by the world.

Columbus was buried in a crypt of a Franciscan monastery in Valladolid, in 1506. Three years later, in 1509, his remains were moved to the Monastery of Santa Maria de las Cuevas, in the river island of La Cartuja, near Seville. His true-born son, Diego, was also buried in las Cuevas monastery in 1526. Ten years later, the third Admiral of the Indies, Luis Colon, transferred the remains of Christopher and Diego Colon, together with those of his brother Bartholomew, to the Cathedral of Santa Maria Menor in Santo Domingo, on nowadays Dominican Republic. Luis himself was buried in the same crypt at the Santo Domingo Cathedral, in 1572.

A century later, in 1697, Spain ceded the eastern part of the Hispaniola to France, which is now Haiti. Later, the rest of the island was also transferred to France. To avoid the remains of the Colon family staying in French territory, the remains were again moved in 1675 to the Havana Cathedral, in Cuba.

However, in 1877, a priest uncovered a lead coffer with bones in the Santo Domingo Cathedral, with an inscription identifying the remains as those of the "First discoverer of America, the Admiral". Inside the coffer was also a lead bullet. Further excavations in the Santo Domingo Cathedral uncovered another sign in the place of that lead coffer, reading, "Last remains of the first Admiral, Sir Christopher Columbus, discoverer." The bishop of Santo Domingo at the time, monsignor Rocco Cocchia, an Italian, offered multiple fragments of the bones and dust from the coffer, scattering the supposed Colon's remains to multiple institutions: Pope Leon XIII, the university of Pavia, the city of Genoa... and the city of Boston!

It is possible that when transferring the remains in 1675 to Cuba, only the top casket was moved, with the remains of the Admiral's son, Diego, whereas those of the Admiral remained in Santo Domingo.

No-one ever understood the meaning of the lead bullet.

After the Spanish-American war in 1898, Spain transported the Cuban remains, continuing to claim they were those of Christopher Colon, to the Seville Cathedral.

Today, both Dominican Republic and Spain continue to claim the remains of Columbus.

Spain considers the true remains of Christopher Columbus lie in the imposing Seville Cathedral, one of the largest Cathedrals in the western world, in a raised bronze sarcophagus on the shoulders of four heralds representing the kingdoms of Spain: Castella, Leão, Aragão and Navarra.

Dominicans claim the Admiral and his grandson Luis are in Santo Domingo, whereas Seville holds his son Diego. In 1992, on the fifth century celebrations of the Admiral's first voyage, *the Dominican tomb was transferred from Santo Domingo Cathedral to the Faro a Colón (literally, Lighthouse to Columbus), a gigantic cross-shaped modern building that houses a museum and mausoleum. There are 157 beams of light that emanate towards the sky from the Columbus Lighthouse and a rotating beam, which can be seen from space.*

When Professor José Antonio Lorente opened Christopher Columbus mausoleum in the Seville Cathedral in 2003, to conduct DNA tests, he found only 200 grams of bone. Most are the size of chickpeas. The largest fragment is the size of a golf ball. This corresponds to only 15% of a human skeleton. So, where are the remaining 85%? It is possible they were lost with all the transfers of his remains, or that Columbus remains are split between two or more resting places.

As in life, so after his death the Admiral continues to elude historians and confuse the world. Even after death, Christopher Colon's remains are clouded in mystery. He remains a voyager, an adventurer who refuses to settle down in a single final resting place.

The lead bullet found on the Santo Domingo casket baffles everyone, another Columbus unsolved mystery.

LISBON, MAY 2019

Savanah loved the early Saturday morning runs. The city was desert and she could enjoy it just for herself, running past the tiny alleys of cobblestones of the old town, the wide avenues drawn by ruler and square by Marquês de Pombal after the 1755 earthquake, and the palatial houses in the noble areas of the city. But mostly, she loved the light, the luminous blue sky reflected by the Tagus river.

Not today though. The weather was changing. You could feel the electrical tension in the air, a strangely warm wind starting to blow from the south. There was a heavy silence, even the usual barking sounds of the dogs had vanished, as if the city was bracing in anticipation for the storm. News reports were announcing heavy rain and winds above 100 km/h, with 10 meter waves in the Atlantic coast. An unusual spring storm. It was expected to hit Lisbon early afternoon and to continue until Sunday morning.

She was doing her usual route, down her apartment in Lapa to the river and then right along the shore, passing under the imposing red iron 25 de Abril bridge and onwards to Belém. The Padrão de Belém, the monument to the discoveries, was already visible ahead, jotting into the sea as if in defiance of the oncoming storm.

Savanah noticed the hundreds of Seagulls on the monument and the pavement around it, landed in a closed group and all facing south. Nature is amazing, it seems to have a sixth sense our human hears and eyes are unprepared to grasp. The skies were still clear and the wind blowing just slightly, but the seagulls seemed to anticipate the southern storm. Thousands of them, in a closed group, facing an enemy that was not yet there.

Then it hit her. "Gosh... It's not what is there, but what is missing!"

Although the southern wind was missing, you could guess it by the seagulls. The relevance of the seagulls was not because of what was there, but because of what was not – the upcoming wind.

Savanah picked her mobile and called an Uber. That would save her the 30 minutes run back. She showered quickly and headed straight to university. Thank God it was Saturday, which avoided suspicious looks as she ransacked the history department library. She looked, trying to recall in which of the dozens books she had been reading, were those images.

Meanwhile, the storm had abated mercilessly over the city, the floodgates of hell sweeping the hilly streets of Lisbon and causing floods in downtown areas. Savanah could hear the rain pounding the windows and the wind growling through the air vents of the old building, but she kept going.

And finally she found them. One book where Raven had circled part of an image in a pencil, with a short note on her methodical calligraphy "The missing X!". And another book with a second image with a circle marking a spot, with a similar short note in the same careful small letters.

"The X marks the spot!", she whispered to herself, half smiling as she remembered the conversation with Sergio and Duma. The images were too dark, the pictures from her iPhone camera got blurred and foggy. So she decided to risk it... with a "hell, fuck it", she switched on the department's photocopy machine, swiped her card and took a copy of each of the two pages.

After putting the books and documents back in their place as best as she could, and sure she had misplaced something, she ran down the stairs. It was still pouring and she decided against facing the storm to walk to the metro, so she booked an Uber. She was desperate to call Sergio and Duma but didn't dare making the call from the car with the driver listening, so she texted both of them.

"Can we meet tonight?"

Sergio answered shortly after: "A date invitation from a beautiful woman in a stormy winter night?"

She didn't particularly fancy these easy flirts, but they were mainly inconsequential and pleasant. In any case, she was in a good mood. So she texted back, with a grin on her face:

"I've got a secret ✖ to show you. Tonight, the △ will finally get the ▽".

Sergio's response took a bit longer than expected. He was probably debating what to answer, maybe writing and deleting sentences back and forth. Finally, it came back, a non-committal response trying to test the grounds: "Ok, sure... Where do we meet?". They always met at Duma's, so this was really just testing his chances...

Duma had tried to call, but she had cancelled it waiting to get home. Closing the door behind her, hair and overcoat soaked from the brief run from the cab to the building door, she called Duma back.

"Dear, I would be happy to meet tonight, but are you sure you want to leave home in this weather? What's going on?"

Sergio would pick her up in 30 minutes, avoiding another Uber ride. As she sat on the sofa and closed her eyes, she realized the morning headache was gone, but also how tired and starving she was. Reluctantly, she picked up the phone and texted Duma saying she would order some pizzas delivered to her apartment.

In the car, Sergio pushed her to reveal the big discovery, but Savanah insisted on telling both him and Duma at the same time.

The delicious smell of freshly baked woodstove pizzas filled the place when they arrived. Although excited and desperate to tell them, Savanah tucked into two slices before she could settle down on the table.

"So, are you going to reveal the mystery or we will just seat here watching you eat?", asked Duma.

"Sorry, I was starving. Skipped lunch... I was all day at the university looking for something I had seen but not related."

Savanah took the two copied pages from her shoulder bag and unfolded them on top of the table. Neither of them seemed to grasp the meaning of what was in front of them. Some silent instants passed until Duma draw a breath and realized what it was.

"Holy heavens! They were in America before Columbus. His mission was to find them. Just as Raven wrote in her notebook!!"

Sergio was still at odds, so Savanah provided him with

the little bit of background information he needed to connect the dots.

"The Columbus signature you know, of course. The little detail we never paid attention to, though, is that the Xs in his signature have the little wiggle on the top right arm, what Duma called quite appropriately a ´hooked X ´. In light of our discussion about the Templar cross being the overlap of 4 runes but missing the hook, this 'detail' becomes relevant. The important thing is not what is there, on the Templar cross, but what is missing... the hook. That's what Raven wrote in her notebook: The X in the Templar Cross is incomplete."

"Now," continued Savanah, "the other image is really what had stuck on the back of my mind until it hit me this morning. This is the Kensington Rune Stone, a 92 kg slab of rock covered in runes similar to the Futhark runes we discussed, the Viking runes of the 9th century. The Kensington stone was discovered in 1898 in... guess what... in Minnesota. The rock has been internally dated to the year 1362, which is..."

"...130 years before Columbus reached America, and right around the time Henry Sinclair supposedly sailed there!", exclaimed Sergio, now seeing the connection. Suddenly he reached out and smacked a kiss on Savanah's cheek, which instantly turned red. "You are a genius, Savanah. This is amazing!" said Sergio retrieving his composure.

It had been a happy kiss, in the spur of the moment. Yet, for her American notion of personal space, it was still a bit too much. Not an air kiss, barely touching skin, but a full smooch, lips to her skin, with a prolonged "schhhhwack" noise.

As if to break the momentary embarrassment that risked descending on the room, Duma said "Raven was indeed asking me a lot of information about this Kensington

Rune Stone. And also Newport Tower. Once, when I asked her why the hell she wanted that for a PhD on Columbus, she confided these were geomarkers of American Templars territory, signalization points to orient the southern line of the European Templars... Now the pieces of the puzzle fit in! If a pre-Columbus Templar settling in America was using the same Hooked X symbol as Columbus used on his signature, maybe these were two sides of the Templars who had separated to protect a secret and were now trying to reconnect in the New World. Does this make sense?"

"That must be it," said Savanah, "This hooked X means something... like a secret sign to recognize each other, unifying in the New World what had been separated in Europe."

Savanah left with Sergio, late evening. Rain was still fustigating Lisbon as they climbed into Sergio's Mini Cooper. They were both silent during the drive to Savanah's apartment, each ruminating their own thoughts. Probably the reminiscence of that kiss still too present on their minds to risk any type of conversation. Sergio parked in front of Savanah's building and she exited briskly, shouting through the noise of the rain on the pavement.

"Thanks for the lift. I guess we made some good progress tonight."

To her surprise, she sat at the sofa mildly thinking about that kiss in a sedated state of reverie. Surely nothing more than a friendly effusive gesture.

At that moment, she got startled at the sudden ring of her mobile. It was Hugh, as if admonishing her for her thoughts.

As it turned out, Hugh was calling to tell her he was thinking of taking a week off and meet her for a tour of Europe, to compensate for the cancelation at Easter. "You know, the key points, Madrid, Paris, Rome. It would be nice, like a second honeymoon. Maybe we can get a baby going. What do you say?"

It sounded like Hugh was making this to be a grand gesture on his part, taking a week off to join her. Indeed, it was, she knew how hard he was pushing now they were a single income couple. But honestly, though Savanah, one week for a full tour of Europe? That's so touristy… ticking boxes and getting Instagram photos. You would need at least a week in each of those places. But Savanah found herself actually smiling and looking forward to a week off with Hugh.

TOMAR, JULY 2006

Raven had just walked out of the Tomar Convent of Christ in a hurry, driving away in her red Fiat Punto. She was furious. Outraged.

The man in long black robes, with whom Raven had been talking in the Convent's library, looked out the window, trailing the red Fiat Punto. He then turned back, looking expectantly at the cardinal, the archbishop and the vicar in his private room.

Early that morning, immediately after reading the American's email, he had called the Secretary of the Congregation for the Doctrine of the Faith. He had kept the Secretary well aware of the American's progress over the previous months, but matters had now escalated and a decision had to be made. The three prelates had moved quickly. The Vatican private jet landed in Lisbon at 12.21pm CET, which was 11.21am in Lisbon, and they arrived in Tomar before 1pm.

"Father Paulo", the Prefect addressed him in a slow, grave voice. "We have considered the matter. The letter you show us is clear about the American's suspicions and intentions."

The younger Undersecretary, Vicar Jerome, continued. "Father, as you know, we have all been expecting the American could discover something and lead us to the forbidden Book. But she is still looking in Tomar, where we know it is not. Allowing this matter to continue can be dangerous. It must end."

"Yes, Excellency. The weed of Heresy cannot be allowed to firm its roots. Does the Holy Father know?"

"That is not of your concern.", answered Vicar Jerome. "Father, I don't need to remind you this matter is subject to the Pontifical Secrecy rules of the *Secreta Continere*." [95]

Father Paulo reached the phone at his desk and dialled a number from memory.

"Professor, good of you to pick up. She knows. She wants to look into the archives in search of the treasure."

"But Father, she will not find it there. For centuries the Convent´s archive has been searched. It is not there."

"Sure, but then she will look somewhere else. What if she finds it and exposes it to the world? Or even if she does not find anything concrete, if she publishes what she has found or starts talking about it, it would be a severe blow to us. We are at our weakest point, the last thing we need is another conspiracy theory undermining the faith. We cannot risk it, Professor. Take care of it."

"Yes, Father. It shall be done."

SEVILLE, 1542

(Fernando)

"Thousands will die, thousands of thousands will die, thousands of thousands of men and women will die, the earth will be filled with screams of pain, howls of agony, the smoke of the burned will cover the sun, their fat will sizzle over the embers, the smell will agonize, and all this will be my fault. Not your fault, because of you. Father, keep this cup from me. That you drink it is a condition of my power and your glory. I do not want this glory. But I want that power."
JOSÉ SARAMAGO, THE GOSPEL ACCORDING TO JESUS CHRIST

Father died in 1506, discredited by the Spanish and abandoned by the Portuguese. He died bitter and delusional, torn apart by the personal and moral sacrifices he had to make to complete his mission, and forced to bear the weight of such hard choices alone and in secret. His true monsters were never those of the physical world: he could sail storms and overcome archaic fears like few others. What tormented his mind were the spiritual monsters of the atrocities he committed or allowed. Very few knew him well. Outwardly he remained confident and stoic until the end, but I know his inner soul agonized with the doubt of whether the great ends justified the means, fearing how God would judge him in the end. His proud bearing asserted his noble origins, a son of kings. But I suspect his arrogance and confidence were just a shield of self-preservation.

Around the same time of Father's fourth expedition, Amerigo Vespucci participated in expeditions to the New World, on behalf of Spain in 1499 and then for Portugal in 1501–1502. Vespucci was my Father's agent and in the pay of the Kings of Portugal, although this must all be treated in much secrecy [96]. Anything the Portuguese say or write is interpreted with much caution by the Spanish, so Father needed foreigners like Vespucci to praise the wonders of the new western continent, to convince the Spanish monarchs that even if the western lands he discovered are not the true India, they are the best and richest of all Indias. Father himself wrote to the Spanish monarchs in a letter dated 7 July 1503, saying "Your Highnesses are in the best of the Indies, Calicut [97] does not matter."

Vespucci produced two amazing books with drawings and colorful descriptions of those exotic lands, which later became popular in Europe and fired the imagination of nobles, adventurers and intellectuals. This all makes the new continent worth defending by the Spanish, at least out of spite and pride not to acknowledge they were deceived by Colon. With this mission, and not bound by the policy of secrecy imposed on the Portuguese sailors, Amerigo could brag about his real or imaginary discoveries. One year after my Father's death, in 1507, Martin Wadseemuller published a map depicting Brazil and parts of the New World, naming it with the Latinized version of Amerigo Vespucci name: America.

Today, more than thirty years later, the name has stuck.

The world is creating a fable around Father. He died dishonored and abandoned by the king, but now he is no longer a threat, the Spanish stir to make him his great hero! God, all this cynical political maneuvering sickens me. I take refuge in my books, for I can't stand all the manipulation and self-interest circulating around Father's memory. Three years after Colon's death, the Spanish king decided to move his remains from Valladolid to las Cuevas Monastery in Seville, with great pomp, as befits a national hero! The chroniclers are creating another farce to hide the farce created by Father!

They say that the Admiral, for all his mistakes and atrocities, broke through the dark ages of mysticism and ignorance. Before him, all men though the world was flat and ships only dared to sail within sight of land. The intrepid, insane adventurer Colon was the first to risk his life, with supreme abnegation, facing perils and myths, to sail across the open sea, proving the world does not end in an abyss of boiling water. Oh, what a fine tale!

Father must be laughing from his grave. His own deceit and lies made him an outcast during his life. The lies of those he so masterfully deceived are turning him into a hero after his death! The ways of the world are indeed strange.

It does not matter. The further away everyone's attention is from my Father and his books, the better.

The secret that consumed Father's life will go to the grave with me. I have spent my life defending his legacy, protecting our family's wealth from charlatans and crooks, studying his journals and trying to understand, reaching deeper beyond the veil of mystery that my Father left behind. What little he told me, I am sure is just a small part of the entire truth. I may never discover the complete truth, and certainly shall never reveal it. But I must understand, I must separate the clear path from the fog with which the Infante, the Portuguese King and my Father intended to hide it.

The generous income from the trade rights inherited from my father have allowed me to continue building on Father's library. This is a personal passion I share with him, collecting, reading and annotating thousands of books. But it is also a necessity, to maintain the charade: as long as the church believes the Book is hidden in my massive library, they will not look elsewhere.

My library is close to 15.000 volumes. For over three decades I travelled throughout Europe gathering books, personally noting and dating each purchase. It is an extravagant number which has attracted the attention and patronage of scholars across Europe, including Erasmus of Rotterdam. I also employ librarians to maintain a storage and sorting system and to write a summary of every book I own. This should facilitate consultation and dissemination of the knowledge and ideas contained within these walls.

It is important to make knowledge accessible outside the monasteries, so Gutenberg's invention is of tremendous importance to disseminate knowledge and ideas. The flow of ideas is the only protection against tyranny and absolutism. A large portion of my library consists of printed books using this marvelous new technology, utilitarian and efficient, instead of the old beautifully decorated manuscripts that take months to reproduce. Knowledge and ideas were hostage to the church monopoly of scribes, but Gutenberg's press shall end that stranglehold.

I hope my descendants are strong enough to preserve the library, but I fear the moment I die the Church will jump over my collection, searching for the Book. They have been looking for it for fifteen centuries, they will not give up easily. God forbid it, they might even be tempted to simply destroy the entire collection, launching all the books to the fires of the Inquisition.

The Holy Grail has many forms, and the most dangerous one is the Book. The bloodline of the Rose can be denied. But the Book is proof, not just of the bloodline, but also of the falsified truth established and endorsed by Popes and Cardinals for over fifteen centuries of denial.

Fernando Colon impressively large book collection includes Christopher Columbus diaries, logbooks of his expeditions and the books Fernando inherited from his father, with extensive

handwritten annotations from Columbus. This is a valuable source – and one of the few first hand sources – about Columbus life and ideas.

Fernando personally annotated each book of his collection, with date, place and price of the purchase, as well as a statement testimony of his motivations: "Fernando Colon, son of Cristobal Colon, the Admiral of the Indies, left this book for the use and benefit of all."

Fernando established provisions on his will to ensure the library would be maintained. The collection eventually passed to Seville Cathedral after his dead. Unfortunately, almost ¾ of this valuable collection was lost, burned on the fires of the Inquisition or victim of poor storage conditions. Less than 4.000 volumes of the original 15.000 books in Fernando Colon library survived the zealous destructive fury of the Inquisition or simple abandonment. The remaining volumes are accessible for consultation in the Biblioteca Colombina in Seville.

The Inquisition priests must have been looking for something! During the Inquisition in Europe, Portugal was the country where the highest number of books was confiscated. By 1624, the Portuguese catalog of forbidden books contained 1048 pages!

SEVILLE, 1542

(Fernando)

> *"Man is the cruelest animal."*
> FRIEDRICH NIETZSCHE

We live momentous times, a defining moment for civilization, a turning point of cultural, scientific and commercial effervescence. I have become a collector of the epic times we live in, amassing one of the largest libraries of modern times. The great discoverers – my Father, Cabral, Gama – played a pivotal role in the events that are reshaping civilization, by opening wide ajar the gates that the church had kept shut for centuries and letting a flood of novelties rush in: new peoples, new languages, new flavors, new cultures. All this quickly disseminated by Gutenberg's marvelous invention.

How extraordinary, this mind turning succession of great men: Father was born in 1451. Leonardo da Vinci in 1452. Amerigo Vespucci 1454. Erasmus 1466. Gutenberg 1468. Maquiavel 1469. Copérnico 1473. Miguel Angelo 1475. Thomas More, 1478. Magellan 1480. Luther 1483. Human voice, silenced for centuries, suddenly cries loud again, despite the ruthless attempt by the Inquisition to stem the barrage of change. Father has conquered his rightful place amongst these great men of freedom and science. His true secret mission is known only to this brotherhood that carries the Templar's secrets, known by many names: The Priory of Sion, the Templars, the Illuminati, the Freemasons...

Christopher Columbus was the last Templar knight, completing the mission of reuniting the Wind Rose with the Rose Line. The secret is now safe in the New World, this new Promised Land of America, away from the shackles of Rome. A land of freedom and reason where heretics, Moors, Jews can take refuge, escaping the fires of Inquisition.

The Book of Prophecies my Father wrote in his final years is a beacon guiding future generations into that Promised Land to the west. I believe this Book of Prophecies is not intended for ourselves, but for the future inhabitants of that New Jerusalem being constructed in the new continent. Almost a sermon, preaching the future peoples of that new Arcadia their responsibilities to respect the land of freedom and reason.

The Book of Prophecies claims the discovery of the Western Indies was prophesized in the biblical texts. father quotes mainly from prophet Isaiah and his predictions of the "discovery of new lands and new skies for the exultation of Jerusalem". In the introductory letter, addressed to the Spanish monarchs, Father states that "the execution of the journey to the Indies... was simply the fulfillment of what Isaiah had prophesied". I believe he was referring to Isaiah 42:1–4: "Behold my servant: I will uphold him. My elect: my soul lighteth in him. I have given my spirit upon him... and the islands shall wait for his law".

Father also quotes extensively St John the Evangelist: "a new sky, new stars and planets in the firmament of the other hemisphere; a new land of the West, a new Jerusalem descending from heaven." This is a true prophecy of the discovery of America. With Jerusalem and the Holy Land lost, the Templars looked west, to Avalon, the new Atlantis, the islands announced by Isaiah and St John awaiting the elected people in a new Promised Land to the west.

The search of a western paradise, a new Arcadia, pervades Christian mythology: Saint Augustine wrote "God's City" after the fall of Rome in 410. In the 6th century Saint Brendan ventured into the Atlantic in search of the "Isle of the Blessed". Even closer to my Father's heart, Saint Bernard of Clairvaux, founder of the Templars, predicted in his sermon "De Natividad": "Three wise kings will come, not from the East but from the West, to spread the faith." The prophecy has been realized: King João II of Portugal, Queen Isabella, and Father, himself a secret king who must remain hidden to the world. The three kings found this new Arcadia, the new Promised Land to the west.

And in 1518, Francis Bacon wrote "Utopia". The message is spreading amongst the Illuminati, emboldened by the discovery of a new continent where their ideas can take hold.[98]

I know Father's life is not consensual. He was a bully, a large bulk of raw energy able to command respect with his imposing presence. He inspired and threatened in equal measure with the almost divine aura projected by his restless, probing blue-grey eyes. When I joined Father in his last expedition I was still a very young man, not yet 14 years old. Father was by then an old man, half-blind, suffering sore rheumatic arthritis and with hallucinating fits of malarial fever. But I can still hear in my mind the way he gave orders in the midst of the chaos of a tropical storm or commanded his officials in a contained but fiercely self-confident voice that accepted no disagreement. Those who conspired against him did so always on his back, at least until his downfall, because it was impossible to any ordinary man to oppose him face to face. Those penetrating eyes and ethereal white hair had a super-natural quality that imposed itself over the trivialities of everyday life – as if he was above the grinding quotidian existence. This was probably much cause of spite and resentment from others.

But he was the harshest judge of his own life. The hallucinations, the obsessive maniac ramblings that consumed his last years are just a small crack on the thick fortress he constructed around himself, a tiny crack through which we can barely grasp the complexities, conflicting demands, opposing allegiances he had to deal with. As I become older, I myself come to realize that the timeline of life is inverted: we live life forwards, but judge it backwards.

Life is, in general, monotonous and ordinary. Father's great conquests appear to most as moments of brilliant inspiration and courage, that hide his mistakes and erratic life. But what they fail to understand is that greatness is made of flitting moments of glory over long years of hard, invisible work.

I must protect his legacy. Ever since my young years, upon returning from Jamaica, I feel a sense of ambivalence from the Spanish nobles towards my family. There have always been his faithful and unconditional supporters. But I also found a lot of contempt. Especially after Queen Isabella died, the support for my father in Spain drained away, forcing him into a secluded retirement in semi house arrest.

I am now older and hopefully wiser. There are always two sides to the same story. The Spanish contempt and hostility towards my father is because they feel he tricked them into the fairy tale of the western indies, or because he truly mismanaged the colonies and abused his power? Colon repeatedly accuses the Spanish of only caring for gold and slaves, and when the Western Indies failed to provide the desired riches, the crews and settlers raised in mutiny. Of the 17 ships that sailed to the Western Indies between 1492 and 1500, 12 returned shortly after, disillusioned and miserable.

There are many contradictions and unsolved mysteries in my Father's life. His actions and letters may look, to those who don't know him or wish his dismissal, the wild divagations of a fantasist, a lunatic unable to find his way on the sea or manage the crews.

True enough...My father diaries of his journeys, the accounts from his brother Bartholomew Colon and the chronicles of Frei Bartolomé de las Casas all confirm Colon was a tyrannical and obsessive Admiral of the Ocean Sea and Governor of the Indies. His brother, the Adelantado [99], was probably even more terrible. Some call Colon and his brother barbaric.

The intentions of the discoveries are clear. Under a veil of religious missionary zeal and peaceful trade, the men that sail in the Caravelas are "Conquistadores", intent on subjugating the natives and take as much riches as possible. They arrive to those distant shores and offer pitiful gifts, trinkets of glass and brass. But these gifts are announced with aplomb – banners with Christian crosses, guns and cannon shots.

Dozens of Spanish men were summarily sentenced to prison, torture or death by Colon. Others died due to the miserable living conditions, hunger and diseases. I guess the mutinies amongst the crew reflect the cruelty and atrocities committed by Colon and his brothers, the obsessive control they imposed in every aspect of life in the Western Indies.

Father was also accused of poor management of the colonies. When Bobadilla arrived in Santo Domingo on 23 August 1500, he faced a horror scene: a line of hanged men rotting under the sun. Diego Colon had hanged 7 men and 5 were waiting in line. Christopher was in the Fortress, its prisons full of Spaniards. And Bartholomew Colon was in Xaragua chasing Roldan and his rebels, with 16 men starving inside a water well. It is not surprising Bobadilla's report about Colon was so damaging, but he goes to great lengths to demonize my Father as the source of all evil in those lands. Bobadilla accused Father of conspiring to take the islands for himself, mobilizing local tribesmen to rebel against the

Spanish settlers. Bobadilla lists Colon's atrocities against the Spanish: jailing, executing, starving or cutting noses and hears in arbitrary and tyrannical decisions.

I cannot believe all this. History is written by the victors, and most of Father's life is being re-written by the Spanish, under the silence of the Portuguese. Father is being discredited. The Spanish "hidalgos", ashamed of being tricked and frustrated for not finding gold and riches, are taking their revenge. They are re-writing history, portraying Father as a lunatic, incompetent and clumsy sailor who navigated by chance, a cruel and despot Governor.

Oh... I am sure that even from his deathbed, Father is laughing at this charade and the extremes of love and hate his name invokes! I suppose Father may have been consciously causing havoc and chaos in the Western Indies during his 1492-1500 rule, keeping the Spanish up to the neck in the West Indies disaster. Father was procrastinating, playing a game of cat and mouse with the Spanish monarchs.

The real cause behind much of the complains and accusations against my Father is simply hypocrite jealousy. The Spanish never accepted him for being a foreigner. Oh, and shame, they are ashamed that Father tricked them, with promises of exotic and rich lands, but taking them only to a land of naked natives and misery.

I have myself been victim of this resentment, insulted and mocked as the "son of the Admiral of the mosquitoes"!

Until his arrest in 1500, Colon attempted to establish alliances with the leaders of local tribes, while preventing active colonization of the islands by Spanish settlers. What was his plan? Was Father planning to establish himself as Lord of those islands, going to war to expel the Spanish?

His tremendous forgery of the Western Indies required an iron fist on the crew so that no one could contradict him. He left prisoners behind in Hispaniola, he killed, forced everyone in the ships to sign vows of secrecy, even kept two separate diaries – so that his account could not be contradicted!

It is not my job to make excuses for my Father's actions. History will judge him. He was in equal measure brilliant and audacious as merciless, paranoid and volatile.

The crews and the Spanish nobles spite and loathe Colon as much for his lies and illusions of a false India as for his tyrannical governance. If left unchecked, the crew would have ransacked, raped and killed the native populations to obtain the gold and slaves they considered their right.

Since Ovando took control as Governor of the Indies, the natives have been slaughtered, tortured and enslaved mercilessly. The Indians are the true martyrs of the brutal, mindless colonization. And the African slaves taken in throes to cultivate the new lands.

Friar Bartolomé de las Casas has just written a most daunting and devastating chronicle of the first decades of the Spanish colonization if the Americas. It is titled 'A brief account of the destruction of the Western Indies' [100]. He is a credible and impartial source, as he has witnessed all of this. He sailed with Father during the second and fourth expeditions and a few years later has been ordained the first priest of the Americas, travelling and preaching through the new lands. We have exchanged extensive correspondence. He is adamant that "the despotic and diabolical behavior of the Christians has, over the past four decades, led to the unjust and unwarranted deaths of more than twelve million souls".

The Friar is devastated by the cruelty of the Conquistadores in the Americas. Ovando in the Caribbean islands and then Cortez in the continent. It is a massacre. In Hispaniola and the other islands, the local Taínos are being decimated by the barbaric killings, hunger and diseases. When Colon arrived to Hispaniola in 1492, there probably were, on las Casas estimate, more than 7 million natives. In the 1514 census, only 22.000 remained. Las Casas now tells me less than 200 remain and will soon be extinct.

Las Casas sent a copy to me of his chronicle. It is, in all manners, a lucid and outraged account of the destruction of paradise. He writes "We know for certain that our fellow countrymen have, through their cruelty and wickedness, depopulated and laid waste to an area that once had more than ten kingdoms, each of them larger than the Iberian Peninsula."

I am ashamed of what has been unleashed by the thirst of glory and gold, killing and destroying just because we have the power to do so. And most ignominious of all, the sheer malevolence is done under cover of the holy church, dressed up as 'Christianization of the savages'. I know the victors collect the spoils of war, it has always been so... but there should be a minimum of decency and humanity.

The Conquistadores massacre at will. We wield the flag of God and thump our chests in missionary zeal, while amassing fortunes from slavery and robbery, slaughtering children and elders, running through mother and her baby with a single thrust of our sword. Las Casas book is a sad rosary of the perversion of the human soul! A carnage is taken place in the Americas. Practices most nobles would repudiate as barbaric in Europe go unpunished in the Americas just because they are far from our hypocrite eyes. Las Casas describes as the natives are "tied to a griddle of pitchforks driven into the ground and then grilled over a slow fire, with the result that they howl in agony and despair as they die a lingering death." God, forgive our collective sins! 'In individuals, insanity is rare; but in groups, parties, nations and epochs, it is the rule'.

But then, why should I be surprised. Isn't the Inquisitorial Court doing exactly the same in the plazas around this country??...

Meanwhile, the lack of labor caused by this mass extermination of the natives is being compensated by the massive introduction of African slaves, who are said to work better than the American natives.

It is a shameful disaster! How can the Church of Rome or any honest man believe this is doing God's work? What is at play is not Christianization of the natives, it is indiscriminate extinction and slavery.

The maritime expansion has become the new Crusade, an escape valve for all the greed and malevolence men are capable of. An epic of navigation, trade, technology and science, political power games, espionage, reckless courage, hardship, disease, greed, fear and extreme violence.

I am disgusted and powerless. I just hope we may all one day be forgiven for these immense sins. I maintain my Father's secret, hoping it may one day justify all the pain and confusion it caused.

Friar Bartolomé de las Casas was a Dominican friar who travelled with Columbus during the second expedition and then with Bobadilla in 1500. He is considered a defender of the native Indians, denouncing the cruelty and atrocities committed in the Caribbean and South America. He preached against the system of "encomiendas" that enslaved the natives. He travelled extensively through Central and South America, denouncing the abuses and preaching his doctrine, but was chased and persecuted by colonizers in several places. He became the bishop of Chiapas, in Mexico, in 1543, but was forced to run away by mutinous settlers due to his doctrine that before starting a confession, the penitent had to release all his slaves. He wrote "Paradise lost: the bloody history of the conquest of the Spanish America", exposing the

cruelty of the "conquistadores".

LISBON, MAY 2019

Savanah continued to go through the material in the Judiciária file in her mind, trying to figure out any additional link she might have overlooked. The material amounted to just three folders of random documents, mainly photographs of the crime scene, results from the forensics lab that didn't find any fingerprints, interviews with witnesses and phone records of her mobile. Nothing to cling to. The middle-aged moustachioed police officer seemed more interested in inviting her out than revisiting a dead-end case.

Maybe Hugh was right. It was time to drop this non sense, take the one-week holiday with Hugh and return to NY. Maybe it was time to think about motherhood.

The only relevant take away from the visit to the Judiciária pointed in one direction: Jaros. "Hi Goat. Is Saint Anne with you?" Raven was addressing the Goat, so it was him approaching her that night. There was only one explanation. The Goat was the assassin. Jaros had the motive and the means and lacked an alibi. And yet, somehow, it didn't fit at all with Savanah's perception of Jaros from their talks. And she still couldn't understand how he had known she would arrive at that hour. People can be deceptive...

She sat on the small balcony of the attic room in Lapa, a fashionable Lisbon neighbourhood she had treated herself to. She could actually get used to living here. The light, the people, the great affordable restaurants and hipster coffeehouses, Lisbon was inviting. She stared downhill over the rooftops into the grey-blue Tagus on the distance.

She stared, vacantly, her mind slowly letting go of the flood of information it had absorbed during the past few months.

Then, it hit her. That email she had found in her inbox after returning to NY thirteen years ago. Raven had sent it in the afternoon before her death. It had looked just another charade at the time. She looked back into her google photos to July 2006 for the screenshot she had taken of the email.

"Go to Santiago to find ⋈ "

The mail had been sent early afternoon, 2.29pm. Probably on her way back from Tomar to Lisbon. So, what had taken Raven so long to arrive at her place only at 3.30am? What had she been doing all that time?

Savanah remembered the conversation with uncle Santiago at her parents' house on Christmas eve, about that cryptic message. The runes "K" and "S" were a message sent in distress by her sister, in the early afternoon before her murder, probably from a service station in the motorway between Tomar and Lisbon. Raven was prompting her twin sister to look for the Secret Columbus. Or Columbus Secret. She couldn't quite grasp why her mind had driven her back to that email. What subconscious association of ideas had her brain done?

She jumped up from her chair and dived for her iMac laptop. Powering it up, she went straight to Gmail and clicked "terminate session" to log out of her personal account. The new login window flashed in front of her eyes. Looking again at the photo on her mobile, she copied the email address Raven had used to send it... that was the strange detail she had missed so far. Raven had not used her usual Gmail address, but her nickname: sarah.jagiello@gmail.com. Savanah was so used to the name she hadn't even noticed! She copied it slowly to the login page on the screen. Then the password request. She typed:

":XpoFERENSSECRETUS" and pressed enter, holding her breath. The Secret Christopher Colon. Instantly, the error message appeared, "Wrong password".

She could feel this was it, though. Going back to the password line, she now wrote:

":XpoFERENSSECRETUM". Not the Secret Columbus, but Columbus' Secret. The name instead of adjective.

The screen blipped for an instant and then the message "loading mail". Oh God!!

The last email on the inbox was dated Wednesday 26 July 2006, at 2.53am… about half an hour before she was killed. What was Raven doing writing emails at the dawn of the day she was murdered? The subject line was blank, it was sent from Raven personal "official" Gmail to her own "alias" account – the same email account with her secret nickname which she had used to send Savanah the message on her way from Tomar to Lisbon that afternoon. The email contained only a word document attached. At least this explained what Raven had been doing between 2.14pm when she probably left Tomar and 2.53am. That was a 12 hours and 39 minutes' timeframe, when she had probably returned to Lisbon and been at university writing up a document, putting together her thoughts and conclusions about the research. A sad presage of the fatidic events that would unfold afterwards.

Savanah clicked to open the word attachment. What she saw dispirited her. Several pages with entire sentences of gibberish, each sentence starting with a vaguely familiar word.

Savanah could not hold herself together. "Really, sis. Another cryptic code? Gosh…"

Then there was a second email on the inbox, dated Tuesday 25th July 2006, at 5.21am… It was also sent from

Raven's personal Gmail account to her alias account. Savanah had been landing at the airport about that time. What was Raven doing writing emails at the dawn of the day before she was murdered? It had been a long day! 21 hours and 32 minutes separated the two emails on the screen.

This second email contained a sequence of messages exchanged between Raven's university email account and a certain Father Paulo. The last email on that exchange was a message from Raven sent on 25 July 2006, at 5.19am, just before she forwarded the entire conversation to her own personal email.

"Father Paulo,

I thank you again for the patience you have shown. I understand your reluctance to allow a commoner to look into the Convento's archives, but you will surely understand the scientific importance of the discovery of the item I believe might have been hidden by the Order of Christ.

You have so far dismissed my ideas as heretic phantasies, but I have recently found undeniable evidence that Infante Dom Henrique and Columbus were the last known guardians of what we might call the Holy Grail. They were under pressure to hide it from the Inquisition, which was ferociously looking for the secret the Templars had discovered in Jerusalem. I believe Columbus intended to take the secret to North America, but he never reached it. If the Inquisition did not destroy the secret, it must still be hidden somewhere, and the best place to start is at the headquarters of the Order of Christ in Tomar.

The finding of such secret can have tremendous importance for the understanding of our cultural heritage. Moreover, the finding of a relic such as the Grail ought to spark faith and revive your church. So, why do you oppose the searches?

I will travel to Tomar today to show you the latest,

irrevocable evidence that Columbus and the Order of Christ were the carriers of a significant Templar secret. I hope you will accept my request. I am willing to take this to the highest ecclesiastic hierarchy, the historical societies, even the press if need be. I will meet you in Tomar by mid-morning, again requesting you not to create further obstacles to the pursuit of the truth.

Kind regards,

Raven Jagiello"

Savanah stared at the message for a while, trying to ascertain the possible implications for the investigation. Raven could be quite a bully. She was pushing Father Paulo to open the Convent of Christ archives so that she could look for a secret or hidden Holy Grail. Poking around on church business had never been smart. It seems this time it had also been rather dangerous. Some things are supposed to be left alone, and plenty of interests are keen on making sure they are left alone.

There was also a third forwarded email of a message sent from Raven's university account to Pedro, around the same time, informing him Raven was heading to Tomar and her sister would arrive that morning from NY, staying at her place, and therefore she might not go to the university for a couple of days.

It seemed Raven had been busy forwarding evidence and information to her personal Gmail account, ahead of heading out to Tomar. Raven probably felt she was taking some risks. It was as if she wanted to keep a private copy of these messages in her own personal Gmail, outside the university, just in case… just in case what? Institutional mail accounts are bleachable, for sure, and Raven was probably a bit paranoid at the time. But not only she sent the information and copies of emails to a personal account, she had actually used her 'alias' name, which would be recognizable only by her family.

Savanah was knackered. She recognized the first word that started each gibberish sentence and could almost bet what the codification system was. But if she was right, decoding would be a lengthy process. As much as she wanted to crack the code and read the document in the 2.53am email, her eyes were aching. She undressed and moved into the bed sheets, planning for an early start in the morning. She fell into an agitated and restless sleep.

LISBON, MAY 2019

S avanah found herself awaken and staring at the ceiling shortly past 5.00am, the room barely illuminated by the night stars from the window. She had not noticed waking up. Her mind was bringing back flashes of the ´ring game´, a game she and her sister used to play with uncle Santiago during school holidays. He would set up a treasure hunt or a "who dun it" mystery for the girls to decipher. Quite often the game included some sort of coded text they had to decipher using the star embossed in uncle's gold ring as the code key. She still remembered it by heart. How could she have forgotten? The ring design formed a winged cross, a wind rose with the NE arm pulling upwards.

She showered quickly and had some cereals and coffee, before seating down again in front of the laptop, staring at the coded document in the last email.

"Ok, sis. It's just you and me. What secrets are you still hiding in this document?"

She stared at the words at the start of each gibberish sentence and smiled. This was an insiders code, only those aware of the secret key for the "ring game" could understand. The first words were wind names, used in the eight-point compass system and the mariner's wind rose: (N) Tramontana; (NE) Greco; (E) Levante; (SE) Sirocco; (S) Ostro; (SW) Libeccio; (W) Ponente; (NW) Maestro.

It looked like each sentence had a different key, which made the text unbreakable for anyone without the ring. She mentally went back to the childhood code from uncle Santiago. There were no letters on the ring, but uncle Santiago had taught them the secret code for the cypher. They were forbidden to write it down and had to visualize it mentally. You needed to spell two words on the wind rose, an inner circle and an outer circle, each letter matching an arm of the wind rose. Each word started on the hooked NE arm and then run clockwise. Savanah could still see vividly the mental picture of the code.

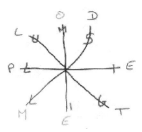

"Sigillum de Templo". Raven had of course been the one to discover the association of the code with the words inscribed in the Templar stamp. The stamp includes two circles, like two sides of a coin. On one side, the inscription reads "De Templo Cristi", a reference to the Temple of Solomon where the Templars had established their first headquarters in Jerusalem and the origin of the Order's name. The other inscription reads "Sigillum Militum", meaning something like military secret. This seal sums up the essence of the Templars: a military brotherhood to protect the secret of the Temple, a kind of Pretorian guard or protective militia of a treasure found in the Temple of Christ in Jerusalem.

The key-code for uncle Santiago ring was a merger of the right half of the inscriptions on the Templar seal: "Siggilum de Templo". The Secret of the Temple.

The coding was simple but unbreakable for anyone

not familiar with the ring-key. The inner circle of the wind rose rotates, the external circle is fixed. As you spin the wind rose, the hooked arm points into a certain cardinal point, determining the right position of the inner circle relative to the fixed outer circle and thus the letter correspondence

You could just refer a wind name or wind direction, the easterlies winds or Levante meant the hook would point straight westwards like in a wind rose. In this case, the S of the inner circle would point to the P in the outer circle. So, you get a correspondence between the 8 inner letters and the 8 outer letters. In the original text you would simply replace the corresponding letters and it would become total mumbo jumbo. You just had to pay attention as there are two Ls in the inner circle and two Es in the outer circle, so you would add some wiggle like * or ' to the second of those repeated letters.

A reference to the trade winds indicates the constant winds that blow in the equatorial region, predominantly from the southeast in the southern hemisphere and from the northeast in the northern hemisphere. A southern trade wind, or Sirocco, blows from southeast, placing the hooked arm of the wind rose S on L, creating a replacing match which would jumble any text.

"The ol a fmckeng pell." Meaning "This is a fucking mess."

Any cypher can be broken if you manage to discover some deciphered bits, allowing for a match of the 8 jumbled letters. But if every text message, or even each sentence within a message, used a different correspondence, you could be comparing messages with a S-L correspondence with others with say a S-M correspondence. The same basic principle of the Enigma coding machine used by the Germans during World War II that twisted the Allies' best mathematical brains for years.

If you know the ring key, though, it is rather easy. Each sentence indicated a wind name, and thus an alignment of the wind rose in the ring inner circle with the fixed outer circle... Excitement grew as the first few words of the first sentence started making sense.

It was a lengthy process which was stressing her out. It took her the best part of the day to decipher the entire document. She took a short break and returned to her laptop, to read finally read Raven's document.

After finished reading it, Savanah stared at the bottom of the screen. "Fuck's sake, Raven!", she let out with a sight. What were her family names doing in a chart about secret orders and Columbus? "Oh Raven, what have you got yourself into?? What have you got *myself* into!!??"

TOMAR, MAY 2019

"The church I mentioned will be established, but its founda-
tion, in order to be truly solid, will be dug in flesh, its walls
made from the cement of renunciation, tears, agony, anguish,
every conceivable form of death."
JOSÉ SARAMAGO, THE GOSPEL ACCORDING TO JESUS CHRIST

Savanah was speechless after reading Raven's email to Father Paulo. The claims and possible consequences were mind-blowing. How could Raven have been so naïve? How could she write such a letter to a priest of the Catholic church and ignore the risks? Just because we live in the 21st century does not mean some people will not resort to 15th century methods to ensure a secret will remain secret. "Gosh, Raven, you can't drop an atomic bomb and then run straight into the centre of the explosion…"

And yet, here she was… doing exactly the same, 13 years later. What was she thinking? "Yeah, sure, just go to the priest, flash him with the print of Raven's letter and wait for a murder confession. That will surely do, Savanah", she thought to herself on the slow train to Tomar. She needed to tread carefully.

At that same moment, a phone call was placed from a Lisbon public payphone. The Professor had not dialled the number in many years, and his hand trembled slightly as he pressed the dialling keys. It was 1.09pm.

"Hi. She is heading towards Tomar. I fear she knows something. It might be better to scare her off."

"Thank you, Professor. I will think about it. Well done, much appreciated."

As Savanah walked slowly down the chapter house of Convent of Christ, approaching the round charola, she tried to act as much as possible like a tourist. Thankfully, it was almost June and the monument was starting to be packed with tourists. She bought a postcard together with the entry ticket which featured the architecture of the church, as well as a small book that explained its history and main features. Most of it she already knew.

The castle and the round charola were the original Templar constructions, sturdy, perennial Romanic-style fortifications, clearly influenced by the Byzantine style of eastern churches the Templars had found during the crusades. The charola replicates the Holy Sepulchre Rotunda in Jerusalem. The cloisters and the sacristy were added by Infante Henry the Navigator during the fifteenth century, revealing early signs of the Renaissance. If Sergio's theory was correct, the sacristy corresponded to what Raven had called the Love Chapel, in reference to the tryptic painting hidden there. Could the sacristy have been built by the Infante, Grand Master of the Order of Christ, purposefully to receive the Grail? Finally, the rectangular chapter house, high choir nave and chancel with a massive window and an oculus combining Gothic and Moorish influences, had been added by king Dom Manuel I during his extensive renovation works. This was the most impressive section of the compound, with a sumptuous gothic-renaissance style fused with elements of the Age of Discoveries, establishing an architectonic style by itself: an intricate and flamboyant stone needlework, reminiscent of the Indian gold filigree work, a tracery of ropes, armillary spheres, anchors, shells, strings of seaweeds and columns carved like twisted strands of rope.

Savanah jumpstarted as a black-clad figure addressed her from behind.

"For a moment I thought I had seen a ghost."

"Oh… you scared me. Sorry, Father, I couldn't see you approaching."

"Sorry if I disturb you. But you do look familiar. You look very much like a young student who used to come here during her PhD research a few years ago."

Savanah heart missed a beat. Think quickly, she though. Better acknowledge it and just explain it away. If he caught her lying, he would suspect she was hiding other things as well.

"Oh, Father, you must have a splendid memory. Indeed, my sister studied in Lisbon many years ago, at the Age of Discoveries history department. I don't know much about it, though, I work in finance and am hopeless in history."

"Yes, I seem to recall. She died in a late night assault in a deserted street in Lisbon… I recall reading about that, so sad."

"Indeed. Family was distraught. I am in between jobs and just decided to take a few weeks off to come to Lisbon and learn a bit about the country. My sister was in love with it and I can understand why. So lovely, so picturesque. By the way, now that you have found me, you won't mind me asking why my sister came here that day? You know, according to what we have been told, she visited Tomar that day and was killed as she returned home late that evening." Go carefully, Savanah, don't push it…

"Well, ehhh. Miss…"

"…Savanah. Mrs Savanah Clifton"

"Nice meeting you. Father Paul. Yes, I do recall several conversations with your sister. If I recall correctly, she had some theories about Columbus being Portuguese and a member of the Order of Christ, thus her interest in this Convent. She was quite a nice young lady. I recall we were talking in my library when she received some message on her mobile phone, this must have been early afternoon. She got quite disturbed, as if something on the message upset her dearly, and she dashed off."

Father Paulo could be trying to fish for what Savanah knew, testing if she had any suspicions. So, she played naïve. "Oh well, father, the police investigated the case and came to nothing. It seems she was the victim of an assault, or, Christ, worst. It's terrible just to think what might have happened."

"Understandably, Mrs Clifton. I was quite shocked myself when I heard about it. I am sure she is in heaven looking after her loved ones here on Earth."

"You are most kind, Father. Thank you for your words. It seems a blessing to travel so far to come to a chance encounter with one of the last persons to talk to my sister."

Savanah left the Convent and took a taxi back to the train station, avoiding to look back. Father Paul was definitely hiding something. She made up her mind to call uncle Santiago. With his high ranking position in the US Capitol, he would ensure her quick access to the American ambassador in Lisbon. Only with the American embassy covering her back would she dare showing to the police the sequence of Raven's compromising email on the 25th and 26th of July. The statements in the email to Father Paulo were farfetched and could hardly be proven, but they were surely damaging enough for some type of secret organization to try to silence her. And Father Paul failing to acknowledge the true reason of Raven's visit that day was suspicious. Her assassination shortly after visiting Tomar could not be a coincidence."

As the taxi drove away, Father Paulo picked up the analogue phone on his desk. Until January, he had not dialled that number for 13 years. Now, it was the second time in less than six months he was forced to call Archbishop Jerome. He remembered well the young Vicar who had sat at this same office in the tragic summer of 2006. Jerome was now Archbishop and Secretary of the Congregation for the Doctrine of the Faith.

Father Paulo felt his hand shacking slightly and he willed it to steady. This was part of the mission he had accepted decades ago, to hold the Church in Tomar and watch over any developments in the departments of Atlantic History of the universities in Portugal. If the forbidden Book of the Templars was not in Tomar, it might have been hidden oversees during the Age of Discoveries. He was still assaulted by remorse sometimes, for what happened in 2006. But for the many to rest at peace, a few had to take the heavy burden on their shoulders.

The conversation was short.

Less than an hour later, the Secretary called him back. "We must handle this situation more tactfully. The Prefect and the Holy Father today are not the same as in 20016. And another… unfortunate disappearance would raise too many eyebrows. The Masonic Grand Lodge of Washington was very suspicious about the events of the summer of 2006, and voiced their concerns to the Holy Father at the time. We must move to Plan B."

After hanging up, Father Paulo called another number.

"Professor, you were right. She suspects something. Your reports that she has been digging around her sister investigations for the past few weeks are quite disturbing."

"Father, that is true. But unlike her sister, she is not a

threat. Too much inside the system, used to playing by the rules. She has not found anything relevant so far and will inevitably conclude her sister was wasting her time. I am sure she will soon go back to her comfortable investment banker life and put this to the back of her mind."

"That may be so. But the American may have left some proof. What if they have a copy of the email she sent me before coming to Tomar? That would not just bring a blanket of suspicion about her death enough to reopen the investigations, but also it would add fuel to all the conspiracy theories already flying around. We must go to Plan B."

"..."

"Professor, it must be done. You have already done a lot in the Church's service. But God requires another sacrifice from you."

TRAIN TO LISBON, MAY 2020

(Savanah)

I must be making up stories. That is outrageous, to think that a man of the church could commit such a hideous crime just to protect some old stories about a centuries-old lost treasure. I must clear my mind. I am letting myself get carried away by my sisters' over imaginative mind.

I try to read Wall Street Journal electronic edition on my iPad, but the thoughts just keep drifting away. I have to keep reading the same line two or three times as the words just don't sink in. I sip the coffee bought at a café next to the Tomar train station before boarding, the flavour mildly tainted by the Styrofoam cup. The mildly undulating green countryside passes by at high speed, cereal fields, fruit orchards and tomato plantations, in a variety of colours that merge in my mind as an indistinct blur of rural life.

What to make of Columbus? I never thought about it more than the dozen or so pages in the high school history book, enough to seat the test with an A-grade, as always. He is a controversial historical figure, not just his life but also his heritage. I now have a deeper understanding of his eight years as governor of Hispaniola, the narcissistic, self-elevating despotic Admiral who portrayed himself as an emissary of God, while at the same time treating his crew atrociously and slaughtering the Indians. Colonization of the Americas was inhumane. As was Africa's. Columbus' settlers and the Conquistadores after him raped, robbed, exploited and massacred entire civilizations, under the hypocrite cover of "Christianisation". We can't change history. Slavery happened and left a dep scar that will take long to heal. We can't change history, but we should avoid re-writing it through the eyes of the winners, ensuring a fair account of what happened. So that it shall never happen again.

Columbus is no longer just a man, but a mythical and idiosyncratic figure, a symbol of perseverance against all odds, bravery and charisma in pursuit of his new world. The European capitals have zillions of their own heroes, martyrs, kings and knights, centuries of history to symbolize national identity. But in the Americas, much like other regions brutalized by the colonial empires, the centuries-old history before colonization was simply wiped out though the sweeping annihilation of local cultures by the European metropolis. Deprived of their own symbols of national identity, the populations throughout the American continent had to create their own myths. Columbus became somewhat of a symbol of self-determination and national identity in the New World. His statues are everywhere, throughout the USA, Caribbean and Latin America. In the United States in particular, Columbus name was given to streets, public buildings, the capital cities of Ohio and South Carolina, the Columbia river, Columbia University, Columbus Avenue in New York and of course, the nation's capital, District of Columbia.

Ironically, Columbus was not even the man's name...

He is the most ubiquitous figure of the continent. Thanks to the children fairy tale of Columbus as a poor Italian wool weaver that ascends to Vice-Roy of the Western Indies, he has gained an aura of super-human courage and determination. Europe has its Hercules. America has Columbus, the heroic figure of the New World epic adventure with almost mystical powers to anticipate storms, survive hurri-canes, control mutineers, overcome near-death wreckage or live like a Robison Crusoe in Jamaica.

The Age of Discoveries opened the door to massacres, exploitation and slavery. The Spanish Conquistadores that followed Columbus were particularly brutal. Columbus bar-baric and oppressive treatment of the natives is in fact a huge magnifying glass, amplifying the brutality, greed, ex-uberance and hypocrisy of the Old World as it emerged from the Dark Ages and discovered a New World.

As the train jerks to a stop at a train station in San-tarem, I catch myself staring blankly through the window. The regional slow-train continues, almost empty.

What was it Father Paulo mentioned about a text message Raven received? A message that disturbed her and made her rush back to Lisbon... I pick up my phone to skim through the pictures I took at the Judiciária when going through the investigation material. The phone log, here it is. Yes, as I thought. The only text messages received by Raven's mobile on the 25th of July 2006 were a text from me to let her know we had just landed, and another one received early afternoon from Pedro, saying "Having a good time in Tomar? Post some pics on Facebook". Quite incon-spicuous... I go into my Facebook to check if Raven posted any photos that day. The data connection on the train is not great, but slowly, pixel by pixel, the pictures download. As I suspected, Raven didn't post anything. That is not surpris-ing at all, sister seldom posted anything on social media. She used to say, laughing, she was a "Facebook parasite", only had an account so that she could spy what others were doing.

Wait a minute... the wide expanse of Mar da Palha, the section of Tagus river that widens immensely just be-fore approaching Lisbon, is drifting away in the window, as the river continues its inevitable path towards the Atlantic, mindless of the human fortunes. Sister didn't post pics to Facebook at all! So how come Pedro texted her that message? He should have known she didn't use social media... Oh, for fuck's sake!

Staring at my mobile screen, I look at my Facebook log of that day. There they are, several of my own pictures with Hugh exploring the city, in Alfama, Terreiro do Paço, Graça, Jerónimos, Belém, and the picture on Sr. António's café under Raven's flat we had taken that morning. Just a normal day, unaware of the Machiavellian clogs at play that would lead to my sister's assassination that evening.

I look closer and enlarge the picture outside Sr. Antonio's café. It is just fucking not possible! I pick up the iPad, thumb out of WSJ app and go to Facebook, so that I can see the picture in a larger format. The time the picture takes to load seems to scorn me. There is no doubt... fuck. The selfie we had taken shows me and Hugh smiling broadly at the camera, happy as newlyweds and looking forward to our two weeks' honeymoon. Reflected on the window of Sr. Antonio coffee shop behind us, there is an image of a person at the other side of the road, looking at the scene. A casual passer-by or another client from the café. I enlarge the reflection... a man with a silver cross on a chain neckless, bald, thin crooked nose and black Linking Park t-shirt. With a goatee.

As the train comes to a halt in Santa Apolónia train station, I am still staring at the picture. I had it all wrong! I have been looking in the wrong place all this time, and the fucking asshole was standing just under my nose this whole time.

LISBON, JUNE 2019

(Savanah)

T he extraordinary thing is... he confessed. I had not expected that at all. The truth is, I was still uncertain
between the two alternatives my mind could conjure:
a conspiracy to silence my sister due to her research and accusations to Father Paulo, or the crime of passion and confounded identities of two twins by Pedro.

Professor Pedro had indeed been a bit strange since I
arrived almost six months ago. He had been helping me to
go through Raven's notes and bibliography, but it felt a bit...
artificial.

The day after my return from Tomar, I went to the Judiciária to have a word with the moustachioed investigator.
I showed him the picture with Pedro's reflection on the window of Sr. António café and mentioned Duma's references to
Pedro as Raven's lover or boyfriend. The policeman took it
from there... "well, well, well", he had said. This could be
the missing link. "If this guy was dating your sister and suddenly, that morning, saw you, whom he surely mistook for
your twin sister, schmoozing with your American new husband in the café under Raven's flat, he probably got jealous
mad. Who knows, maybe mad enough to wait to catch you,

or as it happens, your sister, alone and kill her in an attack of fury. There were no signs of struggle, which suggests she knew her assailant. We never got fingerprints, meaning the attacker wore gloves, so this was not an assault gone rogue. In the end, it seems it all comes down to an old crime of passion and mistaken identities..."

The police officer called Pedro in for questioning. What bugs me is the speed of his confession. It is as if... well, as if he was hiding something else, leading everyone to accept a version of the events and ignore other possible explanations. As if, to protect something or someone, he had come up with a quick and simple explanation, assuming the blame.

Pedro confessed he had gone to Raven's flat that morning to drop some books on her mailbox, when he saw her kissing a tall blond man at the veranda and then basking in the morning Lisbon sunshine at the café. In hindsight, it had been her twin sister. But at the moment, he though Raven had lied, telling everyone she would go to Tomar when in fact she was cheating on him with her American boyfriend. He felt she had been playing with him, her Latin lover toy, to use and discard as she pleased. He went ravenous mad and decided to wait, the steam building up as the day went past. Raven was a deceitful nasty cunt and though to teach her a lesson about Mediterranean ways! Free love my ass, she was putting the horns on him and fucking around like a bitch. He would teach her a right lesson. So he waited in the Alfama streets, bidding his time to catch her alone. That evening, when he saw her red Fiat Punto come up the steep street, he got in front of the car and confronted her. He had gone too far. He just wanted to scare her, scar her skin with a mark she couldn't discard. but he was mad with rage. She had attempted to deny everything with a cockup story about a twin sister... the nerve! The cut had been meant to just scar her skin, but it went too deep in a maddened impulse. It had not been his intention, he just wanted to scare her.

So he got taken into preventive custody, awaiting trial for first-degree murder.

It was just that simple, then. No conspiracy theories, no church assassins protecting century old secret. It was just a crime of passion.

When Raven received Pedro's text message to post pictures on Facebook, she must have found it strange. She rarely used social media, so why was Pedro mentioning that? Looking at her Facebook log, she saw the pictured I had posted and recognized Pedro reflection on the wind, grasping the implied threat, the mess that could come from mistaken identities. She had rushed back to Lisbon trying to untangle the confusion...

Is this it? The whole thing just a crime of passion and mistaken identities?

Something doesn't fit, though. Hadn't Duma said everyone knew about Raven's twin sister and that I would be arriving that morning to Lisbon with my husband? She even had a picture of the two of us at her desk.

LISBON, JUNE 2019

I t was Thursday afternoon when Savanah's mobile rung. It was a Portuguese mobile number she didn't recognize. When she answered the call, a female voice spoke in a very pronounced Portuguese accent.

"God, you are difficult to trace, Savanah!!"

"Who is this?"

"Ana. I used to play guitar with your sister. Saint Anne, from The Goat and the Saints. Jaros, from the rock club, mentioned Sarah's sister was in Lisbon looking around her death. I have been trying to contact you for weeks, but we didn't have your contact. Sarah was always quite secretive about her life outside the rock band. Myself and Jaros knew she was at the university doing some investigation about the Templars and Columbus, so we thought you might have gone to the university to retrace Sarah's steps. We looked at all the professors, research assistants, invited teachers, even the lists of Erasmus students. But nothing!"

"Yeah, I am working with the guys at the university but on an informal role, I'm not enrolled..."

"Right, right. So, there we were, unable to contact you. Until this dumb-ass turns himself in and confesses to the crime. The last few days have been a buzz at The Saints, all the old crew turning up to gossip. That's when, last night, I bumped into Carminho, you have met her right?, and she mentioned she had you phone number. So, here I am."

"Right..."

"You know what… We can meet to chat, but I really thought you should know something. That guy is lying! Pedro! He was never Sarah's – or may I say, Raven, as I recently discovered from the newspapers. He was never Raven's boyfriend. It's bollocks!"

Savanah's mind was running fast, putting the pieces of the puzzle together.

"I'm sending you a picture, Ana. Can you check your messages?" And she sent Ana the Facebook picture of herself and Hugh in front of Sr. Antonio's café, 13 years ago.

"Errhh, what should I be looking for?"

"Enlarge the picture on the right side, the reflection of a man on the café's window…"

A few seconds elapsed. Then Ana came back to the phone.

"Yeah, that's him. The Goat."

LISBON, JUNE 2019

Polícia Judiciária

(Savanah)

I am not fully convinced, and I tend to be a bit of a stubborn when the pieces of the puzzle don't add up. Ok, if Pedro was the Goat, he could have felt threatened by Raven of exposing his drug dealings at the bar. He had the motive and the means, as well as the how: he could have been at university, spying on her until she left. But, fuck, why had he gone to Raven's apartment when he knew she was in Tomar, from the email Raven sent him early that morning? Why had he sent the text message that was bound to alert Raven that something was amiss? And why had he confessed now, when nothing incriminatory against him had been found, besides an innocent picture of him close to Raven's apartment that morning, many hours before she was killed?

I needed to get to the bottom of the story, so I went to see Pedro at the Judiciária, where he was in custody awaiting trial. The Judiciária investigator did not want to allow it, but some flirting did the job. And the subtle threat of talking to the newspapers about the bollocks investigation they had conducted, leaving a crime unsolved for more than 10 years without properly looking into the obvious evidence...

As Pedro entered the room, tall and thin, with his jet black hair and penetrating silver-grey eyes, I wondered how I could have been so naïve. I had completely missed it, reading meaning in mere coincidences and never really considering Pedro, so self-effacing, so gentle, so helpful during my research. The girl in the hard rock club, Carminho, had mentioned the Goat stooping down to kiss Saint Anne and Saint Sarah. Not stretching up. Raven and Ana were tall women. Jaros, the owner of The Goat rock club, was a plump short man. Despite his dubious past, he would never be the one on stage with the two Saints. I had been carried away by motives and means before considering evidence. A rooky mistake.

Pedro sat down, eyed me sidewise while checking the police warden standing up in the corner of the visits room.

"Savanah... you look so much like your sister. It pained me so much, working side by side you for the past months, turning around in my head the times spent with your sister."

I stared at him, blankly. Just curious how long Pedro would keep the farce.

"I'm sorry", he continued. "I didn't mean to, it was in the spur of the moment. When I saw you with that bloke in Raven's apartment, ignoring me, I just went crazy."

I looked at him still, in silence, appraising the extent of the deceit. Pedro repeated the same story about his relationship with Raven, the confused identities of the twins and how he had waited for Raven to return from Tomar, looking for revenge.

"Drop the act, Goat." I finally said.

Pedro stared at me, silver-grey eyes trying to ascertain what I meant. Pedro was different from the photograph. He had shaved the moustache and the goatee, let his black hair grow again, and dressed in formal clothes instead of the metal punk black t-shirts. But there was no mistaking. He was the Goat, as Ana had confirmed.

Pedro run his hand through the sleek black hair, then turned sideways again to eye the police warden in the corner.

I confronted him, trying desperately to force some truth out of guy. "My sister fancied Saint Anna, you two were never lovers! You will be convicted, in the tape recording Raven clearly addresses "the Goat". Even if you drop the lover act, you will still be in for many years behind bars. So, just tell me the truth!"

"My dear, you are still as naïve as when you arrived in Lisbon six months ago. You are dealing with high powers. Just stop looking into it. Go away to your cosy American life. The secret must be preserved. Truth and lie, right and wrong... those are just moral labels. Truth does not exist, only what men do of it. 'He who has a why to live for can bear almost any how'."

"yeah... You may be right. You will be missed in heaven. 'In heaven, all interesting people are missing'."

Pedro smiled slyly, surprised I had just responded to his Nietzsche quote with another one.

"You are a smart ass as well, eh? Raven though she was too, digging out 500 years of Columbus conspiracy. You know what? No one cares any more what happened so many years ago. Facebook, Instagram, Google news... the only truth is the instant soundbite, the world has lost its memory. As for Columbus and his secret...conspiracy theories are out of fashion, they appear and disappear as fast as headlines. For five centuries now, 'those who were seen dancing were thought to be insane by those who could not hear the music'. So, you just keep on dancing, you dance monkey, no one cares."

With that, he rose from the chair and back walked towards the door, singing the Toni Watson hit, arms and head rocking in a sad, mechanic dance:

"Dance for me, dance for me, dance for me, oh oh oh /

Now I beg to see you dance, just one more time."

The interview was over.

Despite the hazing summer heat, I decide to walk for a while before getting a taxi to my apartment. I needed to put ideas in order.

How could I have been so naïve?

I had suspected Professor Noronha because of the ill-explained rape of Duma, his withdrawal from the threatening academic research that could expose secrets guarded for five centuries and sudden enrichment after Raven's death. He had the motives (a bribe) and the how (he could have stayed at the university that night, while Raven was typing up the summary document, spying on her until she left). And he probably had the means as well, not directly but if he is high up in the freemasons hierarchy he surely was a powerful man with the right (or wrong) connections.

I had also suspected Jaros, mistaking him for the Goat. He had the means (access to drugs to sedate Raven) and the motive (unrequited love and what I had thought to be a threat to expose his drug dealings in the club to the police). But he had no 'how', he couldn't know when Raven had left university that night.

So stupid, I had been. It just stared in front of me. I had though Jaros was the Goat because of his dodgy past, being the owner of the club, his crush on Sarah, the heavy metal black t-shirts, the bald head and the goatee he sported in the picture, later shaven. Carminho's boyfriend had listened to Raven threatening the Goat outside the toilet for passing drugs, and I assumed this was Jaros because of his past in drugs. But Carminho had been talking about Pedro all the time, whereas I always fit the image into Jaros. What I missed was quite simple, in fact. In the picture, Jaros was shorter than the two Saints, who stooped down to kiss him on the cheeks. Carminho had said at the end of the show the Goat bended down to stick his tongue on the girls' mouth. The brain only sees what it expects to see...

In the end, I had been looking in the wrong place.

Pedro was the Goat. After Sarah's death, as Duma pointed out months ago, Pedro shaved his beard (she could have been more specific, it was a goatee), let the hair grow back and changed his dress style. He had the means (with a dual life between university and the rock club, he easily had access to drugs), the motive (Sarah's threat to expose his drug dealing) and the how (he could have stayed at the university spying on Raven until she left, then raced her to arrive to her home street before Raven). But still... why had he come up with the claim they were boyfriends and confounded Raven with her twin sister kissing another man? If he had not confessed with that cock-up story, he would never have been exposed and I would never have found out he was the Goat.

I keep walking, unconvinced. The heat is starting to become unbearable, so I signal a taxi on the street, to take me the rest of the way to the apartment. On the middle of the journey, though, I change my mind and ask the driver to take me to The Saints club, instead.

LISBON, JULY 2019

The Saints Rock Club

"I should be judged as a commander who since a long time wields the sword, without leaving it for an instant, of knights, conquests and tradition."
CHRISTOPHER COLUMBUS

T he taxi dropped her across the street from The Saints. It was middle afternoon and the place was, expectably, empty.

There was still something in the story that didn't quite fit, a piece of the puzzle missing. Due to the confusion between Jaros and the Goat, Savanah had assumed Carminho had been talking about the same person, the one who Sarah had threatened outside the toilets (the Goat) and the one behind the bar counter who only served a whatever-brand of Polish vodka and passed Sarah envelopes (Jaros). She had assumed, like Carminho, that Jaros was passing some type of drug... but what if he was speaking the truth, saying Sarah never did drugs. What was in those envelopes?

In the afternoon's heat, the empty bar had a decadent look and smelled stale. Jaros was alone at this time, without the young bored bartender who probably only did part time hours in the evening.

As soon as Jaros saw her, he asked if Ana had managed to talk to her? "There is something odd here, Savanah. The Goat never dated Sarah! What is going on, Pedro taking the blame with a half-baked story of a love crime?"

"That's actually what I'm here about, Jaros. Trying to understand, but the puzzle stubbornly refuses to come together. For instance, Jaros, you guys never though it was somewhat strange that a university assistant professor would be a lead singer in a heavy metal rock band and, you know... do their scene on stage? I mean, Sarah was a 26 years old PhD student, fine, she could still mess around, but Pedro was already a junior professor at the time."

"But we didn't know Pedro was a Professor! Sarah told me about her PhD research, but the Goat and Saint Anne to us were just rock players with a weird past in the seminar and convent. I just realized, from the press reports after Pedro confession, that the guy had an academic career at the same time he played hellfire music here! Honestly, it makes sense. Ana and I have come to realize Pedro was probably just using the band to get to Sarah, to keep her close, spy on her, whatever... soon after her death, Pedro disappeared. We never heard of him again. At the same time, Ana started showing signs of drug withdrawal. She had never consciously consumed drugs, apart from the sporadic weed joint. And neither had Sarah. At the beginning, we though she was just depressed and tired, but the symptoms were too... 'physical'. I insisted she got tested, and yep... there were still traces of cocaine and hashish, which mixed with the weed had most likely kept her in a state of mental delusion and excess. After detox, Ana realized Pedro had probably been secretly drugging her since they had met, started dating and left the seminar. The guy had a big attitude, but it always felt a bit...fake, if you know what I mean. It could just be the seminar education still making him uncomfortable, but, I don't know, looking back it feels more like he was faking, role playing."

That was interesting. It made sense, in fact. If Pedro had wider, deeper secrets... with Professor Noronha he could use threat to force him to abandon the research. Noronha had a lot to lose, the Professorship, a wife, a son. People with something to lose are easy targets to threats. But Raven had nothing to lose, and definitely any hint of a threat or blackmail would just spike her up. So maybe... Pedro surely knew Raven played the guitar and liked metal, she was never reserved about herself. So, maybe all the scene about the Goat and Saint Anne had just been a scheme to get close and spy on Raven. Raven had a bad row with him about dealing drugs, maybe she suspected him drugging Ana without her knowledge. She could be suspecting Pedro was hiding something, or she got too close to whatever secret he was protecting, and so he decided to act.

Savanah moved to the issue that had actually brought her to the bar. "Those envelopes you kept behind the vodka and gave to Sarah, were they drugs?"

"Absolutely not! I told you already your sister didn't do drugs. We had very interesting discussions, about a lot of stuff. Those envelopes...she got very excited about one of the translated excerpts, said it closed the loop, and then suddenly after that... she got killed. I don't understand the whole picture, but the secrets Sarah uncovered may have gotten her killed. I...I just didn't know whom to trust, so I left the documents hidden."

Jaros leads Savanah backstage and in the dark brick wall under the windy staircase that leads to his flat, he pushes inside one of the bricks and uses the space to pull out the brick below. From the hole, he takes a small safe box, which he carries upstairs to his apartment. In the round table they had sat some weeks before, he sets down the safe and a book he pulled from the shelf. He then says:

"I was reading this book about the Jagiellos, who were kings of Poland and the entire Germanic Holy Roman Empire before the Habsburgs. Just, you know, a nationalistic thing. An emigrant sometimes needs these ties back home. Point is, Sarah asks me what it is about, I'm telling her the book is the result of an investigation by the author about a mysterious resident who appears in Madeira around 1450, known as Henrique Alemão. The book establishes that King Ladislau III, who disappeared in the battle of Varna, was later recognized by an Italian merchant and by two Polish monks living in the island of Madeira as Henrique Alemão... well, and then she gets all excited, comes here every afternoon so that I can tell her about the book. It is in Polish, so she asked me to translate some excerpts, the bits about Ladislau III and his travels as a pilgrim until he settles in madeira. Every day I would translate a few pages. That's what was in those envelopes."

"As Sarah was spending her afternoons here, on this table, going through the details of the book with me, she started bringing some of her research stuff. Notes and photocopies she was putting together. She said it all fit together and she had found the final proof. But then, suddenly, she got killed. I was a suspect and interrogated by the police. So I was afraid to show them...", and then Jaros opens the small safe box, taking out several photocopies and images. And, at the bottom, the two pages ripped off from Raven's notebook.

"...this.", Jaros concludes, handing to Savanah two ripped off pages. Savanah takes the notebook and indeed, the two pages match perfectly the zigzagged leftover section where the pages had been cut off.

As Savanah takes the small bunch of documents, Jaros explains that Sarah handed them to him together with the ripped off pages from her notebook, saying they were too precious to go around with them, because there was something she needed to do that could be dangerous. This was Monday, 24 July in the afternoon. On Tuesday she went to Tomar. On Wednesday before dawn, she was killed.

Savanah spreads the several documents on the table. "I refrained earlier from showing this to you, because it may be...because it may have killed Sarah. You must be careful. But something very weird is going on and we need to understand, not least in memory of Sarah. I hope you will be able to make sense of this, I never understood what it means. I'll be downstairs, ok, in the bar."

Besides the two pages of Sarah's notebook, full of notes and references, there were several photocopies of the book Jaros had been reading and which caught Sarah's attention. 'Odyseja Wladyslawa Wrnenczyka', published in 1991 by the Polish academic Leopoldo Kielanowski. Jaros roughly translated the title as 'Odissey of Ladislau, the Varnese'. There were also several handwritten pages, in Jaros careful slightly childish calligraphy, of translated excerpts from the book. One of these translated excerpts was a letter Leopoldo Kielanowski had recently discovered in the archives of the Teutonic Knights. The letter is from a Nicolau Floris to the Grand Master of the Teutonic Order, written in 1472. The key passage reads 'Vladislaus, rex Poloniae et Ungariae vivit in insulis regni Portugaliae". The Odyssey relates how King Ladislau III, after escaping from the battle of Varna, in 1444, goes on a pilgrimage to the Holy Land and then to Mount Sinai where he is armed Knight of Saint Catherine. He then spends a several years as a hermit in the Pyrenees before taking refuge in Madeira island.

This must have meant something to Raven, for her to get so excited and cautious.

The implications dawn on her mind as she reads through the other documents. A second set of copies refer to a book about Nobility Lineages of the island of Madeira, published in the eighteenth century by Henriques Noronha, where two passages were underlined:

"Henrique Alemão arrived in Madeira around 1450, the Prince of Poland who came to the island to conceal his identity."

"Henrique Alemão, knight of Saint Catherine, prince of Poland (...) vowed to pilgrimage and after being knighted in Mount Sinai, came to this island, where João Gonçalves Zarco gave him a large plantation."

A note on Raven's notebook noted that several Portuguese chroniclers declared that, around 1450, arrived to Portugal a high noble, knight of Saint Catherine of Mount Sinai. Despite always publicly denying his true identity, his importance and status were recognized to the extent that Henry the Navigator, Grand Master of the Order of Christ, donated him land in Madeira for himself and 8 knights who travelled with him. King Afonso V regularly sent him ships with provisions. And the king of Portugal arranged the new arrival a high marriage, to a lady of the Zarco family, captain of Madeira. The king himself served as best man at the wedding.

Then, there was a photocopy labelled "Don Tivisco", with a side note saying "Tivisco was the roman name of current day Timisoara, in Romania, a city that was part of Hungary and part of Ladislau III kingdom". Savanah was already familiar with the two books published in the early eighteenth century, by different authors but with the same pseudonym, Dom Tivisco de Nasao Zarco, y Colonna. Raven had underlined the statement "The greatest Portuguese discoverer of all times was the last sprout of Henrique." On the side line, Raven had noted "Sigesmundo Henriques Jagiello Colonna, son of Henrique Alemão (Ladislau III Jagiello) and Senhorinha Anes Colonna."

A colour photocopy showed a coat of arms with a golden cross over a blue field. Next to it, Raven's had written "Ladislau II coat of arms" and then drawn an anchor as a cross imposing over an upwards crescent moon, which combined to make an anchor. Extraordinary... Henrique Alemão had taken his house arms, turned the cross into an anchor, and used it as the Henriques coat of arms in Madeira... which his son Colon then adjusted to five golden anchors in sauterne pattern, over a blue field, as his own "original family arms".

Finally, between the pages in the small safe box hidden for thirteen years behind the bricks of The Saints rock bar, was a photocopy of a chronicle of the Portuguese knights taken in captivity in Ceuta, together with Prince Fernando. João Vasques, married with Guiomar de Sá, granddaughter of Rodrigo Anes de Sá and Cecilia Colonna, with a daughter named Senhorinha Anes... Savanah gasped! This name... sure, it was the name of the wife of Henrique Alemão, father of Segismundo Henriques. The family Anes de Sá was linked by marriage to Zarco, the captain of Madeira who hosted Henrique Alemão. Cecilia Colonna was a Sicilian noble.

This means... Savanah mind was swirling. But it all fit together. If Christopher Colon, Segismundo Anriques, was the last sprout of Henrique Alemão (Jagiello) and Senhorinha Anes (de Sá Colonna), he was not only a Jagiello but also a Anes de Sá, of Italian blood and by all rights a ´Colon'! His father had been a pilgrim and a hermit, living in self-imposed poverty. So, Colon and his descendants had not lied when they said he was of Italian origins of a poor family... they just concealed a lot else!

Several notes on the ripped off pages indicated other leads. The patron saint of the city of Vilnius, capital city of Lithuania and where King Ladislau II was born, is Saint Christopher. Since 1330, the coat of arms of Vilnius depicts Saint Christopher with the infant Jesus in his arms, helping him to cross a river. Cristovão, XpoFerens, means 'Walk with Christ, Carry Christ'. When Segismundo Henriques had to take a fake identity for his mission of deceit in Spain, he picked the patron saint of the city his grandfather was born, Christopher, and the Colonna lineage from her mother, Colon.

Henrique Alemão, Ladislau III, built a chapel in Madalena, Madeira, where he was buried. Savanah was already familiar with the painting of him and his wife, that not only proves the physical resemblance between Alemão and Colon and shows the mysterious pilgrim pouch with the 'Invisible Book'. The new fact on Raven's notebook, though, was quite curious: in the altar of that church there is a carving of a golden eagle with wings spread... quite similar to the symbol of Poland. Ladislau III sword, which is today at the Hermitage Museum in Saint Petersburg, has an eagle with a cross on its chest, engraved in the bone hilt.

Savanah recalled an excerpt that had caught her attention from Fernando's words regarding the "Capitulations of Santa Fé" establishing the agreement between the Spanish monarchs and Colon in 1492: "The said privileges and capitulations were agreed between your Highnesses and my Father, as a Prince and not as a subject". As a Prince!

So, there it was. Professor Noronha had already advanced with the name Segismundo Anriques, or Segismundo Alemão, as the most likely candidate to be the true identity of Cristovão Colón. The documents spread in front of her completed the puzzle. All pieces fitted together.

This also explained the need for hiding or even destroying the true identity of this Prince. His true bloodline was a threat to Emperor Carlos V of Spain and the Habsburg dynasty who took over the crown of the Germanic empire after the disappearance of Ladislau III.

Prince Segismundo Anriques, or Henriques. The S.A. in Colon's cryptic signature. The last sprout of Henrique. Henriques son of Henrique, the secret name adopted by

Ladislau III King of Poland, Lithuania and Hungary, when he took refuge in Madeira island.

Jagiello, Grand Duke of Lithuania, converted to Christianism to be able to marry Jadwiga, heir of the Polish crown, in 1386 and thus become the king of Poland. He was christened as Ladislau II. King Ladislau II sided with the emperor of the German Holy Roman Empire, Segismundo, in the Hussite wars of 1420-1434 against the followers of protestant Jan Huss of Bohemia. Prince Dom Pedro of Portugal, the adventurer brother of Infante Dom Henrique, also took part in those crusades against the Hussite heretics. Ladislau II died in 1434, leaving the throne to his son Ladislau III, King of Poland, Lithuania and later Hungary. The eastern borders of Europe were under several threats during Ladislau III kingdom: The Hussites from north and northwest and the powerful ottoman Turks on the east and southwest. Faced with the threat of the Muslim invaders reaching Constantinople [101] and defeating the Christian Byzantine Empire, the 18-year old King Ladislau III decided to lead an army against the ottomans in 1443. The battle was won, leading to the signature of a 10-year truce treaty. But one year later, war was raging again, leading to the battle of Varna, in Bulgaria, in 1444.

The Christian army of Ladislau III was crushed in Varna, outnumbered massively by the ottoman forces three times larger. Ladislau III was last seen charging against Sultan Murad II. The official version in the story books is that the king was killed in battle. But his body, clothes, sword and shield were never found in the field nor any witness claimed to have seen him dead.

Several clues indicate the King might have survived and escaped the battle of Varna. High nobles from Hungary, Bosnia and Hungary claimed the King was alive. Rumors spread that the King had been seen at the Monastery of Saint Catherine of Alexandria in Mount Sinai. Lord Wawrzyniec

Hedervary of Hungary sent a letter to the German Holy Roman Emperor Frederick III declaring to have received a letter sealed with Ladislau III royal seal, written in October 1445, where the King stated he was in a pilgrimage and his heir should be crowned king if he did not return by the Holy Trinity festivities (a major celebration in eastern orthodox Christianity, celebrated 52 days after Easter, which should be around June 1446). Count Leo de Rozmital, of Bohemia, declared he identified Ladislau III in 1446, living in Spain as a hermit and that he had the King's mark of 6 feet fingers.

In 1444, King Ladislau III was 20-years old and had no sons, so his death would open succession claims. João Hunyadi was only elected regent of Hungary in 1446, after the deadline established by Ladislau. Casimiro Jagiello, brother of Ladislau III, was only crowned king of Poland on 25 June 1447, almost three years after Ladislau III disappearance. If Ladislau III had died, it would be most unusual for Hungary and Poland to have waited 2-3 years to crown the new kings. No-one believed, at the time, that king Ladislau III had died! Only at the end of 1448, the enemies of the Jagiello dynasty, scheming to get the Hungarian crown for the Habsburgs, started spreading the idea that Ladislau III was dead.

Again, history was written by the victors. Despite the official version of Ladislau death, all evidence suggest he survived the battle and run away.

A different version of the facts can be reconstructed, fitting historic evidence. Shamed by defeat and maybe looking to protect a family's treasure from the ottoman threat, King Ladislau III goes on a pilgrimage to Mount Sinai where he is armed a Knight of Saint Catherine. He then travels west and takes refuge in Spain, where he lives as a hermit for several years in the Pyrenees, in the area of Rennes-le-Chateaux and the church of Marie Magdalene where Saunière would find the scrolls more than 450 years later, before finally taking refuge in Madeira, a Portuguese island owned by the Order of Christ. Portugal had sheltered the Templars, so if Ladislau had a Templar secret, it would make sense for him to take refuge in the kingdom. What reason could a king of Poland and Hungary have to give up his throne, assume a new identity and deny his true identity even when identified by Polish monks and nobles? Could Ladislau be the bearer of an ancient secret, and fled to protect it from the threat of the Ottoman invasions or the increasing power of the Habsburgs, aligned with Rome? The secret could have been carried by the Germanic order of the Teutonic knights, created in 1309, two years after the extinction of the Templars. The Teutonic Order was the Germanic equivalent of the Portuguese Order of Christ, with headquarters in Malbork, Poland.

Whatever Ladislau III motives, he arrives in Madeira around 1450, 6 years after the battle of Varna. Despite always maintaining anonymity and the appearance of a pilgrim, he is treated like a high prince, given lands and married to a high noble lady of the Zarco family, captain of Madeira.

A few years later, an Italian merchant declared in Lithuania he had seen the Polish king in Madeira. Emperor Frederico III of the German Holy Roman Empire, married with Princess Leonor of Portugal (sister of king Afonso V), sent two Polish monks to investigate. The monks swore the knight was King Ladislau and begged him to return. In 1466, Count Jaroslav de Rozmital, brother of the Queen of Bohemia, did a long journey around Western Europe. He describes a meeting with a pilgrim in Iberia, asserting he was the former king of Poland Ladislau III.

Historical accounts report the sudden disappearance of both Henrique Alemão, and is son, Segismundo Henriques. As if fate wanted to make these two personages go up in smoke... If the official chronicles are to be believed, Henrique Alemão boarded a ship to Lisbon, headed to meet King Afonso V. A large rock fell off a cliff in cape Girão and landed on Alemão's head, instantly killing him. Puff... one king gone! Cabo Girão in Madeira is one of the highest cliffs in the world, more than 600 meters above sea level. Any ship would surely take a safe distance from the cliff, to avoid shallows and rocks... never would a rock falling from the cliff hit a passing ship. A fantasy spun by the chronicles to make the King vanish from the attentions of the world.

Segismundo Henriques died in another sea accident, a charade as fantastical as the rock from cape Girão... in the case of Segismundo, he was made to vanish hit by a sail mast that broke and hit him in the head. Puff... another king gone!

Were the Portuguese chroniclers so keen on making the trace of these two men disappear that they concoct two bizarre stories to kill both father and son? Suddenly, Anrique Alemão and Segismundo Anriques vanish in a cloud of smoke, never to be heard of again. And out of the mist... appears Cristovão Colon, a man with no past that appears suddenly in 1476 in Portugal, of a ship wreck, swimming 6 miles to the shore near Lisbon. Savanah had trained hard for a triathlon... 800 meters open water swimming is a hard feat that requires a fit body and fine stroke technique. 6 miles in open sea?...

The royal bloodline of Colon would explain many of the otherwise fanciful facts of his life. The deference shown by Portuguese and Spanish lords. His marriage to a high noble lady, Filipa Perestrelo, a Dona of All Saints Covent of the Order of Santiago and daughter of the captain of Porto Santo, the neighbor island of Madeira. Colon's coat of arms where Queen Isabella recognized "the arms your family used to wear", bear the same gold anchor over a blue field as the coat of arms of the Henriques family, which itself is similar to Ladislau II coat of arms. Colon painted in the ceiling of the palace of Mafra amongst the highest Portuguese heroes. Painted by Alejo Fernandez in Seville chapel at the Virgin of Navigators with a hidden crown disguised between the sleeve of his robe. The 'Invisible Crown', as Raven had called it.

Fernando Colon and Friar Las Casas stated that the Colon brothers were from "Terra Rubia", or Terra Rubra. At the time of Ladislau III, Poland included a region known as Rutenia Rubra.

The Columbus Chapel at Boal Mansion contains many enigmatic and extraordinary clues about Colon. The chapel was inherited by Colon's heirs and transplanted, stone by stone, from Asturias in Spain to Boalsburg, Pennsylvania in 1909. The museum exhibits the original desk of the Admiral, with the scallop shells typical of the Order of Santiago. It also contains an extraordinary coat of arms of the Dukes of Veragua: the traditional coat of arms granted by Queen Isabella to Colon, but over-imposed at the center with an oval depicting an eagle with wings spread, exactly like the eagle used by the kings of Poland.

The royal bloodline of Colon would also explain the interest of Spanish kings to discredit the origins of Colon and create the fairy tale of the poor Italian. In fact, the House of Jagiello (Ladislau) and the House of Habsburg were political enemies. Ladislau III had fought the Habsburg to win the crown of Hungary. In 1526, the Habsburg emperor Ferdinand I, brother of the Spanish King Carlos V, took the crown of Bohemia and Hungary from the Jagiello, benefitting from the broken succession line at the Jagiello's. If it was known that a Jagiello Prince, Ladislau III grandson, was alive, this could create a lot of political problems for the Habsburg. So, it would be natural for Carlos V to silence Colon's origins. He ordered Fernando Colon to stop investigating into his father's origins. After 1580, the Spanish Filipine Dynasty, of the House of Habsburg, ruled Portugal for 60 years. During this period, the Spanish kings had plenty of time to rewrite history, destroying, forging or transcribing documents. At the same time, Fernando Colon 'Historia del Almirante' was translated and probably adulterated to Italian and the original disappeared. And shortly after, an Italian merchant comes up, claiming Colon (Member) and Colombo (Pigeon) are the same name and showing documents that try to link Colon to the Italian Colombos – documents that the Spanish court itself dismissed as forged.

Forced to conceal his true identity by the will of his father and the mission of the Portuguese kings, Colon's epitaph on his tomb marks the hope that someday the truth could be found: "I will not be confounded forever!" [102]

LISBON, JUNE 2019

S avanah called an Uber and left The Saints club with a vague mix of ecstasy and emptiness. This was truly extraordinary. She should be thrilled. All the pieces of the puzzle about Columbus were coming together. But she was too tired to feel any elation.

And something was still missing, a final piece of the puzzle. If the 'Invisible Crown' of Colon and the 'Invisible Book' of Henrique Alemão were related, then what was the meaning of the censored tryptic painting in Tomar, restored by the 'Invisible Painter', who had been forced to cover up the words 'Protect the Queen and the Book of Canaan'. Was the Invisible Book on the pilgrim's pouch of Colon's father related to the lost lineage of Christ, the Queen of Canaan?

And why had Pedro taken the blame for Raven's assassination with a cock-up story? The pieces about Columbus could be coming into place, but not Pedro's version of her sister's murder.

Oh, fuck's sake!! She entered the Uber Toyota Prius and let her head rest on the window, watching the normal city life going on as usual, indifferent to the dramas playing out in her mind. The miracle of daily life going by.

The more she thought of it, the more the whole thing seemed bizarre. Duma mentioned everyone at the university research team knew about Raven's twin sister. Actually, Duma said they all knew her twin sister was arriving in Lisbon that day for her honeymoon. And Raven had sent that email to Pedro at dawn, before leaving to Tomar, telling him her twin sister was arriving with her husband and staying at her apartment.

Why had he gone there that morning, knowing perfectly well who he would find? And then texting Raven, alerting her to the photo on Savanah's Facebook post. And why had Pedro confessed to the crime, if there was no new evidence that could prove he had done it? Even if he suspected Savanah had found out about the picture, he could just claim he had not seen the email or was just passing by.

It is conceivable Pedro is taking the blame to cover up a much wider web of secrets to protect... to protect what, or whom? He had the means and the how, but what were his true motives?

Savanah's mind wandered away, until she realised the route the driver was taking was not the one suggested by the app on her mobile.

"Ei, sir, this is not the right way. What are you doing? Stop, let me out."

The driver looked at her through the rear view mirror. "Miss Sophia, your uncle Santiago has asked me to take you to the airport. You are being followed and in grave danger. Do not underestimate the powers at play here. I am a US marine and I am dropping you at the airport. In the back pocket of the seat in front of you there is a ticket to the Azores. You will take it as if you accepted this whole mess as true and decided to take a few days off before returning to the States. An undercover team of the US embassy is at the airport to make sure you board the TAP flight to the Azores without further complications. Your uncle has a team of the Azores US air base at the ready to escort you home."

What the fuck? What had this guy called her? He had addressed her by her childhood nickname only her family knew. Princess Sophia and Princess Sarah, her uncle had called them during those summer holidays sailed around

KARLOS K.

the Caribbean...

GULFSTREAM C-20F, JUNE 2019

Flight from Lages airbase
to Washington

When the TAP flight landed at the Ponta Delgada airport in the Azores island of São Miguel, a short lady with a US military uniform and crisp manners approached Savanah before immigration control and ushered her away to a hangar, where a small executive airplane was waiting for them.

The flight from Ponta Delgada to the US air base of Lages, in the Azores island of Terceira, took less than 40 minutes. The plane had not even reached cruise altitude. The military airbase of Lages was built during the second world war, benefiting from its geopolitical strategic location for the control of the Atlantic. Officially named Air Base 4 of the Portuguese Air Force, it is used since 1945 as a military base by the US Air Force under a cooperation agreement.

Instants after touching down, Savanah was seated in a Gulfstream C-20F, the U.S. military version of the G-IV jet, surrounded by the short woman who escorted her from Ponta Delgada and two other guys with military aspect. The three of them looked stern and professional, like some special unit for extractions. Their destination was only revealed after take-off: Washington DC. "Uncle Santiago, what are you playing at?"

She tried to relax. Realizing there would be little chance of sleeping, considering how active her brain was, she took out her iMac and re-read Raven's document attached to the email of 26 July 2006 sent at 2.53am, which she had painstakingly decoded. By all indications, Raven had been working on it non-stop during the afternoon after returning from Tomar. As if, sensing eminent danger, she needed to write the thoughts and information inside her mind to ensure they would survive even if anything happened to her. Earlier in the afternoon she had sent the coded email to her sister, leaving the leads to access the document.

The first time Savanah read the document, she couldn't grasp its full implications. Only now, after the revelations of the past few days, did the pieces of the puzzle start fitting together. The document was written in a telegraphic manner, crisp and quick, as if Raven had been in a hurry to finish it.

[26 July 2006: Raven's document on the 2.53am email]

Colon's mystery and the 500 years' conspiracy to hide his true identity and mission

1. Colon's identity and true mission

Segismundo Henriques, son of Henrique Alemão. Professor Noronha is right on this.

Names beginning with an S have succeeded in Templar history, from king Solomon to Prince Sinclair and Segismundo Alemão. It is a representation of the serpent of knowledge who took humanity away from the ignorant primitive Eden into self-determination.

Santiago, Sophia and Sarah... continuation of the line that protects the secret?

Colon's mission in Spain is quite clear: to attract the Spanish kings into a wild goose chase for the Indies through a western route, but getting the fleet stuck in the Antilles – which were already known by the Portuguese since at least 1472. Despite being just a few leagues from the huge American continent, he kept the Spanish stuck in the Caribbean islands and only in the third expedition – after D Manuel married the daughter of the Spanish monarchs and thus becoming the first in the line of succession to rule over a united Iberia – did Columbus quickly push forward into the central America coastline.

Colon's expedition was crucial to ruse the Spanish monarchs into signing the Tordesillas Treaty. By doing so, Colon guaranteed for João II the exclusivity of a known India, while offering Isabel and Fernando the possibility of an unknown America.

However, this cannot be the only secret on colon's life! No matter how vilified and shamed the Spanish feel about the deceit, it would not justify 500 years of lies and cover up by everyone, Portuguese and Spanish kings, the Pope, academics... Why continue the charade for 500 years?

There is only one explanation. Colon had another, hidden mission, maybe an immense treasure himself and his Order of Christ were protecting. Only a dangerous or powerful secret of immense magnitude would justify five centuries of controversies, as the powers at play in this secret chess game continued moving the pieces against each other.

2. Colon's signature

Triple S roof represents the Temple of Solomon, protecting an 'A', which in this sense may stand for Arcadia or Avalon: a new Promised Land that Colon was searching, a land of freedom and opportunity for all faiths?

This is the real message in colon's signature: X M Y. Usually considered to be Xrist, Mary and Yosepf. But the 'X M Y' can stand for Christ, Mahommed and Yahweh: Christians, Muslims and Jews living together in Arcadia, the Promised Land in the New World, protected by the Temple of Solomon (Templars). Different faiths as spiritual faces of the same universal Holy Spirit.

There is more to it, though. The signature uses a hooked X, which is a symbol of a female heir (see below). This is critical and has so far been overlooked.

3. The hooked X: a bridge between the Old and New World

The breakthrough is the relevance of the hooked X in Colon's signature and its occurrence in Templar places that until now seemed unconnected.

The X is a representation of the masculine and feminine, upwards and downwards triangles coming together as a symbol of fertility. The hook in the X represents an addition, an appendix, the descendants of the male/female union. As the hook is on the top female triangle, it represents a daughter.

The hooked X of Colon's signature also appears in places far apart, suggesting a current of symbolic meaning uniting sites apparently unrelated: American sites associated with pre-Columbian Templars, like the Westford Knight and the Kensington Runestone; Scotland's Rosslyn Chapel, carved in the wood; Portugal's Church of Santa Maria dos Olivais, carved in the outside wall and pillars.

The hooked X means "masculine/feminine union and their lineage". As X also stands for Christ, this symbol represents "Christ's lineage", most likely "Christ's daughter". The finding of the same fertility symbol in far apart places, each connected with the Templars, suggests the Templars were created in Jerusalem as a kind of Pretorian Guard, a brotherhood to protect and hide the secret uncovered in the Temple of Solomon: the blood line of Christ and Mary Magdalene.

The hooked X in America pre-Columbus can have only one meaning: The Templars were in America before Columbus. The group taken by Henry Sinclair from Scotland Rosslyn chapel, to hide the Rose line, the blood line.

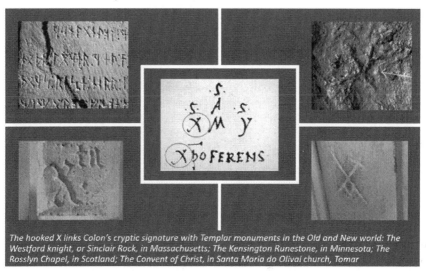

The hooked X links Colon's cryptic signature with Templar monuments in the Old and New world: The Westford knight, or Sinclair Rock, in Massachusetts; The Kensington Runestone, in Minnesota; The Rosslyn Chapel, in Scotland; The Convent of Christ, in Santa Maria do Olival church, Tomar

The link of Templar lore with North America is also trans-mitted in the tales of King Arthur, the knights of the Round Table and Perceval's quest for the Grail in the mystic land of Avalon. Perceval name may be derived from the French 'per cheval' (on horseback), as suggested by Sauniere's parchments, and thus refer to the Templars, whose sigil are two knights on horseback. Avalon refers to North America, more specifically, Newfoundland and Nova Scotia, where the Templar Prince Henry Sinclair disembarked with the Rose Line.

But if the Templar treasure – the Rose Line of Christ and Mary Magdalene – was already safe in America, why did Segismundo (Colon) insist in bearing the Hooked X sigil on his signature? What is the missing link between the southern Portuguese

path and the northern Scottish path?

The Templar seal shows an eight-arched circular tower, a rare design in European churches but replicated both in the Newport Tower near Boston and the Convent of Christ in Tomar. The Temple Church in London also has a round nave.

The northern path taken by Henry Sinclair through Rosslyn Chapel to take the Rose line to protection in the New Jerusalem, America is widely known.

Less explored is the missing link with Columbus and the southern branch of the Templars who took refuge in Portugal. Why do we find the same Templar symbols in Portuguese monuments and in the sails of the Caravelas? Why has Ladislau III (Henrique Alemão), Columbus father, abandoned his crown and riches to hide in Madeira, after spending several years as a hermit in the Pyrenees? Why has a massive conspiracy been created to cover up Columbus true mission?

The simplest explanation is that there was a second secret taken by the Templars from Jerusalem. Two secrets that got branched out during the flight, one taken by the northern path and the other by the southern path. Columbus strived to take the second treasure to the New Jerusalem and probably planned to use his basis in the Caribbean to send expeditions to look for the northern path.

4. The Templar cross in the seal of King Dom Afonso Henriques and the Caravelas of Infante Henry the Navigator

The two secrets discovered in Jerusalem after the first Crusade were separated between the northern path and the southern path, probably in the early fourteenth century after the extinc-

tion of the Order. Since then, the Templar's heirs (Order of Christ, Teutonic Knights…) strived to reunite them in the New Jerusalem, the New World.

The means to complete the mission were the Portuguese Caravelas. The secret mission behind the Age of Discoveries initiated by Henry the Navigator is evident in the Templar cross carried on the sails of the Caravelas: the rose and the cross united!

The seal of the first king of Portugal, Dom Afonso Henriques, is revealing about what would later be concealed in the Templar cross of the Caravelas. Is it a rose? Is it a cross? Is it two chalices overlapped? I guess the true answer is that the seal is all of that – the union of the cross and the rose.

The seal of Dom Afonso Henriques: "Alfonsus Rex Portugalens"

The legend of the Raven Knight in Corvo Island, a statue pointing the way westwards, suggests another origin or hidden meaning for the Templar cross carried by the Portuguese Caravelas of the Age of Discoveries: four Viking runes and the orthodox square cross combined.

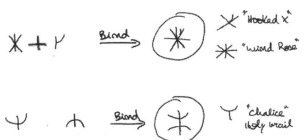

The vertical branch of the Templar cross in the Portuguese Caravelas is the masculine side, uniting the H and K Viking runes. H stands for Homem, meaning "man" in Portuguese. The K rune stands for King and Krist. The combination binds into a Wind Rose with the "hook", the lost "daughter line" of the northern Templars. It also looks very much like an open book, its front and back covers touching and the pages opening like a fan. The southern, masculine branch represents an open book which misses the "hook", the lost daughter of the King.

The name Christopher Colon, the fabricated identity of Segismundo Alemão, can be represented by two mirrored KK (Kristopher Kolumbus), which together with the Greek square cross form a wind rose or an open book.

The painting of Henrique Alemão in his chapel in Madeira suggests a book is hidden in his pilgrim's pouch. The Saunière parchments also indicate that part of the secret (Poussin's Shepherdess and Ark, see below) are in Arcadia (America), but there is still a part of the secret in danger, persecuted by Teniers' demons (a Book).

Several indications thus suggest the secret Colon might have tried to take to America was a Book. His son Fernando's extensive library could also be a way to conceal a secret Book. Inquisition was most extensive and lasting in Iberia, with millions of books destroyed, burnt or censored. Was the church looking for something?

The horizontal branch of the Templar cross in the Caravelas is the binding of the M and R Viking runes. The M stands for Mulher in Portuguese, Woman. The R stands for Real, Royal. So the Royal female line of Christ, Mary Magdalene. The Rose Line, which is symbolized by the rose images carved in Tomar and Rosacruxian lore.

More importantly, the two runes bind to form a clear image of two chalices, an upwards and another downwards. The Holy Grail. It is often depicted as the "last chalice of Christ". The chalice is an ancient symbol of the woman's womb, a symbol of fertility and feminine. The two chalices resemble the cups of two female breasts, source of nourishment for the new-born baby.

The four Viking runes combine into the Templar cross of the Caravelas to represent the reunion of the Wind Rose (Book) with the Rose Line (Holy Grail, royal bloodline). What's missing in the Templar cross of the Caravelas? The hook, the lost daughter.

5. A base to search in North America

During the fifteenth century, Portuguese navigators stubbornly looked for something in Newfoundland and Nova Scotia, secretly, never announcing or claiming those lands.

The 1424 Pizzigano map shows Nova Scotia and New-foundland. In 1473, João Vaz Corte-Real, cousin of Isabel Moniz Perestrelo, Columbus mother-in-law, explored the Isle of Code (Newfoundland) and Nova Scotia. In 1476/77 the Luso-Danish expedition explored Thule, today Greenland (and Columbus claims to have taken part in that expedition). In 1498, João Fernandes Lavrador explored the Labrador Sea. In 1500, Gaspar Corte-Real sailed to Newfoundland and then departed again in 1501 on a second expedition, never returning. In 1502 his brother Miguel also departed, never returning – staying in Canada and descending to Massachusetts where he left the Dighton Rock inscriptions in 1511.

These were uncivilized lands without much opportunities for commerce or loot, so why did the Portuguese keep insisting? They were probably testing a possible passage into the Pacific Ocean. But the search continued long after the Tordesillas treaty established North America in the Spanish hemisphere. Were they looking for the Scottish Templars of the northern path?

The Westford Knight, Kensington Runestone, Newport Tower all suggest North American natives had contact with knights clad in armour and sword long before the seventeenth century settlers arrived.

Columbus needed a base from which to explore North America, in search of the northern path. Most of the ships from Columbus fleets have never been found, despite decades of treasure hunters and marine archaeologists looking for them! A total of 11 ships mysteriously disappeared in La Isabela during the second expedition, in 1494, supposedly *wrecked in a tornado. Colon proved again and again he was a great cosmographer, warning Ovando of the upcoming hurricane in 1502 and later predicting a moon eclipse in Jamaica, so is it reasonable that he lost 11 ships, sunk while at anchor in Isabela Bay? Did all these ships sunk, never to be found, or was Columbus building his own hidden secret armada? In fact, he was accused by Bobadilla of conspiring with the Indians to rebel, aiming to carve out a kingdom for himself in the Caribbean. Was he establishing a base for a North America search?*

Columbus was not just a double agent of Dom Joao II to protect the Indic ocean route to India and ruse the Spanish westwards. He had an additional secret agenda: to establish an outpost as Admiral and ruler of the Caribbean islands from where he could go out and find the lost line of the Scottish Templars.

6. Corte-Real: a desperate attempt to help Columbus complete his mission?

In 1500, Columbus returned to Spain in shackles with the mission unfulfilled, the Portuguese tried a last ditch effort to find Henry Sinclair and deliver the Wind Rose to the Rose Line.

Again they sail to a barren, uncivilized land with nothing to trade or loot. And yet they set sail again to North America... three times! Gaspar Corte-Real, son of João Vaz Corte-Real, led an expedition for King D Manuel II to Newfoundland in 1500 and then a second one in 1501, not returning. In 1502 his brother Miguel Corte-Real, also with Dom Manuel blessing, followed his brother's trail to North *America, also never returning. Other ships on the fleet returned to Portugal and there is no evidence Gaspar or Miguel ships wrecked.*

There are Canadian cities whose names resemble the explorer's: Montreal and Gaspe. The enigmatic Dighton Rock, a 40-ton boulder originally found in the riverbed of Taunton River at Berkley, Massachusetts, contains carved signs which Edmund Delabarre from Brown University interpreted as a Latin phrase and a date which in English would mean "I, Miguel Cortereal, by the will of God, became a chief of the Indians. 1511." The boulder also contains symbols interpreted as a Portuguese coat of arms, a cross of the Order of Christ and a shield. There is a full-size replica in front of the Lisbon Navy Museum.

So, what were Gaspar and Miguel doing when they abandoned high ranking positions as captains of the Azores to settle in North America, more than 100 years before the pilgrims came ashore from the Mayflower on Plymouth in 1620?

7. After Columbus: Saunière parchments, Poussin Arcadia, Teniers Demons

Saunière first parchment dates from the thirteenth century, the second from the eighteenth century.

The first parchment is decoded as "To King Dagobert II and to Sion belongs this treasure and He is dead". This is the treasure of the Merovingian kings who descended from Mary Magdalene bloodline. Also the treasure of Sion, the Templars. The treasure "is dead" or "is death".

My interpretation is the following. At the end of the thirteenth century, under threat and at risk of extinction, the Templars moved the secret in two secret branches: The bloodline (the Grail) taken by the northern path through Scotland and then to Nova Scotia. The southern path protected the Book, the wind rose. But the last part of the treasure, the Ark or tomb where "He is dead", remained in the Pyrenees church. A stone ark is heavy and difficult to move around as the Templars were persecuted. So, the Ark remained hidden in the south of France, protected "By the cross and the horse backed knights (the Templars)", in a place guarded against the demons by the church of blue apples: The Mary Magdalene Church.

I only established the missing link between Colon and the Mary Magdalene church in the Pyrenees over the last few days, after reading passages of a book about King Ladislau III and the Teutonic knights. Emperor Ladislau III (Henrique Alemão, Colon's father) fled Varna to protect a great secret, lived in the Pyrenees as a hermit, near Rennes-le-Chateau and the church of Mary Magdalene, and then took refuge in Madeira waiting to take the Book west, to Avalon, America.

This was the missing link, placing Sauniere's scrolls and the treasure they refer right on Columbus path. Ladislau either brought the secret from the Germanic empire, where it had been protected by the Teutonic knights, or found the secret in the Mary Magdalene church – but in any case establishing this church as a pilgrimage site, which would in the nineteenth century be transferred to the nearby Sanctuary of our Lady of Lourdes.

Less than two centuries later, in 1627 and 1637, Poussin paintings announce the good news to the initiated. The Ark is in Arcadia, next to the Shepherdess – the new Promised Land aspired by the Templars. America, the New World. Poussin's inscription "Et in Arcadia ergo" openly states that "Finally, the Ark is in Arcadia". The inscription is also an anagram for I Tego Arcana Dei, as the Ark conceals the secret of God. I have no proof of what may be in the coffin, but the first parchment refers to the treasure as "He is dead". There is a skull in the Tenier's painting and also in the first Poussin painting. And there is also a skull with crossed bones at the top of the entrance to the Church of Mary Magdalene. Could this be the place where the mortal remains of Christ were kept for centuries in a stone tomb, before being moved to Arcadia, Washington DC? In the Roman empire, death bodies were usually cremated. This was against the Chris-

tians religious beliefs and the first Christians were the first to perform burial rites. So, could Mary Magdalene and her protectors have removed the body of Christ from the obituary and carry Him to ensure a proper burial, later fleeing to south of France and hiding the mortal remains in the ark in the French Pyrenees Mary Magdalene church?

If Poussin shows the good news that the Ark is at its final destination in Arcadia, near the Shepherdess (the bloodline), the scrolls say that Teniers holds the key. In both paintings of the Temptations of St Anthony, the treasure the Saint is protecting is a Book. As if the scrolls were trying to say that the Ark is safe in Arcadia, but the Book is still at risk from the demons in Europe.

But Colon never reached North America! His power dwindled quickly as the Spanish realized they had been deceived by a Portuguese spy tricking them into a wild goose chase west.

So, the Ark was taken to America around the time of Poussin paintings in 1627. But based on Poussin, the Book remained harassed by the demons in Europe – because it never went to the New World and remained where Ladislau III and Colon had hidden it.

The violence of the Inquisition in Portugal, which lasted until the nineteenth century and included a suspiciously enormous list of prohibited books, suggests the church had been desperately looking for the lost Book. Colon's son, Fernando, amassed the largest private library in Europe of his time. Why? Was he trying to hide a secret Book in his massive library, to save it from the claws of the Inquisition fires?

The natural hiding place would be Tomar, the headquarters of the Order of Christ. If the secret found by the original nine Templars in Jerusalem was related to the descendants of Christ, the tryptic painting of the Wedding of Canaan would be an appropriate hiding place. The tryptic had been hidden and only rediscovered in the early twentieth century. Of course, if it was indeed there, it would have been found during the restauration works in

1930 and may have disappeared again.

I have been insisting with Father Paulo, from the Convent in Tomar, to allow me to conduct research on the library and archives. I guess he suspects of something, for he has been adamantly denying any access.

8. Freemasons

Uncle Santiago knows more than what he has been saying. The Freemason's compass and square that are engraved in the stone above our family house in Newport look like a landscape, bringing together Henry Sinclair northern path through the Scottish rugged mountains (the compass) and the hull of the ships Colon took in the southern path (the square).

I have also been doing some gematria work with the symbol. The magic square of the Freemasons, called Square of Saturn, disposes the numbers 1 to 9 in a way that every line, column and diagonal adds 15: the pentagram trinity 5+5+5. In the central line, the numbers 3, 5 and 7 form the number of steps leading into the mid chamber of Salomon's temple. Overlaying the magic square with the pentagram of the square and compass, we get the Venus Pentagram over the Square of Saturn. It creates a numeric code: the pentagram touches 8, 9 and 6 and encircles the 5 (twice, as to draw the pentagram without raising the pen you have to pass through the 5 twice).

*Using a gematria table of the modern French alphabet (Templars being originally French), which links numbers 1 to 9 to letters in sequential rows of 9 letters, we get for the code above: 5 (E O Z); 5 (E **O** Z); 8 (H **R**); 9 (I **S**); 6 (F **P**).*

This allows the construction of "P ROSE", or "Protecteur Rose". The Freemason square and compass symbol emerges from a long line of secret orders starting with the original Protectors of the Rose, the Priory of Sion, the core inner group of the Templars.

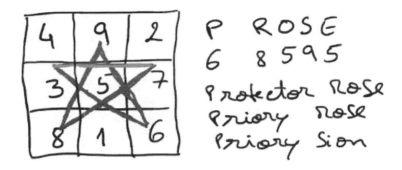

9. Truth is dangerous

The suggestion of a northern path protecting the bloodline of Mary Magdalene from Rosslyn chapel into the New World has been around for decades and that may actually have been positive for the church, bringing a more balanced feminine twist to religion.

But a southern path holding a secret book taken by Colon to America could be dangerous. What is that book, so important to maintain Colon's secret mission hidden for 500 years?

I must be careful. I feel a lot of people following my actions with concern: Professor Noronha, Pedro, Father Carlos in Tomar. I will continue to pretend I am still looking for Colon's treasure in Tomar and convince Father Carlos that is my focus. They surely must know if any treasure was ever hidden in Tomar, it has long been moved, so they should feel safe if they believe I am focused in Tomar.

10. Appendix: The southern and northern paths

X M y

King Solomon + Queen of Sheba

Merovingian dinasty, Kings of Jerusalem
since II a.c.
[under pressure from Muslim invaders, shares secret
with 9 Templar Knights]

Xpo FERENSECRETUM   Xpo FEREN SECRETUS

"Carry a secret of christ"   "carry the secret christ"

ORDER OF CHRIST   TEMPLARS
Segismundo   PRESTER   Sinclair
                    JOHN   Northern Path
Southern Path   tries to   Rosslyn chapel
Tomar covent of christ contact   Scotland
Portugal   by the
                    east, to
Hispaniola   join the   Newport Tower
New World   cruzades   Rhode Island

Rejoined by columbus?
Unik the wind rose *
with the rose line *

Washington capitol

Santiago Jagiello
Sophia and Sarah Jagiello

VALLADOLID, MAY 1506

(Fernando)

*"You have your way. I have my way. As for the right way, the
correct way, and the only way, it does not exist."*
FRIEDRICH NIETZSCHE

F
ather lied in bed, tormented by his arthritis and
blinded from decades on the seas, looking at the sun
through the astrolabe. It would soon be my turn to
take his secret on my shoulders. I would inherit Christopher
Colon's books and riches, but together with the wealth came
a massive conspiracy, the extent of which I was just starting
to grasp.

The metamorphosis of Segismundo Alemão into
Christopher Colon has multiple layers, in a game of mirrors
where reality and shadows mock those who have in the past
or will in the future try to look beyond the carefully crafted
tale created by my Father and his accomplices. The complex web of forgery runs deep and wide and has surely taken
the combined efforts of many. An entire nation, actually, I
suspect. Looking back at all the fragments of information
Father confided in me during our long journey, I guess Father
has been a secret agent of the King of Portugal, D. João II, in
a plot to deceive the Spanish Catholic Kings into taking the
western route to the Indies.

But there is something else… below this top layer of
political conspiracy, there is a deeper mission, to protect
what Father calls the Book of the Queen, the Wind Rose.

Back in 1506, as Father lied in his deathbed, I was still a young man, barely eighteen, and had only a faint realization of these mysteries.

Father's fourth expedition was probably the most bizarre and insane of all his travels. Looking at the logbook, he seemed in a frenzy to meet something or someone in the Terra Firma, going back and forth on those new lands. The tornado at Hispaniola, the push westwards to Terra Firma, shipwreck, mutiny, captivity in a savage island, the moon eclipse, well, it had all the ingredients of a tragi-comedy imagined by a theatre troupe.

Upon my return to Seville, in November 1504, I kept my promise and helped Father recover his possessions. Nicolas de Ovando had been so keen to show off to the Castilian Queen, that he decided, despite Father's warnings of a tornado, to send the fleet with the riches he had so brutally robbed from the natives. Thirty ships departed Hispaniola in 1502, amongst them one that carried the belongings of the previous Governor of the islands, my Father. That's why father was so desperate, ravenous crazy, when he heard the Ovando persisted in sending the fleet. He feared it would be decimated by the storm and his assets sunk. At the time, I attributed his irate rampages to a stingy concern for his jewels and furniture... Father could be quite brutal and tyrannical. I now understand he was desperate not because of the endangered riches but because the secret Book was at risk of being lost.

I guess Father felt vindicated when we found out the only ship that reached Spain was the one with his assets, La Aguja, the Needle. Was this a miracle from God?

I travelled to Valladolid to meet Father on his deathbed. Even though, by then, I already knew about the Father's secret Book, a secret I had sworn to protect, I still failed to understand what it might be, the Book Father so desperately protected and made me promise to continue protecting, keeping his large library where the Book could be maintained inconspicuously hidden.

Was it a map to a secret treasure of the Templars, the Holy Grail found in Jerusalem? In Jamaica, Father made be swear to protect his library, hiding the Book. But over the previous two years, after returning from the Indies, I had looked into all the books and annotations in his recovered library and did find nothing that could be a threat to the foundations of the church of Rome, as Father claimed. In his will, Father has meticulously laid down how he wants to distribute his wealth and titles after his death, and there he clearly stipulates I should use at least 5% of the annual income from his assets to build up "the largest collection of books of our times". Knowledge is the only asset you owe no-one. But Father has another reason to insist I keep building the library: to hide and protect the secret Book, lost amongst millions of other books.

I looked hard, into sleepless nights, trying to identify the secret book so that I could at least know what I was supposed to protect. There are several valuable books and most have extensive side notes from my Father, but I had found nothing that could require such a huge conspiracy and secret. Was Father just fantasizing?

I went all the way from Granada to Valladolid to say goodbye to the Admiral of the Ocean Sea, but also to ask him in confidence about the Book. He lied febrile, a shadow of the strong, imposing man he once had been. I needed to know. When I raised the question, Father looked at me with those deep blue eyes and seemed to mock.

"Oh, Fernando, you are wise and tenacious. That is good, that is good. You deserve to know, indeed. If I have not told you before, it is not because I mistrust you, but to protect you. Ignorance is a bliss. It would be better if you know nothing, for when they come."

"Who will come Father? Rest your spirit, all is done now..."

"Oh, do not fool yourself!! They will come, do not doubt. With flaming torches and righteous priests to burn it down, if need be. They will not stop until they find the forbidden Book. They have already exterminated the Templars, in search for the treasure, but it was useless. They are always looking in the wrong place, because that's where we lead them – feign interest for what you do not want, in order to drive your enemy's attention away from what really matters. The Templars took the necessary measures to protect the secret: The Rose Line was taken to Norway, Scotland and west to Nova Scotia. Rosslyn Chapel, the Rose Line Chapel built by the heirs of Earl Henry Sinclair, stands as gatekeeper for the Northern Path. The Wind Rose was taken to the Germanic forests by the Southern Path, and then hidden by my father at the edges of the world, in Madeira island. When those Pope kneelers arrived in Bourgogne to chase the Templars, they found nothing. Not even the fleet in La Rochelle, those fools. The ships were already secured along the coast of Portugal, the seeds of the largest sea exploration plan of human history. The Age of Discoveries is not just a matter of expanding the Christian faith or conquering lands or trading spices. Many were involved in setting in motion the clogs of a chain of events that will ultimately lead to a new Promised Land to the west, a new world of intellectual freedom, built on the foundations of all faiths – Christians, Jews, Muslims – under the same, single God.

I digress, but you must understand how it all started, the quest for the new Atlantis, the Avalon, the western Promised Land. Once the noise of time passes, it shall all become plain. This plot in which I was central figure, clearing the eastern route for the Portuguese, while controlling the western colonies and thus commanding the route to bring the Wind Rose back to the Rose Line. Those western islands of the Antilles were supposed to be mine!

I strived to command a powerful colony in those islands, believing that would be the best way to reach the Northern Path. I dragged my feet in those sweet islands, avoiding to push forward to Terra Firma, holding the center and blocking a central passage to the southern seas, while establishing a stronghold at my command from which to send secret expeditions in search of the northern Templars.

The plan was to instigate a rebellion and crown myself King of the Western Indies, the front gate for the new Promised Land. But, alas! King Fernando probably suspected my intentions and sent the dog Bobadilla to arrest me, forbidding me from setting foot on Hispaniola! They feared my rebellion would succeed [103]! So Bobadilla arrived, sent me in shackles to Spain, and went on to crush the Indians. A bloodbath... I fear all natives will either be enslaved or massacred."

I was astonished with what Father was telling me. "You mean, during the eight years you governed the West Indies, you sent secret missions to..."

"Yes, son. But that must remain a secret. I am dying and you must know, so that you can understand the need to protect the secret from the devils cloaked in priest robes that will try to find and destroy the Book. In fact, you were present while it happened, but you were too young to comprehend."

"I am older now, Father. I can understand, but I need the true facts! There is so much fog and noise around your name. The "hidalgos" of the Spanish kingdoms hate you, from Andalucía to Aragon..."

"Oh, let them! They have reasons for that!"

Father laughed with a mixture of gusto and bitterness, until a fit of cough interrupted him. Then he continued, telling me the most extraordinary story of his secret life and mission.

"I was wrong, though. The travails and court games to consolidate my position simply delayed me from the true goal. I have to thank the dog Bobadilla for pushing me out of that path. In 1501, the Corte-Real brothers finally found the northern Templars in the New World, many leagues south of Nova Scotia. The Raven Knight, the rock statue in Corvo island, had been showing the way all along: The Rose Line was waiting, at latitude 41º North. So, I had to complete the mission my father and the Old Man had charged me. But the Book was in Hispaniola. In the second expedition I took the small silver casket that contains the Book.

I secretly met Gaspar and Miguel Corte-Real, after Gaspar's first voyage to Terra Nova, Newfoundland. We established recognition signs to ensure I would be able to reach them. Gaspar, and later Miguel, sailed back to the New World, where the round tower of the Templar church is set permanently with a great fire at the top, visible for leagues at sea, like a welcoming statue holding a torch to guide those in search of it. I would take the silver casket myself, or through a messenger bearing my silver bullet as proof of identity. In exchange, they would send back a lead bullet, so that I could be certain the mission had been completed."

My eyes involuntarily fell on the chain around Father's neck, with the lead bullet, as Father continued his amazing story.

"The casket has no openings, built as a solid block of silver with an ancient magnetic mechanism. Only the ring can open the delicate mechanism. There are only two rings. One is carried by the Grand Master of the southern path Templars. The Infante used it. And now I carry it. The other ring is carried by the Grand Master of the northern path, the Scottish Templars."

I looked briefly at Father's left hand, where I had seen the gold ring for years, a simple round sigil with an embossed hooked cross, which I now carry.

"You understand why I had to make that fourth expedition? That was my last opportunity to take the Book to its final destination, reunite it with the Rose Line. I had to find an excuse to stop at Hispaniola, reach La Isabella and then take my ships northbound. The silver casket was in La Isabella, my new town on the north shore of Hispaniola, from where I had been sending exploratory expeditions to the northwestern lands. I had a secret fleet of 11 sturdy caravels in La Isabella, the ships that supposedly drowned in tornados in 1495/96. The settlers moved to the new town of Santo Domingo in the south coast, and neither them nor the Indians approach La Isabella, fearing the spirits of the drowned sailors."

"What do you mean, Father? La Isabella was abandoned, a deserted ghost town ripped apart by hurricanes and disease..."

"Oh, do not believe all you hear! In 1493, during the second voyage, I established La Isabella, west of Natividade. I needed a secret stronghold for my hidden mission, protected from the natives but also hidden from the Spaniards. La Isabella harbored my secret fleet of 11 ships, which between 1493 and 1502 explored the Terra Firma to the north, all the way to Newfoundland."

"You mean, the Lost Armada..."

"My Lost Armada, yes. Oh, they called me incompetent, ignorant, tyrannical... 11 ships, including the flagship

Marigalante, disappeared in 1495 during a hurricane. Do you think I would lose 11 ships??!! I studied the skies and the seas all my life... In 1495 those 11 ships were safely hidden away in a southern bay when the hurricane hit. I claimed they had all been lost during the storm. And they believed it, the fools! Ah, ignorance is so easy to trick.

Then my agents started spreading rumors that La Isabella was hunted by the ghosts of the dead sailors from the Lost Armada. It also helped that the Spaniards can't keep their dicks inside their pants and spread all type of diseases. It was a carnage, unfortunately, but it kept the Spanish and the natives away from la Isabella for many years. No one dared approach the haunted place. Within 3 years, we had a new capital in the south shore, Santo Domingo, and all settlers moved there. La Isabella was deserted, safe for my faithful men to set their base, with the 11 ships. From there they explored the lands to the north, looking for the northern path of the Templars, the heirs of Prince Henry Sinclair."

"... That is... extraordinary, Father."

"Well, finally, in 1501, the Corte-Real brothers found the Northern Path and were at 41ºN waiting for me, with a beacon, a tower of fire to signal the way. I had to reach La Isabella, to retrieve the silver casket with the Book. That meant harboring in Hispaniola, despite the royal prohibition.

I took the Santiago de Palos, the Bermuda, because she was unfit for the perils of the voyage. I intended to have a good excuse to enter Santo Domingo, to trade the caravel. But Ovando refused, and I could not take any of my ships near shore.

So I had no other option. I had to sail the ships so hard, to the utter limit, before returning to Hispaniola in such a state of disrepair and risk to the crew that Ovando would have no choice but to let us enter.

I took the ships back and forth along the Terra Firma coast, looking for the elusive passage westwards. The shipwreck on the coast of Jamaica almost ruined my last hope of accomplishing the mission, but by God's will it actually offered a unique opportunity to drift away unnoticed."

"But... I thought the Book was amongst your possessions shipped by Ovando to Spain in the fleet, whose departure you so desperately tried to avoid. The Book was in a ship bound to Spain, at grave risk of sinking, so how could you plan to take it to that tower of fire in the northwestern lands?"

"Oh, Fernando, you are almost a grown man. Deceit and cunning are the only weapons we have against the immense political and military army of the Bishops if Rome and their European Lords. You must make them look where the treasury is not! The Book was never in those damn Ovando's ships. You can never trust men or fate. The Book was safe in my city of La Isabella."

"I remain at a loss, Father... I never abandoned you throughout those two and a half years, you could not have made such a long trip north without m...."

"But it was not me! Diogo Méndez, remember? He was away for almost 12 months, with a very small retinue of loyal men. Twelve months! What took him so long? Sure, he got stranded more time than necessary by Ovando in Xaragua, but still he had plenty of time to reach La Isabella, sail out and return.

Méndez completed the mission. He took the silver bullet and returned with the lead bullet of the Corte-Real, proving the silver casket with the Book had been delivered.

The Book of the Queen and the Rose Line are finally united in the new continent. Oh, yes, it is an entire continent, Fernando! The Portuguese have been exploring it for almost 100 years and it goes uninterrupted from the icy waters of Newfoundland all the way south of Vera Cruz. Few realized the consequences of Juan de La Cosa's map. It's there, in La Cosa's map... the entire coast of the new continent, from Nova Scotia to Vera Cruz [104].

My son, the New World is ready to emerge as the New Jerusalem. A grand new continent where the descendants of the Rose can establish a land of freedom, away from the shackles of the Vatican, the hypocrite beatitude of the priests and the petty struggles between small kingdoms. A huge country is on the making!"

"You mean, by Cortez, in the Spanish empire, or by Cabral in Brazil?"

"No, no... forget, just daydreaming. Anyway, the mission is done my son, I can rest in peace. You, however, you are the one that must maintain this farce. They will squeeze you, manipulate you in every possible way. So you must keep the plot. They must continue to believe the Book is somewhere amongst my library. The madman Torquemada brainwashed Isabella to expel the Jews and launch the Inquisition, convincing her she is the apocalyptic angel cleaning mankind for the next coming of Christ. So much rubbish.

The Book of the Queen shows all that gibberish is just nonsense fabricated by men to provide hope for the oppressed, hope which is then used by other men to continue the oppression. Now the Inquisitors are burning Jews and witches and throwing books into the flames, for what? We must keep them busy here, looking for the Book in Granada, where it is not.

I will surely roll on my deathbed laughing as those imbecile try, for decades to come, to read meaning in my "Profecias" looking for hints of the treasure. Oh God, how much pleasure I took writing those ramblings of a madman, just to confound them, throwing a bone in one direction and then a hint in another one, making them run around like fools.

They will turn their minds around trying to read hidden meanings."

I had learned to ignore Father's bitterness and to hide his blasphemies. How much of this was true and how much the fabrications of a madman? I have lived all my life with these doubts. Truth is as elusive as the mirage of land in a foggy misty morning at sea. Even now, that I know what the Book contains, I sometimes doubt whether it truly exists, secretly hidden in America, or was just a figment of Father's tired mind.

"Extraordinary, father. You never stop surprising me! So, we were stranded in Jamaica waiting for Méndez to reach La Isabella, and from there sail north with the secret Book?"

"Yes, yes... Oh, how I desired to do it myself. But it could not be. Méndez took a ship in La Isabella and sailed north, for 5 weeks desperately looking for signs. They reached a calm bay brimming with fish and many inland canals. And there it was, in the flat expanse, a round stone tower, similar to the church chancel in Tomar, with a rectangular nave running east-west from the round tower.

A huge fire was burning like a beacon, a welcoming torch, at the top of the tower [105]. For one hundred years, the heirs of the bloodline kept the fire burning at the top of the round tower, which could be seen for miles at sea, waiting for the final reunion of the Northern and Southern Paths.

There, my men delivered the silver casket containing the Wind Rose, the Book of the Queen. It is now safely hidden away, protected by the founders of a new country still in the making. This New World is being built on foundations of truth. And truth is the only protection against tyranny, the safeguard of intellectual and religious freedom and free enterprise. How I wish I could last longer to witness the birth of this New World. That is my true deed. Little else matters. A New World is being created, and it matters not to me if my true name is known to the world or remains hidden. I am ':XpoferenS', Segismundo, Member of the Order of Christ, carry a secret of Christ. Let them turn their brains inside out trying to understand that."

I realize Father was always truthful about his intentions. Again and again, in his letters to the Spanish monarchs, to the Pope or in the journeys logbook, he stated his true purpose: the crusade to rebuild Jerusalem. In the log book of his first expedition, an entry dated 26 December 1492, Father wrote that "all gains for my enterprise shall be used to rebuild Jerusalem".

The references are persistent. In a letter to the monarchs in February 1500 he made another clear reference to his Templar mission: "the Temple of Jerusalem be rebuilt with wood and gold from Ophir, with it restore the Holy Church more glorious than it was." From Jamaica, on 7 July 1503, Father touched the brim of his full secret when he wrote in the logbook "Jerusalem and Mount Sião will be reconstructed". He did not write 'reconquered', but 'reconstructed', as if the old Rome church was decrepit, falling apart at the weight of so much hypocrisy and self-interest, and the only option was to restart again, reconstructing elsewhere from the beginning.

My Father was the last Templar knight, and true to his mission he lived obsessed with rebuilding the Temple... but the Templars and the orders that succeeded them have long ago foregone the liberation of the old city. The last crusade is not about reconquering Jerusalem, but rebuilding it in a New World.

Almost none of the ships from Columbus fleets has ever been found, despite extensive searches from treasure hunters and academics. None of the three ships from the First Fleet was

ever found. Santa Maria was reportedly wrecked on the beaches of Hispaniola and probably burned down by the natives, but what about the Nina and the Pinta?

A total of 11 ships, including the flagship Marigalante, mysteriously disappeared in Isabela Bay during the second expedition, in 1494/95, supposedly wrecked in a tornado. Indiana University's Center for Underwater Science is currently conducting research and excavations in Isabella Bay, looking for those lost ships – but so far, nothing was found.

The "Lost Fleet of Columbus" [106] *has intrigued experts and adventurers for many years, providing ample material for speculation.*

WASHINGTON DC, JUNE 2019

Library of Congress

"Father, forgive them, for they don't know what they are
doing."
LUKE 23:34

"Men, forgive Him, for He does not know what He is doing."
JOSÉ SARAMAGO, THE GOSPEL ACCORDING TO JESUS CHRIST

S avanah landed on Washington DC international airport
shortly after 4.00am, blood rayed eyes and messy hair
from the sleepless night. A non-descript Mercedes with
tainted windows collected her on the runway and drove her
straight to Capitol Hill. The car stopped by the Neptune
Fountain at the front of the Library of Congress Thomas
Jefferson Building. At this hour of the night, the illuminated bronze sculptures seemed to come alive, the majestic,
bearded God of the seas surrounded by muscular tritons and
playful sensual nymphs riding between the jets of water in
galloping sea horses. In the grottoes behind these masters of
the seas, an orchestra of sea creatures, turtles, frogs and sea
serpents, dance and sing their perverse, devilish, never-end-
ing tune, a banter of the fates of the world above water.

Savanah realized the irony... Colon himself had to
fight his own internal and external sea demons and gods. As
she entered the Library building, Savanah felt she was passing a door into another world, governed by ancient myster-

ies and guarded by these sea gods. Would the sea gods let her enter their domains and make sense of the mystery, or reject her as unworthy?

The military intelligence officer who had escorted her from the airport now led Savanah through the corridors of the gigantic building. The Library of Congress is housed in three buildings in Washington DC plus a storage and conservation centre in Virginia. The three Washington buildings are all connected by underground tunnels, so that users need to clear security only once.

The Library of Congress is the research library serving the US Congress and functions as the legal repository of copyright protection in the US, receiving two copies of every publication in the country. The collection extends for about 838 miles. The books alone would amount to 10 terabytes of uncompressed text. It houses more than 32 million books and print materials in 470 languages, 61 million manuscripts, 1 million issues of world newspapers from the past three centuries, and millions of maps, music sheets, photographs, comic books, microfilm reels and sound recordings. The Library of Congress also hosts the largest rare book collection in North America, including the draft of the Declaration of Independence and a Gutenberg Bible, the Betts Stradivarius and the Cassavetti Stradivarius.

The military officer turns into a room she knew well, the Hispanic Reading Room. Four colorful murals in the entryway walls depict scenes of the encounters between Old and New World. The room itself is vibrant with its high vaulted ceilings, large windows and colorful blue and white Mexican tiles on the walls. Running along the walls are the names of great luso-hispanic writers, including Cervantes, Sarmiento, Camões and Dario. At the top of the south wall, the stainless steel mural depicting Columbus' coat of arms contemplates the readers in the heavy wood benches, as if ensuring order over its dominions, although at this early hour the benches were still empty.

Uncle Santiago expected her, standing by one of the windows. When she arrived, Santiago nodded his thanks to the military officer and took Savanah into his private study room.

"Uncle, what is all this? What are you doing?"

"Princess Sophia, I am also happy to see you safe and sound... there are higher powers at play and a secret of our family you probably suspected for long", uncle said flatly. "Sorry, no tea at this time of night. May I get you some other drink?"

"I could use something strong, yes."

Bach was playing on a digital speaker, set on the bookshelf behind his desk. The Chaconne, BWV 1004. 'The soul of the angels', as uncle called it. Spiritually powerful, emotionally powerful and technically transcending. He poured the two of them a large glass of Glenfidish 21-year old Scottish pure malt. Handing a glass to Savanah, he noted: "A person who creates a work like this must feel empty, at the end. As if there is nothing else to do." He was referring to Bach. "The act of creating - writing, painting, composing - is always painful. Probably the closest a man ever gets from the pain of giving birth."

Santiago sat down and looked straight into Savanah's eyes. "Maybe now you will take what happened to Sarah 13 years ago a bit more seriously. Professor Noronha called me when you were on your way to Tomar, pleading me to get you out."

"Professor Noronha called you? You are not going to say he is a US spy in Lisbon, now, will you", said Savanah, remembering her deep suspicions about Professor Noronha.

"Well, kind of. Raven had been working closely with Professor Noronha and we were following it from a distance.

I saw the entire thing as a great initiation for your sister. You see, I was preparing her – both of you in fact, but you then opted to go off and get rich – to take my role as the guardian of the Secret. When she was brutally assassinated, we immediately suspected Father Paulo in Tomar. I had though the Church would clear away from it, as the Secret has not been in Tomar for centuries. But I was wrong. So wrong. And that cost Raven's life. We tried to prove the Church's involvement, but there were no proofs, it was a rather clean job, no fingerprints, no eye witness willing to come forward. We had a quiet talk with Professor Noronha. Although at first he wanted to just forget everything and move into retirement, we convinced him to keep a close look at everyone at the university and in Convento de Cristo in Tomar. I guess the two million dollars we offered him also helped..."

"Ah, so that's how Professor Noronha came to afford the house, but preferred to omit the source of funds" though Savanah, but let it go. Instead, she asked, a bit more strongly than intended "Who are 'we'?"

"Ohh, we have had many names. Once an order got compromised, the group had to disappear and regroup under a new form. The Priory of Sion. The Templars. The Knights of the Round Table. The Illuminati. The Rosacruxians. The Freemasons... Come on, Sarah, you surely have suspected that long ago. You simply could not make you rational mind around it. A small brotherhood who continues to protect the secret of the Book of the Queen."

Savanah sat in silence, wondering. How much, for how long, had uncle Santiago known? She was increasingly tired, from the excitement of the last few days, the air journey and the recent revelations.

"Look, uncle. I am exhausted. I need to go home and put all this behind my back. Hugh is probably waiting for me in the morning."

"Hugh only expects you two days from now" Santiago looked at her from the brim of his glass. "Officially, you have disembarked in the Azores and checked in into a nice cosy hotel for some well-deserved holidays. A young lady with a copy of your passport will board tomorrow a plane from the Azores to New York. That way we put off the trail of those Vatican mice who have been following you. They will think it is all over, you just accepted Pedro's story, took a few days to rest in the beautiful Azores island and boarded home to your husband. I hope that will keep you safe, at least for now."

"And do not worry about Hugh", uncle Santiago continued. "An email has been sent from Mrs Clifton email account telling her husband that outlandish tale of mistaken identities and that you will land in NY in two-days' time..."

"What do you mean? The US military has hacked into my email account to send a false email under my name? Gosh, I will not ask about that..."

"Uhhh, yeah, please don't."

As she sipped though her 21-year old Glenfidish, she felt the Scottish single malt warming her body and mind.

"Sorry, uncle. This has all been a bit... surreal. You are right, though. I suspected something amiss was at play. Pedro confession is odd. He was aware Raven was off to Tomar and her twin sister was arriving that morning to stay at Raven's flat with her husband. There is no way this whole story of mistaken identities is true."

"Indeed, Sophia. And why has he confessed so promptly when there are no fingertips or any other evidence to link him to the murder? He is protecting someone. Indeed, we intersected a call from Father Paulo in Tomar to Professor Pedro's mobile, right after you left Tomar a few days ago, telling him to move to Plan B. When we found Professor Pedro confessed so easily, we knew something was amiss and decided to take you home. Pity in 2006 we didn't have the resources at our disposal we have today. Thank the NSA for that."

"I feel I am telling you what you already know", Savanah said, relaxing a bit into her sofa. "Raven was after something big. There is this treasure, this Templar Holy Grail, whatever it is, hidden in Convento de Cristo in Tomar. With your power, we must dig deeper. We can't let this secret go on, Raven was murdered probably as she got closer to it. We must uncover the secret."

Santiago took a long sip of his whiskey and looked out of the window towards the Potomac river. Night still engulfed the sleeping city, with the lights of Constitution Avenue and Independence Avenue cutting a straight line to the Lincoln Memorial, hidden from where they stand by the Capitol.

"There is no need. The secret is long gone from Portugal." Uncle Santiago stated matter of factly. He seemed to want to leave it there, but Savanah's enquiring eyes forced him to add "The Templar Treasure has never been in Tomar or anywhere near such a high profile and scrutinized place. How could it? There were stories and conspiracy theories and false whispers laid around just to keep the others away, looking elsewhere. We managed to protect the secrets of the Temple of Solomon for 2.000 years, in spite of the furious and sometimes demonical attempts of so many to discover it."

"So...", prodded Savanah, too tired to entertain her uncle's secretive manners.

"It is here.", Santiago finally said, looking deeply into her eyes.

"Here, you mean... in Washington?"

"Indeed."

WASHINGTON DC, JUNE 2020

Library of Congress

*"Give me your tired, your poor, / Your huddled masses yearn-
ing to breathe free, / The wretched refuse of your teeming
shore. / Send these, the homeless, tempest-tost to me, / I lift
my lamp beside the golden door!"*
EMMA LAZARUS, "THE NEW COLOSSUS"

Savanah took her time to let it all sink into her mind. She moved towards her bag and retrieved Raven's notebook, flipping quickly through the pages to those mysterious google maps that had eluded her from the start.

Savanah moved to a table and sat down, flattening the notebook. "Raven's maps seem to suggest some weird connection between Lisbon, in Portugal, the city of Belém in Brazil and Washington DC. I have actually checked this in google maps."

There is a straight line that goes from Belém in Lisbon, where we can still today see the monument to the Age of Discoveries, to Belém in Brazil, passing Madeira where the Slav king Ladislau III took refuge after his disappearance from the battle of Varna. The city of Belém in Brazil is exactly on the spot where the equatorial line crosses the north-south divide of the Tordesillas Treaty. Could this be on purpose? Some mystical considerations that took the Portuguese King D. João II and his agent Christopher Colon to force the

Tordesillas line into its final location, crossing the equator exactly where the Lisbon-Madeira line intercepts the equatorial line? Well, while at the same time guaranteeing for the Portuguese control over Brazil, 6 years before its official discovery by Alvares Cabral.

There is another straight line going from Belém, Lisbon to the Corvo Island in the Azores. Belém in Lisbon, Corvo in the Azores and Belém in Brazil are the vertices of a Pythagorean triangle.

Savanah did a double take. Corvo means "Raven" in Portuguese. The coat of arms of the city of Lisbon includes two ravens. And she could also vaguely remember some story she read about a large stone statue of a horseback knight found in Corvo island by the first settlers, with an outstretched arm pointing westwards.

"Uncle, what is going on? What was Raven hinting at?"

"Sarah had a brilliant mid. And so do you, Sophia.", answered Santiago, prodding her to continue.

It seems that during the Age of Discoveries, while opening the world to new era of science and cultural interchange that culminated in the Renaissance, the Portuguese were at the same time plotting mystic geomarkers on the surface of the world they explored.

But it didn't stop there, the mix between mystic symbology and the most advanced science of its time.

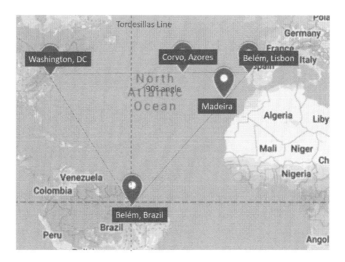

Santiago added, "The founding fathers of this country were well into the plot, in fact. George Washington was a known freemason Grand Master, looking to create this new country on the solid foundations of the Enlightenment, free from the shackles of the Vatican. A country of freedom, a spiritual land where mankind could strive for progress and free thinking. When the American founding fathers were looking for a location to place the capital of this new country, they chose... a swamp, a humid and hot wasteland with apparently nothing to justify the choice. Except that for a master Templar like George Washington, this exact spot where we stand today lies in a straight line from Lisbon to the Azores, forming an isosceles triangle linking Belém in Lisbon to Belém in Brazil and Washington DC. Maybe in honour of the secret places where the forbidden Book had been hidden... Lisbon or Tomar in Portugal, Belém in Brazil and finally Washington in the United States. We have no proofs the Book has been to Brazil, but... Brazil was initialled called by Cabral "Land of Vera Cruz", the land of the True Cross. So it is possible that Columbus, before taking the Book to Newport Tower in 1504, had hidden it in Belém in Brazil. But this is speculation."

"Right, uncle. We will never know... Anyway, this is not really an isosceles triangle, the length of the straight line from Washington DC to Belem in Lisbon is shorter than the line from Belem in Lisbon to Belem in Brazil."

"Do not underestimate how advanced those rough sailors from the Age of Discoveries were. They were probably centuries ahead of their time, and due to the "police of secrecy" enforced by the Portuguese kings, we have only second-hand accounts of their scientific knowledge. Check your google maps. Instead of measuring the distance in a straight line, check for true distances. If you account for the curvature of the planet, the distance from Washington to Belém, Lisbon is 5.845 km. From Lisbon to Belém, Brazil it is 6.068km. Under 4% difference, which is actually quite amazing!"

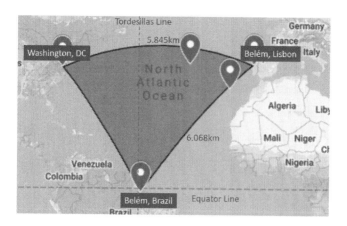

"Gosh, ... I mean."

A few months ago, Savanah would have dismissed all this as just too much imagination by people with too little to do. Now, after all she had seen over the past weeks – she would take anything.

"What you are telling me is that a long line of kings

and Templar knights, from Jerusalem to the German Holy Roman Empire, to Portugal and Brazil and finally the United States have gone to such great lengths to protect this... forbidden Book... while keeping themselves united by a web of secrets, designed by geomarkers into the location of our own capital city. Gosh, that's a bit..."

"Well, even if you don't believe it, our founding fathers did. They were creating a new nation, fuelled by a revolutionary spirit of establishing a new world. The hidden symbolism is everywhere in our national emblems. The European nations have their symbols created through centuries of a complex and bloody history. The nascent U.S.A was a young country. Lacking old symbols, the founders had to resort to new ones. The one-dollar bill is full of this symbology. On the front of the bill you have of course George Washington, a freemason. On the back, the Great Seal is composed of two extraordinary images full of symbolism. To the right, the eagle with 13 arrows on the right claw, 13 leaves and 13 berries on the left claw, 13 stars above and the moto 'E Pluribus Unum' composed of 13 letters. On the left side of the dollar bill, you have the pyramid, a symbol of stability and strength, with 13 layers of brick. Of course, the 13 may be a reference to the original 13 states, but... would they privilege these 13 states against all the others, when the aim was to unite the nation? There is an alternative less publicised explanation... you know, the Templars... "

"What? Here we go again..."

"Just... listen, Sophia. The pyramid is topped by the great seeing eye, a Freemason symbol whereby human action is judged only by God and not by any arbitrary power on Earth. The date below the pyramid in roman numerals MDCCLXXVI, or 1776, is the date of the Declaration of Independence of the US, representing the founding of the nation... if you take out the MCX, which is 111(0), you get DCLXVI, which is 666, the hexagram of the six-pointed Seal of Salomon, the greatest reference to the Knights of the Salomon Temple, or Templars."

Savanah looked doubtful, but too tired to argue. Her mind floated somewhere outside her body, as if watching the scene from above.

"It may be jut coincidences", Santiago conceded. "But there are a lot of coincidences on the founding symbols or our nation."

Santiago continued. "My point is, Savanah...It doesn't matter whether you believe it or not. If others believed in those symbols and were ready to fight for them, making an impact on the world, on your world, then those symbols are very real to you even if you don't believe them! This undercurrent of secret societies and esoteric orders has throughout the ages refused to accept the tyranny of absolute power. Absolut power breeds corruption and curtails innovation. Free spirits, wild as they might be, serve as counterbalance to the mainstream power and the mindless acceptance of the order by the masses."

"I guess...", accepted Savanah with a slight slump of her elbows and a vacant sense of withdrawal. The feeling of emptiness as her mind looked at her body from above was tearing her soul apart, unable to focus.

"The Templars were extinguished and rounded up for massacre by King Philip IV of France on Friday, 13 October 1307. This may be the reason Friday 13 is considered unlucky. Number 13 has always been fateful for the Templars and the secret they protect. The twelve apostles... were in fact thirteen. But the thirteenth was dogmatically excluded from the canons of the Church she helped to found. Atrocities were committed, thousands of men and women and millions of books were burned in a desperate search to find and destroy the forbidden Book containing her word."

Savanah, who had been looking away through the window, turned her head towards her uncle. Their eyes locked, anticipating the meaning of Santiago's cryptic last comment...

WASHINGTON DC,
JUNE 2020

U.S. Congress, Capitol Hill

*Is man merely a mistake of God's? Or God merely a mistake
of man?*
FRIEDRICH NIETZSCHE

Savanah was tired, but curiosity kept driving her mind.

"So, uncle, are you going to show me?"

"What, Sarah?"

"This… Book, the Holy Grail, whatever it is you claim is hidden here in Washington."

Santiago looked away for an instant, lost in his own thoughts and memories.

"Well… it is indeed high time you know the truth, Sophia. All those history quizzes we played when you and your sister were young were not just child plays. You were being prepared to take the command of the ship and continue protecting the secret. I have served my time and must prepare you. Your sister was supposed to take the burden on her shoulders, had it not been for her untimely death. So it lies upon you."

"Oh, don't go there, uncle. You are not going to say me and my sister are the last descendants of Christ on Earth, right? I have seen that movie, for God's sake!"

"Actually, the blood line is long lost. Succession disputes amongst the heirs of the Templars, religious cleansings through the centuries. We have lost track of the true blood line ages ago. It's all just symbolic names, nowadays. Tradition has been maintained by the inner circle who protects the secret to use names with S initials, following from King Solomon and Queen of Sheba, Segismundo, Sinclair... myself, Sarah and Sophia."

He continued, in a calm but assured voice. "What you call the Templar's Holy Grail is in fact the very foundation of this country. Seven centuries ago, chased by Rome for the secret they had been given in Jerusalem, the Templar divided in two secret branches while the main body remained in France, playing a charade with those not-so-secret councils in La Rochelle. The Northern Path took the blood line of Christ and Mary Magdalene, the Rose line, to Scotland and hid the heirs of Christ's in Rosslyn Chapel - the Rose Line chapel. From there, Sinclair sailed west to the New World. These early New World settlers may have descended as far south as Rhode Island, building Newport Tower, a round tower that still survives today near you parents' house in Massachusetts. Legend has it the tower was in fact a beacon, with a fire burning day and night to signal the location for the rendering... waiting patiently for the Southern Path: The Book of the Queen, the Wind Rose. The bloodline may be lost, but the Book of the Queen has endured. And it matters much more than the blood line! Come. I guess at this time of night it will be safe."

Santiago got up from his chair, stretching his muscles. He was tired. For ages he had been tired. Savanah followed him through the rows of ancient books of the Library. It was, Savanah tough has she followed her uncle, the perfect place to hide a secret Book, in the middle of millions of other books. But Santiago kept walking past the rows of books, entering an underground path that links directly the Library to the Capitol. Santiago walked purposefully, used to the corridors of power and those Washington passages.

Ever since Savanah could remember, uncle Santiago had been a US general permanently stationed as head of security in the US Capitol. He exited the passage from the underground corridor by swiping a security pass and ascended, continuing to walk purposefully towards the large rotunda. They were directly under the dome of the US Capitol, the walls around them covered in frescoes. During the day it would be virtually impossible to stand here, in this empty wide rotunda, as thousands of visitors pass through it.

Above them, Savanah knew, was the crowning feature of the US Capitol, the female bronze statue of Armed Freedom.

Santiago and Savanah climbed to the first floor and rounded through the veranda towards the Senate hall. Instead of entering the large wooden doors, Santiago entered through a barely distinguishable side door, concealed in the wall behind the large statue of Neil Armstrong. He used his security pass and then a heavy key kept at his neck to enter a windowless, controlled atmosphere room, empty except for a round table in the middle. On the table was a stand with a small silver ark, protected under a glass dome.

"Although many people believe the Templars took the Covenant Ark from Jerusalem to the New World, this is actually the true Ark bough to America by the last Templar... Columbus. He reunited the Wind Rose with the Rose Line."

He carefully opened the glass dome. The silver ark was entirely carved with symbols. At the front, the two mirrored chalices. The Holy Grail symbol. The ark had no visible locks or keyhole.

"The Book is the Wind Rose that shows the way, the true original word before the adjustments made during the first centuries of Christendom."

Uncle Santiago respectfully touched the embossed hooked wind rose on the gold ring of his left-hand finger to the mirrored chalices in the ark, and with his right hand carefully opened it. The wind rose and the Chalice joined together to open the ark. The southern path and the northern path re-joined. Male and female reunited.

"This is an ancient magnetic mechanism. Each Freemason Grand Master has a similar ring to this one, with the exact magnetic metal embedded in the seal. Only this exact magnetic force pulls the mechanism inside the ark to open it. When the Wind Rose seal in the ring touches the Rose Line symbol on the ark, the mechanism is activated and it opens."

Inside the ark stood a small ancient book. On top of the book, a silver bullet.

Santiago took a pair of white cotton gloves from a drawer and picked up the bullet. "The silver bullet of Columbus. A lead bullet, exactly the same size and shape of this one, was found together with Columbus remains at the Santo Domingo Cathedral. No-one has yet understood the meaning of the bullet."

"Seville, you mean...?", interrupted Savanah.

"Well, that's... debatable. But let's not go there", stated Santiago.

"Yes, let's not.", agreed Savanah, resigned. There are only so much mysteries one can handle for a night.

Then, Santiago carefully picks up the Book. "A newly elected US President is required by Constitution to swear an Oath before exercising any presidential powers. It traditionally takes place on the twentieth of January of the year after the election, during an inauguration ceremony. George Washington, a Grand Master of US Masons and the first US

President, was sworn into office on April 30, 1789, the same year as the French Revolution as you surely know. Incoming presidents swear their oath to "protect and defend the Constitution of the United States", raising their right hand while placing the left hand on a Bible. George Washington swore on a Bible borrowed from St. John's Lodge Number 1, the Ancient York Masons Lodge in New York, the largest and oldest organization of Freemasons in the US and for a long time the largest grand lodge in the world in terms of membership. At the end of his oath, he kissed the Bible."

Savanah looked from her uncle towards the old book in his hands, while recalling the stories told by uncle Santiago throughout her childhood. Despite much bogey mumbo-jumbo and weird rituals invented by senile old men just to convince themselves of their own importance, the Masons inner circle have throughout the ages protected the Book. All the lore, tales and conspiracy theories about the Masons... it is mostly fog to confuse those who have tried to destroy the Book. All the esoteric rituals are simply a charade, a farce to hide the only important truth.

"What you see here, Sophia, is the original Bible upon which the first president of this country took his solemn oath. And ever since it has been so. With a few exceptions of presidents who chose not to use a bible, every president of the US is sworn in on this Bible. The Book is kept here, in the US Senate, and it is shown to the world every four years during the inauguration ceremony. Only a few Presidents actually know they are swearing on the Holy Grail, the secret book kept hidden for centuries until it could be taken into daylight and shown to the world by our first President. The true quest of the Holy Grail had been achieved – the creation of a nation of free men, independent from oppressive powers, a nation turned to the future. This is the Book of the Queen, the only remaining complete Bible that preserves the fifth Gospel, eradicated by the Vatican."

He pointed Savanah towards another pair of white cotton gloves in the drawer. She held her breath and carefully takes the Book on her hands, marvelled at it. So... simple, plain, small. The cover of the small book was leather, clearly more recent than the ancient papyrus pages. The front cover leather pictured an image: an embossed rose, on top of an engraved Templar cross with arched arms, as if reaching for the rose.

"The rosacrux, the seal of the first Portuguese kings and the hidden symbol of the Templar Cross carried on the sails of the Caravelas. The Cross of Jesus and the Rose of Mary Magdalene, united.", commented Santiago. The image can be formed as a chalice, rotating over the axis of the cross. The Grail is the Book... but the Grail is also the Chalice, as many have thought. Not the cup of the last supper, but the chalice engraved in the cover of the forbidden Book.

Savanah opened the delicate book and stared blankly at the text. She could not understand the words.

Guessing her incomprehension, uncle Santiago explained. "It is written in a form of Koine Greek, the common language of the Eastern Mediterranean between century 4B.C. and 6A.D. The texts of the New Testament were written in Greek, which was part of the Hellenistic Jewish culture during the Roman empire. Greek was, at the time, spoken by more Jews than Hebrew." Santiago expertly turns the ancient pages, stopping at the first page of each of the 4 Gospels, Matthew, Mark, Luke and John. Until a fifth Gospel...

"The Gospel of Mary Magdalene, the companion and wife of Christ. The Queen. It is the most passionate, clear minded of them, showing us a facet of Christ unknown from the other Gospels, the doubts, the anguish, the fears of Jesus as He looked to find His path. It includes the most complete collection of Jesus's sayings and quotations, many of them recounted, word by word, in Mark, Matthew and Luke. This was the earliest canon, written shortly after Christ's death, used as a common source by the other Gospels." Santiago looked intently as Savanah, to check if she understood what he was about to say. "This is the Q Source... the Book of the Queen!"

Savanah released a slow breath. She had not noticed she had been holding her breath for quite so long.

The Q Source, also called the Q Gospel, is a hypothetical written text that precedes the other Gospels. By 1900, Bible scholars established the foundations of the modern understanding of the New Testament. The widely accepted view today is that Matthew and Luke Gospels both used Mark and an unknown Q as common sources, in addition to their own individual sources. The nearly identical word-for-word similarities between Matthew and Luke in quotations from Jesus, not found in Mark, imply an earlier Q source. Scholars suggest the Q source was probably written in the 30s to 50s, making it the earliest Gospel. Mark was written in the 70s. Matthew is believed to have been written in the 80s and 90s. Luke was probably written around 80 to 110

AD, but there is significant evidence of extensive revisions to Luke's Gospel and also his Acts of the Apostles well into the second century.

It has always been recognized the existence of other non-canonical Gospels, often with different theological views: besides the "approved" 4 Gospels, many others have been rejected as heretic or apocryphal: Thomas (discovered in 1945), Peter, Judas, Mary, James, Nicodemus... The New Testament is a selection of texts approved and arranged by the early Church to sanction the approved view selected by the Clergy. The earliest known complete book with the 27 texts that currently compose the New testament dates from 367AD, arranged by the Bishop of Alexandria. This "official version" of Jesus life and Christian theology was formally approved during the Councils of Hippo in 393 and Carthage in 397AD, and finally Pope Innocent I ratified it in 405AD. It took 4 centuries to select, refine, adjust and finalize the New Testament, setting the canons of Christianity.

If what Uncle Santiago was saying was true, Savanah was holding a version of the New Testament that included the original Q source, the Book of the Queen. Why has the earliest and probably most accurate Gospel been excluded from the New Testament approved 400 years later? Omitting what should have been the most reliable and valuable document...

Savanah leaves, lost in her thoughts. She has much to digest, indeed.

As Savanah walks away, Santiago seats on the sofa, alone with his own secrets. He would have liked to take the discussion with Savanah to the next level. More than the facts, what matters is their meaning. Homo Sapiens, 'homo knowledgeable', is a dated terminology. Computers accumulate terabytes of knowledge and are today more 'Sapiens' than humans. Homo Dubium or Homo Curiosum would be a fitter designation.

Sophia and Sarah had figured out most of the truth. There was still a remaining secret, which was probably too soon for Sophia to take in. His eyes gaze out of the Capitol window, down Union Square gardens, until they land on the Washington Monument.

It is a 555 feet tall obelisk with walls 15 feet thick at the base. The interior stairs have 50 sections. The entire obelisk is a massive symbolic pentagram, pointing towards the sky, reaching God.

The Ark rests in New Arcadia... At the northeast corner, the foundation stone of the obelisk, 21 feet below ground and encased in thick concrete, rests the stone tomb. The ark lies buried under the immense obelisk, reaching the sky.

In 1620, the Pilgrims of the Mayflower established the first successful settlement of what would become the United States, in Plymouth. Besides the Pilgrims, the Mayflower carried a secret load: a stone Ark. Shortly after, in 1627, Poussin announced to the initiated the good news: The Ark of Rennes-le-Chateau was finally at safety, in the New World, away from the greedy and hypocrite claws of the church crawlers.

Et in Arcadia Ego

I Tego Arcana Dei

Christ's mortal body stands as a symbol of the unity of the human and the divine, one and the same. The divine flame that ignited in the steppes of Africa, marking the dawn of the self-aware and self-doubting Homo Sapiens. The sparkle of curiosity and free will that makes humanity an always evolving miracle. But the divinity of the body and the mortality of the divine were unbearable to the church.

Down the avenue linking the Capitol to the Lincoln Memorial, lie a series of living monuments that evoke the artistic, scientific and technological achievements of the unquiet human soul, the divinity and fallibility that makes our humanity. Our capacity to do great good and great evil: The National Gallery of Art, the Air and Space Museum, the National Museum of Natural History, the National Academy of Sciences, but also the Vietnam Memorial.

The pyramidal capstone of the obelisk is the same All Seeing Eye that features at the top of the pyramid in the dollar bill, although the original capstone (and several other after that) has been melted down by lightning and replaced.

The mortal nature of Christ was the truth revealed in the Book of Baptismal by Fire, written by the Templar Grand Master Roncelin de Fos in 1240. "No prince or high priest knows the truth, for if they had, they would not have worshiped the cross of Christ" (article 4: mortal nature of Christ). "God does not distinguish between Christians, Saracens or Jews... as all men who pray to God shall be saved" (article 5: salvation comes from faith, not by paying indulgences or by sexual abstention or whatever other foolish dogmas). The true mission of the Templars is not to protect the pilgrims to Jerusalem – for the old Jerusalem as a symbol of the old world was long lost –, but to "conquer a New World and establish a united kingdom" (article 4: the coming of the fifth empire).

No wonder the Pope accused the Templars of Satanism, excommunicated their leaders and extinguished the Order.

Santiago turns the pages of the old script to the end of Mary Magdalene Gospel, a drawing that shows a woman in tears exiting the catacombs at dawn, carrying a death man on her arms, accompanied by a few other people. Was this drawing a depiction of herself, Mary Magdalene, rescuing the body of her death husband to conduct a proper burial after crucifixion?

"Queen Mary Magdalene, we will never know, will we?"

ACKNOWLEDGEMENT

I am in no way a historian. But I enjoy reading a great novel. At the beginning of 2019, an extraordinary book ended up in my reading pile: "Columbus – the untold story", by Professor Manuel da Silva Rosa. Besides being a reputable and detailed historic analysis, the culmination of twenty years of in depth research on the life of Columbus, the book read like a fascinating tale. Indeed, sometimes reality can be more creative than fiction.

This book has much to thank to Professor Rosa work as a basis of many of the facts that constitute the underlying inspiration to the fictional narrative. After Professor Rosa, and with the basic plot of this book developing in my mind, I set out in a ferocious mission to read all that I could find about Columbus and the Age of Discovery.

I have used many books and sources in a more or less free-flowing way to set up historic context. In particular, I would like to mention:

- Columbus, the untold story (Manuel da Silva Rosa)

- The Portuguese Columbus (Mascarenhas Barreto)

- Columbus, the four voyages (Laurence Bergreen)

- Conquerors, how Portugal forged the first global empire (Roger Crowley)

- The Templar Meridians, the secret mapping of the New World (William Mann)

- The first Global Village (Martin Page)

- Christopher Columbus, the last Templar (Ruggero Marino)

- The Portuguese Empire (Russell-Wood)

- A wind from the North (Ernle Bradford)

ABOUT THE AUTHOR

Karlos K.

Karlos K. lives in Oporto, Portugal, in a house with a large window over the sea. From that wideness, sometimes stormy and threatening, other times pleasant and joyful – of sea and life alike – are born his books.

He was born in Oporto, where he currently lives with his family. Graduated from Oporto Economics University (António de Almeida award for academic achievement) and MBA from London Business School (Distinction, Dean's list). He worked in Mergers & Acquisitions in London, Lisbon and Madrid and was invited teacher in post-grad programs at the Portuguese Catholic University.

Karlos K. received the António Nobre National Literary Award and the Ferreira de Castro National Literary Award. He published a finance book on cross-border M&A by Euronext. He did a double debut in 2021, publishing two novels: Todos os Caminhos and The Columbus Conspiracy.

END NOTES

---

[1] The pan-European emergency number, equivalent to the 911 in the U.S.

[2] Today Guiné-Bissau

[3] Description by Fernando Colon, "Historia del Almirante"

[4] A carrack. The "nau portuguesa" was the 15th and 16th century merchant ship, a larger vessel than the caravels, bulkier to transport cargo but also slower and less nimble

[5] Currently Martinique, north of Trinidad

[6] The symptoms that afflicted Columbus were probably caused by a severe case of rheumatic arthritis

[7] The long sought strait linking the Atlantic with the Pacific. The Strait of Magellan would be found in 1520 by the Portuguese sailor Ferdinand Magellan.

[8] Corte-Real family of Azorean explorers. João Vaz Corte-Real reached Greenland in 1473 and later took part of the Luso-Danish expedition of 1476-77 that chartered the Canadian Atlantic coast, crossing from Greenland to Newfoundland. Columbus claims to have taken part on this expedition. Gaspar Corte-Real, João's son, landed and explored Newfoundland in 1500/1501. Historical records indicate only two of Gaspar's three ships returned to Portugal. In 1502, his brother Miguel Corte-Real set sail from Lisbon to search for his brother with three ships, but again only two returned. In 1912, Edmund Delabarre concluded that the inscriptions on the Dighton Rock, Massachussets, were carved by Miguel Corte-Real in 1511. Delabarre interpreted the abbreviated Latin message as: "I, Miguel Corte-Real, 1511. In this place, by the Grace of God, I became

a chief of the Indians".

[9] La Isabella, in Puerto Plata province of the Dominican Republic, was the first Spanish settlement in the Americas, located in the north shore of Santo Domingo island. The island is today politically divided between the Dominican Republic and Haiti. La Isabella was established by Columbus in his second voyage, in December 1493, to replace the initial attempted settlement (the Fort of La Natividad, left with a small garrison on Columbus first expedition, had been destroyed by the local Taino natives). La Isabella, battered by hurricanes and disease, was abandoned a few years later and replaced by a new capital in Santo Domingo, on the south shore of the island.

[10] Letter from Columbus to a friend written in Cadiz, upon his return from the third voyage in chains, after being arrested in Santo Domingo, Hispaniola (nowadays Dominicam Republic) by the new Governor of the Indies Francisco de Bobadilla.

[11] The only legitimate son of King João II, who died in a mysterious horse fall during a ride by the Tagus, in 1491. King João had promised his cousin Manuel he would be king in the event he did not have a son to succeed him.

[12] Brazil

[13] Fernando Colon describes this episode with much relish, probably referring to a giant manta ray

[14] A manatee, a large, aquatic, herbivorous marine mammal

[15] Brazil

[16] Testimony account, probably written by a priest who accompanied the knights to battle. The text is today at the Corpus Christi college, in Cambridge.

[17] This would continue with Dom João II until is death in 1495. His successor, Dom Manuel II, dramatically changed the country's foreign policy regarding the Vatican and Spain

[18] Nowadays Cape Chaunar on the shouthern atlantic coast of Marrocco. Until the 15th century it was considered impassable by Europeans and Muslims, hence its name: "Cape Not". This was considered the "non plus ultra", the limit beyond which ships would slide down the curvature of the globe like dropplets on the surface of an apple. In 1434, Portuguese ships under Gil Eanes sailed 180 miles south of Cape Não until Cape Bojador, until then considered the southern limit of the physical world.

[19] 'Pleyto sobre la sucession en possession delmestado y Mayorazgo de Veragua (...) y Almirantazgo de las Indias y demás bienes y rentas que fundó Christoval Colon, primero descobridor, Almirante, Virrey y Governador dellas'. Conducted by the Real y Supremo Consejo de Indias.

[20] The Segismundo Henriques theory is based on Manuel da Silva Rosa research published in 2006 and 2016

[21] Quote from José Saramago, Blindness

[22] History of the Conflict Between Religion and Science, by John William Draper (1874) and A History of the Warfare of Science with Theology in Christendom, by Andrew Dickson White (1896).

[23] Currently the city of Huelva, in the Spanish Mediterranean coast, near the border with Portugal.

[24] Japan

[25] Today Lagos in Nigeria

[26] Today Cameroon

[27] Today Ireland

[28] Situated in today's Haiti

[29] Bartolomé de las Casas took part of Colon's second expedition. He returned to Hispaniola in 1502 with Nicolas de Ovando, and not in Colon's fourth expedition. He later became a Dominican monk and returned to Hispaniola in 1510 as a missionary. He was bishop of Chiapas, a chronicler of the first decades of Spanish rule of Central and South America and a great defender of the rights of the Indians

[30] When Columbus arrived in Hispaniola, the island was divided into 5 kingdoms: Xaraguá, Maguana, Higuey, Magua and Marien

[31] Guanaja, one of the Bay Islands off the coast of Honduras

[32] Probably Mayan, or Aztecs

[33] Probably Puerto Limon, off the coast of Costa Rica

[34] Peccaries, or New World pigs

[35] Spider monkeys, indigenous to the New World

[36] During these two months, Columbus explored the coast of Honduras, Nicaragua and Costa Rica.

[37] In today's Panama.

[38] In today's Panama.

[39] Letter written by Colon to the Catholic Monarchs, Jamaica, 7 July 1503

[40] In today's Panama

[41] Maybe a reference to tobacco leaves

[42] In today's frontier between Panama and Colombia

[43] Nowadays the Cayman Islands.

[44] From the Italian: Piccione (male dove) and Colomba (female dove)

[45] The activity Guillaume de Casenove Coulon is well documented. Known as Coulon, the Elder, systematically attacked Italian and Spanish mercantile ships in the Mediterranean. He may have worked with Portuguese king Dom Afonso V, helping him to counter a combined attack by Spanish and Moors in Ceuta. In 1470, the Senate of Venice has documents about an attack by Coulon and Portuguese pirates. In 1474, the city of Venice wrote to Dom Afonso V asking to contain the activities of the pirate Coulon. In 1476 there was a large pirate attack around Cape Saint Vincent against Flemish and Genoese ships. The "official version" recounted by Christopher Columbus son and by Friar las Casas is that Columbus had drowned and swam 6 miles to shore, arriving in Sesimbra, south of Lisbon. However, the documented 1476 battle was much farther south, in the shores of the Algarve. Some historians have claimed Christopher Columbus was himself this pirate Coulon, the Elder.

[46] Letter from Paolo Toscanelli transcribed in the "Historia Rerum Ubique Gestarum", written by Pope Pio II: "from the city of Lisbon, straight to the West, in said map are 26 spaces each with 250 miles...and the island of Antilia, of which I have information (...) Written in Florence on the 25th of June 1474".

[47] Nowadays Iceland

[48] Nowadays Japan

[49] A note on the 1530 Globe of Frisius and Mercator refer to the straight in the north pole by which the Portuguese attempted to reach the Indies

[50] Nowadays Greenland

[51] This would correspond to the Labrador Sea, which would later be explored in 1498 by Portuguese sailors joão Fernandes Lavrador and Pedro de Barcelos

[52] Corvo Island literally means Raven Island or Crow Island. The statue, if it ever exhisted, was destroyed or removed long ago. There is controversy, as some historians consider the references to a horseback knight relate to a natural rock formation. However, the 15th century historian Damião de Góis clearly describes the statue and the mysterious symbols on its base.

[53] The 7th constable of the kingdom, like his great grandfather, Dom Nuno Álvares Pereira. Dom João of Braganza married Dona Isabel Enriques de Noronha, half sister of Filipa Moniz Perestrelo (daughters of the 2nd and 4th wives of Bartolomeu Perestrelo).

[54] Garcia de Resende

[55] Professor Ralph Penny, from Queen Mary University in London, in his article "The Language of Christopher Columbus" demonstrates Colon's writings in Spanish have clear Portuguese influences. The Spanish historian Menéndez Pidal concluded the same thing, the non-spanish words found in Colon's writings are based on the portuguese language. Consuelo Varela also notes in the very few instances Colon tries to write in Italian, he commits gross errors that reveal Colon was never used to the language.

[56] River Congo is also called River Zaire, which is a portuguese adaptation of a Kikongo word, nzere, which means 'river'. It is the second longuest river in Africa, behind the Nile. It crosses the equator twice in a U-shaped course. The sedimentary basin of the Congo covers all equatorial Middle Africa from the Gulf of Guinea to the African Great Lakes.

[57] D João of Aviz, great-grandfather of D João II, was the bastard son of [xxxx] and in [xxxxx] in a succession crisis was acclaimed King of Portugal, thus ending the Bragança dinaty and starting the Aviz dynasty.

[58] The Granada War took much longer than initially expected, lasting 10 years until the final capitulation on 2 January 1492 and annexation of the former emirate to Castella

[59] In 1487 Gonçalo Eanes and Pêro de Évora sailed inland through river Senegal reaching Tumbuctu

[60] Diogo Cão would reach Cape Cross

[61] Beheim would produce a globe representing the world as a sphere but grossly underestimating the size of the Atlantic Ocean, making the Indies reachable in a much shorter westbound route

[62] José Vizinho, Afonso de Paiva and Duarte Pacheco reached Benin, where they were able to trade pepper and other spices

[63] Letter signed by El Rey Dom João II on 20th March 1488 and sent to Xpovam Collon in Seville. Original letter kept in the Archive of the Indies in Seville

[64] Bay of Saint Blaise. Dias named the capes and bays using the name of the Saint of the day it was discovered.

[65] Great Fish River

[66] Nowadays Great Fish River

[67] Letter from Colon to the Spanish kings, transcribed by Bartolomeu de las Casas, book I, chapter XXI

[68] Cited by David A. Shugarts, "Secrets of the Code", edited by Dan Burstein

[69] Garcia Hernandez, doctor and fisician of Palos, in the hearings for the "Pleyto con la Corona" (1515)

[70] Martin Behaim, or Martinho da Boémia, was a Germanic cartographer and creator of the famous Globe of Nuremberg. This is the oldest known globe, built in Germany by Martin Behaim, and currently exhibited in the Germanic National Museum. He died in 1507 in Lisbon in the german hospital of San Bartolomeu.

[71] Initially published in 1410

[72] Amerigo Vespucci was an official of Colon during his 4th expedition in 1502 and also integrated several Portuguese maritime fleets. History would perpetuate Amerigo by naming the new continent America, due to a well disseminated and popular letter he wrote describing the new lands.

[73] Columbus first fleet was composed of a carrack (Nao in Spanish or Nau in Portuguese) and two caravels (Caravelas). The Nau, named Santa Maria, was owned and piloted by Juan de la Cosa. It was the largest ship, slower but necessary to carry supplies. The two caravels, smaller but faster, were piloted by the Pinzón brothers. One was named Santa Clara, nicknamed Niña (in reference to her owner Juan Niño). The other's name is lost, but is known by her nickname Pinta.

[74] Tables written in Hebrew which can today be found in the Hebraic Theology Seminary Museum in New York.

[75] Roncelin de Fos was Grand Master of the Templar Order from 1252 to 1259. The primitive, or original, Rule of the Knights Templar was written by the Council of Troyes in 1129. However, according to Templar lore, a Secret Rule of the Order was set down in The Book of Baptism of Fire by Master Roncelin. Quotes refer to article 4 and 5 of the Secret Rule of the Order.

[76] Translated from the official logbook records of the jouney.

[77] Translated from Columbus entry on his personal logbook.

[78] A small coral island in the Bahamas or Turks and Caicos

[79] Cuba

[80] Probably Bahia Bariay in Cuba

[81] This entry in Colon's journal is probably the first reference to tobacco, a plant unknown until then in Europe

[82] Natividade means Christmas, in Portuguese.

[83] Beatriz Enriquez de Arana, Colon's companion and mother of Fernando Colon

[84] At the same time, on his personal log book, Colon wrote he was close to the Flores islands, in the Azores. The Admiral was never lost!

[85] These are the actual entries in Colon logbook, proving that since leaving the Azores Colon set a straight course to Lisbon. The storm he claims to have led him out of the way to Castella and into Lisbon is an obvious ruse, the Admiral always wanted from the beginning to go nowhere else but Lisbon.

[86] The Count of Penamacor was arrested in the Tower of London in 1492, at the request of King João I. He was later released and run to spain. He was murdered on May 8, 1493 after the long unsigned warning letter to Queen Isabella (now known as the Portuguese Memorial)

[87] Vera Cruz, located in nowadays Brazil. On April 22, 1500, the fleet of Pedro Álvares Cabral reached Monte Pascoal, which they called island of Vera Cruz. The expedition was made in haste to claim the territories for the Portuguese crown, because the Spanish Vicente Pinzon reached cape Santo Agostinho (south of today's Brazilian state of Pernambuco) on January 26, 1500. In fact, the final destination of the 1500 Cabral expedition was India, sent soon after the return of Vasco da Gama in July 1499 to consolidate the Portuguese trade rights in Calecute (where Gama had disembarked in May 1498). Cabral fleet did a quick detour, stopped in Brazil for just 3 days between 24 and 26 April 1500, went ashore to say mass on Sunday 26 April, and soon after departed to India, sending only 1 of the 13-strong fleet back to Portugal to confirm the discovery. The Portuguese probably knew those lands since before the Tordesillas Treaty in 1494. At least an earlier expedition to Brazil is documented, by Duarte Pacheco Pereira, in 1498. In his logbook, Pacheco Pereira clearly states he had found "terra firma" on the southwest Atlantic... but the discovery again was kept secret until the "official" discovery by Cabral in 1500. The Portuguese kings took no risks, no risks whatsoever, that could destabilize the equilibrium of the Tordesillas Treaty by announcing lands on the west before firmly establishing the dominance of the maritime trade route to India in 1499. There is also strong evidence the Portuguese were aware of the southwestern lands long before, though: maps depicting the Antilles

and the Sargaço Sea, references to a secret "terra firma" and the insistence of King João I in 1493 during the negotiation of the Tordesillas Treaty to push the dividing line to 320 leagues west of Cape Vert, pushing the limit 120 leagues westwards.

[88] Now Greenland

[89] For the second expedition, Colon never delivered to the pilots of the large fleet the coordinates of their destination. Instead, he provided each a sealed letter with indications of their destination, to be opened only in case Colon perished.

[90] The southern passage from the Atlantic to the Pacific Ocean would be found only in 1520, by Portuguese sailor Fernão de Magalhães, known to the world as Ferdinand Magellan, who crossed the Strait of Magellan – also known as the Dragon's Tail – during his circun-navigation expedition.

[91] A total moon eclipse indeed occurred on the night of 29 February to March 1, visible at sunset in the Americas, during the night in Europe and near sunrise in Asia.

[92] The tobacco plant was described in Colon's diary of the first voyage. It is probably one of the oldest crops known to humanity but was unknown in Europe at the time.

[93] Torre do Tombo is the National Archive of documents from the IX century to today. It functioned as the official Royal Archive from 1378 to 1755. Originally located in one of the towers of the Castle of S. Jorge, in Lisbon, which crumbled in the 1755 earthquake, the Archive moved between several places until its current location in a dedicated modern building in Lisbon's university quarter.

[94] Dom Manuel I married two of Isabel and Fernando daughters (Isabel in 1497, who died in 1498 after birth of the first son, and Maria in 1500) and made a third marriage with one of their granddaughters (Leonor da Austria, in 1518). In 1498 he succeeded in making himself named as the successor of the Spanish crown. He never achieved the throne of the Spanish kingdoms, but opened the door for 60 years of Spanish rule over Portugal between 1580 and 1640.

[95] The instruction Secreta Continere was issued by the Secretariat of State of the Vatican on 4 February 1974. The text is published in the Acta Apostolicae Sedis, and it details the matters subject to Pontifical Secrecy under cannon law.

[96] A letter written by Christopher Colon to his son Diego, dated 5

February 1505, very clearly identifies Vespucci as a secret agent of Colon, in the payroll of the Portuguese king, with the mission of boasting the wonders of the western lands. By 1505, after Vasco da Gama arrival to the true India in 1499 and 6 years of very profitable trade in spices and silk, it was evident Colon had not arrived even remotely close to the true India. In the letter, Colon described Vespucci mission as to make "His royal highness (King Fernando, as Isabella died in 1504) believe his ships were taken (by me) to the best and richest of the Indies."

[97] City in western India where Vasco da Gama arrived in May 1498

[98] The utopic dream continued. Francis Bacon was a defender of reason and empiricism, credited as the founder of the scientific method and also considered a founder of the Rosacrucian movement. He wrote New Atlantis, published in 1626.

[99] Bartolomé Colon stayed as Governor of the Indies in 1496, after Colon's return to Spain

[100] The book was banned by the Inquisition

[101] Nowadays Istambul

[102] Extensive evidence of the theory that Christopher Colon was Segimundo Henriques, son of Ladislau III and Senhorinha Anes, was published by Manuel da Silva Rosa in "Columbus Secret Revealed" (2006) and "Columbus the Untold Story" (2016)

[103] Christopher Colon was often accused by the Spanish of intending to foster a revolution in Hispaniola. Nicolás de Ovando, stated, during the transfer from Bobadilla as governor, "the Admiral (Colon) intended to rebel with this island, and he would have already done it by now (if he had not been arrested)." This probably explains Ovando's suspicions about Colon's intentions in 1504, when Colon's fourth fleet was refused to enter the harbor of Santo Domingo despite an upcoming tornado.

[104] Juan de la Cosa map produced in 1500 shows the first known sketch of America, from Canada to Florida and Brazil.

[105] Reference to the Newport Tower, near Boston. It is described as a 17xxx old windmill, but carbon dating of the lower stone structure suggests it may date from the XII th century. Although today only a round arched tower remains, there are archaeological signs of a rectangular chancel facing east. This disposition (nave facing west and rectangular chancel running east) is traditionally been attributed to Templar buildings, like the Temple Church in London and unlike most gothic churches

where the nave faces east to receive the morning sun.

[106] National Geographic special documentary, 2012

Printed in Great Britain
by Amazon